Praise fo
NO JOURNEY 1

"No distance is too great for love, a truth beautifully laced into *No Journey Too Far*. Bringing to life the little-known story of British Home Children, Turansky creates a tale of love, loss, and reunion for the continuing saga of the McAlister family as they search for one another after years of separation. Readers will not want to miss this gem—heartwarming and full of grace."

—J'NELL CIESIELSKI, author of *Beauty Among Ruins*

"Carrie has penned another stirring tale of the heart, spanning two continents and the all-too-real lives of those caught up in the challenges of the British Home Children. The issues of prejudice, privilege, and powerlessness speak as much to us today as in the past, and encourage us to seek the Maker of all, whose love shows that there is no journey too far for finding His children and bringing them home. Thank you for making this important part of history come alive to us, Carrie."

—CAROLYN MILLER, Australian author of *Dusk's Darkest Shores*

"Cruelly separated and spread across Canada as British Home Children, the McAlister family have never given up their determination to be reunited. Following WWI, Carrie Turansky continues their heart-wrenching search through a riveting plot and the well-drawn characters we've come to dearly love. *No Journey Too Far* reminds me of the extent our Lord goes to seek us out, win our hearts, and draw us safely home. A beautiful and satisfying conclusion by a wonderful author."

—CATHY GOHLKE, Christy Award–winning author of
Night Bird Calling and *The Medallion*

"In *No Journey Too Far*, Turansky continues the stirring McAlister family saga and the journey to reunite their family, separated when three of the siblings were mistakenly sent to Canada as British Home Children. The sequel to *No Ocean Too Wide* begins ten years later, focusing on Garth McAlister's attempt to find his youngest sister, Grace, the only sibling adopted into a Canadian family. The author skillfully depicts the terrible prejudice the British Home Children faced, yet the story is one of hope, illustrating that in the end faith and determination can overcome any obstacle. A wonderful conclusion to this moving family drama!"

—SUSAN ANNE MASON, author of the
Canadian Crossings and Redemption's Light series

"*No Journey Too Far* is a formidable story that is genuinely touching, telling of a desperate fight to reunite a family and the extreme difficulties encountered along the way. This book touches upon the shame, abuse, and stigmatization felt by many Home Children, mixed with a loving family bond on both sides of the ocean. Carrie brings the continuing story of the McAlister family to life in a compelling way that descendants will appreciate, and all readers are sure to be moved. Heartfelt, real, and poignant."

—LORI OSCHEFSKI, CEO of the
award-winning British Home Children Advocacy
and Research Association (BHCARA) and author of
Bleating of the Lambs: Canada's British Home Children

"A sweet and gentle tale at heart, *No Journey Too Far* features endearing characters who live out their faith in difficult circumstances. The story also casts light on the prejudices faced by the British Home Children in Canada, even as they entered adulthood. Carrie Turansky's writing pulls the heartstrings in all the right ways!"

—SARAH SUNDIN, bestselling and Carol Award–winning author of *When Twilight Breaks*

"A delightful story that explores the fascinating history of the British Home Children, *No Journey Too Far* is a touching tale filled with excitement, drama, mystery, romance, and faith. Through the McAlister family, Carrie Turansky weaves the hopeful message that God does not let us go, that His grace and acceptance defy all stigmas and prejudices, and that He always keeps His promises. A beautiful novel that historical fans are sure to appreciate."

—HEIDI CHIAVAROLI, Carol Award–winning author of *Freedom's Ring* and *The Orchard House*

Books by Carrie Turansky

Novels
No Ocean Too Wide
Across the Blue
Shine Like the Dawn
A Refuge at Highland Hall
The Daughter of Highland Hall
The Governess of Highland Hall
Snowflake Sweethearts
A Man to Trust
Seeking His Love
Surrendered Hearts
Along Came Love

Novellas
Shelter in the Storm, in *A Joyful Christmas*
Waiting for His Return
Moonlight over Manhattan
A Trusting Heart, in *Mountain Christmas Brides*
Wherever Love Takes Us, in *Where Two Hearts Meet*
Tea for Two, in *Where Two Hearts Meet*

No Journey Too Far

No Journey Too Far

A Novel

McAlister Family,
Book 2

Carrie Turansky

MULTNOMAH

No Journey Too Far

The characters and events in this book are fictional,
and any resemblance to actual persons or events is coincidental.

Published in the United States by Multnomah,
an imprint of Random House,
a division of Penguin Random House LLC.

MULTNOMAH® and its mountain colophon are registered trademarks
of Penguin Random House LLC.

LIBRARY OF CONGRESS CATALOGING-IN-PUBLICATION DATA
Names: Turansky, Carrie, author.
Title: No journey too far / Carrie Turansky.
Description: Colorado Springs : Multnomah, [2021]
Identifiers: LCCN 2020051762 | ISBN 9780525652953 (paperback) |
ISBN 9780525652960 (ebook)
Subjects: GSAFD: Christian fiction.
Classification: LCC PS3620.U7457 N58 2021 | DDC 813/.6—dc2
LC record available at https://lccn.loc.gov/2020051762

Printed in the United States of America on acid-free paper

waterbrookmultnomah.com

9 8 7 6 5 4 3 2 1

First Edition

Interior book design by Virginia Norey

To the descendants of British Home Children: may this story highlight the courage shown by your relatives and the challenges they overcame as they built new lives for themselves and for future generations.

The LORD is a refuge for the oppressed,
a stronghold in times of trouble.
Those who know your name trust in you,
for you, LORD, have never forsaken those who seek you.
—PSALM 9:9–10, NIV

No Journey Too Far

Prologue

Belleville, Ontario, Canada
May 1909

Grace McAlister held tight to her sister Katie's hand as they slowly walked across the large open room in the Belleville Town Hall.

"It's all right, Grace. We're going to meet our new family this morning." Katie smiled down at her, but it didn't look like her real smile.

Grace swallowed hard and pushed out her words. "What if they're not nice?"

"Anyone who would take in children who are not their own must have a kind heart." Her words sounded brave, but she still looked worried.

Grace matched Katie's steps as they followed the line of girls who had come with them on the big ship from England to Canada and then on the train to Belleville. She wished she had eaten more of the porridge at breakfast that morning, but her tummy felt funny, and she'd pushed her bowl aside after a few bites. She missed Mum, Garth, and Laura. Where were they? Why didn't they come and take her and Katie home?

Grace and Katie joined the line of girls along the back wall of the room. Miss Delaney, the tall lady with red hair who had come over on the ship with them, talked to two men and an old lady sitting at a long table in the front of the room.

Who were they? Where was her new family? Would they like her? When could she and Katie go home and see Mum?

A buzzing began in Grace's head like there was a bee inside. She squeezed her eyes tight until the buzzing finally went away. Taking a slow deep breath, she opened her eyes. Everything would be all right. Katie promised it would.

She smoothed the pinafore over her green dress. All the other girls were dressed the same, and each wore a blue jacket and straw hat like hers. Most of the girls were bigger, like Katie, who was fourteen. She looked down the row, searching for Millie, the only girl in their group younger than Grace. Millie was six, and Grace was seven. They'd played together on the ship. Would Millie find a new family too? What if no one wanted her? What if no one wanted Grace and Katie?

The buzzing in her head came back. She stepped closer to Katie and leaned against her side. Her sister's arm felt warm like when they used to sit together in the big chair at home and Katie would read her a story.

Miss Delaney crossed the room and stopped in front of Grace. She wore a plain brown dress and small hat, and her pink cheeks were covered with freckles. "All right, girls. I want you to stand up straight. Look smart and be quiet and respectful to the people who come in to see you."

Grace's tummy tightened. She peeked up at Katie. Her sister stood taller and lifted her chin like Miss Delaney.

A side door opened, and a man and lady walked in and came toward the line of girls. The man was tall and wore a black suit and hat. He looked at each girl as he and the lady moved down the line. The lady wore a dress the color of pennies. Her big hat was the same color, with lots of flowers and feathers on top. She had a pretty face and blue eyes. As the lady came closer, Grace could see she had brown hair under her hat.

The man and lady stopped in front of them. The lady looked down at Grace for a few seconds and smiled. She turned to the man. He nodded and then took the lady's arm and they moved down the row.

"They didn't like us?" Grace's voice felt tight and shaky.

Katie put her arm around Grace. "Don't worry. I'm sure there are more families coming in soon."

Grace fiddled with the edge of her pinafore and counted the boards on the floor around her. She thought about Mum and the times they used to go to the park near their flat over the dress shop. Grace liked feeding the ducks and chasing Garth and Katie across the grass. Mum would smile as she watched them from the bench in the shade of the big tree by the pond. Grace wished they could all go to the park again.

"I'd like you to come with me, Grace."

Grace sucked in a breath and looked up. Miss Delaney stood in front of her.

Katie gripped Grace's hand. "Why? Where are you taking her?" Her voice sounded high and scared.

Miss Delaney motioned toward the front of the room where the man and lady stood. "That couple would like to talk to her."

Katie pressed her lips together for a second, then nodded. "Go ahead, Grace." Katie let go of Grace's hand. "Just be sure to tell them I'm your sister and we have to stay together."

Before Grace could answer, Miss Delaney took her hand and tugged her across the room. Her face felt hot, and she could feel her heart beating hard. Why couldn't Katie come with her to talk to the man and lady? What did they want to say to her?

"This is Grace." Miss Delaney gave her a little push toward the man and lady. "She's seven years old."

The lady in the penny-colored dress smiled. "Hello, Grace. I'm Mrs. Hamilton, and this is Mr. Hamilton."

Grace knew she should say something, but she couldn't make her voice come out. She bit her lip and looked at the floor.

"Have you been to school yet?" The man's voice was strong and loud.

Grace kept her eyes down. If she said yes, would they ask her to count or recite? She could do that with Katie but not with people she didn't know.

The lady bent down toward her. "Can you tell us something you enjoy doing?" Her voice sounded nice, but when Grace glanced at her face, there were lines across the lady's forehead. Was she mad because Grace didn't answer?

Grace peeked over her shoulder at Katie. Her sister sent her a pleading look, but Grace wasn't sure what she was supposed to say or do.

"Mr. Hamilton and I have a dog named Cooper," the lady continued. "He's a very pretty collie. We like to take him for walks in the park or spend time with him out in our garden. Do you like dogs?"

Most of the dogs Grace had seen in London lived on the street and weren't very friendly. Her mum had always told her to stay away from them. What should she say?

"What's your favorite food?" the lady asked.

If she said Mum's meat pies, would they know what she meant? Grace shrugged.

The man frowned. "Why won't she speak to us?"

Mrs. Hamilton patted Grace's shoulder. "I'm sure this is all a bit overwhelming." She turned to Miss Delaney. "Do you have information about her background and family? Is she in good health?"

"She's in excellent health. All the children are given examinations before they leave England and on arrival in Canada." Miss Delaney opened a file and sorted through some papers. "She's an orphan from London with no relatives who can care for her. She was born on May 16." She closed the file and looked up at Mrs. Hamilton. "I can assure you she will have more to say once she feels comfortable. Isn't that right, Grace?"

"Yes ma'am," Grace whispered.

Mr. and Mrs. Hamilton looked at each other. Mr. Hamilton nodded and then turned to Miss Delaney. "Very well. We'll take her."

Grace gasped. They were going to take her? What about Katie? She turned and looked toward the back wall. Her sister watched her with wide eyes.

Mr. Hamilton stepped up to the table and signed a paper. Mrs. Hamilton took Grace's hand and started toward the side door.

Grace pulled back. "Wait!"

"It's all right, dear." Mrs. Hamilton gripped harder and continued toward the door. "Our motorcar is just outside. Have you ever ridden in a motorcar?"

"No! No!" She screamed and tried to wriggle away.

Mrs. Hamilton held on tight. "There's no need to make a fuss."

Grace's eyes burned and overflowed, and her cries turned to jerky sobs.

"That's enough! Settle down, Grace!" Mr. Hamilton scooped her up and hurried across the room.

Grace tried to get away, but Mr. Hamilton's strong arms pressed her hard against his chest. She jerked her head up, searching for her sister as they passed out the door. Katie stood by the wall, a wide-eyed, fearful look on her face. Grace's heart lurched, and she screamed her sister's name. But the door slammed behind them, and she couldn't see Katie anymore.

1

Toronto
February 1919

Grace Hamilton shifted her weight from one foot to the other. How much longer was this going to take? They couldn't expect her to stand perfectly still on this footstool forever. She shot a look at the dressmaker, kneeling at her feet, and then at her mother. "Are we almost finished?"

Impatience flashed in her mother's eyes. She crossed the parlor toward Grace but then pressed her lips together and held her peace.

Mrs. Wilson pulled a pin from her lips. "It shouldn't be too much longer. I'm almost done pinning the hem."

Grace turned and glanced at the clock. "I'm supposed to meet Abigail Gillingham at one to work on our plans for the church charity sale supporting injured veterans."

Mother's eyebrows arched. "Abigail can wait. This final fitting is more important."

Grace twisted around. "But, Mother—"

"For goodness' sake, Grace, stand still! You're almost eighteen. You must learn to have patience and conduct yourself like a proper young lady!"

Grace froze in position, her frustration simmering just beneath the surface. Being forced to pose like a statue had worn her patience thin. But if that was what it took to be free to meet her friend and have some time away from home, then that was what she would do.

Mrs. Wilson poked the next pin into the sky-blue satin fabric and looked up at Grace. "I must say this color is a perfect match for your eyes, and it highlights your blond hair very nicely."

Mother sent Grace a pointed look, her expectation clear. Grace swallowed her frustration and gave the expected response. "Thank you, Mrs. Wilson."

Her mother nodded, seeming satisfied. "Grace will be wearing this gown when she makes her debut at the St. Andrew's Ball in April."

Mrs. Wilson turned toward Mother. "I didn't realize she was coming out this spring."

"We had planned to bring her out next year, but now that the war is over and the soldiers are coming home, her father and I have decided it's best not to wait."

Grace lifted her eyes to the ceiling. All this fuss and bother about making her debut and finding a husband. She wouldn't turn eighteen until mid-May. Why were they in such a rush?

Mrs. Wilson added another pin. "I'm thankful the war is finally behind us. But what a terrible cost our men had to pay for the victory."

The dressmaker's words sent a pang through Grace's heart. Here she was frustrated about this dress fitting when so many brave men were still recovering from injuries they had suffered in the Great War. How courageous and noble they were to serve their king and country. And some would never come home, including her cousin Rodney, who had died at Passchendaele.

Her eyes grew misty as she thought of how she and Rodney had laughed and played together when they were younger. He might not be her cousin by blood, but they'd shared a close friendship ever since she'd joined the Hamilton family. Now he was lost to her forever.

Mother stepped forward and touched Grace's back. "Stand up tall. No man wants a wife who slouches."

Grace straightened her shoulders and tried to ignore her mother's stinging words, but it wasn't easy. No matter how perfectly she tried to follow every rule of etiquette, she couldn't seem to please her mother.

"With so few men of marriageable age left, the most promising prospects will be snatched up this spring." Her mother fingered the satin fabric of Grace's skirt. "That's why Grace must make the best impression possible at the ball. We don't want her to miss the opportunity to find a suitable husband."

Mrs. Wilson looked up at Grace. "With her natural beauty and this lovely gown, there's no doubt she'll attract a long line of suitors."

Was that true? Grace shifted her feet and looked away. The idea of dressing up and attending balls had sounded exciting and romantic when they'd first discussed moving up her debut. But now that the time was near, she wasn't so sure.

How would she know which young men she ought to encourage? What were the most important qualities she should look for in a potential husband? And when someone did pursue her, how would she know if he truly loved her or if he was more interested in her family's wealth and position in society?

Her mother focused on choosing the right gown and making the most influential social connections. Surely there were other things that were more important.

She pushed that thought away. Her parents had provided every advantage for her, including the best education a governess could offer, as well as years of piano, voice, and dance lessons. She should feel grateful and confident about the future, but somehow she couldn't help feeling unsettled, like something wasn't quite right about her life.

Faded memories of her early years in England and her family there drifted through her mind. Her father had died when she was five, and she wasn't sure what had happened to her mum. She could barely recall her parents' faces now, and that thought pierced her heart. Why had she been sent to Canada? Weren't there any relatives in England who could have taken care of her and her siblings?

She was the youngest of four, she remembered that much. Her brother, Garth, and sister Katie were twins seven years older than Grace. They would be in their midtwenties now. Were they still living in Canada, adopted into families as she had been, or had they finished their indentured contracts and struck out on their own?

And what had happened to their oldest sister, Laura? Was she still working as a lady's maid on a large estate in England, or was she married and caring for her own family now?

Her throat tightened as she recalled other memories of her brother and sisters. They had been so close when they were young. She thought they had shared a bond that would never be broken. Yet they had been separated soon after they came to Canada, and none of them had ever written to her or visited her.

She blew out a breath to release the painful ache in her chest. It wasn't right. They were older. They should've searched for her and made sure she was safe and well cared for, but they hadn't. She'd been taken in by strangers and expected to accept them as her new mother and father.

Her parents said they knew nothing about her birth family and had forbidden her to tell anyone she was adopted. Most people didn't approve of taking in a Home Child with an unknown background.

She lifted her chin, and a wave of determination coursed through her. She might be a British Home Child, but she was not ashamed of that fact, or of her birth family, no matter what her adoptive parents said.

If she could find her siblings and discover the truth about her family and life in England, maybe she could make peace with her past. That seemed the only way she could live an open and honest life rather than feeling she must hide her history from everyone she met. But would connecting with them finally fill the aching void in her heart?

"Turn, please." The dressmaker looked up at her.

Grace blinked and shifted her gaze to Mrs. Wilson.

"Really, Grace, you must put aside your daydreaming! Soon you'll become a wife and then a mother, though I can hardly imagine my little girl is all grown up." Her mother's eyes filled, but she sniffed and looked away.

Grace sighed softly. Her mother was often sentimental and dramatic, praising her one minute and criticizing her the next.

Footsteps sounded in the front hall, and her father strode into the parlor. Tall and glowing with good health and confidence, he was dressed in a fine charcoal suit and carried his black leather briefcase. Threads of silver glistened in the black hair at his temples and in his full beard and mustache.

His assistant, Richard Findley, followed him through the doorway dressed in an equally fine fashion.

"Ah, Judith, here you are." Father greeted Mother with a brief smile, then looked across the room at Grace. His eyebrows dipped into a slight frown. "It looks as though we're interrupting."

"It's all right." Mother glanced at Grace before she turned to the dressmaker. "Mrs. Wilson is just pinning the hem."

Mrs. Wilson rose. "Yes, the dress is finished. I was just checking to make sure the hem is the proper length."

Richard flashed a confident smile at Grace. "You certainly look lovely this afternoon, Miss Hamilton."

Her cheeks warmed as she stepped down from the stool and returned his smile. "Thank you."

Richard was ten years her senior and worked as her father's assistant manager at Hamilton's, the second-largest department store in Toronto. He was a handsome man with reddish-brown hair and deep-set brown eyes. Lately, he seemed to take more notice of Grace, paying her compliments and sending her teasing smiles whenever he visited their home.

"Is that dress from our store?" Her father's serious tone and frown made his suspicions clear.

Her mother moved next to Grace. "No, it's one of Mrs. Wilson's designs."

Father's frown deepened. "We have the entire contents of our store at your disposal and you bring in a private dressmaker?"

Mrs. Wilson's face reddened. She turned away and began putting her supplies in her sewing basket.

"Howard, can we discuss this later?" Her mother's uneasy gaze darted from the dressmaker to Grace's father.

He huffed. "Very well."

Mother thanked Mrs. Wilson and turned to Grace. "Please go upstairs and change. Mrs. Wilson will want to take the gown with her."

Grace nodded and followed the dressmaker toward the parlor door.

Richard smiled again as she passed. She averted her eyes but couldn't suppress her smile. When she reached the door, she looked over her shoulder, and Richard's gaze followed her. Their eyes met, and he winked.

She pulled in a sharp breath and hurried through the doorway. What did he mean by that wink? Was he flirting with her, or was he simply in a lighthearted mood?

Would Richard attend the St. Andrew's Ball? If he did, would he ask her to dance? Her father said he was intelligent and hardworking. Surely, those were two important qualities to recommend him as a potential beau. She didn't know anything about his family, but the fact he had been given such an important position at Hamilton's seemed to indicate that her father trusted and respected him.

A sudden thought struck, and her steps slowed. Would Richard still send her those teasing smiles if he knew the truth about her past? How could she step out into society and keep her background a secret? Building a secure future on the shifting sand of lies and secrets would be difficult, if not impossible.

And even if she could, was that the kind of life she wanted?

A few minutes later, Grace slipped out of her gown, and Mrs. Wilson helped her into her day dress.

"It will still be chilly in April," the dressmaker said as she tied the sash at the back of Grace's dress. "Would you like me to design a cape to go with your new gown?"

Father's disapproving expression flashed across Grace's mind. "No, thank you. Mother has a blue-and-silver shawl that will match the gown."

"Very good, miss. I'll finish the hem and send the gown to you as soon as it's done." Mrs. Wilson placed the gown in a large cloth bag and draped it over her arm.

Grace thanked her and followed her into the upper hallway. As the dressmaker descended the stairs, Grace looked over the railing to the entry hall below.

Richard followed the butler to the front door, accepted his hat and coat, and walked out.

Grace released a soft sigh. She'd missed her chance to speak to him. It didn't matter. She wasn't sure what she would say if he had lingered, waiting for her.

Mrs. Wilson followed Richard out, and as soon as the front door closed, Grace's father's voice rang out from the parlor. "Honestly, Judith, do you think I am made of money?"

Grace bit her lip, but she leaned forward to hear more of her parents' conversation.

"Howard, please. There is no need to raise your voice."

"It seems that is the only way I can convince you to listen."

"I don't understand why you're so upset. We can certainly afford a new gown for Grace."

"But I own a store full of dresses. You could choose any one you want. Why on earth do you insist on calling in a private dressmaker?"

"If Grace is going to make the right impression at the St. Andrew's Ball, then she must have a unique gown—one that sets her apart from all the other young women. We can't simply choose a gown off the rack at Hamilton's."

Her father grumbled something Grace couldn't hear.

"We must dress Grace like a princess to make sure no one suspects her background."

Grace stifled a gasp. Was that why Mother brought in the dressmaker? She feared someone would guess she wasn't a native-born Canadian?

"No one suspects Grace was a Home Child."

"They might if we don't make sure she looks like she was born into our family."

"I don't know why I ever let you talk me into this scheme," her father growled. "We should never have hidden the fact that Grace was adopted."

"How can you say that? She'd be an outcast from society if the truth were known. Then she'd never find a suitable husband."

Grace clutched the railing as pain pierced her heart. How could her mother say such a thing? Surely, that wasn't true, was it?

Her father continued, "Grace is an attractive and accomplished young woman, and we are a respected family. That should be enough to impress any young man."

"Not in Toronto society. If we are going to secure Grace's future and protect our reputation, then no one must ever know the truth."

A few seconds ticked by before he answered. "That's a foolish choice, Judith, and one I'm sure we'll come to regret." The parlor door slammed, and he strode across the entry hall toward the library.

Grace pulled back into the shadows and held her breath. When her father's footsteps faded, she peered over the railing. The entry hall was empty.

Was her mother right? Did her past make her unworthy of love?

If only her father's opinion were true and she could be accepted into society based on her character and accomplishments rather than pretending she had been born into a wealthy, upper-class family.

But her mother's fearful words struck her heart again. If the truth became known, she would be an outcast. She had no choice.

She would have to continue the charade and make sure no one, including her future husband, ever suspected she had come to Canada as a British Home Child.

Ten minutes later, desperate to distract herself from the memory of her parents' heated conversation and the turmoil in her heart, she set off down the upper hallway in search of their maid. She found her putting away clothing in her mother's dressing room. "Hello, Sylvia."

The maid nodded to her. "Good day, miss. Can I help you?"

"Yes, I'm looking for my mother's blue-and-silver shawl, the one with the silver fringe."

The maid's brow creased. "Mrs. Hamilton told me to put it in storage in the attic with a few other items. Would you like me to fetch it for you?"

"No, that's all right. I'll get it. Thank you, Sylvia."

"Of course, miss."

After returning to the hallway, Grace climbed the stairs to the top floor and slipped into the attic storage room. Dust motes floated in the shafts of sunlight streaming through the only window, but the room was still cold. Grace shivered and rubbed her arms. She'd have to make this a quick search.

Extra furniture and stacks of boxes filled most of the space beneath the exposed rafters. Two old wardrobes stood against one wall with several trunks and boxes stacked around them. The family stored out-of-season clothing in those wardrobes, and she hoped to find the shawl in one of them. She crossed the room and opened the first wardrobe. It held her father's suits and overcoats. She opened the second wardrobe and looked through the row of her mother's dresses, including a few that she'd outgrown, but found no shawls.

Grace lifted the lid of the closest trunk and found that it contained neatly folded blankets. She lowered the lid and searched three more trunks. No shawl.

With a sigh, she stood, looking across the attic. It had to be here somewhere. In the corner, a blanket was draped over what seemed to be a smaller square trunk. Two other boxes were stacked on top. She set the boxes aside and pulled off the blanket. Underneath was a simple wooden trunk with words stenciled across the top in black paint.

Grace scanned the writing and pulled in a sharp breath. She blinked and read the words again: *Grace McAlister, Care of the Matron, Pleasantview Children's Home, Belleville, Ontario, Canada.*

This was *her* trunk, the one she'd brought from England!

Her fingers trembled as she lifted the lid and peered inside. Several child-sized dresses, aprons, petticoats, and stockings were folded in neat piles. A packing list was attached to the inside of the lid. She quickly read the items listed, and memories came rushing back.

Her sister Katie had helped her pack this trunk before they sailed to Canada. She carefully pushed the clothing aside and looked deeper inside. She spotted a small black Bible in the bottom corner and carefully lifted it out.

She had just been learning to read when she'd taken that voyage across the Atlantic, but Katie had told her she must take good care of the Bible and read it often. The bittersweet memory brought tears to her eyes. She blinked them away and smoothed her hand over the cover.

Her parents had a large leather-bound family Bible downstairs in the parlor, but she couldn't remember them ever opening it. She didn't have a Bible of her own, or at least she'd forgotten she had one until now.

Her throat tightened as she remembered how Katie had held the Bible and told her to treasure it. Closing her eyes, Grace lifted it to her lips and kissed the cover. This Bible was a connection to her family in England. She would take it to her room, start reading it tonight, and keep her promise to her sister.

She lowered the trunk's lid and studied the writing on top: *Grace McAlister.* Like a surging wave, images from her life in London flooded her mind. The butcher, the dressmaker, and the reverend at church had all called her mum Mrs. Edna McAlister. The memory was as clear as day now.

They'd lived in a small flat above a dress shop where her mum worked as a dressmaker's assistant doing hand sewing until she fell ill. Grace could picture the table where they ate their simple meals and the bed she'd shared with her sister Katie.

She stared at the words stenciled on the trunk once more, trying to recall the Pleasantview Children's Home in Belleville, but the three children's homes where she'd stayed all blurred together.

An idea struck, and she laid her hand on top of the trunk. Now that she knew the name of the children's home in Belleville, she could write to the matron and ask for information about her birth family.

Joy tingled through her, and her smile spread wide. Perhaps the matron would write back and tell her how she could find Garth and Katie, and through them, she might learn how to contact Laura in England. At last she might be able to find out if Mum was still living.

But her joy quickly faded as new questions stirred her heart. Why had her adopted parents told her they knew nothing about her family or the circumstances that brought her to Canada? Surely, they remembered that her trunk was stored in the attic with this information stenciled across the top. Had they purposely kept it from her so she wouldn't ask questions? What would they think about her delving into her history and searching for her family?

Grace straightened and turned toward the window as one thought connected to the next. She had a right to know about her background, even if her adoptive parents wouldn't approve. She would write the Pleasantview Children's Home and ask how to contact Garth and Katie.

Finding the trunk and learning the name of the children's home she'd passed through was thrilling, but there was so much more she wanted to know, so many questions that needed to be answered. Most of all, she longed to see Katie and Garth again. Maybe then she'd finally feel the heart-to-heart connection she'd been missing for so many years.

That evening, after dinner, Grace crept down the back servants' stairs and peeked into the kitchen. The maid stood at the sink, washing the last of the pots and pans that had been used to prepare the family's dinner.

Grace scanned the room to make sure they were alone, then cleared her throat. "Good evening, Sylvia."

The maid spun around, her eyes wide and her hands dripping dishwater. "Oh, Miss Hamilton! Can I help you?" She quickly wiped her hands on her apron.

Grace smiled. "I wanted to ask if you might do an errand for me tomorrow."

Sylvia's golden-brown eyebrows rose. "You want *me* to do an errand for you?"

"Yes, if you don't mind." It was an unusual request to make of the maid, but Grace needed help and there were few members of the staff she could trust.

"What would you like me to do, miss?"

Grace took the letter she'd addressed to the Pleasantview Children's Home from behind her back. "I'd like you to mail this letter for me."

Confusion filled the maid's eyes. "Why don't you give it to Mr. Harding?"

The butler usually handled all the family's mail, but he was loyal to her father and she couldn't risk him seeing the address and reporting it to her parents.

"I'd rather you take it to the post office."

Sylvia blinked, looking uncertain.

Grace wished she could go herself, but her parents rarely allowed her to leave the house without a chaperone. "It's a private letter. I'd rather Mr. Harding didn't see it."

Sylvia slowly nodded. "All right, miss. I'll post the letter for you."

Relief rushed through Grace. "Thank you." She took two coins from her pocket and held them out with the letter. "This should be enough to pay for the stamp, and a bit extra for your trouble."

The maid's eyes widened again. "Oh, thank you, miss. That's more than enough." Sylvia accepted the envelope and tucked it into her apron pocket along with the coins.

"Thank you, Sylvia. I appreciate your help."

The maid dipped a slight curtsy. "Of course, miss. You can count on me. I'll keep your secret."

A smile rose from Grace's heart as she walked out of the kitchen. She'd just taken the first step to reconnect with her family, and it made her feel so light and hopeful, she could almost dance up the stairs. Perhaps in a few weeks she'd be able to write to Garth and Katie and then make plans to see them. At last she'd find the answers to her questions and know what it felt like to be part of a real family.

St. Albans, England
March 14, 1919

Garth McAlister grabbed his military-issued duffel bag from the overhead rack and adjusted his stance to steady himself while the train rocked and swayed down the tracks. He studied the passing countryside, then turned to his friend Rob Lewis. "We're getting close."

Rob grinned and rose to his feet. "I'm glad to hear it." He slung the strap of his duffel bag over his shoulder and tugged his olive-drab uniform cap down over his dark-blond hair. "Are you sure your family won't mind my arriving unannounced?"

"Positive. My mum and sisters will be happy to welcome you to Bolton."

"But what about your brother-in-law? It's his family's estate."

"Andrew Frasier has always been very hospitable."

"I'm looking forward to meeting your family. I remember Katie from our voyage to Canada and that one time we saw her at church. But that was almost ten years ago."

The conductor poked his head into their compartment. "St. Albans is next."

"Thank you, sir. That's our stop." Garth placed his uniform cap on his head.

"Welcome home, boys." The conductor smiled and gave them a jaunty salute. "You've won a great victory. We're all very proud and grateful."

Garth nodded to the man, but uneasiness tightened his chest. His role, caring for horses used to transport equipment, had kept him out of the trenches, while many of his friends had fought on the front line and sacrificed their lives.

He gave his head a slight shake and pushed away those grim thoughts. The war was over now. It was time to move forward and forge a new life for himself and Emma.

The memory of his sweetheart in Canada sent a pang through his chest. He took her photograph from his shirt pocket and studied her heart-shaped face, soft round cheeks, and gentle brown eyes. Others might not see it, but to him there was no one more beautiful. He swallowed hard and tucked the photo away. It had been more than three months since he'd heard from her. It didn't make sense. Before that, she'd written to him faithfully and always closed her letters by telling him how much she looked forward to his safe return. He'd thought they had an understanding, but now he wondered if he'd clung to her memory and imagined more than she had intended in order to keep the horror of war at bay.

When her letters had stopped in December, he told himself that they were delayed because his unit had moved and divided after the war ended. But as the weeks passed, his concern had grown.

Had she met someone else? If so, why hadn't she written and told him? What if she'd taken ill or . . . He slammed the door on that dreadful thought. She couldn't have perished at home in Canada while he had survived the gruesome battles in France. That was not possible.

He would visit his family at Bolton for a short time, secure their help, and then go to Canada and find Emma. His heart couldn't chart any other course.

The train brakes squealed. Rob motioned toward the passageway, where several people already waited. "After you, my friend."

Garth exited the train and stepped down to the platform. It had been almost a year since he'd come through St. Albans and visited his mum and his sisters Laura and Katie on a short leave. Then he'd returned to France and continued serving with Princess Patricia's Canadian Light Infantry.

The railway station bustled with activity as troops returned home and men, women, and children set off on their travels. Garth pulled in a deep breath and filled his lungs with crisp fresh air. It was good to be back in England, especially in a picturesque city like St. Albans. The branches on the nearby trees were still bare, but a few spring flowers brightened planters on the platform.

Garth and Rob made their way through the crowded station and out to the street. After a few inquiries, they found a farmer with a wagon headed in the direction of Bolton and caught a ride in the back between crates of cheese and baskets of wool.

Twenty minutes later, they hopped down from the wagon, thanked the farmer, and started up the long drive toward the main house at Bolton. Garth nodded to a stone cottage on the left. "My mum and sisters stayed there for a few months until Laura and Andrew were married, and then they all moved up to the main house."

"That looks like a nice place."

Garth grinned. "Wait until you see where they live now."

They walked on, and the view of the parkland opened up before them with spacious lawns dotted by several large trees. Sheep grazed in the pastures, and birds darted in and out of the trees along the drive. They rounded the bend, and in the distance the three-storied manor house came into view. It was built of honey-colored stone and had a large gable in the front, at least a dozen chimneys, and rows of mullioned windows extending along two wings at the north and south. Terraced gardens surrounded the house, and a small lake to the left of it reflected the blue sky above.

Rob halted in the middle of the drive. "Saints alive! That's your sister's home?"

"Yes. Rather grand, isn't it?"

"I should say so." Rob brushed his hand down his rumpled uniform jacket. "I'm not dressed to visit a place like that."

"Don't worry." Garth grinned and motioned toward the house. "I'm sure they'll be happy to see us no matter how travel weary we look." He set off, and Rob fell in step beside him. As they approached the massive oak front door, energy thrummed through Garth like a buzzing current. He could hardly believe he was finally going to see his mum, his sisters, their husbands, and his four young nieces and nephews again.

He knocked, and within seconds a tall, thin butler opened the door. "Good day, Mr. Sterling," Garth said, smiling.

The butler quickly pulled the door open wider. "Mr. McAlister, please come in. We weren't expecting you until tomorrow."

"Yes, we made all our connections more quickly than we expected. This is my good friend Rob Lewis."

Mr. Sterling offered a brief nod. "Welcome to Bolton, Mr. Lewis."

Rob returned the nod. "Thank you, sir."

Garth's gaze darted around the entrance hall, past the butler. "I'm eager to see my family. Are they at home?"

"Mrs. Tillman is in the library. If you'll follow me, sir."

As soon as the butler finished his sentence, the library door flew open and his sister Katie rushed out. "Garth!" A joyful smile lit up her face as she opened her arms and hurried toward him.

"Katie!" Grinning, he caught her up and swung her around. He could barely contain his joy at the sight of his twin sister. Their connection ran deep, and though they hadn't seen each other since his last visit, it felt like no time had passed at all.

Katie let go of Garth and stepped back. Pride and affection glowed in her hazel eyes. "You're too thin, but we'll take care of that. Our cook, Mrs. Drummond, is a miracle worker. You won't believe the lovely meals she makes even though so many items are still rationed."

Garth's smile spread wider as he noticed Katie's softly rounded midsection. "My goodness, Katie. Look at you!"

Her cheeks flushed pink, and dimples creased around her smile. "Yes, we're expecting an addition to our family in May."

"That's wonderful! I'm so glad for you and Steven." Knowing that his sister was happily married and expecting her second child was a great comfort to him.

She glanced at Rob, then back at Garth. "Please introduce me to your friend."

Garth chuckled. "Don't you recognize Rob Lewis?"

Her eyes widened. "Why, Rob, is that truly you?"

Rob smiled and nodded. "Yes ma'am."

"We'll have none of that. You're an old friend. Please, you must call me Katie." She smiled. "I hardly recognized you in your uniform. And you're so tall."

"I suppose I have grown a bit since our time in Canada."

"It's wonderful to see you again. I'm so happy you've come with Garth."

"Thank you. I'm very glad to be here."

Garth glanced past her shoulder. "Where are Mum and the rest of the family?"

Katie tucked her arm through Garth's and led them into the library. "Mum and Laura have taken Laura's two boys out for a walk, and my little Cecelia and Laura's Lillian are upstairs napping. Andrew and Steven are meeting with the estate agent, but everyone is due back in time for tea."

Garth tried to recall the names of Laura's sons but came up blank. He rubbed his forehead, weariness coursing through him. He'd looked forward to this reunion for so long. Why was he feeling befuddled?

Understanding lit Katie's eyes. "You must be tired, Garth. Why don't I show you and Rob up to your rooms? Then you can rest for a couple of hours before the family returns."

Garth nodded, grateful for Katie's kindness and insight. Ever since they were young, she'd had the ability to read his moods, sometimes before he was even aware of them. Their mum said it was their special twin connection. Perhaps that was true, but it also came from the deep bond that had developed since they were children. "Thank you, Katie. We *are* tired from our travels."

He ran his hand along his bristly chin. It would be good to rest and clean up before he saw Mum and the rest of the family and stepped into his roles as son, brother, and uncle.

As he and Katie climbed the stairs, memories of their life in London and the events that had taken them to Canada ran through his mind. They were only fourteen when their mother had become ill and had been taken to the hospital. He and Katie had tried to manage on their own and care for their sister Grace, but they were so hungry, he'd stolen a loaf of bread one day and been caught by a policeman. After that, they were taken to a children's home and eventually sent to Canada. He'd lost touch with Katie for a time, but the Lord orchestrated events, and they found each other one Sunday at church.

Their older sister, Laura, followed them to Canada and searched for them with the help of Andrew Frasier, who was now her husband. Katie had been found and freed from her indentured contract. She returned to England with Laura and Andrew, but Eli Gilchrest, Garth's employer, had refused to free him from his contract.

He clenched his jaw as he thought of his hard-hearted employer. Laura and Andrew had taken the matter before three judges, but in the end, Garth had been required to stay in Canada and finish his contract as a laborer at the Gilchrest farm and sawmill. Those events and the ones that followed had altered the course of his life forever.

He pulled in a steadying breath. Leaving the past behind, including his harrowing experiences in the war, and reuniting with his family might not be as simple as he'd imagined. He glanced at Katie, thankful for the chance to see her first and reestablish their special connection. But apprehension rippled through him. What would his family say when he told them of his plans to return to Canada?

Later that afternoon, Garth took a seat next to his mum on the library sofa. Rob and the rest of the family were gathered around them, seated on comfortable chairs. A wave of emotion tightened Garth's throat. What a gift to all be together. Only Dad and Grace were missing from the family circle. The addition of Rob was a comfort, and once again he thanked the Lord for such a faithful friend.

Laura sat across from him, next to Andrew, looking happy and contented in her roles as wife, mother, and mistress of the manor. A few fine lines around her eyes were the only changes he noted in her delicate features.

Andrew and Laura's three children occupied a small table near the end of the sofa, eating scones while the adults carried on their conversation.

Eight-year-old Andy was a near-perfect reflection of his father with light-brown hair and a winsome smile. The shape of five-year-old Matthew's nose and his large blue eyes made him look very much like his mother. Three-year-old Lillian's honey-blond curls reminded him of his sister Grace.

He turned to Laura. "Is there any news in the search for Grace?"

Laura's face clouded, and she shook her head. "We haven't heard anything from our contacts in Canada for several months."

Andrew laid his hand over Laura's. "Now that the war is over, we hope it will be easier to send and receive mail from Canada. That should help us renew the search."

Garth nodded. The Germans sunk several ships crossing the Atlantic, and the letters those ships carried had gone down with them. That made every letter he'd received from Emma a treasure. Now that the danger from German U-boats had passed, all the mail should get through. So why hadn't he heard from her?

Mum searched his face, and her eyes misted. "Oh, Garth, I can't believe you're really here with us."

Garth sent her a grateful smile. "I've dreamed of this reunion for a long time."

"And so have we." Mum squeezed his hand.

Surviving the war and reuniting with his family was a miracle. So many lads in his unit would never return home to see their loved ones. But the Lord had kept him safe. That meant He had a purpose and plan for Garth's life. Returning to Canada to marry Emma seemed to be the path he should take. But was it fair to leave his family so soon, especially after so many years apart?

Garth glanced at Steven, seated beside Katie. He held their little daughter, Cecelia, on his lap, though it was a challenge for him. He'd been injured in the Battle of Verdun and now wore a sling to protect his damaged left arm.

Before they gathered for tea, Katie had told Garth about Steven's injury. He needed help with some tasks, like buttoning his shirt and tying his shoes. But she was thrilled to have him home. Garth was deeply grateful as well. He would have hated to see his dear sister suffer the loss of her husband after all she'd endured in Canada when she was younger. Katie deserved to enjoy her family and a peaceful, happy life in England.

Andrew refilled his teacup and then turned to Garth. "Have you thought about what you'd like to do now that the war is over?" He glanced at Laura, who nodded. "We want you to know you're very welcome to stay here at Bolton as long as you'd like. We want to offer you a position on the estate, if you're interested."

"Thank you. That's very kind, but I have a plan in mind."

Mum looked his way. "What is that, dear?"

Garth braced himself, hoping Mum would not be too disappointed. "One of the officers in my unit is an experienced veterinarian. He appreciated the way I worked with the horses and offered to help me continue my veterinary training."

"Here in England?" Katie asked.

"No, his home is north of Toronto, near Orillia."

Mum's face fell. "You're going back to Canada?"

He turned to Mum. "It sounds like a good opportunity for me to get the training I need to establish my own veterinary practice. When I'm finished, I could work in Canada or England." He shifted his gaze away. "But there are other reasons I need to go back."

"Are you thinking of Emma?" Katie asked softly.

Garth nodded, his neck heating. He had told them a little about Emma in his letters, but his sister had always been able to read between the lines.

The tension in Mum's face eased. "Well, I don't like the idea of you being so far away to do that training, but I'm happy to hear you've found someone special."

"Nothing is settled between us yet." Garth debated what else to say and finally added, "I haven't heard from her in quite a while."

Katie's brows dipped. "How long has it been?"

He hesitated, then said, "About three months."

Katie exchanged a worried look with Laura. "Her letters were probably just delayed or misdirected. The military mail system must have been disrupted with the end of the war and so many troops returning home."

"That could be the reason, but I received letters from you and Mum right until the day our ship crossed the Channel." Garth shook his head. "I don't understand it. Honestly, I'm concerned."

Andrew shifted in his chair. "Are you thinking something may have happened to her?"

Garth's chest tightened, and a sense of foreboding filled him. That was exactly what he was thinking, and he hated to admit that it might be true. "Emma works on the same farm where I worked. Verna Hathaway, the cook and housekeeper, looked out for Emma and treated her well." He frowned. "I can't say the same for Mr. Gilchrest or the other two men working there."

He grimaced as he recalled the men's rough ways. Their coarse language, drinking, and carousing made him wish Emma could work somewhere else. But her indentured contract required her to stay until she was twenty-one, and that date had passed while he was in France. "It's not the best situation, but I thought she'd be safe there with Verna to watch over her until I returned. I never would've enlisted if I thought she was in any danger."

Katie's forehead creased. "Then you must go back and make sure she's all right."

"That's what I plan to do." Garth turned to Andrew. "I have some money saved, but I wanted to ask if you might cover part of the cost of the trip. I only need a small loan. I can repay it as soon as I'm working again."

Andrew nodded. "Of course. We'd be glad to help."

Garth released a deep breath, relieved his request had been made and that Andrew was agreeable. "Thank you."

Mum's eyes lit up. "Perhaps you can deliver a letter and packet to the man in Toronto who is overseeing the search for Grace."

Garth straightened. "I'd be happy to." If he could somehow help in the search to locate his younger sister, he was more than willing.

"But I hope you won't leave right away." Mum laid her hand on his arm. "We've missed you so much."

Garth smiled, warmed by his mum's kind words and gentle touch. "Rob and I would like to stay for at least a week or so. It will take that long to make our arrangements for the trip."

Mum patted his knee. "That's not very long, but I'll try to be grateful and enjoy each day."

Garth slipped his arm around Mum's shoulders. "Thank you, Mum. I hope you know how much I love you and all the family."

"I do, son." Her eyes glistened with unshed tears, and she quickly blinked them away. "You'll always have a special place in my heart."

Gratefulness flowed through him like a warm wave. His mum

had waited so many years for his return to England, and she'd covered him in prayer all that time. He would make the most of these days and show her how much she meant to him.

It would be hard to leave them all, but he couldn't ignore the urgency he felt to return to Canada. He would deliver the packet to the private detective overseeing the search for Grace and then look into what was required for his veterinary training. But first he had to keep his promise to Emma and make sure she knew how much he cared.

3

Belleville, Ontario

Emma Lafferty knelt on the kitchen floor of the Hazelton Boardinghouse and dipped her scrub brush in the bucket of cold gray water. She wiped her sleeve across her damp forehead, then pushed the brush over the next few feet of pine planking. Her light-brown hair fell forward, and with a weary sigh, she tucked it behind her ears.

Her shoulders and knees ached from all the tasks she'd done that day, but her heart ached more. Why hadn't Garth replied to her letters? That painful question cycled through her mind every day as she tackled the cleaning and laundry at this drafty old boardinghouse.

It had been four months since she'd received Garth's last quickly scrawled note, dated 5 November 1918, from Armentières, France. The war officially ended a week later, and with each passing day, the possible explanation for why she hadn't heard from him grew from a nagging worry to a dreaded fear.

Garth couldn't be gone!

Even after everything else that had happened to her in the past few months, losing him would be the worst blow of all. No one else loved her the way Garth did. And few seemed to care what happened to her since she'd fled Mr. Gilchrest's farm in mid-December.

The memory of the frightening events that sent her running through the night tightened her throat. She swallowed hard, trying to hold back tears, but a sob escaped. *Oh, Garth, where are you? Why don't you come? Every day with no word strains my heart near to breaking.*

Was she a fool to hold on to the hope that he still loved her and would make it home from this terrible war? He'd told her that his duty, caring for the regiment's horses, kept him out of the trenches and away from the line of fire, but that didn't mean he was never in danger. Even now, he could be injured and languishing in some military hospital in France or England.

She closed her eyes. *Please, Lord, if he's been hurt, watch over him and restore him to full health. Send some word. Let me know he's still alive.*

Could there be some other explanation for his silence? Had her letters to him been lost? If that were the case, then he wouldn't know that the terrible flu epidemic had sickened her and claimed Verna's life. He wouldn't know she'd run away to save herself from Mr. Gilchrest's terrible threats and vile intentions.

Emma shuddered and dipped her brush back in the bucket. After she'd found her way to Belleville and made an agreement with the owner of the boardinghouse to work in exchange for her room and meals, she'd written to Garth again and told him what had happened, and she'd continued writing every week. Still, she'd heard nothing.

Please, Lord, help my letters reach him so he'll know where to find me. I can't bear the thought of going on without him.

As her silent prayer faded away, another fearful thought rose and threatened to quench her last flicker of hope. What if Garth had received every letter she'd sent but he'd finally decided what everyone else said was true—that she was only a poor orphan, an outcast from the slums of London, a British Home Child no one could ever love? She lowered her head, anguish twisting her heart.

No! Garth wasn't like everyone else. He knew her, truly knew her. He'd promised he'd come home and they would be together again. She would not fail him now by doubting his love. She would hold on to that promise, treasure it in her heart, and let it carry her through these difficult days.

The kitchen door swung open, and Mrs. Ruby Hazelton, owner of the boardinghouse, strode in wearing a stained apron over her wrinkled brown dress. A scowl lined her haggard face, and her frizzy gray hair puffed out from her head like a misshapen steel-wool scrubber.

Mrs. Hazelton's scowl deepened. "How do you expect me to cook supper in here when the floor is wet and slippery?"

"I'm sorry." Emma wiped her forehead again, feeling dazed. "I'll be done soon."

"Well, don't just sit there staring at me. Get to it!"

A cheeky reply rose in Emma's throat, but she swallowed it down. She dared not anger Mrs. Hazelton and lose her place here. She had no real friends in Belleville and nowhere else to go.

Mrs. Hazelton shook her head. "I don't know why I took you in. You're hardly able to do a decent day's work!"

Emma pressed her lips tight, dipped the brush in the bucket once more, and went back to scrubbing. It wouldn't do any good to remind Mrs. Hazelton she was still recovering from a dreadful case of the flu that had nearly taken her life. She needed time to rebuild her strength, but the woman kept her busy all day until late in the evening and barely gave her enough food to keep going. It was no wonder her recovery was taking so long and she was slow to finish her tasks.

"This floor better be done and dried in fifteen minutes or you can pack your bags and leave!" Mrs. Hazelton stomped out of the kitchen. The door swung back on its hinges, squeaking in her wake.

Emma sighed and sat back on her heels. Her irritation with Mrs. Hazelton faded as thoughts of Garth returned. There had to be some way she could find out what had happened to him. Even if it would lead to the news she dreaded, at least she would know he'd died loving her rather than broken his promise and left her behind like everyone else.

A strangled cry startled Emma awake. She sat up in the dark, her heart pounding hard, and clutched the blankets to her chest. Another muffled cry rose from somewhere in the house, and then seconds later, hurried footsteps ran down the hall and descended the stairs.

Emma froze, trying to make sense of the sounds. Mrs. Hazelton's room was just across the hall. Had something happened to her, or had the cry come from one of the four boarders on the floor below? She slipped out of bed, crept across the room, and put her ear up to the door. All was quiet now. She pulled the door open a crack and peeked out.

Darkness engulfed the upper hallway. Nothing moved, and the only sound was the eerie whistling of the wind under the eaves. She wanted to climb back into bed and pretend she'd heard nothing, but she couldn't ignore the fearful cries or the mysterious footsteps.

She walked back to her bedside table. Her fingers trembled as she struck a match and lit her small lantern. She slipped on her robe and pulled in a deep breath. "Lord, give me courage," she whispered as she left her room, crossed the hall, and knocked on Mrs. Hazelton's door.

No one answered. She knocked again and leaned toward the door. "Mrs. Hazelton, are you all right?"

When no one replied, she tried the doorknob. After finding that it was unlocked, she pushed open the door and held up the lantern.

The faint light spread shadows across the sparse room, revealing a wooden chair in the corner with a tall dresser next to the window. A rumpled bed sat against the far wall with a still form beneath the blankets. On the floor next to the bed lay a pillow.

Emma strained to listen, but no sound came from the bed, not even a soft snore.

A chill traveled down her back, and she forced herself to move closer. "Mrs. Hazelton?" Her voice shook. "I heard someone cry out. I thought I should check on you."

The lantern light fell across Mrs. Hazelton's face, and Emma froze. The woman stared at her, wide eyed and unseeing.

Emma gasped and jumped back, almost dropping the lantern. Frightening questions darted through her mind, followed by a wave of nausea and dizziness. She spun away and ran from the room.

As the sunrise turned the sky pale gray, Emma sat in the boarding-house kitchen with two constables and Margaret Clarkson, the kind silver-haired widow who was the only other female boarder.

Constable Fieldstone and his partner, Constable Burton, had already questioned the three male boarders and sent them away. Now Constable Fieldstone directed his stern gaze toward Emma. "You say you heard footsteps in the upper hallway outside your door?"

"Yes sir." She'd already told him everything she could recall. Why did he keep asking her the same questions?

"Describe them for me."

"They sounded hurried as they went past my door, and then they faded away as the person went down the stairs."

"Past your door, you say?"

Emma nodded.

"But Mrs. Hazelton's room is directly across the hall from yours."

Emma hesitated, feeling a bit confused. "I thought they ran past my door, but it might have just been the sound of the person running down the hall, away from my room."

Constable Fieldstone leaned forward. "Which was it, Miss Lafferty? Did the person run past your door or not?"

Emma rubbed her forehead. "I'm sorry. I don't know. As I said, I was startled awake by a loud cry, and I was trying to make sense of it all when I heard the footsteps."

The constables exchanged glances.

Constable Fieldstone focused on Emma again. "Tell me, Miss Lafferty, how long have you been working for Mrs. Hazelton?"

"I started here about a week before Christmas, so about three months."

"And where did you work before that?"

Emma paused. If she told him the truth, would he send her back to Mr. Gilchrest? Her indentured contract was finished, but even if it weren't, she couldn't go back there. Not ever. "I . . . worked on a farm near Roslin."

"As a domestic?"

"Yes sir."

"And why did you leave that position?"

She glanced away, wondering how to explain it without giving him too many details. "The woman I worked for died." That was true, but it wasn't the whole story. Verna Hathaway, Mr. Gilchrest's housekeeper, assigned Emma's tasks and watched out for her, but Mr. Gilchrest was her true employer.

The constable frowned. "Your former employer died as well?"

Emma nodded. "We both came down with the flu after caring for our neighbors during their illness. I recovered, but Mrs. Hathaway did not."

He continued to frown, even after her explanation. "Is Roslin your hometown?"

Emma pulled in a breath to steady her nerves. "No sir."

He cocked his eyebrows. "Where were you born?"

She wished she could give a different answer, but there was no way around the truth. "I was born in London, England."

"I thought you had an English accent. When did you come to Canada?"

"When I was fifteen."

"You and your parents?"

"No, my parents died in a carriage accident when I was three. I lived in a children's home until I came to Canada with a group of children sponsored by Dr. Barnardo's Homes."

Constable Fieldstone's mouth drew down at the corners. "So, you're a British Home Child." His grim tone made his disapproval clear.

Emma looked away, her heart sinking. How many times had she been taunted or shunned when people learned she was a Home Child from England? Many believed only the dregs of society were sent across the sea to Canada and that they were not worthy of friendship, acceptance, or even a kind word.

Margaret straightened. "She may be an English orphan, but

she's a good girl, and she's always been kind and respectful to me. You've no cause to think poorly of her."

The constable turned to the widow with a skeptical lift of his dark eyebrows. "You can vouch for her character?"

"Yes sir, I can. Emma is a hard worker. She never argued with Mrs. Hazelton or had a harsh word to say about her, even though the woman worked her like a slave."

He narrowed his eyes. "So, you believe the girl wasn't well treated and had a reason to dislike Mrs. Hazelton? Perhaps she even had a reason to strike back at her?"

Emma pulled in a sharp breath. Did he really think she might be responsible for Mrs. Hazelton's death? Was that why he continued questioning her after he'd dismissed the three male boarders?

Margaret's face flushed. "That's not what I said, nor what I meant. That girl wouldn't harm Mrs. Hazelton or anyone else. You can dismiss that thought right now."

Constable Fieldstone stroked his mustache, looking unmoved by Margaret's firm words. "Nothing seems to be missing from Mrs. Hazelton's room, which makes me doubt robbery was the motive." He focused on Emma again. "What would make a person so angry they'd want to kill Mrs. Hazelton?"

Emma pulled back. "I'm sure I wouldn't know."

He leaned closer to Emma, his gray eyes steely. "Who held a grudge against Mrs. Hazelton or had a reason to harm her?"

Emma raised her hand to her heart. "I don't know. Mrs. Hazelton never confided in me. She only told me what chores to do. That's all we spoke about."

The constable glared at her a few more seconds, then stood up. "Very well. That's all the questions we have for you now, but we'll be in touch." He nodded to his partner. They put on their hats and walked out the back door.

Emma crossed to the window and watched the two men set off down the back alley.

"Well!" Margaret huffed. "What a dreadful man. The idea of him interrogating you like that!"

"I suppose he has to question everyone to find out who's responsible for . . . what happened to Mrs. Hazelton."

"Perhaps, but he seems set against you, especially now that he's aware of your background." Margaret shook her head. "That kind of prejudice is intolerable."

Emma stared out the window as all that had happened in the past few hours rolled through her mind. Finding Mrs. Hazelton lifeless in her bed had been so shocking, she'd nearly fainted. Somehow she'd found the courage to run downstairs and wake all the boarders. Mr. McDonald, one of the boarders, had gone for the constables, and they'd arrived within the hour and begun their questioning.

It all seemed like a terrible nightmare, and she wished she could wake up and find that it wasn't true. Who could've done such a thing? She'd never liked Mrs. Hazelton, but she'd never wished her any harm.

How could that constable think she might be responsible for Mrs. Hazelton's death? What if they arrested her?

Margaret rose from her chair. "This is certainly a sorry kettle of fish."

Emma turned toward Margaret. "What are we going to do now?"

"Well, I'm not wasting another minute in this dreadful place. I plan to pack my bags, and you should do the same."

"Where will you go?"

"My sister, Lucy, lives in Kingston. She's been asking me to come and stay with her, and I suppose now is as good a time as any."

Emma bit her lip. "I don't have any family." The only folks she knew lived in and around Roslin. But if she went back there, Mr. Gilchrest would hear of it, and there was no telling what he would do to her.

"Why don't you come with me to Kingston? It's a bigger city with more possibilities for work. I'm sure my sister wouldn't mind. She owns a café, and we could help out. That would give you time to search for a new position and make a fresh start."

"But what about Constable Fieldstone? What if he wants to ask me more questions?"

Margaret shook her head. "You've done nothing wrong. If we leave this morning, he'll be none the wiser."

A shiver raced down Emma's back. Wouldn't disappearing from Belleville make it look as if she were guilty of Mrs. Hazelton's murder? But what other choice did she have? She couldn't stay at the boardinghouse now that Mrs. Hazelton had passed away, and she couldn't go back to Roslin.

"I'm sure that as soon as you're gone, Constable Fieldstone will focus on finding out who is truly responsible for what happened. You'll be doing him a favor by coming with me to Kingston."

Emma wasn't sure the constable would see it that way, but she didn't see any other option. Staying in Belleville and being blamed for a murder she did not commit would be foolishness. She wrestled with those thoughts a little longer, then blew out a deep breath. "All right. I'll go with you."

"Good." Margaret plucked two oranges from a basket on the counter. "We better get packing. The sooner we leave this town, the better."

Emma nodded, hoping and praying it was the right decision, but a niggle of fear wove around her stomach and cinched it tighter.

4

G arth lifted his hand to shade his eyes and followed the kite as it flew up into the sky. The bright-red diamond rose on the breeze, its cloth tail fluttering as it swooped closer to the ground and then flew toward the clouds again. "That's the way!"

"Yes! Good job, Andy!" Katie's voice rang out.

The young lad set his mouth in a firm line, reeling out the string and looking determined to master the kite. Rob stayed behind Andy, holding the string, his grin wide as they ran across the lawn. Matthew and Lillian ran alongside, cheering their brother on.

"Andy's a strong young lad, but I don't think he could manage that kite without some assistance from Rob. Not on a windy day like this." Katie shifted her gaze from the kite to her little daughter, Cecelia, who toddled across the grass.

Garth looked up at the billowing clouds as he followed Katie and Cecelia into the shade of a large cedar tree. "It's a fine day for flying kites and letting the children run off some energy."

Katie smiled. "Yes, it is." She reached down and quickly plucked a small stick from her daughter's hand before she could put it in her mouth. "It's kind of Rob to lend a hand. He seems to have a special way with children."

"Yes, Rob's a fine fellow. I couldn't ask for a better friend." Garth smiled, remembering how he and Rob first met at the children's home in Liverpool when they were fourteen. Even then,

Rob had always been the one to look out for the younger boys. They'd sailed to Canada on the same ship and been taken in by families on adjoining farms near Roslin, Ontario.

Katie looked his way, emotion flickering in her eyes. "I'm glad you've had a good friend like Rob, especially since we've been separated for so long."

Garth nodded, sobering as he remembered all that had happened to him and Katie in the past few years. "We've each been on a unique journey, haven't we?"

"That we have." Her eyes misted, and she laid her hand on his arm. "But God answered our prayers. He kept you safe and brought you home to us, and that's a great blessing."

Emotion clogged Garth's throat, stealing away his words. He slipped his arm around Katie's shoulder and pulled her against his side, grateful beyond words to be with his sister again.

Cecelia tripped and thumped down onto the grass. She looked up at her mother with a trembling chin but didn't cry out.

Katie leaned down and held out her hand. "What a brave girl you are, Cece. Come on. Stand up and try again."

The little girl grabbed hold of her mum's fingers, rose to her feet, and let go. Two steps later, Katie had to reach for her again. "No, Cece. Don't put that in your mouth. It's dirty." She took a small stone from the little girl's hand.

Garth grinned. "She certainly keeps you busy."

Katie smiled and brushed an auburn lock of hair away from Cece's cheek. "She does, but she's such a sweet, cheerful baby, I can't complain."

Garth studied his sister, noting the tired lines around her eyes and the slope of her shoulders. Perhaps it was time for her to go back to the house and rest. He pulled his watch from his pocket.

"It's almost twelve. Shall we go in and give the children time to clean up before lunch?"

"Good idea. We don't want to keep the rest of the family waiting."

"Time to go in," Garth called before taking off across the lawn to round up his niece and nephews.

Rob helped Andy reel in the kite, and then he challenged the children to race back to the house. With laughter and shrieks, they tore across the lawn, climbed the terrace steps, and dashed toward Bolton's front door. Garth scooped up Cecelia and followed at a slower pace for Katie's sake.

As soon as they walked inside, Mr. Sterling crossed the great hall and held out a silver salver toward Katie. "The morning post arrived, ma'am."

"Thank you, Sterling." Katie accepted the letters and flipped through the pile. She pulled in a sharp breath and looked up at Garth. "This one is from the Hughes Home in Liverpool."

Energy zinged through Garth. "Do you think it's about Grace?"

"It must be, but it's addressed to Andrew and Laura." She spun to Mr. Sterling. "Where are Mr. and Mrs. Frasier?"

"In the drawing room with your mother and Mr. Tillman."

Katie and Garth hurried to the drawing room.

Katie held up the envelope. "A letter has arrived from the Hughes Home in Liverpool!"

"That sounds promising." Andrew rose from his chair. "Open it, Katie."

Her fingers fumbled as she tore at the envelope. "My hands are shaking. Here, Garth. You do it."

Garth took the thick envelope and tore it open. Inside he found two letters. He unfolded the first and read it aloud:

"Dear Mr. and Mrs. Frasier,

We kept your letter on file requesting information about your sister Grace McAlister, who passed through the Hughes Home in 1909 on her way to Canada. I'm writing today to pass along a letter we received from your sister, who now goes by the name Grace Hamilton and lives in Toronto, Ontario."

Garth stared at the words, too stunned to go on.

Laura lifted her hand and covered her mouth. "Oh my goodness! Grace found us!"

Andrew motioned toward the letter. "Is there more?"

Garth nodded and continued reading:

"Grace wrote to the address of the old Pleasantview Children's Home in Belleville, Ontario, requesting information about her siblings. That home was destroyed in a fire, but it has been rebuilt at a new location. The letter was redirected to that address. The matron at the new Pleasantview Home had no information about the family because the records were destroyed in the fire, so she sent your sister's letter to us. We are enclosing that letter so you can be in touch with her if you so choose.

Sincerely,

Mrs. Wilma Rogers

Matron of the Hughes Home, Liverpool"

Katie leaned toward Garth. "Read Grace's letter."

He took out a thick sheet of stationery, unfolded it, and read the letter out loud:

*"To the Matron of the Pleasantview Children's Home,
Belleville, Ontario*

Dear Madam,
    *I am writing to request information about my sister Kath-
erine McAlister."*

Katie gasped and lifted her hand to her heart. "She remembers
us!"

"Of course she does." Laura reached for Katie's hand.

Garth continued:

    *"My sister and I came from London, England, to
Pleasantview in the spring of 1909. We were separated
and sent to different families a few days after we arrived.
I have not heard from my sister since then. I only recently
learned that I passed through the Pleasantview Home
before I was placed with my adoptive parents, Judith and
Howard Hamilton of Toronto. I would like to contact my
sister Katherine, who goes by the name Katie, and I'd
also like to contact my brother, Garth McAlister."*

He looked up. "I guess she remembers me too." He pulled in a
deep breath to steady his voice and continued reading:

    *"If you know where they were sent or how I might con-
tact them, I would very much appreciate that information.
Thank you for your help in this matter. You may write to
me at this address: 421 Teasdale Street, Toronto, Ontario.*
    Yours sincerely,
    Grace McAlister Hamilton"

Garth lowered the letter and glanced around the circle of astonished faces.

"It's too wonderful!" Laura's voice trembled. "I can hardly believe it. After ten years of searching for her, she writes to us!"

Garth sat back, waiting for the two footmen to finish clearing the luncheon dishes from the table. Their conversation over the meal had focused on how they ought to respond to Grace's letter. Opinions varied, and Laura had flashed a silent warning around the table, stopping the conversation until the servants left the dining room and the door swung closed behind them.

Katie leaned forward. "I don't think we should send Grace a telegram. That seems too impersonal after so many years apart. It would be much better if each of us wrote her a letter and told her what's happened in our lives since we were separated."

Mum looked around the table, hope and uncertainty in her eyes. "A letter from each of us would help, but my main concern is her present situation. Is she well treated? Is she safe? That's what we need to know."

Garth tensed as memories flooded his mind. Mr. Gilchrest had been a harsh master who had little compassion for the boys he took in to do the hard labor on his farm and less compassion for Emma. But his sister Katie had fared far worse with the two families who'd taken her in to work in their homes. "Mum's right. Grace's safety is what's most important."

"She's not of age yet." Andrew's brow creased as he looked across the table at Garth. "She may still be working under an indentured contract as you were."

Laura laid her hand on Andrew's arm. "But in her letter, she said she was adopted. Wouldn't that mean she's been accepted into a family and has been treated as a daughter rather than a servant?"

"I hope so. We have no way of knowing what her situation is truly like until one of us goes there." Andrew rubbed his chin. "But I have two complicated cases right now, and I'm not sure how long those will take."

Katie tossed her napkin on the table. "Then I'll go. I don't want Grace waiting one more day, wondering where we are or if we care about her."

Her husband reached for her hand. "I know you love your sister, but a sea voyage at this stage of your pregnancy wouldn't be safe or wise."

Laura turned to Katie. "Steven is right. We'd all worry if you went now, and for good reason."

Katie sat back with a resigned sigh. "I suppose you're right."

Garth looked around the table. "I'm already headed to Canada. It makes sense for me to take our letters to Grace. Then I can assess the situation and see what we can do for her."

Katie's face brightened. "That would be wonderful, Garth. Then, as soon as you see her, you could send us a telegram so we won't have to wait and worry until a letter arrives."

"And you must tell her we've been searching for her all this time," Laura added. "I don't want her to think we abandoned her."

"Oh dear." Mum clutched her napkin to her chest. "She didn't say anything about me in her letter. Do you think she believes I died from that illness?"

Garth grimaced as a painful memory rose to the surface. Those in charge at the Grangeford Children's Home in London had told him his mum would never come for him and he should go to

Canada and make a new life for himself. They'd led him to believe she'd passed away, and that's what he'd told Katie. He hadn't learned his mother survived her illness until Laura found him in Canada.

Katie shook her head. "I never could bring myself to tell Grace we thought you died, and then we were separated just a short time later in Belleville."

Mum turned to Garth. "You must tell Grace I'm alive and well and that we all want her to come home to England."

Garth's throat tightened, and he nodded. Grace needed to know she was a cherished member of the family. He would make sure that message was delivered, and then he would do whatever was needed to see that she was safe. That was his duty to Grace and to their family.

"I'll help you make the arrangements." Andrew took a pen and small notebook from his jacket pocket and began writing on the first page. "You'll need sufficient funds for the trip and return passage for you and Grace."

Mum turned to Garth. "You will escort her home, won't you?"

Conflicting thoughts darted through his mind. Sailing to Canada and traveling to Toronto would take at least ten days, maybe longer. Contacting Grace and escorting her back to England would more than double the time. And what about Emma? He had to find out what had happened to her and see if there was still hope for them to have a future together.

Katie looked his way, concern reflected in her eyes. "What's wrong, Garth?"

He shifted in his chair. "I want to take our letters to Grace and escort her home, but I have to see Emma, as well."

"Why not go to Toronto first?" Katie suggested. "If Grace is free and willing to travel to England, she'll probably need time to prepare for the trip. That would give you a chance to go to Roslin and see Emma."

Katie's plan made sense, but would that give him enough time to make things right with Emma? That would depend on why she'd stopped writing and if she still cared for him. If she'd fallen in love with someone else, one brief visit would be all that was needed to hear that painful news. But what if she was ill or needed his help for some other reason? How would he care for Emma and see that his sister was safely reunited with the family?

Garth clenched his jaw, debating his best course of action. His youngest sister needed to know she was not forgotten. Her safety and well-being had to take priority over his desires. Helping Grace would change his plans, but it wouldn't stop him from finding Emma and making sure she knew how much he loved her.

5

Grace looked out the window and spotted the postman coming up the front walk. She hurried down the main staircase. She would have to be quick if she was going to intercept the afternoon post before it was given to her parents.

It had been more than a month since she'd written to the matron at the Pleasantview Home in Belleville, but so far she'd heard nothing.

Why didn't the matron reply? Surely, there were records of all the children who had passed through the home. Even though it had been ten years since she and Katie stayed there, the matron should know where Katie had been placed. Was there some rule that prevented her from giving the information? Was that why she hadn't responded?

As Grace reached the landing, the butler exited the morning room and crossed the main hall toward the front door. Apparently, he'd also seen the postman's approach through the morning room windows.

She slowed to a more ladylike pace but continued down the steps, intent on her goal.

Mr. Harding opened the door, greeted the postman, and accepted the small stack of letters. He placed them on a silver salver and started back toward the morning room.

"Are there any letters for me?" Grace asked.

He lifted his chin. "I wouldn't know, miss."

She suppressed a grin, knowing Mr. Harding usually looked through the post when it arrived, but only if he thought no one was watching. "I'll take them." She slipped the stack of letters off the tray before he could stop her.

His eyebrows dipped, and he pursed his lips. "Very well, miss." But disapproval filled his voice.

She waited for him to leave the hall before she flipped through the letters. If she found the one she was hoping for, she couldn't risk him reporting it to her father.

She read the address on the last letter and released a frustrated huff. Nothing! Perhaps she would have to write a second letter or try something else, but she had no other clues to follow.

Her mother walked into the hall from the morning room. "Is that the post?"

Grace's face warmed. "Yes, it is."

Her mother sent her a curious glance. "Well, don't just stand there. Bring it here."

Grace handed her mother the letters.

Her mother quickly sorted through them, and her eyes lit up. "Oh, here it is!" She tore open a square cream envelope, took out the card, and read the message with a smile.

"What is it, Mother?"

"An invitation for us to attend Agatha Pendleton's garden party."

Grace tensed. "Do we have to go?

"Yes, of course we do. Her son, Alfred, is one of the most eligible young men in Toronto. He recently returned from Oxford."

Rumors about Alfred swirled through her mind and unsettled her further. "I met him at Julia Milford's home, and I don't really care for him."

"Don't be silly, Grace. He's from one of the finest families in the city. His father is a chief shareholder of the Canadian Pacific Railway."

That might be true, but he was also one of the stuffiest and most self-absorbed young men she'd ever met, yet she couldn't very well say that to her mother. "I understand he's from a fine family, but I'm not interested in him as a possible suitor."

Her mother's eyebrows drew down in a V. "That's nonsense. Alfred Pendleton is an intelligent and respected young man. You will go to the party, and you will be polite and attentive when he speaks to you."

Grace looked away and pulled in a slow, deep breath. Why wouldn't her mother listen to her? Alfred Pendleton had a reputation for breaking hearts, and she did not want to be numbered among the young women he pursued and then quickly discarded.

"If he shows the slightest bit of interest, you will be encouraging and do everything you can to let him know you would welcome his proposal."

"But, Mother, I don't want to mislead—"

"Grace, you don't seem to understand the situation! There are very few young men of marriageable age left. The war has taken away your option to be choosy."

Grace's throat burned. "So, you're saying I should just settle for any man who shows the slightest bit of interest in me?"

"If he has the right background and social standing, yes!"

"Surely there are other qualities that are more important for a happy marriage."

"A secure future is the goal." Her mother's tone grew insistent. "Happiness is a by-product for a fortunate few."

Grace turned away and strode toward the window. Folding her

arms, she stared outside and tried to calm her stormy emotions. She'd always dreamed of marrying for love and being cherished by a man who accepted and appreciated her regardless of her background.

"You need to be sensible, Grace. Marriage to the right man will give you a place in society, a home, and a family. And most of all, it will give you a way to put your past behind you once and for all."

Grace swung around. "That's what this is really all about, isn't it? You don't want anyone to know I wasn't born into this family!"

"Grace, lower your voice! The servants will hear you."

There was no stopping her rush of words now. "That's why you moved up my debut and why you're pushing me toward an early marriage. You don't want it known that I'm a British Home Child!"

"Calm down, Grace. You're being overly dramatic." Her mother crossed the room and closed the door.

"What do you expect me to tell the men who come calling? How do you suggest I keep my background a secret?"

Her mother's stern expression firmed. "I expect you to avoid the subject as long as possible. Most men are happy to talk about themselves, if you ask them the right questions."

Grace clenched her fists, determined not to back down this time. "What if he asks me directly? What am I to say?"

Her mother fluttered her hand in the air. "Tell him you were born in Hampton, New Brunswick. That's where your father and I met and married. Your father had a shop there for three years. Then we moved to Kingston, where he expanded his business. Finally, we moved to Toronto when you were seven, and he founded Hamilton's."

Grace stared at her mother. After ten years, she thought she knew her. Now she wasn't certain at all. "You truly want me to lie to my future husband."

Her mother clicked her tongue. "There is no need to think of it that way. You're simply protecting your reputation and ours. That's what is best for everyone, and it's the only way I can see you having any hope for a promising future."

Grace shook her head. "Do you hear yourself, Mother?" Her voice rose. "Is that what you really want for me? A future built on lies?"

She grabbed Grace's arm. "Don't use that tone with me!" Grace tried to pull away, but her mother tightened her grip. "After all your father and I have done for you, the least you could do is show a little appreciation and do as we ask!"

Hot tears filled Grace's eyes. "I won't deceive my suitors! It's not right!"

"You will do as I say!"

"No! I won't! You don't care about me. You're only concerned about your precious reputation!"

Her mother's eyes flashed, and she slapped Grace hard across the cheek.

Grace gasped and pressed her hand to her stinging face.

Her mother's chin trembled and her eyes glittered with angry tears. Without a word, she spun away and marched out of the room.

Grace stared after her, too stunned to think clearly. She pulled in a shuddering breath, her thoughts slowly coming back into focus.

Judith Hamilton might have cared for her the past ten years, but she didn't truly love her. It was clear now that she cared more about appearances and the opinions of society than giving Grace a chance to find love and live an honest life.

A piercing pain shot through her heart as tears burned her eyes. She was not truly a member of the Hamilton family, and she never would be.

———◉

Grace rested her arms on her bedroom windowsill and looked at the twinkling lights of the city. Toronto was beautiful at night, but the awesome view did little to ease her aching heart. Her cheek still throbbed where her mother had slapped her that afternoon.

How could she treat her that way? Especially when Grace had worked so hard all these years to fit into the family and do everything her parents asked. She'd tried to be their ideal daughter to please them and make them proud.

Perhaps that was the problem. Truly fitting in and trying to win her mother's approval was futile. Her father had been somewhat easier to please, though he held back his affection when she did something he didn't like.

She could never be the daughter they wanted because she was not their daughter by birth. She was a Home Child, and they were ashamed of her and intent on making her keep that secret.

A tear rolled down her cheek, but she didn't bother to wipe it away. She might have been adopted into the Hamilton family, but she didn't belong to them. She was a McAlister, and somewhere out there she had two sisters and a brother. They had a shared heritage and memories of their life in England with their mum, who had truly loved them, faults and all.

She reached for the Bible on the window seat beside her and ran her hand across the cover. Each evening since she'd found it in the old trunk in the attic, she'd read a few pages from the gospel of John, which told the life story of Jesus. What He'd said and done seemed to leap off the pages and flow straight into her heart.

Jesus's actions were motivated by His devotion to God and His love for people, yet He was despised and rejected by many who heard Him teach, even after all the miracles He performed. He led a sinless life, but He faced endless opposition that took Him all the way to the cross.

If He faced so much trouble, should she be surprised by the problems and heartaches she had to endure? Her life certainly wasn't sinless. Every day she struggled against resentment toward her adoptive parents and the selfish desire to run her own life without yielding her heart to God and His will and plans for her. Yet she still sensed His love and call to come closer and trust Him.

She sighed and looked out the window again. *Father, there's so much I don't understand. I want to honor my parents and please them, but carrying on this masquerade to deceive the man I will marry isn't right. If I give in and follow that path, it will surely lead me into more trouble. But if I stand up against my parents and let the truth be known, they'll be angry and reject me.*

She pondered that for a moment. Hadn't they already rejected her by demanding she hide her true identity? They gave only partial approval to the dishonest version of their adopted daughter.

She closed her eyes against her tears. *Give me courage, Father. Help me find the right path forward. Lead me toward the life You have for me.*

A whisper of peace flowed through her, and for the first time in weeks, she felt the burden begin to lift off her shoulders. She didn't know how He would lead or where that would take her, but she believed the answer to her prayer was on the way. She would trust Him and wait with hope filling her heart.

Emma pushed the rolling pin over the piecrust with careful strokes, and the buttery yellow dough spread out in a neat circle.

Margaret smiled as she watched from across the worktable in the kitchen of Morton's Café. "Lucy will be pleased. We can't seem to make enough of these apple pies to satisfy all her customers."

Emma nodded, then sprinkled a little flour over the dough and continued rolling. It had been a busy day at the café. Finally, the last of the customers had finished dinner and gone home. As soon as she put these pies in the oven, she and Margaret could sit down to take a rest.

Lucy, Margaret's sister and the owner of Morton's Café, had gone upstairs around three to lie down and relieve her headache. The poor woman was plagued with them. Emma couldn't imagine how Lucy had managed the café before she and Margaret had arrived to help with the cooking and serving.

Emma glanced into the dining room, where Peter Morton swept the floor to prepare for tomorrow morning's breakfast crowd. Lucy's tall, lanky son sent her a quick smile before he went back to sweeping.

Emma looked down, uncertain what to think of Peter or that smile. She shook off her reaction and continued rolling and turning the crust to make a perfect circle.

Her thoughts drifted back to the Gilchrest farm, where she'd worked from age fifteen until she was twenty-two. Verna had taught her how to bake all kinds of bread, cakes, cookies, and pies.

How many times had she rolled out a piecrust and baked a pie just like this one? Apple pie was Garth's favorite. And when one of those pies came out of the oven, golden brown and steaming with the sweet scent of cinnamon, their mouths would water. After supper some nights, she and Garth would sit out on the porch and enjoy a piece of pie and a cup of coffee. Mr. Gilchrest rarely allowed him in the house. Garth slept in the bunkhouse by the barn with Harry and Jason, the other two men who worked for Mr. Gilchrest.

During those evenings on the porch, Garth would always smile and praise her, saying she was the finest baker in all of Hastings County. His eyes would shine with life and good humor, and she'd feel so proud and happy. There was no one like Garth, no one so strong and caring. He appreciated and treasured her, or at least she thought he had.

Tears stung her eyes. She swallowed hard and blinked them away. It was best not to think about him now or her tears would overflow and Margaret would want to know what had upset her. Emma carefully folded the piecrust and slid it into the pie pan.

"What's wrong, Emma?" Margaret asked as she sprinkled cinnamon into a bowl of sliced apples.

"Nothing." She hadn't told Margaret about Garth. If she kept him a secret, she wouldn't have to admit she hadn't heard from him since November. That seemed the only way she could protect her treasured memories and hold on to hope he would return. Was that the only reason she kept silent, or was it because she was afraid Margaret would make her face the fact that Garth might never be coming back? She clenched her jaw and pushed that thought away. She wouldn't accept that—not yet.

"I can tell you're carrying a burden," Margaret continued with a gentle tone. "I can see that as plain as day. What's troubling you, child?"

Emma straightened her shoulders. "Don't worry about me. I'm all right." She'd always kept her worries to herself, and she didn't see any reason to open up now. Telling Margaret wouldn't change anything.

A shadow crossed Margaret's face. "Well, if you ever do want to tell me, I'll be glad to listen."

Peter walked into the kitchen carrying the broom and dustpan. "I'm all done in the dining room."

Margaret motioned toward the front room of the café. "Everything looks good, Peter."

But his attention seemed to be on the pie that was ready to go in the oven. "My, that sure does look good."

"It won't be ready for another hour, but I saved you a piece of chocolate cake." Margaret nodded toward the metal dome covering the cake plate on the counter.

"Thank you, Aunt Margaret. That's real nice of you." He ran his hand over his lean stomach. "But I'm still full from that fine supper you and Emma prepared." His gaze darted to Emma.

"I'm glad you liked it." Margaret smiled. "I'm always happy to hear someone enjoys my cooking."

"I do, and I know my mother does too." His smile faded. "These last few months have been real hard on her. Since Dad passed away, she's been suffering more with her headaches." He shook his head, as though he were trying to banish those memories. Then he looked at Emma. "I'm real glad you came . . . both of you."

Emma knew all too well how painful it was to lose a dearly loved family member. Both her parents had passed away when she was a young child. Peter was older, but that didn't make the loss any easier. He not only had to grieve his father's death; he had to step into the role of caring for his mother and helping manage the café. Emma studied him more closely. He might be twenty-one, but with his blond hair, light-blue eyes, and softly rounded face, he looked younger.

"It's a nice night, warm for this time of year." Peter glanced at Emma again. "Would you like to step outside and take in some fresh air?"

Emma blinked, surprised by Peter's suggestion. He'd never asked her anything like that before. "I need to finish this last pie."

"Don't worry about the pie." Margaret waved her hand and shooed them toward the door. "I'll finish up. You two go on outside and take a look at the stars."

Emma's cheeks warmed. "All right." She rinsed and dried her hands, wondering what she ought to say to Peter. Maybe she was fretting over nothing. He probably just wanted some fresh air and friendly conversation. She turned from the sink and met his gaze.

Peter stood by the side door, her shawl in his hand and an expectant look in his eyes.

Emma tensed. His expression seemed to say he was hoping for more than just fresh air. She crossed the kitchen and met him by the open door.

He draped the shawl around her shoulders. "There you go. We don't want you to get cold."

She turned away from his smile and stepped onto the porch. The soft song of the crickets greeted her as she crossed to the railing and looked down Central Street. The hush of evening had settled over the city.

Across the street, the shades had been pulled over the windows of Miss Barnet's Millinery Shop. Most of the other businesses were closed and dark as well. Only a few lights glowed in the second-story windows above the boot shop and Swanson's General Store. Many of the other shop owners had homes away from their businesses, unlike Peter and his mother, who lived above the café.

Peter joined her at the porch railing. "I sure do appreciate the way you and Aunt Margaret have stepped in and helped us. It's been a huge relief. I want to thank you, Emma."

She shook her head. "It's no trouble. I'm glad to help, and I'm grateful to have a safe place to stay."

He tipped his head and studied her face. "You haven't told us much about your family or where you're from."

Emma bit her lip and looked away.

"I mean . . . I know you met Aunt Margaret in Belleville. Is that where you grew up?"

She hesitated, wishing she could avoid answering, but there didn't seem to be any way around it. "No. I worked on a farm near Roslin for several years before I came to Belleville."

He watched her, waiting for her to explain. When she didn't, he blew out a slow breath. "It's all right. You don't have to tell me any more if you don't want to."

She clutched the shawl tighter around her. "It's not that I don't want to. I'm just not sure you'll like what you hear if I do."

He frowned. "What do you mean?"

She released a soft sigh. There was no use keeping her past a secret from Peter. The truth would come out sooner or later. It always did. "I was born in England. My parents died when I was young. I came over to Canada with a group of girls from a children's home when I was fifteen."

Questions lit up his eyes. "You're an orphan?"

"Yes, I am." She looked down, fingering the fringe on her shawl, knowing full well what that admission would cost her. "I know what people say about British Home Children—that we're all street urchins, tainted by our parents' sin, and destined to pollute Canada." She grimaced, hating the bitter words she'd heard directed at her for so many years.

"Whoever would say something like that about you is foolish and ignorant."

"You really mean that?"

"Of course I do. It doesn't matter to me where you're from or how you came to Canada. You've obviously worked hard to make a new life for yourself. That's quite an accomplishment. You should be proud of it."

The tightness in her shoulders eased a bit. "That's kind of you to say, but I'm afraid most people wouldn't agree with you."

"Well, I'm not most people." His forehead creased, his eyes searching. "I hope no one is giving you trouble at the café."

She shook her head. "I haven't told anyone else here in Kingston about my past."

A warm glow filled his eyes. "Well, if anyone *does* give you trouble, just let me know and I'll straighten them out."

A smile tugged up the corners of Emma's mouth. "Thank you, Peter."

"No need for thanks. I'm glad to do whatever I can for you." He took a step closer and leaned on the porch railing. "I want you to feel at home here, Emma."

Her smile faded, and she glanced away. Had she said too much and given Peter the wrong impression? She was glad to have a friend who thought well of her, but she didn't want to encourage him in a romantic way. That wouldn't be fair. She'd given her heart to Garth years ago, and even though she wasn't sure where he was or if he was coming for her, she couldn't imagine ever loving anyone else.

6

Garth led the way across the platform at the St. Albans railway station with Rob, Laura, Andrew, Katie, and Mum close behind.

Mum reached for his arm. "Do you have your tickets?"

Garth turned toward her with a reassuring smile. He pulled the envelope Andrew had given him from his suit-coat pocket. "They're right here, Mum."

"Good." Mum's expression eased, but a few lines still creased her forehead.

Garth's chest tightened. He didn't want to add another burden to his mum's heart. "We'll be fine. Please don't worry."

She sent him a tremulous smile. "I'll try, but it's hard for a mother not to worry when she loves her children so much."

Laura slipped her arm through Mum's. "Garth is an experienced traveler. Andrew made sure he and Rob have everything they need for their journey."

Mum shifted her attention to her son-in-law. "Thank you, Andrew. I'm very grateful."

"Glad to do it." Andrew turned to Garth, his tone and expression serious. "When you arrive in Quebec City, you can make inquiries and purchase your train tickets to Toronto. All the funds are in the envelope."

Garth nodded, grateful for his help. They'd gone over all the travel arrangements a few times, but it was reassuring to hear them again. He knew doing so would comfort his mum as well.

Katie stepped forward. "As soon as you can, let us know how the meeting goes with Grace." She clasped her hands together. "I'm so anxious for her to know we've never stopped searching for her."

He touched Katie's arm. "I'll tell her, and I promise to send word after I see her."

"Thank you, Garth." Katie rose on tiptoe and kissed his cheek. "We'll be praying for you every day, and we'll be eager to hear your news."

He pulled her in for a gentle hug. He loved all his family, but he would always share a special bond with Katie. He held her close and had to swallow before he could speak. "Take care of yourself and the baby."

"I will." Katie stepped back, her eyes glistening, and rested her hand on her rounded midsection. "You better hurry back to England so you and Grace will be here for the arrival of your next niece or nephew."

"I wouldn't want to miss that." Garth forced a smile while fighting off his own concern. Childbirth was never easy, and there was always some danger for the mother and infant. He'd have to pray for Katie even more than he usually did.

Garth turned to his brother-in-law and extended his hand. "Thank you, Andrew. I appreciate everything you've done to make this trip possible."

Andrew gripped Garth's hand, his expression warm. "You're a good man, Garth. Thanks for taking this on for the family. I'm confident you'll manage everything well."

Garth nodded, hoping he could live up to their expectations.

What if Grace didn't want to leave her adoptive family and come to England, even for a visit? If that were the case, it would put him in an awkward position with her and their family. But he had no more time to consider that possibility, as one by one his family members gave him a final hug or pat on the back and wished him well on his journey.

Rob put out his hand toward Andrew. "It's been a pleasure meeting you all. Thank you for your hospitality."

Andrew shook his hand. "I'm glad you and Garth can make this trip together. It's always helpful to travel with a friend."

The train whistle blew, and the conductor called for the passengers to board.

Mum pulled Garth in for one more hug. "Goodbye, son. You're always in my heart and prayers. Please give my love to Grace and tell her how much we long to see her."

"I will." He kissed Mum's cheek and sent her a last look, then followed Rob toward the train.

Rob looked over his shoulder as they boarded. "You have a fine family."

"Yes, the finest." Garth stepped into the first-class compartment Andrew had reserved for them. He lowered himself onto the padded bench seat and looked out the window. Mum, Andrew, Laura, and Katie stood together on the platform, waiting to see them off. A bittersweet pang filled his chest as he lifted his hand and waved to them.

How long would they be separated this time? Only a few weeks, or would connecting with Grace and Emma take longer? Would his veterinary training make him claim Canada as his future home, or would he find his way back to England to build a future there?

He studied the faces of his family once more, treasuring their images in his heart to carry with him no matter how far the journey.

With Rob at his side, Garth walked down Teasdale Street, taking in the large stately homes on his right and left. Most were set back and surrounded by tall trees, manicured lawns, and flower beds filled with early-spring flowers. "I had no idea Grace lived in such a prosperous section of Toronto. Growing up here must have been very different than what we experienced."

"I'm sure you're right about that." Rob pointed to a three-storied red-brick house. "Is that the one?"

Garth's steps slowed as he studied the large Victorian home with its wide covered porch and stained-glass windows on the main floor. He checked the plaque posted by the front gate that read *Number 421*. "Yes. That's it."

Seeing the address reminded him of Grace's letter, and he straightened his shoulders. There was no need for him to hesitate. His sister had written and asked for information about the family, and he'd come to bring her their replies. That was invitation enough to approach this impressive house.

Garth pushed open the gate, and Rob followed him up the steps to the porch. Garth breathed out a silent prayer, lifted the brass knocker, and rapped three times. He glanced at Rob, and his friend sent him a confident smile.

After a few seconds, the door opened and a young woman wearing a maid's uniform looked out at them. "May I help you?"

Garth quickly searched the maid's face, and relief rushed through him. Though she had blond hair like his sister, her eyes were brown. She wasn't Grace. He cleared his throat. "Yes, we'd like to see Miss Grace . . . Hamilton."

The maid sent them an anxious look, then glanced over her shoulder. Finally, she turned back to Garth. "I'm not sure if Miss Hamilton is receiving callers today."

Garth tipped his head to listen and looked past her shoulder. Piano music drifted out from somewhere in the house.

"We've come all the way from England," Rob said. "I'm sure you don't want to turn us away."

Garth nodded. "That's right. It is important that we see Miss Hamilton today. Is she at home?"

"Mr. Harding, the butler, usually takes charge of guests, but he's not feeling well today." She hesitated, then leaned forward and lowered her voice. "I've only been working here three days, and I'm not sure what's proper."

Garth smiled, hoping to put the maid at ease. "I'm sure it will be all right. Please tell Miss Hamilton that Mr. Garth McAlister and Mr. Robert Lewis are here to see her."

"Very well." The maid pulled the door open wider. "You may come in and wait here." She ushered them into the large entrance hall, then scurried off through a doorway at the end of the hall. It sounded as though that was the room where the piano was being played.

Garth studied the dark-paneled walls and imposing staircase with carved oak railing and banisters. A plush red carpet covered the center portion of the stairs leading up to the next floor.

"Someone is certainly a talented musician." Rob nodded toward the doorway where the maid had disappeared. "Does your sister play the piano?"

Garth blinked. He had no idea. "She didn't play the piano when she was seven."

The music stopped, and Garth heard the maid's voice. "There are two young men here to see you, miss."

Garth leaned forward, straining to hear his sister's reply.

"Two young men?"

"Yes, miss. I can't recall their names, but they look respectable."

Rob grinned and winked at Garth. Garth shoved his friend's arm.

"Did they say why they were calling?"

"No, miss. They only said they've come from England and they want to speak to you."

Garth held his breath as the grandfather clock to his left ticked off the seconds.

"All right. You may show them in."

The maid appeared again. "Miss Hamilton will see you now." She motioned toward the open doorway.

Garth and Rob crossed the entrance hall and entered a large sunlit room. Garth quickly scanned the elegant furniture and marble fireplace. Light streamed through tall windows on the right. A grand piano sat in front of the windows, and a young woman with long blond hair turned on the piano bench, questions hovering in her violet-blue eyes that strongly resembled Laura's.

She rose from the piano bench with a slight smile. "Good morning, gentlemen. You asked to see me?"

Garth watched her closely, hoping for a look of recognition, but none crossed her face. "Are you Grace Hamilton?"

"Yes, I am. And you are?"

A myriad of emotions rushed through Garth. "I'm your brother, Garth."

Her eyes widened. "My brother?"

"Yes." His heartbeat pounded in his ears as he took her envelope from his inside jacket pocket. "I've come in response to your letter."

She blinked. "My letter?"

"Yes, the one you sent to the Pleasantview Home, asking how to contact your siblings. It was forwarded to our family in England." His eyes burned, and emotion clogged his throat.

Her chin wobbled and tears filled her eyes. "Oh, Garth, is it truly you?"

"Yes . . . yes, it is." He started across the room toward her.

She hurried forward, and he opened his arms to her. She stepped into his embrace and leaned against him with a gentle sob.

He hugged her tight, waves of relief washing over him. He'd finally found his little sister. Soon she would be reunited with the family, and they would all be together at last. He held her close, silently lifting prayers of thanks.

"I can't believe you're really here," she whispered.

"We've been searching for you for the past ten years."

She stepped back and gazed up at him, wonder in her eyes. "You've been looking for me all this time?"

"We've all been part of the search. Laura followed us to Canada only a few weeks after the three of us were sent away. She found Katie and rescued her from a terrible situation on a farm near Roslin where she was working. They found me on a nearby farm and tried to free me, but I had to stay and fulfill my indentured contract. Laura tried to find out where you'd been placed, but there was a fire at the Pleasantview Home, and all your records were destroyed."

Grace lifted her hand to her heart. "The home burned down?"

"Yes, only a few days after Laura found Katie. No one remembered who had taken you in or if you'd stayed in Belleville or gone to another town. Katie needed to recover from her ordeal, so they returned to England, but Laura and her husband, Andrew, hired private investigators to continue searching for you. Of course, the war made communication between Canada and England difficult, but we've never given up hope that we'd find you someday."

Grace still looked dazed. "This is so . . . I don't know where to start. I have so many questions. Do you and Katie and Laura all live in England now?"

He nodded but then shook his head. There were so many details he needed to explain. "Laura and Katie do, but I've been away in France for three years with my regiment, fighting in the war. Laura and Andrew live on his family estate with their three children."

"Laura is married and has children?"

"Yes, two boys and a girl." Garth grinned. "You're an aunt."

Grace's eyes lit up, and her smile returned. "I'm an aunt? Oh, that's wonderful. I'm so happy for her."

"Katie lives there too, with her husband, Steven, and their daughter. The estate is near St. Albans, north of London, and Mum is there with them."

Grace gasped and raised her trembling hand to her mouth. "Mum . . . is alive?"

"Yes." Garth pulled the letters from his family members out of his other pocket and held them out to her. "Each one of us wrote you a letter telling you about our lives since we were separated."

Grace accepted the four envelopes with shaking fingers. "You all wrote to me?"

"We debated the best way to explain everything. We knew you'd have a lot of questions and that it would be a challenge for you to take it all in. We thought the letters would give you a chance to hear from each of us."

Tears glistened in her eyes again. "Thank you, Garth. That's so very kind."

He swallowed hard. "Mum especially wanted me to tell you how much she loves you and misses you. Her dearest wish is to see you again and have all our family reunited in England." He tapped the top letter in her hand. "The blue envelope is from Mum."

Grace swiped a tear from her cheek. "I always hoped Mum had recovered and was alive and well, but ten years is a long time to wait to hear from your family. I'd almost given up hope."

Regret dampened Garth's spirit. It had obviously been difficult for Grace to be separated from them. "I'm sorry it took so long. But you must believe you've always been in our thoughts and prayers."

Her tremulous smile returned. "I believe it now. Please take a seat. I'm sorry to have kept you standing so long."

Garth released a deep breath and settled on the settee facing the piano. Rob joined him.

Grace shifted her gaze to Rob. "I'm sorry. I don't recognize you. Are we somehow related as well?"

Rob smiled. "No, I'm Garth's friend."

"Rob is more like a brother," Garth said. "We met in Liverpool at the children's home when we were fourteen, and then we sailed to Canada together. We ended up working on adjoining farms for a few years. Then in late 1915, we decided to enlist. We served together in Princess Patricia's Canadian Light Infantry for the past three years."

Grace said to Garth, "If you had to go to war, I'm glad you were able to go together." She looked at Rob again. "Have you reconnected with your family in England?"

Emotion flashed in Rob's eyes, and he shook his head. "My parents died in a fire when I was young. I lived with my grandmother for a few years, but when she passed away, I was sent to the children's home. Garth arrived about the same time. We've been watching out for each other ever since."

"Yes, we have. And it's a good thing." Garth clamped his hand on Rob's shoulder. "Rob saved my life in France. I'll never be able to repay him for all he's done for me."

Admiration shone in Grace's eyes. "You saved Garth's life?"

Rob glanced away, looking embarrassed. "That's a story for another day. But I will say this: Garth has done more than his share to keep me alive and well these past few years."

Garth studied Grace, making careful note of her pink cheeks, shining hair, and vibrant eyes. She seemed healthy and content, but he had to be sure. "I need to ask, Grace . . . have the Hamiltons treated you well? Are you safe and happy here?"

She pressed her lips together and averted her eyes.

He tightened his grip on the arm of the settee. "What is it? Please tell me."

Slowly, she looked up and met his gaze. "My adoptive parents have given me a good education, fine clothing, and music and dancing lessons . . . but they've forbidden me to tell anyone I was a British Home Child."

Rob's face darkened. "Too proud, are they?"

Grace sighed. "I suppose that's part of it. My father owns one of the largest department stores in Toronto, and they're respected members of society. They said it would damage my reputation and diminish my chances of making a good match."

Garth's gut twisted. "So they don't want anyone to know the truth?"

She nodded. "They said I'd never find anyone willing to marry me if my past became known."

Garth shook his head. "How do they expect you to never speak about the first seven years of your life or your family in England?"

"They insist that's the only way I'll ever find a husband. And tomorrow night I'll have to continue the charade when I make my debut at the St. Andrew's Ball." Her shoulders sagged. "My mother says it's time I enter the marriage market and find a respectable suitor."

Garth frowned. "But you're only seventeen. That seems awfully young to be pushing you toward marriage."

"I'll be eighteen soon, and many young women marry at that age. At least that's what Mother says."

Rob sat forward. "That may be true, but what do you think of the idea?"

"I don't know. Tomorrow night will be the first time I've attended a ball or taken part in a large society event. I've never even been to the Houghton Hotel before."

Voices sounded in the entry hall. A middle-aged man and woman walked into the room, and their steps stalled.

Grace's gaze darted from the couple to Garth and Rob. "Mother, Father, I didn't expect you'd be back until this afternoon."

Garth rose to his feet, and Rob stood up beside him.

Mr. Hamilton's forehead creased as he looked at Garth and Rob. "Grace, who are these men?"

"This is Robert Lewis and Garth McAlister . . . my brother."

Mrs. Hamilton gasped and stared at Garth with wide eyes.

Mr. Hamilton's face reddened as he strode across the room. "Your *brother*?"

Garth stepped forward. "Yes sir. Grace is my youngest sister. She was born into the McAlister family in England. I've come to bring her news about her mum and sisters."

"I don't believe this!" Mr. Hamilton scoffed. "How dare you barge into my home with such a deceitful story!"

Garth froze, stunned by the man's response. "I'm not trying to deceive anyone. I simply want—"

Mr. Hamilton sliced his hand through the air. "What proof do you have to substantiate your claims?" Before Garth could answer, Mr. Hamilton jutted out his chin and continued. "Tell me the truth. What do you *really* want?"

Garth straightened his shoulders. "As Grace already told you, I am her brother. We came to Canada on the same ship in 1909."

Mr. Hamilton huffed. "That's a likely story."

"It's the truth!" Garth shot a glance at Grace, then at Mr. Hamilton. "I've come to see my sister and make sure she is being well treated."

Mrs. Hamilton's face flushed, and she quickly moved to stand beside her husband. "I don't believe a word of this! You must have learned some details about Grace's past, and now you want to use them against us."

"No ma'am. I came to bring my sister letters from her family and take her back to England to be reunited with them if she chooses."

Grace's mouth dropped open.

"So *that's* what you've planned!" Mr. Hamilton glared at Garth. "You want to sway my daughter into believing your lies so you can blackmail us or spirit her away and hold her for ransom."

"No sir. That's not it at all!"

"I've heard enough! It's time for you to leave." Mr. Hamilton pointed to the door.

Grace shook her head. "Please, Father, you don't under—"

Mr. Hamilton scowled. "Let me handle this, Grace."

She reached for his arm. "But what he's saying is true!"

"No!" He shook off her hand and turned to Garth. "Leave this house immediately! If you ever try to darken our door again, I will contact the constables."

Garth stood his ground, his anger seething. How could Mr. Hamilton dismiss everything Garth said? Was he truly so stubborn and prideful that he'd forbid them to see Grace?

He glanced at his sister. Tears glittered in her eyes as she looked from Garth to Mr. Hamilton.

Garth didn't want to hurt Grace or make this situation more difficult for her. It seemed he had no choice. "All right, I'll go, but this is not finished. I *am* Grace's brother, and I won't let you keep us apart."

Hot tears flooded Grace's eyes as she watched Garth and Rob stride out of the drawing room. She gulped down the knot in her throat and swung around to face her father. "Please call them back!"

Her father shook his head, his expression firm. "That young man is *not* your brother."

"But he is! I remember him and my sisters."

"You mustn't believe his lies. He's not who he says he is."

"But he knows how I came to Canada. He told me about my sisters, Katie and Laura, and about my mum. She's alive and well in England. She loves me and wants to see me."

"That can't be true!" Her mother quickly closed the door, then spun and faced Grace. "The authorities in Belleville told us you were an orphan with no relatives who could care for you."

"Then they're the ones who lied! Please, can't you see how important this is to me?" She searched her mother's face and then her father's. There had to be some way to make them understand. "For years I've longed to know more about my family and understand who I truly am. Now, the day my prayer is finally answered, you tell me it's all a lie!"

"Grace, calm yourself." Her mother took her handkerchief from her sleeve and dabbed her glowing cheeks. "This incident has been upsetting for us all. But we must put it behind us and focus our thoughts on your debut tomorrow night. Why don't you go upstairs and lie down? I'll have Sylvia bring you some tea."

Grace clenched her hands. "I don't want to lie down, and I don't want tea! You have to listen to me. I won't let you sweep this under the carpet and pretend it didn't happen!"

Her father shook his head, his expression firm. "You're young, Grace. You don't understand the way some people devise all kinds of schemes to swindle those who are wealthy. But I won't be fooled by that young man or anyone else. You must trust me to handle your affairs as I see best."

"The same way you've *handled* my affairs for years—lying to everyone we know, pretending I'm your daughter by birth? And now you're *handling* it by banishing the only true relative I've seen in ten years!"

Her father's face darkened. "We are your parents. It's our job to protect you, and that's what we intend to do."

Grace's face burned. She crossed her arms and turned away. It was useless to try to reason with them. They'd told themselves the lie for so many years, they actually seemed to believe it was true.

Her mother stepped in front of her. "We've given you every advantage so you could forget your shameful past and build a respectable future. That should inspire gratitude and loyalty rather than this defiant and disrespectful display."

Grace tried to calm her racing heart. "I *am* grateful for all you've given me. But that doesn't mean I agree with you or want to continue this charade."

Her mother's nostrils flared. "If this is a charade, then you're just as responsible for carrying it out as we are for suggesting it."

She gasped as though her mother had slapped her. "I've only gone along with it to please you. Now I see that's impossible."

Her father stepped closer. "Consider what's at stake, Grace. You're about to launch into society so you can marry and establish a home and family of your own. Surely, you don't want to throw all of that away to chase after some foolish schemer with questionable intentions."

Grace shook her head. "How can you expect me to pretend my birth family doesn't exist?"

Her mother gripped her arm. "You'll do what's needed to give yourself the best chance for a decent future. Now listen to us and put this foolishness out of your mind."

Grace pulled her arm away and locked eyes with her mother. "I know what you want me to do. But I can't ignore my conscience, and I *won't* ignore my brother!"

She turned and strode through the doorway. But as soon as she reached the entrance hall, her legs went weak and she almost stumbled. Pulling in a shuddering breath, she focused on the stairs and continued toward them. Each step forward renewed her strength and determination.

She had no idea how to contact Garth, but she would not give up her search until they were reunited and she was on her way to England to see her mum and sisters.

7

Kingston, Ontario

E mma tilted her letter to Garth toward the lantern light. She hoped what she'd written didn't make her sound foolish or weak, but she missed him terribly and couldn't hide her feelings. She bit her lip and read the words once more:

Dear Garth,

I hope and pray this letter finds you well and you're on your way back to Canada. Each day that passes, I miss you more. I long to hear from you and know that you're safe, but I have not received a letter from you since November, before I left the Gilchrest farm. That makes me concerned for you and eager for news. Please write as soon as you're able in care of the new address below.

I hope you have been receiving my letters and understand why I had to leave the farm. With Verna's death and Mr. Gilchrest's threats, I was so frightened, I didn't know what else to do.

Last month, Mrs. Hazelton, the woman who owned the boardinghouse where I was working, died unexpect- edly. Soon after that, I left town with my friend Margaret Clarkson. She's a very kind middle-aged

woman who was also staying at the boardinghouse.
Her sister, Lucy Morton, owns a café in Kingston. That
is where I'm working now.

I've been putting my cooking, baking, and cleaning
skills to good use here, and that seems to please Lucy
and her son, Peter. I haven't received any wages, but
they've given me my own room and plenty to eat. Best
of all, I feel safe here while I wait to hear from you.

Now that the war is over, it's wonderful to see some
of the men returning home. Just yesterday there was a
wonderful celebration here at the café for a returning
soldier. I was so happy for his friends and family. But it
made my heart yearn to see you walk through the door.

Oh, Garth, I hope and pray that day will come soon.
It will be so wonderful to see you again and finally
be together. Holding on to that dream is what keeps
me going.

Until then, know that my heart belongs to you
while I wait for you in Kingston at Morton's Café,
42 Central Street.

All my love,
Emma

She laid the letter on the desk and folded it in thirds. The only address she had for Garth was the one in France with his regiment. Was he still there, or had he been discharged? How would the letter reach him if he was no longer stationed in France? Would they forward it on? How long would that take?

She sighed, then slipped the folded letter into an envelope. There were no answers for any of those questions. All she could do was seal the envelope and send it off with a prayer.

Closing her eyes, she held the letter to her heart. *Please, Lord, guide this letter and let it reach Garth. Watch over him and help him know how much I miss him. If he's injured or has lost a limb or is scarred in some way and wondering if I'll still love him, please help him believe that wouldn't matter to me. Give him courage and show him the way home.*

Hot tears welled in her eyes. As she reached in the drawer for a handkerchief, a knock sounded at her door. "Yes?" She quickly swiped the tears from her cheeks.

Margaret walked in and her steps stalled. "Oh dear, what's wrong?"

Emma shook her head. "It's nothing. I'm all right."

"I can see you're not." Kindness softened Margaret's voice. "Don't you think it's time you told me what's going on? I'd gladly help you carry the burden if I can."

Emma released a shaky breath. Perhaps it would ease the pain if she told Margaret about Garth. She pressed her lips together and lifted the envelope. "I was just writing to . . . a young man who has been serving in the war in France."

Sympathy filled Margaret's eyes. "Someone special?"

"Yes, very special. His name is Garth McAlister. We worked together on the farm before I came to Belleville. I've known him since I was fifteen."

Margaret nodded, encouraging Emma to continue.

"He came to Canada as a Home Child a few years before I did, so that gave us a common bond. We became good friends, and then as we grew older, we became closer."

"Has he been writing to you?"

"Yes, ever since he enlisted, but . . ." Emma hesitated and looked down. "I haven't heard from him since November. I don't know what to think."

"Maybe he sent his letters to the farm where you used to work."

"I gave him my new address as soon as I moved to the boardinghouse in Belleville."

Margaret rubbed her chin for a moment, then looked back at Emma. "Did you have an understanding with each other before he left?"

"I thought we did, but now I'm not so sure. Maybe I was just wishing . . ."

"When he came back, you'd have a future together?"

"Yes." Emma's voice broke, and a new wave of tears overflowed.

Margaret wrapped her in a gentle hug. "There now, child. Don't despair."

"But I don't know what's happened to him."

Margaret released her, then sat on a corner of the bed. "And you're worried he might be injured or missing?"

"Either that or . . ."

Margaret raised her hand. "Let's not assume the worst. Perhaps you can write to the Red Cross. They help loved ones find information about missing soldiers. You could also write to the commander of his regiment. Surely, he'll be able to help."

Emma sat up straighter, a wave of hope lifting her spirits. She knew about the work of the Red Cross. During the war, many women in and around Roslin had done their part, knitting and sewing for the men in uniform. They'd packed parcels for prisoners of war and visited wounded soldiers. Some had even gone off to become drivers who transported the wounded from the front line to field hospitals. Maybe the Red Cross could help her locate Garth.

Margaret reached over and squeezed Emma's hand. "You'll find your young man. Now dry your tears and say your prayers."

———⟨©⟩———

Emma picked up a large wooden tray and walked into the café's dining room. All the tables were empty except for one in the corner, where a man sat hunched over his plate, finishing his dinner.

She set down the tray and started clearing the table closest to the kitchen. As she stacked the dishes and silverware, her thoughts drifted to the letters she'd mailed earlier that day: one to the Red Cross headquarters in Toronto and the other to the commander of Garth's regiment in France. How long would it take to hear back from them? She sent off another silent prayer for Garth as she finished loading the tray.

The man at the corner table looked her way. "Miss, could you bring me some more coffee?"

She met his dark-eyed gaze, and uneasiness rippled through her. She'd felt him watching her since he'd first walked in the door. It wasn't right to judge a person by his appearance, but the man's rumpled clothes, pockmarked face, and dirty dark-brown hair gave the impression he lived a hard life. Who was he? Why didn't he clean up before he came to dinner at the café?

Pressing down her questions, she nodded to him. "Yes sir. I'll be right back."

She returned to the kitchen and lifted the coffeepot from the counter. It felt almost empty, so she crossed to the stove, where a second pot was brewing.

Peter stood at the sink, up to his elbows in dishwater, scrubbing a large baking pan. He looked over his shoulder with a grin. "I didn't realize there were so many dirty dishes when I sent Aunt Margaret upstairs to spend some time with Mother."

Emma returned a smile. "That's what you get for being so nice."

He chuckled, then glanced at the coffeepot in her hand. "You're still serving? I thought everyone would be gone by now."

"There's just one man left. It looks like he's almost finished, but he wants another cup." She poured the steaming coffee into the serving pot and wiped the side with a cloth. "As soon as he's done, I'll bring you the rest of the dishes." Her tone was playful, reflecting their growing friendship.

Peter groaned. "Thanks a lot." But his smile let her know he enjoyed their good-natured banter.

She returned to the dining room, and the man's steady gaze remained on her as she approached the corner table. Once again, a flicker of unease traveled through her.

"Here you go." She filled his coffee cup. "Can I get you anything else?"

He looked up at her with a slow, suggestive smile that revealed crooked, stained teeth. "As a matter of fact, I was hoping you'd ask."

Emma blinked. "I'm sorry?"

He pulled some folded dollar bills from his pocket and laid two on the table. "This is for the meal." He held out the rest of the money. "And this is for you, if you'll meet me at my hotel later."

Emma gasped and stepped back. "No sir. I'm not that kind of girl."

He tipped his head and looked her over. "Come on. I know who you are, and I know what girls like you want."

She shook her head, fear tightening her stomach and stealing her voice.

He cocked his eyebrows. "Don't look so surprised. Your accent gives you away. You were a Home Child, weren't you?"

Emma bristled. "Who I am or where I'm from is none of your business."

"I'm not so sure about that." He took a folded paper from his jacket pocket and opened it up. "There's a constable in Belleville searching for a girl with a British accent who fits your description. She used to work at a boardinghouse there, but she left town in a hurry." He paused and looked her in the eye. "It seems she's wanted for questioning about a murder."

Emma's legs went weak. "What makes you think that has anything to do with me?"

"Before she left Belleville, she told one of the men at the boardinghouse she was going to Kingston to stay with the Mortons." He tapped his finger on the words *Morton's Café* printed boldly across the top of the menu she'd left on his table.

A shiver raced up her back, but she lifted her chin and infused strength into her voice. "I think you should leave."

He rose from his chair and stepped toward her, a wicked glimmer in his eyes. "I'm not leaving unless you're coming with me."

"I'm not going anywhere with you!" She spun away, but he grabbed her arm, pulling her back. Hot coffee splashed her sleeve, and burning pain shot up her arm. "Ow!"

Peter strode into the dining room, a fierce look on his face. "What's going on?"

The man tightened his grip. "Nothing that concerns you."

Peter's startled gaze darted from the man to Emma. "Let go of her now or I'll—"

"Or you'll what?" The man sneered and pulled Emma closer.

Peter jerked a knife from his pocket, and the blade sprung out, glinting in the sunlight streaming in from the window. "I said let her go!"

"Peter!" Emma shook her head. The man outweighed Peter by at least fifty pounds, and he would have no trouble taking Peter down in a fight. The last thing she wanted was to see her friend injured on her account.

The man scoffed. "You think that little blade scares me?"

"It should." Peter widened his stance and lifted the knife. "I've been known to throw my knife from twenty yards and hit the bull's-eye, and I'm a lot closer to you than that."

A slight tremor traveled through the man's hand. He shifted his weight to the other foot but held tight to Emma's arm.

Peter narrowed his eyes. "Now, unless you'd like to see a demonstration of my knife-throwing skills, I suggest you step away from Emma and walk out that door."

The man huffed, but his bravado faded. "No need to take offense. The girl and I were just having a conversation. If she's not interested—"

"I'm not!" Emma pulled away from the man and strode toward Peter. Her arm throbbed from the coffee burn and the man's rough grip, but that didn't matter. She was free of him now, thanks to Peter.

The man took his hat from the table, placed it on his head, and looked at Emma. "I'll be going now, but don't forget what I said."

Emma clenched her jaw and glared at him, refusing to reply.

He sauntered out the front door, closing it with a bang.

Peter lowered his knife and turned to Emma. "Are you all right?"

"Just a bit shaken." Her arm stung, but that seemed unimportant after what had just happened.

Concern shadowed his eyes as he searched her face. "What was *that* about?"

She swallowed, debating her reply. Margaret had urged her not to say why they'd left Belleville, and Emma had agreed. Peter had no idea a constable there suspected she was responsible for Ruby Hazelton's murder.

She glanced away. "He heard my accent and realized I came to Canada as a Home Child."

Peter's forehead creased. "But why would he want you to remember what he said?"

She crossed to the corner table and started stacking the dishes. "He's just . . . a man looking for . . . companionship."

"Emma." Peter's tone made it clear he knew there was more to the story.

She slowly turned and faced him, still torn about how much to say.

Compassion shone in his eyes. "If you're in some kind of trouble, you can count on me to help."

Her defenses melted, and she lowered herself into the nearest chair. "It's a long story."

Peter sat across from her. "I have all evening."

"All right." She started from the beginning, telling him about the flu epidemic and her reasons for running away from the Gilchrest farm and then about her time at the boardinghouse in Belleville.

Peter listened quietly with no judgment in his eyes. "So, that man knows you were questioned by the constables about Mrs. Hazelton's murder?"

"Yes. He must be connected with them somehow."

Peter frowned. "Do you think he'll send word back to Belleville?"

"I don't know."

"Well, even if he does contact them, you've done nothing wrong. I'm sure it will all blow over."

"I hope so." But Emma's arm continued to throb, reminding

her of the man's strong grip and frightening threats. She would have to be careful and do everything possible to avoid another confrontation with him.

Garth turned into the alley at the back of the Houghton Hotel and scanned the side of the tall brick building. Shifting clouds hid the moon from view and made it difficult for him to see. Up ahead, a gaslight spread a faint glow on the damp pavement.

It was the night of Grace's debut, and he and Rob had tried to enter the hotel ballroom through the lobby, but a haughty maître d' at the door had turned them away when he saw that their names were not on the St. Andrew's Ball guest list.

"How are we going to get in now?" Rob sidestepped a broken bottle as he kept pace with Garth.

"There's got to be another entrance." Garth frowned as he peered around the large trash bins.

"Even if we find it, how will we get past that man checking names at the door?"

"The ballroom has to have other doors. I'm sure we can find another way to slip in."

"But didn't you see how everyone was dressed? The men are all wearing Scottish kilts or white tie and tails."

"There's nothing wrong with our suits."

"They won't pass for dinner jackets or Highland dress, that's for certain."

Garth strode on. "Well, I'm not giving up. I have to speak to Grace tonight."

Up ahead, two men leaned against the wall, smoking. They wore long white aprons and white caps that made them look as though they worked in the hotel kitchen.

The taller man glanced their way. "You fellows lost?"

Garth slowed, considering his words. His father had always said that honesty would take him much further than a lie. "My sister is making her debut upstairs at the St. Andrew's Ball. Our names aren't on the guest list, so they turned us away. We're trying to find another way in. Can you help us?"

The man smiled. "A rift in the family, eh?"

"Something like that," Garth replied.

The man pointed to the right. "Just past that alcove, you'll see a door used for deliveries. That will take you down the hall past the kitchen. At the end, you'll see the stairs going up to the main floor. Across that upper hall is a set of double doors that lead into the ballroom. If you're careful, you can probably get in that way without anyone noticing."

Relief rushed through Garth. "Thank you."

"Glad to help." The man nodded. "But keep an eye out when you go down the hall. The chef doesn't take kindly to strangers near his kitchen."

Rob grinned and gave the men a salute. "We'll be careful. Thanks very much."

Garth and Rob set off down the alley and soon spotted the door for deliveries. Garth quietly pulled it open and looked into the dim hallway. No one was in sight. He stepped inside, and Rob followed close behind.

Down the hall, voices drifted out of the kitchen, along with the clatter of meal preparations. Garth put a finger to his mouth as he held out his arm to stop Rob.

His friend nodded and softened his steps. They kept in the shadows on the far side of the hallway, made their way past the kitchen, and started up the stairs.

"Can I help you?" a female voice called out behind them.

Garth froze on the fourth step, then turned.

A young woman in a maid's uniform looked up at them from the bottom of the stairs, suspicion in her eyes.

Garth pulled in a quick breath. "Yes, thank you. We're looking for the ballroom."

"The ballroom?" She studied them warily.

Rob moved down one step, bringing his face into the light hanging above the stairway. "You see, miss, our friend is making her debut tonight in the ballroom, and even though we're not on the guest list, we hope to see her presentation." His tone was warm and friendly. He glanced at his watch. "I'm afraid if we don't hurry, we'll miss it."

Rob's charm seemed to do the trick, and the maid smiled. "All right. I suppose I can show you the way."

"That would be much appreciated." Rob grinned at Garth as the maid passed them, and they followed her up the stairs.

When they reached the main floor, she pointed across the hall. "The ballroom is just through those doors." Rob stepped forward, but she lifted her hand. "Let me take a look first."

Rob nodded. "Good idea."

The maid pulled the door open a crack and peeked through. Just then, the blast of bagpipe music burst out from the ballroom.

"Whoa." Garth stepped back.

The maid turned and motioned them closer while the loud pipers' music continued. She leaned toward them. "This is a good time. Everyone is watching the Highland dancers and listening to the pipers."

Garth sent her a grateful smile as he stepped through the doorway into the ballroom. Rob followed Garth in and softly closed the door behind them.

NO JOURNEY TOO FAR 95

The lights had been lowered around the large room except for those over the center of the dance floor, where a group of eight young women dressed in Scottish tartan skirts and billowing white blouses danced in unison to the lively music. Onstage at least a dozen men in full Highland dress played bagpipes and drums, blasting out a traditional Scottish song that vibrated through Garth's bones.

He looked around the room, searching for Grace, but didn't see her. There were at least two hundred men and women seated at round tables surrounding the dance floor. The women wore elaborate gowns with sashes in various tartans. How would he ever find Grace in that crowd?

"What do we do now?" Rob whispered.

Garth motioned to the right. "Let's move over there, behind that palm. That should give us a better view."

Rob nodded to Garth, and they stayed in the shadows as they crossed to stand behind the large potted plant.

Garth searched the faces of those seated at the tables again, but even from this new location, he didn't see Grace.

The final note of the pipers' song hung in the air, and the dancers took a bow. Polite applause filled the ballroom. The dancers left the floor, and the pipers marched off the stage.

A distinguished older man wearing a green-and-black-tartan kilt and a black jacket strode to center stage. "Thank you to those talented young ladies from the Glenview Scottish Dancers for their lovely performance. And we also thank the men of the Forty-Eighth Highlanders Pipe Band for providing that wonderful music. And now it's my pleasure to introduce the young women who are being presented to Toronto society for the first time this evening."

The lights dimmed, and a spotlight shone on the far end of the ballroom. A young couple stepped through the open doorway and started toward the center of the room with the spotlight following them.

"Miss Regina Helena Randolph is the daughter of Mr. Reginald Randolph and his wife, Mrs. Jane Randolph. Miss Randolph is an accomplished rider and a member of the First Presbyterian Women's League. She is escorted by Mr. Charles Lennon Jr., son of Mr. Charles Lennon Sr. and his wife, Mrs. Eugenia Lennon."

The young woman reached the center of the dance floor as the master of ceremonies finished his comments. Her anxious expression made her uncertainty painfully clear. She stepped to the side and then lowered herself in a wobbly curtsy. The audience applauded and she rose, looking relieved. She walked with her escort toward the stage as the spotlight returned to the door at the far end of the ballroom.

Rob grabbed Garth's arm. "There's Grace!"

Garth turned to the doorway as his sister stepped out with her tall escort.

"Next, we have Miss Grace Louise Hamilton. She is the daughter of Mr. Howard Hamilton and his wife, Mrs. Judith Hamilton."

"They're not her only family, and that's not her real name," Garth whispered under his breath.

"Miss Hamilton is a talented pianist and vocalist," the master of ceremonies continued. "She is also a Red Cross volunteer who knitted more than two hundred pairs of socks for the brave men who fought in the Great War."

Garth watched her glide across the dance floor beside her escort. She looked like a princess in her pale-blue gown with her golden hair piled up and her necklace and earrings sparkling in the spotlight. Mum would be proud of how she carried herself with such poise and confidence.

"Miss Hamilton is escorted by Mr. Alfred Pendleton, son of Mr. Archibald Pendleton and his wife, Mrs. Agatha Pendleton."

Garth frowned as he studied the young man who escorted Grace. He walked with a prideful strut and a raised chin, giving the impression he thought a lot of himself. Garth shook his head. Her escort was the least of their worries. Now that they'd spotted Grace, they had to find some way to get her attention.

Grace and her escort reached the center of the ballroom. Her cheeks were flushed and her blue eyes sparkled as she gracefully lifted her hand and made a smooth and elegant curtsy. She rose with a smile and slipped her hand through her escort's arm.

Applause filled the ballroom, and Garth released a deep breath.

Grace and her escort walked toward the stage and joined the other young couple waiting there.

Eight more young women were introduced, and Garth used the time to search the room for Mr. and Mrs. Hamilton. He finally spotted them at a table only a few yards away. Both were seated with their backs to Rob and Garth, facing the stage.

The spotlight shone on the master of ceremonies. "Let's give one more round of applause for these beautiful and gracious young ladies and their handsome escorts." When the applause died down, he continued. "And now we'd like to invite these young couples to return to the dance floor for the first dance."

Garth leaned toward Rob. "Keep an eye on Grace. We have to catch her attention when Mr. and Mrs. Hamilton won't notice."

Rob nodded, but his stern gaze seemed to be focused on Grace's escort rather than Grace. "I don't like the look of that fellow."

"Neither do I." Garth's frown deepened as he studied Alfred Pendleton. "The sooner we can get her away from this crowd, the better."

8

Grace tried to relax her shoulders and keep in step with her partner and the music, but dancing the waltz in the spotlight made her head spin and her steps falter.

Alfred Pendleton—or Freddie, as he insisted she call him—tightened his hold and drew her into the next turn as they waltzed across the dance floor. "Relax. I won't let you fall." His words sounded more like a reprimand than reassurance.

She lifted her chin and silently counted the steps she'd learned from her dancing instructor. Waltzing should come naturally after taking six months of lessons. But dancing with Freddie felt so different, especially knowing so many people were watching her every step, judging her performance, and weighing her in the balance.

Freddie lifted their arms, and she twirled underneath. "That's better," he said, offering her a slight smile, but it did little to ease her quivering stomach.

She'd made it through her entrance and curtsy. Now, if she could just finish this first dance without making a major mistake, she'd be able to step out of the spotlight and catch her breath. But even if she made it through the dance, she wasn't sure how she could truly enjoy the evening when her whole life felt like a complex charade. She had to conduct herself like a proper young lady, guard every word of conversation, and remember every detailed instruction her mother had given her.

She glanced past Freddie's shoulder and noticed two men

standing at the side of the room, partially hidden by a large palm. One of them looked like Garth. She blinked and looked again. That couldn't be right. Freddie spun her, and she almost lost her balance.

"Focus, Grace," he hissed under his breath. "You don't want to make us look like fools, do you?"

"No, of course not."

"Then pay attention and follow my lead." The muscles in his jaw jumped as he looked down at her, his expression full of disapproval.

That look was enough to let her see past his proud, confident exterior. Underneath, he was just as anxious as she was to make the right impression. The expectations of his family and pride in his position in society motivated him to perform, while she played her part to keep her true identity a secret. That painful thought pierced her heart.

The next time they circled the floor, she searched the shadows at the side of the room. The two men stepped out from behind the palm again, and her breath caught in her throat. It was Garth! He nodded to her, and she returned a nod and brief smile before Freddie spun her away.

Her heartbeat picked up speed. How could she break away to speak to Garth? What would she say to him? How could she keep his presence a secret from her parents?

The song finally ended, and Freddie escorted her to the table where her parents were seated.

"Thank you." She nodded to him and turned to face her parents and the other guests at their table.

"You did well, Grace." Her father sent her a confident smile, but she sensed he was pleased with the impression she'd made rather than with her.

Her mother focused on her with a serious gaze. "You look quite flushed. Are you feeling unwell?"

"No, I'm fine. It must just be all the excitement." Grace glanced at the palm, and Garth motioned her over before stepping back into the shadows. She fingered the button at the wrist of her elbow-length gloves. Her parents would not want her to speak to Garth, but how could she refuse to see her brother? She pulled in a steadying breath and turned to her mother. "Excuse me. I'll be right back."

Her mother frowned. "Where are you going?"

Grace gestured toward the ladies' lounge. That seemed to satisfy her mother, and she released Grace with a nod, then returned to her conversation with the woman seated beside her.

Grace's heart pounded as she slowly made her way between the tables toward the side of the room. She smiled at those who looked her way, but she didn't rush, lest she make someone suspicious.

Garth beamed when she stepped into the shadows. Rob's expression was equally warm.

"I can't believe you're here," she whispered.

"You mentioned the ball, and I didn't want to miss this opportunity to speak to you." Garth clasped her hand tightly.

"I'm glad you've come." She looked over her shoulder, grateful to see that the feathery fronds of the palm hid them from view. "I'm sorry for the dreadful way my parents treated you yesterday. I'm afraid they're so wrapped up in their own world, they don't want to see the truth."

Garth shook his head. "It's not your fault. What did they say after we left?"

"They don't want to believe you're my brother." Her voice faltered. "And now everything has taken a turn for the worse."

Garth frowned. "What do you mean?"

"Last night, as I was coming downstairs to try to reason with them, I heard them talking." She swallowed hard at the painful memory, struggling to go on.

Garth leaned closer. "What did they say?"

"Father wants to send me away to British Columbia with his sister Eloise, but Mother says that if I leave town now, I'll ruin my chances for making a good match."

Rob's eyes widened. "Why would they send you away?"

"They want to keep me from seeing Garth." She turned toward her brother. "They still have this foolish idea you're trying to steal me away and extort money from them."

Garth's eyes widened. "That's crazy!"

"They've already spoken to Aunt Eloise. The arrangements aren't complete, but we could leave as early as Tuesday."

"That soon?"

"Yes." Grace released a weary sigh. "My parents will do whatever it takes to keep my past a secret."

Rob stepped toward her. "So you're just going to give in and do as they say?"

Grace bristled. "I've been trying to appeal to them, but nothing I've said has convinced them to change their minds."

Garth rubbed his forehead. "I never expected them to react like this." He looked down for a few seconds, then focused on Grace again. "You've told me what your adoptive parents want and what they've planned, but what do *you* want?"

She pressed her lips together as ideas spun through her mind. Could she really choose? It was almost too wonderful to think she might actually have the freedom to make up her own mind about her future. She would turn eighteen in May. Her parents thought she was old enough to enter society, entertain suitors, and marry. If that was true, then she was old enough to make this decision.

Confidence and strength flowed from Garth's gaze, encouraging her to take hold of those same qualities and make them her own. Her heart swelled, and the answer became clear. "I want to see Mum, Laura, and Katie."

Garth's expression brightened. "Truly? You want to travel to England to see the family?"

"Yes. That's what I want, but I don't know how I'll ever achieve it."

"We'll take you," Garth said without hesitation. "We have the funds and can make all the arrangements."

Grace bit her lip. Could she really walk away from the privileged life she'd lived for the past ten years? Could she leave it all behind for the chance to see her mum and sisters again? And what about her adoptive parents? "I can't imagine going against my parents' wishes."

Garth's expression hardened. "It will take courage."

"And determination," Rob added.

"My father is a very powerful man, and my mother is equally strong minded," Grace explained. "If I leave home without their permission, they'll most likely search for me."

"I'm sure they will." Garth stood shoulder to shoulder with Rob. "But we've been through a war together, and we've learned a bit about courage and determination. We'll help you find a way."

Grace sat in her dark bedroom, waiting and listening. The clock on the upper landing finally chimed midnight. She quietly opened her door and looked into the dim hallway. No one was in sight, so she picked up her traveling case and tiptoed down the hall. As she approached her parents' bedroom door, the floor creaked beneath her feet. Her heart jumped and she froze. The sound of her father's soft snores drifted out past her parents' partially opened door.

Could she really leave the house without her parents' permission? What would they do in the morning when they discovered her note and realized she was gone? A tremor traveled through her. If she turned around now and went back to her room, her parents would never know she'd rather leave with her brother than submit to their plans for her future.

But this was her chance to travel to England and experience a genuine, close relationship with her mum, sisters, and brother. Her heart ached for that, more than she feared her parents' disapproval.

Her mother would probably swoon when she learned Grace had left in the middle of the night with two young men and no chaperone. But Garth was her brother, and it was perfectly respectable for an unmarried young woman to travel with her brother as her escort.

Pulling in a deep breath, she started down the hall again. She took the back servants' stairs and slipped past the kitchen. It was a good thing she'd made a habit of coming down for late-night snacks and could easily find her way without much light.

When she reached the back door, she stopped and looked over her shoulder. The dim light in the kitchen sent a faint glow over the lower hall. This might be farewell to her life in Toronto and to her place in the Hamilton family. She pressed her lips tight and shook her head. She was not truly a Hamilton. She'd only been a placeholder for the daughter who had never been born to them.

"Give me courage, Lord," she whispered. "Guide me to the life

You have for me." She stood in the open doorway for a few more seconds, waiting for an answer and confirmation that this was the right decision, but the only sounds she heard were the soft whisper of the wind in the fir trees and the lonesome hoot of an owl.

She pushed away her doubts and stepped out into the cool night air. Bright moonlight shone down on the garden. She closed the door softly and crept around the side of the house and down the gravel path toward the back gate.

Garth stepped out of the shadows, his serious gaze meeting hers. "Here, let me take your bag." He kept his voice low and held out his hand.

She passed the case to him with a tremulous smile. "Thank you."

Rob stood next to Garth and glanced at the house. "You made it downstairs without anyone hearing you?"

She nodded. "My parents are sound asleep, and I didn't see any of the servants."

"Good." Rob motioned to the right. "There's a cab waiting for us at the end of the street."

Garth took her arm and guided her down the alley. Rob fell in step beside her.

"Where will the driver take us?"

"We'll go to Oshawa tonight," Garth said. "Then we'll catch a train east to Belleville just after five tomorrow morning."

She nodded, thankful her brother was an experienced traveler and had made all the arrangements for their journey.

Garth tugged down the brim of his hat. "If Mr. Hamilton searches for us, I suspect he'll go to Union Station."

Grace's stomach contracted. "But you don't think he'll find us in Oshawa?"

"We'll be on our way out of the town before he wakes up."

Rob looked her way. "Don't worry, Grace. We'll be safely away on the train before he even realizes you're gone."

She hoped they were right. Her father was a powerful man, and he had a temper to match. She was glad she would not be there when he learned she'd left and was intent on traveling to England with her brother.

That was a stormy encounter she was happy to miss.

Grace gazed out the window of the train as pale-pink clouds brightened the eastern sky. She lifted her hand and stifled a yawn, then stretched her tired neck and shoulders. She hadn't slept more than an hour since they boarded the train in Oshawa, but the excitement of finally beginning her journey to see her mum and sisters had given her a boost of energy and kept her awake.

Garth and Rob sat across from her in the train compartment. Garth's eyelids drooped, and his head tipped to the side, swaying slightly with the movement of the train. Tenderness and gratitude warmed her heart as she watched him. He'd traveled all the way from England to find her, bring her letters from the family, and plan her journey home. How would she ever repay him?

Rob glanced at her sleeping brother, then at her. They exchanged a smile.

"Garth can sleep anywhere." Rob kept his voice low. "When we were in France, cannons and rifles would be firing in the distance, but he'd sleep right through it. Once, he even slept through roll call." Rob sent her a playful grin. "But I always covered for him and kept him out of trouble."

Grace smiled. Rob's good humor had eased the tension on the

long ride last night from Toronto to Oshawa. He'd kept a friendly conversation going while they waited in the dimly lit station to board the first train traveling east that morning. She sensed he'd done it to help her calm her fears on the journey, and she was grateful.

When Garth stretched out across the seat, Rob shifted to make room. He looked across at Grace. "May I sit with you?"

"Yes, of course." She scooted over to make room for him.

Rob settled in next to her, leaving a proper distance between them. "Thank you."

"You're not tired?" she asked.

"A little, but I'm fine to let Garth take his turn first and get some rest."

His words caught Grace by surprise. Had he and Garth agreed one of them would stay awake to watch out for her? A shiver traveled down her back. "I wonder if my parents found my note yet."

He offered a gentle smile. "They're probably still sound asleep, and we're already miles away from Toronto. Don't worry, Grace. We'll keep you safe."

She pulled in a slow deep breath, letting Rob's words sink into her heart and bring her a measure of peace. "I believe you will."

Rob settled back and watched out the window as the countryside raced past.

She took a moment to study him. He was taller than Garth but just as lean and strong. He was handsome in a rugged way, with sky-blue eyes, dark-blond hair, and broad shoulders that made him look as though he could chop down a tree or plow a field with no trouble at all. He was dressed in a modest suit and looked nothing like the polished young gentlemen in Toronto society, but he had a peaceful presence and confident strength that made her feel safe and protected.

He glanced at her as though he sensed she'd been studying him. Her cheeks warmed and she looked down. "Garth said we're going to stay with the Chapmans. They're the family you worked for, aren't they?"

"That's right. Mabel and Chester Chapman are two of the finest folks you'll ever meet. They took me in when I was fifteen, fresh off the ship from England. They expected me to work hard on their farm, but they treated me like a son—certainly much better than the way Eli Gilchrest treated Garth."

Surprise rippled through Grace. "Garth wasn't treated well?"

Rob shook his head. "Mr. Gilchrest only took in Home Children so they could do all the work on his farm. He didn't treat them kindly or care about their future. If Laura and Andrew hadn't insisted he abide by the terms of the indentured agreement, he probably wouldn't have let Garth attend school or given him enough food and clothing."

Grace shuddered and rubbed her arms. "I didn't realize his growing-up years were so difficult."

"How could you, separated as you were? But Garth wouldn't want you to feel sorry for him. He says those trials made him a stronger person and better able to endure the hardships of war."

Grace's heart ached as she pondered Rob's words. It sounded as though her brother had suffered a great deal as an indentured Home Child, while she'd had all the toys, clothing, and schooling any child could want. Their lives had been so very different, but they had both longed for love and acceptance and close family ties that would've made their childhood easier.

"I'm sorry, Grace. Maybe I shouldn't have said anything about how Garth was treated."

"No, it's all right. It helps me understand him better."

"Mr. Gilchrest gave him time off on Sundays. He usually came to our farm after church. Mabel and Chester always treated him kindly and gave him a refuge away from Gilchrest."

"I'm glad to hear it. I'm looking forward to getting to know Mr. and Mrs. Chapman. How long has it been since you've seen them?"

"I left the farm three years ago, but I had a short leave last year." Grace's hand rose to her heart. "Still, that's a long time."

"We exchanged a lot of letters, and that kept us close while I was away."

"I remember you said you lost your parents and grandmother when you were young. Do you have other family in England?"

He looked her way again, resignation in his eyes. "I have an uncle and a few cousins in London, but I haven't seen them in years. When things are more settled, I'll write to them."

She nodded. "Now that you're released from your military service, do you plan to stay in Canada?"

He shifted his gaze to the view out the window. "I'm not sure. Chester and Mabel told me I'd always have a home with them, and working on the farm is a good life. That's what I've always wanted . . . but I'm still waiting to hear from the Lord to know what He has planned for my future."

His words stirred Grace's heart. She already admired Rob because of his loyal friendship with Garth. Knowing he had faith in God deepened her admiration. Perhaps spending time with Rob would help her understand more about how God could lead her.

"What about you, Grace?" Rob shifted in his seat to look her way. "Will you stay with your family in England or return to Canada after your visit?"

She met his gaze. "I . . . don't know. I'm not sure what the future holds."

He nodded. "That's all right. You've stepped out in a new direction by agreeing to visit them. The Lord knows what comes after that. He'll show you the way."

His calm words soothed her ruffled spirit. She might not know exactly what the future held, but with the help of her brother and a friend like Rob Lewis, she was headed in the right direction.

9

Emma bit her lip and cast her fishing line into the stream again. The baited hook sank into the rippling water and disappeared.

"That's the way." Peter sent her an approving smile. He stood a few feet away on the stream bank, holding his own fishing pole with a relaxed stance. He was an experienced fisherman, and he seemed to enjoy teaching Emma this new skill.

Margaret and Lucy sat on a blue-plaid blanket beneath the shade of the tall trees several yards up the hillside from the stream.

The sun warmed Emma's shoulders, and a refreshing breeze carried the scent of new grass and unfolding leaves. She lifted her gaze to the blue sky, streaked with feathery clouds. What a beautiful place to spend their Sunday afternoon.

"Watch the bobber," Peter called softly.

Emma stilled and focused on the small red ball attached to her line. It floated on top of the water and slowly moved downstream with the gentle current.

"As soon as you see it jiggle up and down, give it a gentle jerk to hook the fish, and then reel it in."

"You make it sound so easy." She'd already had two bites, but both times the fish had escaped before she'd managed to hook it securely.

Peter grinned, his eyes dancing. "Fishing isn't hard. It just takes practice. You'll snag the next one."

She hoped so, because her poor fishing skills were embarrassing. She sighed and shook her head. This was the first time she'd ever tried to catch a fish. Why was she being so hard on herself? She supposed it came from all the years she'd worked for Mr. Gilchrest. If she didn't learn a new skill perfectly the first time he explained it, he would belittle her in front of the others, call her degrading names, and treat her like she was a worthless fool. She pushed those painful memories away and sent off a prayer of thanks that she would never have to see that awful man again.

The bobber jiggled, and she felt a tug on the line. She gasped and gripped the pole tighter. "I've got a bite!"

"Pull up just a little." Peter's voice was calm and steady.

Emma lifted her pole a few inches, a thrill racing through her as the line went taut. "I can feel him!"

Peter set down his pole and stepped up next to her. "Is he still there?"

"Yes!" She looked at Peter, eager for his help.

He seemed to read her mind and placed his hand over hers. "Let's give it a jerk."

She nodded, every nerve in her hand and arm tensing. He gave a quick tug to the side. "You've got him! Now reel him in!"

She cranked the handle, and the dripping fishing line came rolling in. A beautiful silver trout flipped and splashed to the surface of the water.

"Oh, look at him!" Emma's voice rang out.

"That's the way. Bring him closer!" Peter grabbed the fishing net and knelt on the bank. He dipped the net into the stream and scooped up the flapping fish. "Well done, Emma! He's a winner."

She laughed, her heart racing. "I caught a fish!"

Peter's grin spread wider. "You certainly did." He held up the line with the fish attached and turned toward Margaret and Lucy. "Emma caught a big one!"

Margaret clapped and nodded her approval. "Look at that! Great job!"

"That will make a fine supper, Emma," Lucy added with a smile.

Emma's heart warmed at their praise, and she rose up on her toes, still holding tight to her fishing rod. What a joy to hear their compliments and realize she could learn something new. Through her work at the café and the encouragement of her friends, she was learning new skills and building her confidence. The other day, Margaret said she was like a rose just beginning to bloom. That memory made her smile.

Her life was changing, and everything she learned would help her when she had her own home and family someday. That was all she wanted: a peaceful home where she could feel loved and secure with Garth at her side. If only he would return from the war and make that dream come true.

In the next thirty minutes, Peter caught two more fish, and Emma cheered him on each time he reeled one in. They placed Peter's fish in a basket along with Emma's, which was the largest catch of the day, and then Peter carried the basket and their poles up the hill. Margaret and Lucy had laid out their picnic lunch and greeted them with cheerful smiles and more compliments on their fishing catch.

Emma and Peter joined Margaret and Lucy, and they feasted on cold roasted chicken, canned peaches, and thick slices of bread slathered with butter and strawberry jam. Emma savored every bite, thankful for the warm spring sunshine and a chance to enjoy a restful day with her friends.

When they finished eating, Peter stood and brushed off his hands. He motioned toward the hill behind them. "That path takes you up to a great viewpoint. Would you like to go up and take a look?"

Emma glanced up the hill. "Do you think the landowner will mind? I'd hate to be caught trespassing."

Peter chuckled. "Uncle Theo owns this land. He said we can come here whenever we like."

"Oh, I didn't realize this was your uncle's land."

Peter cocked his head. "Do you think I'd go fishing in someone's stream without asking?"

Emma's cheeks warmed. "Of course not. I wasn't thinking." Peter was honest to a fault. She should've known he'd never invite her to fish there if he didn't have permission.

"Don't look so worried. I'm just teasing." Peter held out his hand to her. "Come on."

Emma took hold and rose from the blanket, then turned to Margaret and Lucy. "You're coming too, aren't you?"

Margaret started to rise, but Lucy reached for her arm and stopped her. "You two go ahead and enjoy the view." She sent Margaret a pointed look. "Margaret and I will stay here and pack up the food."

Emma's stomach tensed. She looked at Margaret, silently urging her to join them. She usually tried to avoid being alone with Peter. Not that she didn't trust him. She did, but she could tell his feelings for her were growing, and she didn't want things to become awkward between them.

Margaret met her gaze but quickly looked away. "Go on and enjoy the walk." She reached for the leftover pieces of bread and wrapped them in a dish towel.

A ripple of unease traveled through Emma. There was no way around it now.

"We'll be back in a while." Peter turned to Emma. "Ready?"

She forced a smile and crossed the grassy slope after him. They followed the twisting dirt path uphill through a wide meadow and into a shady wood with tall fir trees.

Emma listened as Peter told her about going there as a child and following the same path with his cousins many times. While he talked, she focused on the shifting scenery rather than making eye contact.

Finally, they stepped out of the woods and into the sunlight. Emma's breath caught. She shaded her eyes and took in the view of the wide valley. "Oh, it's amazing! I don't know if I've ever been up this high."

Peter placed his hands on his hips, taking in the green-and-gold fields dotted with trees. "You can see the St. Lawrence River." He pointed to the southeast, where the river twisted through the land like a shimmering silver ribbon and opened to Lake Ontario in the far distance.

Emma studied the land beyond the river to the west. Could she see Roslin from here? If she looked far enough, could she spot the Gilchrest farm?

Bittersweet memories filled her mind. Mr. Gilchrest had been a strict master, and the work had been demanding, but she'd shared many happy times there with Garth. Riding together around the farm, sharing quiet conversations on the porch as the sunset faded in the western sky, walking to church together, and spending Sunday afternoons with Rob at the Chapmans' farm were all treasured memories.

Thoughts of the Chapmans eased her painful recollections of Mr. Gilchrest. She had loved visiting Mabel and Chester's home with Garth. The atmosphere there was always warm and welcoming. Mabel and Chester treated each other with thoughtful consideration, and they extended the same kindness to Rob, Garth, and Emma. They'd always viewed Rob as a son rather than an in-dentured farmhand.

Watching Chester and Mabel together was her first experience of seeing how a loving husband and wife treated one another, and it touched her deeply. Their lives were based on their commitment to faith and family. She'd learned so much from them, and she'd tried to follow their example as she and Garth grew closer.

Peter turned toward her and took her hand. Emma stilled, and her heartbeat picked up speed. She ought to say something to stop him, but her throat constricted and cut off her words.

He looked into her eyes, his expression earnest. "I'm glad we have a few minutes alone. I've been wanting to speak to you."

Emma slipped her hand out of his. "Peter, I'm not—"

"I don't want to rush you, Emma. But I must tell you how much I've come to care for you."

She swallowed and prayed for the right words to explain the situation.

His forehead creased. "I know you might think it's too soon for me to speak or that I'm not good enough for you, but—"

"Oh, no, Peter. You are very good, and you've been so kind to me. I'm grateful we've had a chance to become friends, but . . . my heart is promised to someone else."

Confusion filled his eyes. "Someone else?"

She nodded. "Remember me telling you about the farm where I worked before I went to Belleville and met Margaret?"

His face darkened. "Of course, and I remember why you had to leave."

A shiver traveled down her back, and she had to swallow before she could go on. "A young man worked there named Garth McAlister. He's also from England, and we became friends. Over time, our friendship grew much deeper, but when the war went on and on, he felt he had to enlist. He's been away since the fall of 1915, fighting in France."

"But the war is over now. Where is he?"

Emma released a shuddering breath. "I'm not sure. I haven't heard from him since November."

"That's five months. Surely, if he truly cares for you, he wouldn't stay silent that long."

Emma folded her arms across her middle and turned away from Peter.

He laid his hand on her shoulder. "I'm sorry, Emma. I shouldn't have said it that way. But it doesn't make sense that you haven't heard from him now that the conflict is over."

She slowly turned around to face him. "It *has* been a long time. I'm not sure if he's injured or a prisoner of war and still on his way home. I just don't know."

"There has to be some way to find out."

She nodded. "Margaret encouraged me to write to the Red Cross and to the commander of his regiment."

"So, you're waiting to hear from them?"

"Yes."

"How long will you wait?"

She met his gaze. "Until I know for sure where he is and what's happened to him."

Peter studied her face. "You must truly care for him."

"I do, very much. I made him a promise, and I have to keep it."

Pain etched his face, but he finally nodded. "I understand, and I admire your loyalty. I just hope you're not waiting in vain."

Her heart seized. "That's my hope and prayer as well."

Peter's jaw firmed, and he looked her in the eye. "I care for you, Emma. You're gentle and kind and so very pretty. I know we could have a good life together." He reached for her hand again. "I'm willing to wait."

Tears pricked her eyes, but she didn't pull her hand away this time. Peter was a good man, and he had become a dear friend. He was offering her his heart and a chance for a safe and secure future. She didn't love him, not like she loved Garth. But in time could she learn to love him?

The promise she'd made to Garth filled her mind. What if he never came back to claim her as his beloved? What would she do then?

"Whoa." Garth pulled on the reins and halted the rented wagon, thankful they'd made it safely to the Chapmans' farm. He turned to Grace and Rob with a tired smile. "Here we are." Then he hopped down and headed around to the back of the wagon.

Rob climbed down on the other side and offered Grace his hand. "This is home." He motioned up the hill toward the Chapmans' large white house.

Grace nodded as she looked around. "It's all so . . . lovely."

"That it is," Rob replied with a warm smile.

Garth grabbed his bag and Grace's from the wagon bed, then turned and looked across the farm. Several tall maple trees surrounded the simple farmhouse. Vegetable and flower gardens were laid out to the right, and beyond the garden fence sat the chicken coop, the large red barn, and the corral. A sense of peace washed over him as he took it all in. Everything was just as warm and welcoming as he'd remembered.

Rob grabbed his bag from the back of the wagon and turned to Grace. "I'm eager for you to meet Chester and Mabel."

"So am I." Grace brushed her gloved hand down the skirt of her blue traveling suit and adjusted her hat.

Garth dipped his chin toward Rob. "Lead the way."

Rob strode up the path and mounted the wooden steps to the front porch. He stopped at the door and glanced back at Grace. "I don't usually knock, but this will be a fun way to surprise them."

Grace looked from Rob to Garth with a smile.

Rob rapped on the door three times, and a few seconds later, the door swung open.

Mabel Chapman looked out, and her eyes widened. "Oh, the Lord be praised! You're home!" Her brown hair showed new streaks of silver since Garth had seen her last, but her rosy cheeks and plump figure were unchanged. She pushed open the screen door and lunged for Rob.

Rob dropped his bag and wrapped Mabel in a tight hug and then stepped back. "I made it back safe and sound just like I promised."

Mabel beamed and grabbed Garth for a hug as well, then looked them over with glistening eyes. She turned and called over her shoulder, "Chester, come quick and see who's here!"

Chester came around the corner from the kitchen, wearing faded overalls, a blue shirt, and sturdy work boots. His wrinkled face lit up, and his gray mustache twitched into a smile. He grabbed Rob and slapped him on the back, and then he gave Garth a hug. "Welcome home, boys! Come in, come in."

Mabel led them inside. "What a wonderful answer to prayer to have you both home again." She turned to Grace. "And who is this?"

Garth nodded to Grace with a proud smile. "This is my youngest sister, Grace."

Mabel gasped. "My goodness! The same one you and your family have been searching for all this time?"

"Yes ma'am." Garth shifted his gaze back to Grace. "These are my good friends Mabel and Chester Chapman."

Grace nodded to the couple and offered her hand. "I'm very pleased to meet you both. Garth and Rob have told me so much about you."

"We're glad to meet you as well." Mabel looked her over with an approving smile. "You're a real beauty, and I can see the family resemblance."

Grace's cheeks glowed as she thanked Mabel.

Mabel placed her hand on Grace's back and guided her into the warm kitchen. "Where have you come from? How long was the journey? Please sit down and let me get you something to eat. You must be famished. Then you can tell me all about it."

Mabel motioned to the long table and six wooden chairs in the center of the room. A neatly pressed ivory cloth covered the table, and a jug of daffodils and hyacinths sat in the middle.

Rob pulled out a chair for Grace.

"Thank you." She nodded to him as she took a seat, looking pleased by the thoughtful gesture.

Garth sat next to Grace and released a happy sigh. "You don't know how wonderful it feels to be here at last."

"Like heaven on earth," Rob said as he took a seat on the other side of Grace.

Chester sat across from Rob, while Mabel bustled around, stoking the woodstove and putting on the coffeepot.

Chester looked from Garth to Rob. "So, you've both been discharged from your regiment?"

Rob nodded and briefly filled them in on their last few weeks in France and then told about their stop in England to see Garth's family.

Mabel placed a mug of coffee in front of Garth. "How did you find Grace? That's what I want to know."

"We didn't find her. She found us!" Garth grinned as he stirred cream into his coffee. He nodded to Grace. "Tell them the story."

Grace seemed a bit hesitant at first, but soon her words began to flow, and she told them what had happened since she'd found the old trunk in the attic at her home in Toronto.

Mabel shook her head, looking mesmerized by the story. "Now, if that isn't divine intervention, I don't know what is." She placed a plate of sliced bread on the table along with a bowl of butter and another of blackberry jam. Next, she added a plate of ham and another of cheese. Soon they were all filling their plates and enjoying the simple meal.

Chester leaned forward, his gaze intent on Garth. "What will you do now?"

"I plan to take Grace back to England so she can be reunited with our family. But first I need to go to the Gilchrest farm and see Emma."

Chester shot Mabel an anxious look.

Garth tensed. "What is it? What's wrong?"

Mabel placed her hand over Garth's. "I'm sorry, dear, but Emma's not there."

Garth sucked in a breath. "Where is she?"

"We don't know," Chester said in a solemn voice.

A worried frown creased Mabel's forehead. "She disappeared about a week before Christmas."

Garth looked back and forth between Chester and Mabel. "What do you mean? How could she disappear?"

Mabel lifted her hand. "We'll tell you all we know." She glanced at her husband. He nodded to her, as though encouraging her to tell the rest of the story. "In late November, the flu struck down many in and around Roslin. I suppose you heard it has killed almost as many people as died in the war . . . Emma and Verna took on nursing duties for the Spielman family. You remember them, don't you? They live about two miles down the road from the Gilchrest farm."

Garth and Rob nodded.

"Verna and Emma visited night and day, doing all they could, but after two weeks, Mary Spielman passed away, and soon after, two of their six children followed her to heaven. Her husband and the other four children slowly recovered. Soon after that, Emma and Verna both came down with the flu."

Mabel sighed and shook her head. "It's a terrible sickness. The doctor came, and Chester and I did what we could for them, but we lost Verna, and we almost lost Emma."

Garth clasped his hands under the table, worry gnawing at his stomach. How could he not have known Emma was so ill? He swallowed hard and looked at Mabel. "But she recovered."

"Yes . . . but the day after we buried Verna, I went to the farm to check on her, and Mr. Gilchrest said she'd run off." Mabel's frown deepened. "That didn't make sense. Emma was barely well enough to attend Verna's funeral. How could she run off? Where would she go? And why on earth would she leave when the weather was turning so cold, unless . . ."

A terrible wave of dread washed over Garth. He leaned forward. "Go on."

"Unless she was fearful of staying at the farm without Verna's protection."

Mabel's words hit Garth like a punch to his gut. He clenched his jaw as fearful thoughts raced through his mind.

"Eli Gilchrest is a hard man, but I don't think he'd hurt the girl." Chester rested his elbows on the table. "But I'm not so sure about those other two young men who worked for him."

Fire flashed through Garth and he jumped up. "I'm going over there now."

Chester rose from his chair. "It's almost dark, Garth. You'd best wait until morning when you've had time to rest and collect your thoughts."

Rob nodded, worry shadowing his eyes. "Chester's right. You'll handle this better after you get some sleep and take time to think through what to do."

Garth clenched his fist. "I'll tell you what I'm going to do: if anyone hurts Emma, I'll make them pay."

Chester walked around the table and laid his hand on Garth's arm. "Now, son, that's exactly why you have to wait until morning. You need to control your anger and prepare yourself if you're going to get anything out of Eli or those other two."

Rob rose and stood beside Garth. "I'll go with you tomorrow."

Garth shook his head, his anger still simmering. "I'll wait until morning, but this is something I want to do on my own."

10

Emma lifted the damp tablecloth from the clothes basket and plucked a wooden clothespin from her apron pocket. She tossed the white fabric over the clothesline, tugged one side down to match the other, and pinned it securely in place.

Stopping for a moment, she massaged her shoulder and gave her arms a rest. A warm spring breeze lifted the row of tablecloths and they swayed gently back and forth. They'd be dry in no time at this temperature, and then she'd bring them in and press them so they'd be ready to use in the café tomorrow.

Margaret walked around the side of the café at a quick pace and lifted her hand. "You have a letter!"

Emma gasped and dropped two clothespins into the basket at her feet. Was it from Garth? Or could it be from the Red Cross or Garth's commander?

Margaret strode toward her, holding out the white envelope. "It's from the Red Cross office in Toronto."

Emma's heart lurched. She took the letter with a shaky hand. For a second, she stared at her name typed on the front of the envelope, then tore open the letter and pulled out the folded sheet of paper. The words swam before her eyes, and she had to pull in a calming breath before she could read them aloud:

"*Dear Madam,*
We are writing in response to your request for information

*about Corporal Garth McAlister of Princess Patricia's Cana-
dian Light Infantry. We have no record of him being a prisoner of war. He is also not listed as missing in action,
wounded, or killed."*

Her voice faltered as the news raced through her mind. She
gulped in another breath and forced herself to keep reading:

*"We suggest you contact his family members. They may
have more information. We are sorry we cannot provide more
help at this time, but it may be considered good news that he
is not on the lists mentioned above.
Sincerely,
Mrs. Elizabeth Sherwood
Family and Friends Correspondent
Canadian Red Cross
Toronto, Canada"*

Emma looked up and met Margaret's gaze.

"I'm sorry," she said. "I know you were hoping to learn more
from them."

Emma swallowed, trying to banish her disappointment, but
that was impossible. "How can they say he's not missing? He's
missing to me." Her voice cracked, and tears stung her eyes.

Margaret rested her hand on Emma's shoulder. "I know this is
difficult, but they're right: he's not on one of those dreadful lists,
so that gives us hope."

"But we still don't know where he is or why he hasn't come to
see me."

"True." Margaret lifted her hand to her forehead. "Can you

think of any family members you could contact? Anyone he mentioned?"

Emma paced across the yard, trying to recall their conversations about Garth's family. "He has three sisters. Two are in England, and one's in Canada, but he lost touch with her soon after he arrived."

"The two in England—did he say where they live? Even if you know just their names and the town, a letter might reach them."

Emma closed her eyes, searching her memory. "Katie—she's his twin—and Laura, who is older. Both are married, so their names have changed. They left London and moved to a large estate north of there." Frustration burned her throat. "But I don't remember the name of the estate or the town."

Margaret sighed. "I wish there was more I could say or do to help."

"I know you do." Tears filled Emma's eyes as she folded the letter and slipped it into her apron pocket.

Margaret wrapped her arms around Emma. "Don't give up hope. You may still receive an answer from his commander."

Emma held on to Margaret, soaking in her warmth and concern. Where would she be without the kindness of her friends?

Garth clicked his tongue, urging his horse around the edge of Chester's newly planted field. He followed the path downhill to the small stream that separated the Chapmans' land from the farm owned by Eli Gilchrest. The old tree that had fallen in a windstorm long ago still spanned the stream from one bank to the other.

He'd run across that log more times than he could count when he was younger. Each time, he'd felt like he was fleeing the gray gloom of the Gilchrest farm and bursting into bright sunshine at the Chapmans'. But this time, he'd cross the water in the opposite direction.

He halted the horse and looked across the shallow stream. Everything in him was repulsed by the thought of returning to the farm and speaking to Gilchrest, but for Emma's sake, he'd face the hateful man and make him tell the truth.

As he rode up the opposite bank, painful memories from years of ill treatment at the hands of Eli Gilchrest filled his mind. Gilchrest had worked him hard and treated him more like a slave than a hired boy. He clenched his jaw against the resentment rising in his chest. He needed to forgive Eli Gilchrest. His faith demanded it, but that was a battle he still fought in his soul.

Meeting Emma was the only good thing that came out of Gilchrest's decision to keep Garth on the farm. After all he'd suffered at Eli Gilchrest's hand, Garth considered getting to know Emma his reward—God's way of taking something painful and turning it around for good.

He'd just turned seventeen when Emma came to work at the farm. She was fifteen, small for her age, and shy from the hardship she'd suffered as a Home Child. They struck up a friendship right away, and he became like a big brother to her, teaching her how to do farm chores and avoid Gilchrest's wrath.

As he got to know Emma, he soon realized she was a sweet girl with a kind and caring heart. In time, their connection grew stronger and his affection deepened into love. He became her protector and stood up for her when Gilchrest treated her harshly. Doing so had earned him a few whippings, but he'd gladly do it again to keep Emma safe. That was his priority—at least it had been until he'd felt called to enlist and fight in France.

Regret swamped his heart. He'd convinced himself Emma would be all right while he was away. Verna had always been kind to Emma, and she'd promised to watch out for her. He never imagined Verna would become ill and pass away before he could return or that Emma would run away.

What had happened? Why had she been so frightened that she'd fled the farm? He had his suspicions, but he intended to find out the truth. And if anyone had harmed Emma in any way, he'd see that justice was done.

The low gray farmhouse came into view. Garth straightened in the saddle and rode across the open field toward the house. It was odd Gilchrest hadn't already plowed and planted the field. As he drew closer to the house, he frowned. Weeds had grown up and choked out the spring flowers Verna usually tended. One of the black shutters by the front window hung loose and swung on a broken hinge. Dirt, leaves, and a crumpled newspaper littered the front porch. He'd never seen the place in such disarray. Gilchrest had always taken pride in all he owned, and he'd ordered those who worked for him to keep everything neat and orderly.

Garth halted the horse in front of the house and stepped down from the saddle. Squinting, he searched the side garden, corral, and area around the barn. There was no sign of Gilchrest or the other men who worked for him. The hair on the back of Garth's neck prickled. What was going on here?

He walked up to the door and knocked, then steeled himself. No one answered, so he knocked again. Finally, he heard shuffling footsteps inside, and the door slowly swung open.

Gilchrest looked out at him through dark, bloodshot eyes. His gray hair was mussed, and his shirt and trousers were stained and wrinkled. He cocked one bushy gray eyebrow at Garth. "Well, look who finally came home." But there was no warmth or welcome in his voice.

Garth shook his head. "This isn't my home. I came to see Emma."

The old man hesitated and shifted his gaze away. "She's not here."

Garth knew that much, but he would go along with it to see what he could learn. "Where is she?"

Gilchrest rubbed his chin. "Well, that's what *I'd* like to know. She ran off a while ago, and I haven't seen or heard from her since."

"Why did she leave?"

"How should *I* know?" A nervous tic started at the corner of Eli's left eye, and he took a step back. "One day she was baking bread in the kitchen and doing the laundry, and the next day she was gone."

"When did you see her last?"

He rubbed his hands together. "I don't know . . . Around the middle of December. It was right after Verna died." He met Garth's gaze, but there was no sorrow in his eyes. "You heard about that, didn't you?"

"The Chapmans told me."

"I should've known you'd go there first," Gilchrest muttered.

"Why shouldn't I? They treated me with more kindness than you ever did."

Gilchrest shook his head. "You always were a weakling. Too soft for farm life."

Garth glared at him. "Three years fighting the Kaiser's troops in France toughened me up."

"Is that right?" Taunting skepticism filled the old man's voice.

"Yes, and I'm done playing guessing games." Garth stepped toward Gilchrest. "Why did Emma leave? What did you do?"

Gilchrest's face colored as he stepped back. "I didn't do anything! She must have been tired of the work and wanted a change."

"Her indentured contract with you was finished. She could've given you notice and left whenever she wanted, but she told me she planned to stay here until I came back."

"I guess she changed her mind."

"There's more to it than that, and you know it!"

"I saw all your letters. They kept coming here even though she was gone." His mocking tone grated across Garth's nerves. "I guess she just didn't care enough to tell you where she was going."

Heat surged through Garth. "That's not true!"

Gilchrest grinned, looking satisfied that he'd riled Garth's anger. "I knew you were sweet on her. But three years is a long time to expect a girl to wait."

"You don't know what you're talking about!"

"I know Jason and Harry took off that same night. Not one word of explanation. They all left me high and dry!"

Surprise shot through Garth. Jason and Harry had come to the farm as indentured Home Children before Garth arrived. They were a few years older than Garth, and they'd done all they could to make his life miserable.

"Maybe she just got tired of waiting for you and decided to find herself another fella—one with a little more gumption."

Fire flashed through Garth. He grabbed Gilchrest by the shirtfront and pulled him up close. "Tell me the truth! Did Emma go with them?"

Gilchrest huffed, and his foul breath clouded the air between them. Then he clamped his mouth closed and turned his face away.

Garth shook him loose, his breathing heavy. "Where did they go?"

Gilchrest waved his arm toward the barn. "If I knew where those two no-good skunks were hiding, I'd drag them back here and make them do their job."

"Listen to me!" Garth jabbed his finger at Gilchrest. "Emma's missing! That's what matters!"

Gilchrest raised both hands. "I don't know anything about that. Like I said, she ran off, and I haven't heard from her since."

Garth turned and paced across the porch. Was Gilchrest lying, or was he just as clueless as Garth?

"There's a group of Home Children coming into Roslin next week. I'll be taking three boys and two girls. That will get things back the way they should be."

Garth spun around. "Is that all you care about? Getting the work done around here?"

Gilchrest lifted his grizzled chin. "This farm is all I've got. That's what matters to me!" He waved his arm. "Go on! Get off my land! And don't come back here or I'll forget who you are and meet you with a shotgun next time."

Garth shook his head. "Don't worry. I'm not planning on ever coming back here." He turned and stomped down the steps, his heart pounding.

Twenty minutes later, Garth rode into town, searching the streets for any sign of Emma. Where would she go? Who would she turn to?

His mind shifted back to their time at the farm. They worked six days a week and attended church on Sunday mornings. Emma greeted the girls and women she saw there, but her only friends were Verna Hathaway and Mabel Chapman. Verna couldn't help him, and Mabel had already told him she knew nothing other than *when* Emma disappeared.

Frustration cinched his chest tight, making it hard to pull in a deep breath. There had to be someone in this town who could help him. He rounded the corner, and the church steeple came into view. Had Emma turned to the church in her time of need?

He stopped by the parsonage and asked to speak to Reverend Paxton. The kind older man invited Garth into his study and listened to his story with patient concern but told him he hadn't seen Emma since Verna's funeral. He'd also wondered what happened to her, but no one had mentioned her to him in the past few months.

The reverend sent him a sympathetic look. "If I hear anything about Emma, I'll send word to the Chapmans."

"Thank you."

"Before you go, why don't I say a prayer?"

"I'd appreciate it." Garth bowed his head.

Reverend Paxton rested his hand on Garth's shoulder. "Father, You know what's become of Emma. We ask You to look after her, wherever she is, and help Garth locate her. Give him clear direction as he conducts his search. Open the way and make his path straight. Help him put his full trust in You and remember that You are good and faithful and able to do exceedingly more than we can ask or think. We ask You to show Yourself strong on their behalf, and we pray this in the name of Jesus. Amen."

Garth thanked him and left the parsonage. He appreciated the reverend's willingness to listen and pray, but he felt just as uncertain about how to find Emma after the meeting as he had when he'd arrived. If the reverend hadn't seen or heard from her, who else could he ask? He mounted his horse and rode back toward the center of town.

He replayed the reverend's prayer in his head as he studied the businesses on each side of the street. His gaze lingered on O'Leary's Public House, and he slowed his horse. Maybe he was following the wrong track, asking the wrong questions. He turned his horse aside, dismounted, and tied him to the hitching post in front of O'Leary's.

When he stepped inside, he blinked and waited for his eyes to adjust to the dim light. The dark paneled walls, large stone fireplace, and long bar on the side of the room made O'Leary's look like an old English pub. Men and a few women were gathered at several tables, eating and carrying on quiet conversations.

Garth stepped up to the bar and waited for the barkeeper to turn his way. "Good day, sir. I'm looking for Jason Martin and Harry Fisher. Have you seen them?"

The balding man lowered his gaze and continued drying the glass in his hand. "Who's asking?"

"My name is Garth McAlister. I used to work with Jason and Harry at the Gilchrest farm. I've been away for the past three years in France with Princess Patricia's regiment, and I just got back."

The man's suspicious look faded. "You fought with Princess Patricia's infantry?"

"That's right."

The barkeeper seemed impressed. "Good work, young man. You made us proud."

Garth shifted his stance, uncomfortable with the praise. "Thanks." Then he glanced around the room once more. "So, do you know where I can find Jason or Harry?"

The barkeeper set the glass on the counter and tossed the towel over his shoulder. "We've got a private room for card games in the back. I believe you'll find Jason there."

Garth blinked, surprised he'd located one of the men so quickly. Maybe this was an answer to the reverend's prayer.

The man pointed to the left. "It's back that way."

Garth nodded his thanks, then made his way between the tables toward the dim hallway. Voices reached his ears, leading him to the second door. It was open a crack, so he gave it a push and stepped into the doorway.

Four men were seated around the table in the center of the room. Each held a few cards in his hands. They all looked up, and Garth pulled in a quick breath. Jason Martin sat on the far side of the table, facing the doorway.

He studied Garth for a split second and frowned. "McAlister, is that you?"

Garth's shoulders tensed as he stepped forward and studied the man who'd often ridiculed him, making his time at Gilchrest's farm even more difficult. "That's right."

"What are you doing here?"

"I want to talk to you."

"I'm in the middle of a game right now. Pull up a chair and we'll deal you in."

Garth shook his head. "This is important."

Jason looked at his cards with a mocking grin. "That's right. You never did want to play poker with us." He glanced around the table at the other men, then sighed and laid down his cards. "I fold."

Garth released a breath.

Jason rose from his chair and crossed the room to meet Garth. "I had a pretty good hand. You better make this worth my time."

Garth pushed the door open wider.

Jason sauntered past. "Buy me a drink and we can talk."

"What do you want?"

"Whisky, but they don't serve that anymore." He grimaced. "Just give me a cider."

They stopped by the bar, and Garth slid two coins across to pay for Jason's drink.

Jason looked his way. "You don't want one?"

"No, I don't." Garth chose the closest table and sat down.

Jason joined him and tossed back the cider in one long gulp. "So, what's on your mind?"

"I want to know what happened to Emma."

Jason shifted in his chair. "I'm not sure I know what you mean."

"She's not at the farm. Gilchrest said she ran away the night of Verna's funeral. He told me you and Harry took off the same night." He watched Jason carefully. Would he tell the truth?

Jason tipped his chair back and grinned. "Harry and I had enough of Gilchrest's crazy temper."

Garth forced his voice to remain steady. "Did Emma leave with you?"

Jason chuckled, then cocked his eyebrows. "Worried about your sweetheart, are you?"

Garth's chest burned and he leaned forward. "Tell me what you know. Now!"

Jason lifted his hands in surrender. "No need to get riled. I've got nothing to hide. Emma was real sick for a while. She caught the same flu that killed Verna. Mrs. Chapman came over every day and nursed her for at least two weeks, maybe three. Emma perked up enough to go to Verna's funeral, but she still looked pale and sickly. That night, Gilchrest went crazy—drinking, cursing, storming around the house, and breaking things."

Sickening memories flooded Garth. Gilchrest was a hard man, but when he drank too much, he was a terror. They all took off and made themselves scarce every time he went into one of those rages.

"He came out to the barn and lit into Harry and me for no reason. We tried to get him to settle down, but he took a pitchfork and almost pinned me to the wall. That was it for me. I told Harry I was leaving."

"Harry agreed to go too?"

"That's right. Said he was going to pack up and take off that night."

"What about Emma? Did you tell her you were leaving?"

Jason's mouth hiked up on one corner. "I didn't, but Harry was sweet on her. He told her he'd take care of her."

Pain shot through Garth's chest like a searing arrow. "She left with Harry?"

"I don't know. I got tired of waiting around and took off as soon as the moon rose. Harry was still jawing with Emma, trying to convince her to come along."

"Did he say where he was going?"

Jason shrugged one shoulder. "He talked about going up to that hunting cabin outside of Tweed. Said he'd look for work up that way. I got a job here in town at the livery. I haven't seen Harry or Emma since I left the farm."

Garth clenched his hands, trying to fight off the painful questions racing through his mind. Had Emma fallen in love with Harry? Was that why she'd stopped writing? Had they run off together to that hunting cabin without telling anyone where they were going? It didn't seem like something Emma would do, but had three years' separation and desperate circumstances forced her to make such a terrible choice?

Garth swallowed hard. "Where is this hunting cabin?"

Jason squinted and looked off toward the bar. "It's east of Tweed about three miles downriver. Harry and I went there last fall, and I shot a nice six-point buck."

"Can you think of anything else that might help me . . ." He couldn't say "find Harry and Emma." He just couldn't.

Jason shook his head. "Nope. That's all I know."

Garth rose. He ought to thank Jason, but he couldn't push those words past his tight throat. He nodded to him instead and strode out the door, his heart heavy and his mind swirling with anguished thoughts.

11

The front door to the café opened, and Emma looked up from setting one of the tables. It was just after three, and the café was empty except for two women at a corner table who lingered over plates of berry pie and steaming cups of coffee.

Peter stepped inside, closed the door, and crossed the room toward her. His solemn expression sent a tingle of apprehension through her. He held out a white business-size envelope. "This letter is for you."

Emma's heart leaped. She quickly set down the stack of napkins and took the envelope. "Thank you." Her gaze darted to the return address: *Col. Edward Cummings, Princess Patricia's Canadian Light Infantry, 1st Battalion: Edmonton, Alberta.*

Margaret looked out from the kitchen doorway, then walked toward Emma, concern lining her face. "Who is the letter from?"

"I think it's from Garth's commander." Emma's fingers fumbled, but she finally tore open the envelope, unfolded the sheet of stationery, and read aloud:

"Dear Miss Lafferty,
I received your request for information regarding Corporal Garth McAlister. I made inquiries and learned Corporal McAlister listed you, along with his mother, Mrs. Edna McAlister, and his sister, Mrs. Katherine McAlister Tillman,

as his next of kin. That gives me permission to share the following information with you.

Corporal McAlister served honorably with his battalion and was discharged from duty on 6 March 1919. He asked that his final pay be sent in care of Mr. Andrew Frasier, Bolton Estate, St. Albans, England."

Emma released a deep breath and looked up. "At least we know he was alive and well in March."

Margaret motioned toward the letter. "And now you have the names of his mother and sister and the estate where he intended to go."

"Yes." Her voice trembled slightly. "I can write to them. They must know how to reach Garth."

Margaret leaned closer. "Does he say anything else?"

Emma continued reading:

"I hope this information will be helpful to you in locating Corporal McAlister and establishing contact with him again. We appreciate his service and wish you well.

Sincerely,

Col. Edward Cummings"

She turned over the paper to see if he'd written anything else on the back but found it blank.

Margaret looked from Peter to Emma, then smoothed her apron. "Well, this is good news. He's not a prisoner of war or suffering in some French hospital. He's probably in England with his family." Her cheerful tone didn't match her forced smile.

Emma swallowed hard. "Yes, that's probably where he is." But waves of disappointment nearly swamped her heart and drowned out her voice. He'd been free of his military responsibilities since early March. Why hadn't he answered her letters? And more importantly, why hadn't he come back for her as he'd promised?

She bit her lip, refolded the letter, and slid it into the envelope. She was glad he wasn't injured or a prisoner of war, but she couldn't deny the pain twisting her heart or the tears stinging her eyes. Did Garth still love her? Had he ever? Should she keep hoping he would return, or was she just holding on to a daydream that was never going to become a reality?

"Excuse me." She strode past Peter and Margaret toward the back door, blinking back her tears. She needed time to think and pray. That was the only way she would be able to make sense of her jumbled feelings and find the strength to carry on.

Grace dabbed her mouth, then laid her napkin beside her empty plate and smiled across at Mabel. "Thank you, Mrs. Chapman. Everything you prepared was delicious."

"You're welcome, dear. I'm glad you enjoyed it. And please call me Mabel."

Grace nodded, pleased by the request. "Thank you, Mabel."

Rob glanced toward the window. "I'm surprised Garth isn't back yet. He's not usually one to miss a home-cooked meal."

Chester set his coffee cup on the table. "That boy is intent on finding Emma."

Rob nodded. "I hope Mr. Gilchrest was willing to talk to him."

"Gilchrest doesn't have a reputation for being helpful," Chester added, "but I think he'll tell Garth what he knows. He owes that boy a great deal for all the work he did over the years."

"That he does." Mabel rose from the table and reached for one of the empty serving bowls and the water pitcher.

"Let me give you a hand." Rob stood.

"No, you sit down and enjoy your coffee." Mabel walked into the adjoining kitchen, carrying the items she'd cleared from the table.

"I don't mind helping." Rob picked up his plate and Mr. Chapman's, then looked across the table at Grace with a steady gaze.

What was he trying to communicate? Grace sent him a tentative smile, grateful that he'd gone out of his way to help her feel comfortable since they'd arrived at the farm.

Mr. Chapman rose and reached for Grace's plate and silverware. "I'll take that."

"Thank you." She sat back, noting the older man's slight frown. A ripple of unease traveled through her. Something wasn't right. What was she missing?

Mabel returned from the kitchen and gathered up the water glasses.

Rob entered the dining room again. This time he looked at Grace with lifted eyebrows.

She sucked in a sharp breath. "Oh, I'm sorry. I should've offered to help." She quickly rose and reached for the butter plate, one of the few items left on the table.

"That would be appreciated." Mabel's lips pressed into a firm line, and she bustled off with the glasses. Chester followed her out with the last load of dishes and napkins.

Grace sighed and turned to Rob. "I'm afraid I offended them."

His expression softened. "Don't worry about it."

"At home it was always drilled into me that I had to remain seated until the table was cleared by the servants."

His eyes widened for an instant, and then he looked away.

"I'm sorry. I don't think of you or Mr. or Mrs. Chapman as servants. That's not what I meant." She looked around the empty table, her frustration matching her embarrassment. "I want to fit in and do what's expected, but everything is so different here."

Rob stepped closer and gently nudged her shoulder with his. "Stop fretting. It's all right. You'll get used to things in time."

"Before or after I wear out my welcome?"

He chuckled. "Long before, I'm sure."

"I don't want them to think I'm just a pampered young woman from the city who expects to always be served."

His expression softened. "They don't think that, and neither do I."

She stilled, surprised by the tender look in his eyes. Should she tell him how much she appreciated his kindness and understanding? If she did, would he think she was inviting him closer and opening the door to more than friendship? She reached for the breadbasket and carried it and the butter plate into the kitchen.

Why was she even asking herself those questions? In a few days, she would sail away to England, and Rob would stay behind in Canada. She didn't want to mislead him or damage her relationship with her brother by hurting his friend.

No matter how much she admired and respected Rob or how much she longed to feel loved and accepted, she shouldn't let her feelings lead the way. She would treat Rob as a good friend and hold on to her heart.

Emma sat at the small desk in her bedroom and stared at the blank stationery before her. What should she say to Garth's family? How could she frame her words so she would not look like she was a foolish girl chasing after a young man who didn't seem to care about her anymore?

She closed her eyes. *Help me, Lord. I'm so tired of writing one letter after the next and receiving only disappointment and heartache with every reply. Should I even write this letter? Do You want me to keep searching for answers, or does Garth's silence mean I should let him go and move on with my life?*

But giving up on Garth didn't feel right. If she was lost to him, would she want him to give up the search? No! She'd want him to keep looking until he knew for sure what had happened to her and how she felt about him.

She sighed and resumed her prayer: *I suppose that's Your answer. I must keep my promise to wait for him and keep seeking answers until all is made clear.*

She took up her pen and began her letter:

Dear Mrs. McAlister,

My name is Emma Lafferty. I worked at the Gilchrest farm with your son, Garth, from the time I was fifteen until he left for the war. Garth and I became very good friends, and we corresponded while he was away in France. I sincerely care for him, so I was very sorry to lose touch with him when I had to leave the farm.

I've sent him several letters since then, mailing them to his military address in France, but I have not heard from him for many months, and I'm not sure why. I understand he planned to visit you at the Bolton Estate after he was discharged, and I am hoping you can let him know where I am and how he can be in touch with me if he would like.

After I left the farm last December, I worked for a time at a boardinghouse in Belleville. More recently,

I've been working at Morton's Café in Kingston,
Ontario, and I live in a room above the café at
42 Central Street.

If you could please pass this information on to
Garth, I would be most grateful. I would like to know
that he is well and learn what his plans are now that
the war is over. I would very much like to see him
again.

Thank you for your kind assistance. I appreciate it
very much and look forward to hearing from Garth.
Yours truly,
Emma Lafferty

She read the letter again, trying to imagine what his mother would say and do when she read it, but there was no way to know what her response would be. She folded the letter and placed it in an envelope. Tomorrow she would walk to the post office and send this message across the ocean to England. Hopefully, Garth's family would send her information and address on to Garth.

How long would it be until she heard from him? If he was at the Bolton Estate and responded right away, she might receive a letter in about three weeks. It could be much longer if his family had to send a letter on to him.

She lifted her gaze to the window and looked out at the dark-blue-velvet sky. A small star winked back at her through the silver clouds, and just for a moment, that little beacon of light brought a small ray of hope to her heart. Maybe this time her letter would reach him and bring him back to her.

The scent of hot coffee perking and bacon sizzling on the stove greeted Grace as she walked into the Chapmans' kitchen. "Good morning, Mabel. Breakfast smells wonderful."

"Thank you." Mabel held out an apron. "I could use your help with these biscuits."

Grace's steps stalled and she stared at the apron. Not only had she never worn an apron, she'd rarely set foot in a kitchen. But if she was going to fit in with the Chapmans and let them know she appreciated their hospitality, it was time to change her ways and learn something new. She took the apron and met Mabel's gaze. "I've never prepared biscuits before."

Mabel's lips twitched up at the corner. "No time like the present to learn." She motioned toward the kitchen table. "I already mixed the dough. Now it's time to roll it out."

Grace slowly tied on the apron. "I'll be glad to help. Just show me what to do." Preparing biscuits couldn't be that hard. She crossed to the table and stared at the large lump of white dough in the ceramic bowl.

Mabel dusted the table with a little flour. "Place the dough on the table and turn it a few times to mix in the flour."

Grace reached for the dough.

"Wait! You have to put some flour on your hands first so the dough won't stick."

"Oh yes, of course." Grace dipped her fingers in the flour container and sprinkled some of the white powder over her hands. She plopped the spongy dough on the table, patted it a few times, and looked up at Mabel, uncertain what came next.

"Turn it and fold it over until most of the flour is absorbed, but be gentle. You don't want to overwork the dough."

Grace pressed her lips together, folded the dough in half, and patted it again.

Mabel smirked, appearing to hold back a chuckle. "Here, let me show you what I mean."

Grace sighed and stepped aside. She was making it painfully obvious she'd never prepared anything more than a cup of tea.

Mabel dusted her hands with flour, then quickly folded, turned, and patted the dough, forming it into a smooth circular mound. "There. Now you can roll it out."

Grace pushed the rolling pin across the dough and flattened it in a smooth oval. "Look! I did it!" She sent Mabel a triumphant smile.

Mabel nodded. "That's the way. But don't press too hard. You want the biscuits to be layered and fluffy, not thin like hardtack."

Grace eased back and lightly rolled the pin across once more.

Mabel showed her how to use the biscuit cutter, and Grace pressed it into the dough, making a dozen circles. They transferred those to the pan, and Grace slid the pan into the oven.

Mabel dusted off her hands. "Now, why don't you clean off the table and then set it for breakfast? I need to collect the eggs and look in on Chester. He and the boys are out taking care of the animals."

Grace glanced out the kitchen window toward the barn, but she didn't see Rob, Garth, or Chester. She'd heard Garth come in late last night after she'd gone to bed. He and Rob shared the room next to hers, and she'd heard them talking again that morning, but their conversation hadn't been clear. She was eager to see her brother and hear what he had learned about Emma when he visited the Gilchrest farm.

Mabel rinsed her hands at the sink, then said to Grace. "I'm worried about Chester. He wasn't feeling well this morning, but he insisted on going out to the barn." She sighed and shook her head. "I told him Rob and Garth could take care of the animals, but he wouldn't listen."

"You go ahead. I'll make sure everything is ready for breakfast."

"Thank you." Mabel took her sweater from the hook by the back door and slipped it on. "Keep an eye on those biscuits."

"I will." Grace took a damp cloth and wiped the table, but that just smeared the wet flour across the tabletop. She hurried back to the sink, rinsed her cloth, and tried again, this time with success.

A few minutes later, she spread a tablecloth over the clean surface and then found the plates, cups, and silverware. She hummed as she arranged each place setting and folded the cloth napkins next to the plates. Everything looked correct, but the white plates on the white tablecloth seemed quite plain.

She looked around the kitchen, and her gaze settled on a pretty blue pitcher. What this table needed was a bouquet of fresh flowers. She searched again until she found a pair of scissors and a basket. Wouldn't Mabel be pleased when she saw the extra touch Grace had added to brighten the table?

She hurried out the front door and down the path to the large lilac bush, savoring the sweet fragrance while she clipped several stems. She placed the fluffy bunches of lavender blooms in the basket, then turned toward the side garden to find another type of flower or some greenery to add to her bouquet.

She spotted some small blue flowers shaped like bells, clustered on slim green stalks. She didn't know their name, but they were just what she needed to add color and dimension to her arrangement. She crossed the lawn to the garden, snipped several stems, and placed them in the basket with the lilacs.

"Morning, Grace," Garth called as he walked toward her from the barn. Rob walked beside him and looked her way with a smile.

"Good morning." She returned her brother's greeting and included Rob in her smile and nod.

"Those look nice." Rob motioned to the flowers she had collected.

"They have a lovely fragrance." She held out the basket.

Rob bent and sniffed. "Mmm. They do smell good."

She turned toward Garth. "How did it go yesterday? I was concerned when you were gone so long."

"Sorry. I didn't mean to make you worry." He shifted his stance, and a shadow seemed to pass over his face. "Gilchrest confirmed Emma left the farm in December without giving notice. Two men who worked for him left the same night."

Grace pulled in a breath. "Did Mr. Gilchrest know where she went?"

"No. I found one of the men, Jason Martin, playing cards in town. I learned a bit more from him, but none of it was very encouraging."

The sorrow lining Garth's face cut her to her heart. "What did he say?" she asked softly.

"After Verna's funeral, Gilchrest was drinking and went into a rage. He threatened both of his hired men, and heaven only knows what he did to Emma."

Grace clutched the basket tighter. "Oh, Garth, I'm so sorry."

"Emma left that night." He looked away, the muscles in his jaw twitching. "She might have gone with one of the men—Harry Fisher. It doesn't seem like something she would do, but if she was desperate to get away from Gilchrest . . ."

Rob's eyebrows dipped. "Did Jason know where Harry planned to go?"

"He thinks Harry went to a hunting cabin up north, near Tweed." Garth crossed his arms. "I'm going to speak to the constable in Roslin after breakfast and let him know Emma is missing. I'm not sure what he can do now, since so much time has passed, but I have to try that first."

He shifted his gaze to Grace. "Would you feel all right staying here with the Chapmans while I ride up to Tweed? I'll be gone two or three days."

Grace nodded. "I'll be fine."

"I'll go with you," Rob said, his expression serious.

Garth shook his head. "There's no need."

"I don't think you should go by yourself."

"I'll be all right. I could use some time on my own to think things through."

A door slammed, and Mabel screeched. "Land sakes! Where is that girl?"

Grace gasped and spun around.

The front door flew open, and a smoky blue haze billowed out.

"Oh no! The biscuits!" Grace dashed toward the house, silently scolding herself every step of the way. Mabel had asked her to keep an eye on the biscuits, and Grace had failed to keep her word. Why couldn't she get anything right? This was one more disappointing mark against her. How long would it be until they asked her to pack her bags and return to Toronto?

12

Grace pressed her lips tight and tried not to breathe in too deeply, but the strong odor of animal dung, hay, and horseflesh filled the Chapmans' barn. She looked around and spotted cobwebs hanging from the walls and rafters. She thought of the spiders that had spun them, and the hairs on the back of her neck rose.

An assortment of tools she couldn't name hung on the far wall, along with saddles and horse trappings. Four horses stood in stalls on the left, and two cows munched on feed in their stalls on the right.

Grace stifled a yawn and blinked a few times, hoping to clear her senses. The air was chilly this morning, and she wrapped her borrowed sweater tighter around her.

When she'd come down to the kitchen that morning and announced she wanted to help with the chores, Rob had smiled, approval reflected in his eyes.

Mabel had surveyed what Grace was wearing and offered to loan her a plain brown skirt and a cozy sweater, saying that would be a more practical outfit for chores, and glancing around the barn now, she realized Mabel was right.

Rob passed Grace a small metal bucket, then grabbed a low stool and a larger bucket. "There's nothing to milking a cow once you learn a few tricks."

"I'm not so sure about that." Thoughts of yesterday's biscuit catastrophe filled her mind, and her face flushed. Even the pigs wouldn't eat those burnt black rocks.

"Don't worry. I'll teach you everything you need to know." Rob smiled, and her stomach did a funny little flip. As she studied him, the sights and smells of the barn faded from her notice. He was clean shaven, and his damp hair was neatly combed back. He wore faded denim overalls, sturdy work boots, and a green shirt with the sleeves rolled up, revealing his strong forearms. How could he look so wide awake and handsome this early in the morning?

He pulled open the half door to the nearest stall and motioned her to enter first. A large golden-brown cow raised her head and watched them with dark soulful eyes surrounded by long lashes.

Grace clutched the sides of her skirt and suppressed a shudder. She'd never been this close to a cow. But she wanted to do her part and learn how to help rather than waiting for others to take care of her every need. She could do this. She just had to have courage and determination.

"This is Elsie." Rob set down the stool and bucket and squatted next to the cow. "She's a Jersey, and she gives the best milk you've ever tasted."

Grace crossed her arms and stayed a few feet away by the stall door.

"Come closer." Rob motioned her over.

She took a few reluctant steps toward him.

"First, you have to wash her off so you don't get any dirt in the milk." Rob took a cloth from the smaller bucket they'd brought from the house and gently wiped the cow's udder. He held out the rag to Grace. "Here, you try."

Grace hesitantly took the warm rag. She knelt next to Rob and followed his example, but the cow bawled and Grace jerked back. "Did I do something wrong?"

Rob's eyes twinkled and he grinned. "No, Elsie is just saying good morning." He nodded toward the cow. "Go on. Finish up."

Grace took a few more swipes with the cloth.

"That's good. Now put the cloth in the small bucket, and I'll show you what's next."

She dropped the cloth and scooted back.

Rob positioned the stool next to Elsie and sat down. "You place your hands here, like this." He looked up at Grace. "See?"

"Yes." Grace's cheeks warmed. What would her mother say? No doubt she'd be horrified. But Rob didn't seem the least bit embarrassed to be touching the cow's udder. He acted as if milking were the most natural thing in the world.

"You let the first few streams of milk go before you start collecting."

Grace leaned closer. "Why is that?"

"To make sure the milk is clean and pure." He squirted some of the creamy liquid by Elsie's back hooves. "Now put the clean bucket underneath."

Grace grabbed the large metal bucket and set it under the cow.

"There's a rhythm to milking once you learn what you're doing." He squeezed and pulled with two hands, and streams of milk squirted into the bucket with a *ping-swish* sound.

Elsie bawled again, and Rob slowed the milking for a moment. "It's all right, Elsie. You'll feel fine as soon as we finish." He winked at Grace, then returned to his rhythmic work, sending the foamy white milk shooting into the bucket at a steady pace.

Her discomfort faded as she watched Rob. He did the task with such ease and familiarity, it made her smile. He was home, and this was the life he enjoyed. What would it feel like to be that comfortable with your daily routine and truly feel you belonged somewhere?

For so long, she'd tried to fit in with the Hamilton family and their Toronto life, but she'd always felt at odds with it, as though she were acting a part—one that wasn't right for her. It left her conflicted and, even now, uncertain about who she was and what kind of life she wanted in the future.

When the bucket was about a third full, Rob looked up. "Your turn." He rose from the stool and stood back.

Grace bit her lip and lowered herself carefully onto the stool. She adjusted her skirt to keep it out of the way.

Rob knelt beside her and leaned in close. "Let me help you get started." He took her hands and guided them into place. "Now, remember, just pull and squeeze like I showed you." His warm breath brushed her cheek, and a shiver traveled through her.

She turned slightly and looked into his blue eyes. Only inches separated them now. A sweet feeling washed over her, spinning her thoughts and senses.

His smile slowly spread wider and his eyes shone, conveying his pleasure and maybe something more. He nodded to her. "Go ahead."

She cleared her throat and turned away, trying to remember everything Rob had showed her. She squeezed gently, and a long stream of milk flowed into the bucket, and then another followed. She laughed and looked his way. "I'm doing it! I'm milking a cow!"

He joined in with her laughter, sharing her delight.

But with her next squeeze, some of the milk sprayed sideways, and she gasped. "Oh, I'm sorry! I shouldn't have done that."

"It's all right." He reached for her hands again and guided her back to hold on and pull in the right direction.

She focused her attention again, determined to master milking and make Rob proud. She continued for a few minutes, but soon her fingers and arms grew tired. She stopped and shook out her hands.

Rob bent closer. "Are your hands hurting?"

"I'm sure I'll get used to it."

"Would you like me to finish?"

"No, I can do it." She took hold again and squeezed out another stream of warm milk. Soon she was back to the rhythmic motions, though her pace was slower than when she'd begun.

When the foamy milk had almost reached the top, Elsie bawled and kicked her back foot. Grace gasped, the bucket toppled, and milk poured out on the barn floor.

"Oh no!" She jumped up as Rob lunged forward and righted the bucket, but most of the milk spread out in a big puddle around the cow's feet.

Hot tears pricked Grace's eyes. How could she be so inept? She couldn't even manage to keep the bucket upright and in place! What would Rob think of her now? She shot him a fearful glance. "I'm hopeless. You might as well send me back to the kitchen to burn another batch of biscuits!"

Rob's gaze softened as he looked at her. "You're not hopeless, Grace."

"But all that milk is wasted! What will Mabel and Chester say?"

"They'll say not to worry. It's happened before, and it will probably happen again."

"I should've grabbed the bucket. But I was so surprised, I didn't know what to do. That was foolish, I know."

"Grace, stop being so hard on yourself. You've never milked a cow before. No one expects you to do it perfectly the first time."

"But Chester and Mabel have been so kind to me." That

thought pushed her over the edge, and she couldn't hold back any longer. She lifted her hand to cover her mouth as tears rolled down her cheeks.

"Hey, don't cry. They'll understand."

She sniffed. "Truly?"

"Yes. I know they will. And there's no need for any more tears, unless they help ease a deeper pain."

She stilled. A deeper pain? Was that why she was so tearful this morning? Maybe it wasn't just the spilled milk that brought her emotions to the surface. Maybe it was the regret and confusion she felt for leaving her life in Toronto that made her tears over- flow. But what other choice did she have? Her adoptive parents never would've agreed to let her go to England to see her mum and sisters. They hadn't even acknowledged that Garth was her brother. She pushed those bewildering thoughts away.

"I just feel so useless and out of place here." Her chin trembled.

"Oh, Grace, it's all right." He gently brushed a tear from her cheek. "You have time to learn what's needed here. And before you know it, you'll be on your way to England to see your mum and sisters. You've got a whole new life ahead of you."

He'd meant to comfort her with those words—she was sure of it—but they brought a new round of fears and questions to her mind. If trying to adjust to life at the Chapman farm was chal- lenging, what would it be like when she traveled to England and was reunited with her family? Would she finally feel that sense of belonging and acceptance she longed for?

The hinges on the barn door squeaked, and footsteps ap- proached. "Rob?"

"That's Chester," Rob said softly, and he stepped back.

She brushed the last of her tears from her cheeks.

"We're in here," Rob called.

Chester appeared at the stall door. "Breakfast is ready. Mabel says come in as soon as you finish milking." His gaze shifted from Rob to the puddle of milk on the floor. "What happened here?"

Grace cringed, reluctant to admit what she'd done.

"Elsie was in a mood this morning." Rob shook his head as he patted the cow's back. "She kicked the bucket over, and I hardly had time to catch it."

"Crazy cow." Chester waved it off as though it wasn't important. "That's the second time this week. Mabel says we ought to sell her, but I can't quite bring myself to do that yet." He turned to Grace. "I hope Rob showed you how to steer clear of Elsie's hooves."

"Grace is doing just fine." Rob looked her way with a smile and wink. "If I can just keep Elsie in line, we may have some milk to bring inside in a few minutes."

Chester chuckled and turned away. "Don't take too long. The pancakes are hot."

Gratitude welled up in Grace's heart. Rob had taken the blame for the spilled milk and preserved her dignity. "Thank you for not telling Chester I'm the one responsible for this mess."

Rob turned toward her. "Elsie is the one who kicked over the bucket. It's not your fault. Just be on your guard next time."

Grace blinked. "Next time?"

"Of course. You're not getting out of chores just because of one mishap." The humor in his voice and the twinkle in his eyes washed away the last of her embarrassment. Maybe it wasn't such a disaster after all. Come to think of it, if Elsie hadn't kicked over that bucket, Rob might not have brushed the tears from her cheek and she'd have missed his comforting touch.

"Rob!" Chester's faint voice drifted toward them.

Rob frowned and stepped out of the stall. "Chester?"

"Out here." The old man's voice sounded hoarse and strained.

Rob headed for the barn door, and Grace hurried after him, questions tumbling through her mind. As soon as she stepped outside, she spotted Chester lying on the ground, and panic flashed through her.

Rob dashed over and knelt beside him. "What happened? Did you fall?"

Chester lifted his hand to his chest. "I had a sharp pain, and it knocked the wind out of me."

Grace looked around, trying to think how she might help.

Rob took Chester's hand. "Can you sit up?"

Chester nodded, and Rob slipped his arm under the man's shoulders and slowly lifted him to a sitting position. Chester's face was pale, and his breathing was labored.

Rob kept his arm around Chester's shoulders. "If I help, do you think you can walk to the house?"

Chester lifted a shaky hand. "Let me catch my breath first."

Rob shot Grace a concerned look. "Go get Garth and Mabel."

Grace nodded, but just then the back door flew open. Mabel hurried outside and ran down the path toward them. "Chester! What happened?" She lowered herself to the ground beside him.

"Just a little dizzy spell. I'm all right."

"I looked out the kitchen window and there you were on the ground!" Her voice sounded ragged from her run. "It nearly frightened me to death." She looked across at Rob. "Let's get him into the house. Then I want you to ride over to Dr. Hooper's and bring him back."

"You don't need to go for the doctor," Chester insisted. "I'll be fine as soon as I rest for a few minutes."

Mabel shook her head. "Don't argue with me, Chester. We're sending for the doctor."

"Mabel's right," Rob added. "We'll all feel better if he pays you a visit."

Chester sighed. "All right, but I'm only agreeing so you won't worry."

The back door opened again. Garth looked out, then hurried over. He took his place on Chester's left side, opposite Rob. Together they lifted Chester and helped him slowly walk up the path to the house.

Grace ran ahead and opened the door.

When Chester was settled on the sofa with Mabel hovering nearby, Rob, Garth, and Grace gathered in the kitchen.

Rob looked from Grace to Garth. "I'll ride over to Dr. Hooper's and bring him back."

Garth nodded. "I'll stay here until you return."

Grace's heart clenched as she watched Rob head toward the back door. He loved Chester like a son loved his father. It would be a terrible blow to him if Chester didn't recover. She crossed to the window and watched Rob disappear into the barn. "How far is it to Dr. Hooper's?"

"About three miles. It won't take him long."

Grace clasped her hands. "I've never done any nursing, but I'd be glad to do whatever I can for Mabel and Chester."

Garth touched her shoulder. "That's kind of you, Grace. I'm sure Mabel will let you know how you can help."

Her thoughts flashed back to yesterday's burned biscuits and the half-empty milk bucket in the barn. So far, her efforts hadn't been much help, but she would keep trying to do what she could to support the Chapmans through this difficult time.

She met her brother's gaze. "I'll check with Mabel and then head out to the barn to finish milking Elsie."

Garth's brows rose. "You know how to milk a cow?"

"I'm learning." She glanced toward the sitting room, then back at Garth. "What will you do about the trip to Tweed?"

Emotions flickered across Garth's face and he rubbed his jaw. "I won't leave until we hear what the doctor has to say about Chester and we make a plan."

Grace nodded, thankful for Garth's reassurance. But she could tell he was torn about delaying the search for Emma. What would he discover when he finally made the trip to Tweed? Was Emma there with that other man? Her heart clenched, and she prayed that her brother's hopes would not be crushed when he made his journey.

Two hours later, Garth followed Rob and Dr. Hooper down the porch steps. As they walked with the doctor toward his one-horse gig, Garth noted the lines of concern around Rob's eyes.

Rob shook the doctor's hand. "Thank you for coming."

"Glad to do it." The doctor rested his hand on the side of the gig. "I'll be back tomorrow morning. Until then, make sure Chester follows my instructions. He needs complete rest. No work of any kind, and no upsetting conversations."

Rob nodded. "I'll make sure of it."

"Good. And see that Mabel gets some rest as well. Neither one of them is as young as they used to be." A worried frown settled on the doctor's face. "You know, this isn't Chester's first heart attack. I've told them they need to consider moving into town and taking life at a much easier pace."

Rob's eyes widened. "This happened before?"

Dr. Hooper nodded. "His first attack was last October at harvest time. Chester works too hard for a man his age. If he wants to enjoy a few more years, then he needs to seriously consider giving up farming." The doctor climbed into the gig and tipped his hat to them. "Good day to you."

Rob thanked the doctor again and lifted his hand in farewell.

Garth crossed his arms and watched the gig roll down the drive. He seemed like a skilled physician, but his advice about giving up the farm would be difficult for Rob and the Chapmans to accept.

Rob ran his hand through his hair. "They wrote to me every week. I can't believe they never told me Chester had a heart attack."

"They probably didn't want you to worry."

"They should've said something." Rob stared off toward the field for a few seconds, then turned back to Garth. "I've got to make them understand they need to take the doctor's advice."

"That won't be easy."

"No, it won't, especially when Chester is not supposed to have any upsetting conversations." Rob huffed and shook his head. "I can't imagine they'll ever agree to leave this farm."

"It looks like they might not have a choice."

Rob grimaced. "Farming is their only income. I don't see how they could afford to live in town unless they sell the farm."

Garth nodded. Moving to town would be hard enough, but this farm had been in the Chapman family for three generations. Selling it would be a painful blow for Chester and Mabel.

Rob turned, as if taking in everything—the house and land around it. "All through the war, the thought of coming home and running this farm with Chester was what kept me going. It's going to be hard to let that go."

Garth placed his hand on Rob's shoulder. "I know that was your dream, but home is not just a place. It's the people you care about. And right now you still have time with Chester and Mabel."

Rob blew out a shaky breath. "You're right. They're more important than a house or fields. I need to be grateful and focus on helping them find a way through this."

Garth squeezed Rob's shoulder. "You're a good man, Rob Lewis. They're blessed to have you in their lives."

"I'm the one who has been blessed. And now I have a chance to return their kindness. It's the least I can do." Rob started back toward the house, and Garth fell into step beside him. "Do you have what you need for your trip to Tweed?" Rob asked.

Last night Garth had gathered his supplies and gained permission from Chester to borrow two horses: one for himself, and the other in the hope that Emma would return with him. "I'm all set. I've spoken to Grace, Mabel, and Chester about the trip. Grace understands why I have to go to Tweed, and she's eager to help Mabel, especially now."

"I'll watch out for Grace."

"Thanks. I know you will."

When they reached the front door, Rob turned to Garth with a serious look. "Be careful."

Garth nodded. "I will."

"I'll be praying for you."

"Thanks. I'll need it, that's for sure." Garth gave Rob a brotherly hug and thumped him on the back. They had been through so much together. Soon they'd be parting ways. Garth didn't want to think about that.

Rob stepped back and looked Garth in eye. "I'll be storming the gates of heaven for you."

"I'm counting on it."

They pushed open the door and walked into the kitchen.

Grace rose from her chair. "What did the doctor say?"

Rob moved to her side and lowered his voice as he relayed the doctor's parting words and the warning he'd shared.

Garth shifted his gaze away, his thoughts already carrying him down the road toward Tweed and his hopes of finding Emma. Would she be glad to see him, or would she tell him she'd given her heart to another man and turn him away?

13

race carefully lifted the wooden tray filled with steaming coffee cups and a plate of apple-cinnamon muffins she had just
taken out of the oven. Their spicy scent tickled her nose and made
her mouth water. They looked perfect! She couldn't wait to offer
one to Rob and see his reaction. Maybe this would show him
she'd finally mastered some cooking skills.

She walked into the sitting room, where Chester rested on the
couch with a pillow beneath his head and a blanket tucked around
him. Rob and Mabel sat in the two chairs by the fireplace.

Rob put down the book he was reading and smiled as she came
closer. "Something sure smells good."

Grace's stomach quivered, and she returned his smile.

Mabel looked up from her knitting and surveyed the tray.
"Those muffins look wonderful, Grace. Why don't you set the tray
on the table by the sofa?"

Grace lowered the tray and then held out the plate toward Rob.
"I hope you like apple-cinnamon muffins."

He grinned as he took one. "You bet I do. Thank you, Grace."

Chester slowly sat up, eyeing the muffins. "I'm not sure my
doctor would approve, but I'd like to try one of those."

Mabel frowned. "Now, Chester, I don't think that's the best
idea."

"One muffin is not going to set me back." He motioned Grace
closer. "Bring that plate over here."

Mabel finally gestured her consent, and Grace held out the plate to Chester. He selected a muffin and nodded his thanks. As Grace turned to serve Mabel, Chester gasped and sputtered. Grace spun around.

Chester's lips puckered and he held out the muffin, minus one big bite off the side. "Saints alive, Grace! What did you put in these?"

Grace's thoughts tumbled. What had she done wrong? She'd been so careful to follow every step in the recipe Mabel had written down for her.

Mabel picked up a muffin, took a small bite, then coughed. "Mercy's sake! How much salt did you add?"

Grace blinked, trying to recall. "Just one spoonful. That's what your recipe said."

Mabel's eyes widened. "One teaspoon, one tablespoon, or one serving spoon?"

Grace's face flushed. "I'm not sure. I just took a large spoon from the drawer and used that to measure the salt and baking soda."

"Well, that's the problem. The recipe calls for one teaspoon of salt, and you put in at least four times that amount."

"Oh no. I'm so sorry. I didn't realize the difference."

Chester tossed his muffin back on the tray. "Well, don't worry about it, Grace. Any new cook could make a mistake like that. It's not your fault." He sighed and settled back on the couch. "It was probably the Lord's way of reminding me I shouldn't be eating sweets. The doctor told me they're not good for my heart, but they smelled so good, it was hard to resist." He looked her way with a teasing smile. "Next time you make them, use a teaspoon, and then hide them from me."

"You're not upset with me?"

Chester laughed. "Upset? Over a batch of muffins? Never!"

Grace glanced at Rob and then Mabel, thinking one of them would scold her for her foolish mistake. But Rob's eyes glowed, and Mabel's mouth twitched up at the corner.

Grace blew out a breath. "I suppose the pigs won't mind salty muffins."

Mabel's laughter broke out, and she shook her head. "Oh, Grace, you do beat all!"

Rob chuckled and sent her an approving nod.

Grace finally joined in the laughter, grateful for such kind and accepting friends. They hadn't scorned her for ruining the muffins. Instead, they'd made light of her mistake as though she was more important than her poor baking skills.

What would it have been like to grow up in a home like this, where mistakes became lessons to learn from rather than failures that brought condemnation and shame? The Hamiltons had always insisted she perform perfectly or at least project that image. Remembering their high expectations and critical attitude stung a bit, but not as much as it had in the past.

The Chapmans seemed to have a totally different view of how family members ought to treat each other. Kindness and respect were given and received by everyone.

Was that what had made Rob so patient and encouraging? The love and acceptance he'd received from Mabel and Chester had obviously made a deep impact on him. But his good qualities reflected more than a loving upbringing. He had an inner strength and self-assurance that made him at ease with himself and others.

Where did that inner strength come from? How had he become so confident yet humble and considerate of others? She needed to know the answers to those questions because those were qualities she lacked in her heart and life.

Garth slowed his horse and sniffed the air. Behind him the second horse nickered. The scent of wood smoke drifted toward him through the trees, and his shoulders tensed. He must be close to the cabin. Would he find Emma there with Harry? *Lord, please give me the wisdom and courage to handle whatever I'm going to find at that cabin.*

He clicked to his horse and continued down the narrow trail, scanning the forest on the right and left, his senses on alert for any sign of movement.

Earlier that morning, he'd stopped at Rider's General Store in Tweed and spoken to the owner, Mr. Rider. That conversation rolled through his mind as he rode on.

"Good day, sir." Garth slipped off his cap and nodded to the proprietor behind the counter. "I'm wondering if you could help me."

Mr. Rider looked him over with a brief smile. "I will if I can."

"Thank you. I'm trying to find a man named Harry Fisher. He's in his early thirties, around five foot ten, with red hair and a full beard and mustache. He came to this area about four months ago. Have you seen him?"

Mr. Rider listened closely, then nodded. "There's a gruff fellow who has come in here a few times. He never bothered to introduce himself. He just gathers up his supplies and pays for them without any conversation. But he fits your description."

Garth braced himself. "Was there a young woman with him? About five foot two with golden-brown hair and brown eyes?"

Mr. Rider tapped his fingers on the counter. "No, I don't recall seeing a woman. He always comes alone."

Hope surged in Garth's chest, but it receded just as quickly. Even if Harry hadn't brought Emma to the store, that didn't mean she wasn't with him. Maybe he'd forced her to stay at the cabin and never allowed her to come to town or see anyone. "Do you know where he lives?"

"This is a small town, and we take note of strangers." Mr. Rider walked to a map posted by the door. "He rented the old Fillmore cabin. It's about three miles east of town." He pointed to the location. "Now that old Walter Fillmore has passed on, his widow rents it out."

"What's the best route to the cabin?"

Mr. Rider slid his finger down the map. "We're here, and you can take the road down to the river, then turn right and follow the river for about three miles. You'll see a waterfall, and just past that is a trail on the right that leads uphill. The cabin is at the top of the ridge."

The screech of a crow broke through Garth's thoughts, and he focused on his surroundings again.

A light wind ruffled through the fir trees above, making a shushing sound. Up ahead a dog barked. The hairs on the back of Garth's neck rose. He pulled back on the reins and strained to listen.

Footsteps sounded across wood, followed by an odd rustling sound. The dog continued barking. Soon a man's voice rang out: "Get back here, you blasted hound, or I'll tan your hide!" The dog yelped. More scuffling and a round of curses followed.

Garth dismounted and quietly tied his horse to a nearby tree. The second horse dipped his head and chomped on the grass at his feet. Bending low, Garth crept several yards ahead through the underbrush and finally spotted the old cabin built of rough, unpainted wood in the middle of a clearing. A thin cloud of gray smoke rose from the stone chimney, and moss covered more than half the wooden shingles on the sagging roof. A rusty metal pail sat on the narrow porch, along with some wooden crates stacked beside the partially open front door. He peered into the dark interior of the cabin, but he couldn't see any movement.

His pulse thumped loudly as he scanned the area around the cabin. The dog and the man were nowhere in sight. Had they gone back inside, or had they headed off into the forest? He stood still and listened again, but the only sounds he heard were the wind in the trees, the rippling of the stream in the distance, and a few lonely birdcalls.

He circled around behind the cabin, hoping there might be another window that would allow him to look inside, but all he found was solid wall and a foul-smelling outhouse.

He made his way around the far side of the cabin and knelt behind a bush, waiting and praying for direction. There seemed only one thing to do. He had no weapon, nothing he could use but his words to confront Harry. Hopefully, that would be enough to gain Emma's freedom.

He rose and walked up to the open front door. "Hello?"

No one answered.

He pushed the door open the rest of the way and walked inside. One sweep of the room revealed a small rickety table, a wooden stool, and a single folding cot covered with rumpled blankets. A pile of dirty clothes lay in one corner, and a few cans of food lined the rough wooden mantel over the fireplace. A blackened pot hung above the small fire, and the smell of burnt food hung in the air.

Reality struck him like a hard blow: Emma wasn't there.

"Hey! What do you think you're doing?" a harsh voice barked behind him.

Garth spun around and froze.

Harry Fisher held a rifle aimed straight at Garth's chest. His dirty overalls, stained gray shirt, and muddy boots reflected the same sorry state as the cabin.

Garth slowly lifted his hands. "Harry, it's me. Garth McAlister."

Harry lowered the rifle an inch and studied him. "Garth?"

"That's right. Sorry to surprise you like this." He lightened his tone, hoping to put the big man at ease.

Harry huffed and lowered the rifle. "You ought to make yourself known before you sneak into someone's place. Next time you might get yourself killed."

"You're right. That's good advice."

Harry frowned as he looked Garth over. "What are you doing up here? How'd you find me?"

"I saw Jason in Roslin. He told me you talked about coming up this way. I asked in town, and Mr. Rider at the general store gave me directions to the cabin."

Harry scowled. "Can't keep nothin' a secret in Tweed." He shifted his weight to his other foot. "So, you made it back from the war in one piece."

"Yes. The Lord was watching over me."

Harry motioned toward the stool. "You want to sit down?"

The stench inside the cabin was turning Garth's stomach, but he was eager to question Harry and learn what he knew about Emma. He glanced toward the door. "Why don't we sit out on the porch?"

"All right." Harry laid his rifle on the bed and walked outside. Garth joined him, and they each turned over a crate and sat down.

"So, why'd you come all the way up here? Did old man Gilchrest send you to try and convince me to come back and work at the farm?"

"No, he didn't send me." Garth straightened. "I'm looking for Emma."

Harry cocked an eyebrow. "She's not at the farm anymore?"

"No, she's not. Jason thought she might be with you."

Harry grimaced and shook his head. "I tried to get her to leave. Gilchrest didn't treat her right. And with Verna gone and us taking off, I was afraid for her to stay on by herself."

Garth nodded, the truth cutting him to the quick. Why hadn't he taken more pains to make sure Emma was safe?

Harry leaned back against the cabin. "How long since you heard from her?"

"Not since December. The Chapmans said the last time they saw her was at Verna's funeral. Gilchrest says she disappeared that night."

Harry sat forward. "The same night Jason and I left?"

Garth nodded and watched Harry closely. He seemed genuinely surprised she was missing, not like he was hiding anything.

Harry scratched his chin. "I asked her to come with me, but she said she was waiting for you, and with the war being over, she expected you to come back any day."

Guilt swamped Garth again and he lowered his head. Emma had stayed at the farm, hoping for his return, until she'd had no choice except to run away. He focused on Harry once more. "Did she give you any idea where she might go or tell you about any friends she'd made since I left?"

"You know how it was. Gilchrest kept us on the farm, working our tails off. She didn't have much chance to make friends, except on Sundays, and she spent that time at the Chapmans' or church." Harry shook his head, looking grim. "You came all this way, thinking she was here with me?"

Garth nodded, hating that it was the truth. "It was the only lead I had. Now I don't know where to look."

"I'm sorry. Emma's a sweet girl. I tried to woo her, but she had her heart set on you."

Garth's spirit plummeted again, and a powerful ache filled his chest. Emma must have been in a desperate situation, longing for his help and protection. But he'd failed her when she needed him the most.

What would he do now? How would he ever find her? And even if by some miracle he did, would she ever forgive him?

Grace finished setting the breakfast table and looked out the kitchen window. Rob stood near the lilac bush with his arms crossed and his gaze focused on the fields. From this angle, she could only see his profile, but his sagging shoulders stirred her concern. Perhaps she should find out what was troubling him.

She turned to Mabel. "I'll go out and tell Rob breakfast is almost ready."

Mabel looked up from stirring scrambled eggs on the stove. "It's not quite time yet. The biscuits need a few more minutes."

Grace nodded and looked out the window again, watching Rob and pondering their growing friendship. A few times each day, she'd look up and find him watching her. He'd smile and go back to what he'd been doing, but she couldn't help wondering what thoughts were behind his smile. Was that the way a friendship between a man and woman naturally progressed? Did it mean he had romantic feelings toward her? And if he did, what should she do about that?

She sighed and brushed a few crumbs from the table. She liked Rob. The more time they spent together, the more reasons she found to admire and appreciate him. But their lives were headed in different directions no matter how much she wished that wasn't the case. If only her heart would listen and stop tugging her toward him.

Mabel stepped up beside her and glanced out the window. "Maybe you should speak to Rob. He could probably use a kind word or two."

"I was thinking the same thing." She hurried out the door.

Rob looked over his shoulder as she approached. "Morning, Grace." His half smile didn't erase the serious look in his eyes.

"Good morning." She stopped beside him. "You seem deep in thought. Is everything all right?"

"I was just thinking about Garth, wondering if he'll make it to Tweed today." He glanced her way. "Harry is a big man, and he has quite a temper. I hope he'll listen to Garth and they can re- solve things peacefully." He shook his head. "I shouldn't be wor- rying about it. That won't change anything. What I need to do is pray, and the sooner the better."

Grace blinked. He was going to pray right now?

"Would you like to join me? I could pray first, and you could pray after."

Her eyes widened. She'd prayed silently before meals when she was a guest in someone's home or at church, but she'd never prayed outside, standing by a field. Was that even proper?

"I don't mean to put you on the spot if you'd rather not."

"No, I'm just not used to saying a prayer aloud."

Rob nodded. "All right. I'll pray aloud, and you can pray along silently and add your amen at the end. How does that sound?"

She gave a hesitant nod and was surprised when he slipped his hand into hers. His fingers were warm and a bit rough, and his touch sent a delightful tingle up her arm.

He closed his eyes and bowed his head, and for just a moment, she studied the handsome planes of his face, his strong straight nose, his deep-set eyes, his firm square chin, and . . .

"Dear Father . . ."

She sucked in a breath and lowered her head. She needed to focus!

"We ask You to watch over Garth today and guide him on his journey. Please keep him safe and help him find Emma. Give him courage and grace to deal with whatever he encounters in Tweed, and bring him safely back to us. Thank You that You love Garth and have good plans for his life. Keep him on the right path, moving toward the life You have for him. We know You are faithful, and we entrust him into Your care. We pray all this in the name of Jesus . . ."

Grace had to swallow before she could whisper, "Amen." How could such a simple prayer touch her so deeply? She lifted her head and looked at Rob through misty eyes. "That was beautiful. How did you learn to pray like that?"

"I don't know." He offered her a gentle smile. "That's just the way I've always prayed."

"But it sounded like a conversation with a friend rather than any prayer I've ever heard."

"I suppose that's because I consider Jesus my friend as well as my savior."

She paused, remembering the images of Jesus she'd seen in the stained-glass windows at the church she and her parents had attended in Toronto. Those images had stirred her curiosity about God and faith. The long sermons she'd heard on those occasions were usually difficult for her to follow. But then she'd found her old Bible in the trunk in the attic and recalled her sister Katie's plea to read it often. She'd taken her sister's encouragement to heart. Now she looked forward to reading a section each evening.

The Jesus she read about in those passages was bold and courageous yet loving and caring, especially toward those who needed His help or healing. He told the truth, even at great cost to Himself. He loved His friends deeply, so deeply He was willing to die for them. That was the Jesus she was getting to know, and He was changing her view about so many things.

She looked up at Rob. "When I lived with the Hamiltons, they never read the Bible or prayed, except when we attended church, which wasn't often. We didn't even pray at meals as some families do."

A touch of sadness crossed his face. "I'm sorry they didn't give you much of a foundation for your faith. But that's in the past. You can choose your own path now."

"That's true."

"Your brother has a strong faith, and from what he's told me, the rest of your family in England does as well."

She pressed her lips together, pondering his words. The letters from her mum and siblings had told her about some of the events that had happened since they'd been separated, but she wanted to get to know them and learn how faith was woven into their lives. "I see what you mean. Even a girl who is almost eighteen and has little training in spiritual matters can learn to pray."

His smile brightened. "Yes, she can."

The kitchen door opened behind them, and Mabel looked out. "Breakfast is ready."

"We're coming." Rob turned toward the house with his relaxed smile back in place.

Grace's heart lifted. "Thank you, Rob."

He lifted one eyebrow. "For . . ."

"For shining a light on the path ahead and helping me see my way."

His eyes glowed. "You're welcome." He touched her gently on the back as they started toward the house.

Pleasant warmth spread through Grace. Rob's caring words and actions were a comfort, and her attraction to him deepened every day. How much more time would they have together? She wanted to travel to England and be reunited with her family, but the thought of saying goodbye to Rob sent a pang through her heart. Did he feel the same about her, or were his thoughtful gestures just a reflection of his kind heart?

14

Emma placed three onions in her basket on top of the two bunches of carrots and turned toward the counter. "Mr. Swanson, do you have any peas?"

The bald, bespectacled grocer offered her a warm smile. "I believe we just had some delivered not an hour ago. I'll bring some out for you."

"Thank you. That's very kind. Mrs. Morton is making beef stew at the café, and she said your spring peas are always the best."

He puffed out his chest. "Well, you tell Mrs. Morton I'm pleased to hear she likes our peas. I bring them in from Bill Conroy's farm. He and his wife, Judy, have the best produce in these parts." He started toward the back of the store, then looked over his shoulder. "Tell Mrs. Morton I'll be coming by this evening for some of her delightful stew."

Emma smiled. "I will."

Mr. Swanson disappeared behind the curtain. Emma checked her list and then glanced around the store. Canned goods filled the shelves against the far wall, and bins of potatoes and onions were stacked next to the front door. Sacks of baking supplies on the shelf behind the counter caught her eye.

Yesterday, Peter had eaten a large slice of her chocolate cake and said it was the finest he'd ever tasted. She smiled at the memory, but a wave of confusion quickly followed. She shouldn't be thinking about baking cakes to please Peter. She'd made a promise to wait for Garth, and though she'd had no word from him or his family, she wanted to remain true to her word. She turned away from the baking supplies, her heart sore at the memory of Garth's silence.

Mr. Swanson stepped out from the back room carrying a large basket of bright-green peapods. "Here we are." He tipped the basket for her to see.

"Oh, those look lovely. I'd like two pounds, please."

He scooped up the peas and poured them into the basket on the hanging scale. "I've noticed you have a nice accent. Where are you from?"

Emma stilled, and her heart pounded as she stared at the grocer.

He tipped his head and studied her. "Nova Scotia or Prince Edward Island? I can usually guess someone's accent."

She shook her head. "I'm not from there."

He lifted his eyebrows, obviously expecting her to answer his question.

She couldn't lie, so she met his gaze. "I'm from England, but I've lived in Canada since I was fifteen, and always in Ontario."

"Hmm, that's interesting. I have family in Essex, England. Is that where your family is from?" He slid the peas into a paper sack and held it out toward her.

Her fingers trembled as she took the sack. "No, we're not from Essex."

His eyes narrowed as he studied her more closely.

Did he suspect she was a British Home Child? Did he hold the common opinion that all Home Children were street rats who should be shunned? Would he spread the word about her background and cause her to lose the few friends she'd made in Kingston?

She dropped the sack of peas into her basket. "I should get back to the café. I don't want to keep everyone waiting. They count on me to help prepare lunch, and I'm sure Mrs. Morton wants to get that stew started." She was rambling now.

"All right. Let me total your order and add it to the café's account."

"Yes. Thank you." Emma set her basket on the counter and turned away so she didn't have to meet his eyes again.

He jotted down the price of each item and showed her the total.

"Thank you." Emma grabbed the basket and hurried out the door. She scolded herself as she rushed down the steps. She needed to work harder to cover her English accent. When she focused on it, she could hide it fairly well. But if she wasn't careful, she reverted to her normal way of speaking and still sounded very British.

She sighed and trudged down the street. Why couldn't people mind their own business and not ask her personal questions? If only there wasn't such a strong prejudice against British Home Children. Then she wouldn't have to hide her accent and background.

As she hurried around the corner, she bumped into someone. "Oh, I'm sorry." She looked up and gulped in a breath.

The man who had come to the café and threatened her sneered at her. "Well, if it isn't just the girl I'm looking for." He smelled of sweat, tobacco, and strong drink, and his hair and clothes were just as dirty as they'd been the first time she'd seen him.

Emma pulled back, clamped her jaw, and tried to step around him, but he blocked her way.

"Where do you think you're going?"

"That's none of your business." She tried to force strength into her voice, but her tremble betrayed her.

He grabbed her arm. "You listen to me, girl. You better act nice or you're in for a whole world of trouble."

She lifted her chin. "Let go of me."

He gripped her arm tighter. "Don't tell me what to do."

"What do you want?"

His slow, suggestive smile returned. "That's better."

She tugged her arm away, her stomach swirling.

He looked down at her with narrowed eyes. "I sent word to the constables in Belleville and asked them for more information. I told them I might have seen the girl they're searching for."

A jolt of fear shot through her, but her anger rose and overcame it. "How dare you!"

He laughed. "I thought that would get a rise out of you."

She bolted around him and strode toward the café.

"Don't turn your back on me!" He quickly caught up, grabbed her arm again, and jerked her around. "If you want me to keep quiet, then you better reconsider my invitation."

Emma's heart pounded in her throat. She couldn't do what he asked. But if she didn't, how could she stop him from telling the constables she'd run away to Kingston?

He cocked his head. "Well? What's it going to be? You coming with me to the hotel, or am I heading over to the telegraph office?"

A dizzying wave of panic swept over her, nearly knocking her off her feet.

"Let go of her now!" Peter's voice rang out from down the street.

Blessed relief poured through her. Peter ran toward them, an angry scowl on his flushed face.

The man growled and dropped her arm. "What is he—your blasted watchdog?"

Emma hurried toward Peter and met him in front of the barbershop two doors down from the café. The man's solid footsteps followed her.

Peter looked her over. "Are you all right?"

"Yes." But her voice trembled.

Peter scowled at the man. "I thought I told you to stay away from her."

"She's the one who ran into me." He sent them a wicked smile. "But I don't mind. Not at all."

Revulsion rolled through Emma, and she turned her face away.

"I meant what I said," Peter insisted. "Leave her alone."

"And I meant what *I* said. It's none of your business."

The two men stared each other down while Emma leaned against Peter's arm and fought to keep down her breakfast.

"Emma hasn't done anything wrong. You've no cause to keep bothering her."

"There are some constables in Belleville who might disagree with you about that."

"Then they're on the wrong track, and so are you." Peter slipped his arm behind Emma and turned her toward the café. "Let's go."

"This isn't over," the man called. "You haven't seen the last of me."

Peter strode on, his arm protectively guiding Emma down the street. She kept pace and tried to calm her racing heart, but it continued beating at a frantic rate. Peter pulled open the café door and motioned her inside.

Emma looked back, and a cold wave of dread washed over her.

The man stood where they'd left him, watching them with a piercing glare.

15

The April sunshine warmed Grace's shoulders as she inspected the neat row of radishes growing in the Chapmans' garden. It was a lovely morning, and there was nowhere she'd rather be than out in the garden with Rob. She plucked another plump red radish from the soil, wiped it off, and dropped it in her basket. It made a pretty contrast to the bright green-leaf lettuce she'd already cut.

She rose and held out the basket toward Rob. "This is going to make a nice salad to go with the chicken soup I helped Mabel prepare this morning."

His eyes glowed as he looked her way, admiration and maybe something more shining in his eyes. "You've been a good help, Grace. I know Mabel and Chester are grateful, and so am I."

Her cheeks warmed as she returned his smile. "I'm glad I can return some of the kindness they've shown me."

She was thankful for this time with Rob and the Chapmans. Each day, as she learned new skills, she felt like she was making a difference. Many of the confusing thoughts she'd struggled with after leaving Toronto were fading. Time with Rob and the Chapmans had shown her what life could be like when she was surrounded by loving friends and family who lived out their faith and valued each other.

"I think we need just a little more lettuce." He squatted and inspected the row.

She knelt across from Rob, taking in his handsome features and the way he focused on his task. He'd shown her how to tell which radishes were ready to be picked and how to clip the lettuce leaves and let the plant continue producing.

Rob added a few more lettuce leaves to his basket. "That should be enough. Let's head back to the house."

"Sounds good." Grace stood and stretched. She'd worked off her breakfast some time ago and was looking forward to lunch.

Rob pulled a rag from his pocket, wiped off a big red radish, and popped it into his mouth. "Mmm. These are good."

Grace glanced down at her basket. Was it all right to eat a radish without washing it off? Rob didn't seem to mind, and her stomach was growling. She chose one of the largest, then wiped it on her apron, twisted off the stem, and took a bite. It was crisp, and the slightly sweet and spicy flavor burst on her tongue. She looked at Rob and laughed. "Oh my goodness. These are delicious."

"You've never had a radish before?"

"I have, but this one tastes so much better."

Rob chuckled and popped another into his mouth. "Fresh from the field. You can't beat that."

Side by side, they left the garden and walked up the path toward the house.

The sound of an engine approaching reached Grace, and she looked up as a man on a motorcycle rode toward the house.

"That's Ethan Swope." Rob picked up his pace. "I hope it's not bad news."

Grace hurried along beside him. "Who's Ethan Swope?

"He delivers telegrams." Rob lifted his hand and called out to Ethan.

Ethan hopped off his motorcycle and waved to Rob with an envelope in his hand. Rob and Grace walked over to meet him.

"Morning, Rob. I have a telegram for Garth McAlister in care of the Chapman family."

Grace stared at the envelope as questions darted through her mind. Only a few people knew Garth was staying with the Chapmans.

Ethan's gaze shifted past them to the house, and then he looked at Rob again. "I remember Garth. Didn't he used to work for Mr. Gilchrest?"

"That's right, but he's been staying here with the Chapmans since he got back from the war."

Ethan looked at the envelope. "I didn't see what it says. My father took the message. I hope everything is all right."

Rob held out his hand. "I'll see that Garth gets it."

Ethan pulled the envelope back toward his chest. "I ought to deliver it to him directly."

A hint of impatience flashed in Rob's eyes. "He's not here at the moment, but I'll give it to him as soon as he returns."

Ethan stroked his chin. "Well, I don't think I can do that. I should put it in his hand. But since it's in care of the Chapman family, I suppose I could give it to Chester or Mabel."

Grace stepped forward and offered him her sweetest smile. "I'm Grace McAlister, Garth's sister. I'll accept the telegram for him."

Ethan's eyes lit up. "You're his sister?"

"That's right."

He cocked his head. "I didn't know he had a sister. I thought he was an orphan, one of those British Home Children."

Irritation rippled through Grace, but she didn't let her feelings show. "I can assure you, Garth is not an orphan. He has a very loving mother in England and three devoted sisters. I am the youngest." She tipped her head and kept her smile in place. "May I have the telegram, please?"

"Oh yes, of course." He passed it to her, then gave a slight bow and touched the brim of his cap.

She nodded. "Thank you, Mr. Swope. You're very kind."

The young man's face flushed, and he almost fell over his feet as he backed up toward his motorcycle. "Thank you. Good day, Miss McAlister." He climbed aboard and turned on the engine with a roar. Grace waved to him as he started off.

Rob huffed and crossed his arms. "Well, it's a good thing *you* were here. I don't think he would've given me the time of day or that telegram without a tussle."

She laughed softly. "I suppose all those lessons about meeting and greeting people were finally put to good use."

"You charmed him, that's for certain." Then his expression sobered. "Now, what should we do with the telegram?"

Her sunny mood melted away. "It's probably from our family in England. I think we should open it. It might need an immediate reply."

Rob considered it a moment, then nodded. "If it's an urgent matter, I can ride up toward Tweed and look for Garth."

She slipped the basket over her arm, opened the envelope, and pulled out the telegram. Her eyes darted over the words and she gasped.

Rob leaned closer. "What is it?"

Grace read it aloud:

"EMMA LAFFERTY WROTE TO US. SHE IS NOW LIVING AND WORKING AT MORTON'S CAFÉ, 42

CENTRAL STREET, KINGSTON, ONTARIO. SHE IS
VERY EAGER TO HEAR FROM YOU.
LOVE, MUM AND FAMILY"

She smiled at Rob. "Oh, isn't that wonderful?"

"Wait until Garth hears this. He'll be over the moon."

"When do you think he'll return?"

Rob's eyebrows dipped. "I thought he'd be back by now."

She glanced at the telegram again. "I hope he's all right."

"If he's not back by tomorrow noon, I'll ride up that way and
look for him."

Possible reasons for his delay rolled through her mind, and her
shoulders tensed. Had he been hurt or lost his way? She pushed
those worrisome thoughts aside, tucked the telegram back in the
envelope, and held it out to Rob. "You keep it then."

He took the telegram from her and clasped her hand. His expression softened, and tenderness filled his eyes.

Her breath caught, and time seemed to slow around them.

"Grace, there's something I want to say, but I'm not sure—"

The door squeaked open behind them. "Lunch is ready," Mabel
called.

Rob's tender expression faded, and he released her hand.

Questions swam in Grace's mind. What was he about to say?
She glanced past his shoulder. "I suppose we should go in."

He gave a brief nod, and some other emotion she couldn't quite
read filled his eyes. He turned and walked toward the house without waiting for her.

Her heart fell. What had she done? She hated to disappoint
Rob. His friendship and opinion had become so very important
to her. She followed him back to the house as more questions
tumbled through her mind.

Cold rain drizzled down the back of Garth's neck. He shifted in the saddle and pulled up the collar of his coat, but it didn't do much good. He was wet clear through. The rain had already delayed him two days, and his only choice was to keep on riding until he reached the Chapmans' farm. He blew out a breath, resisting a shiver. This miserable journey was a perfect reflection of how he felt about his life at the moment: cold, soaked, and heartbroken.

His trip to Tweed had been useless. All he'd gained was an aching body and a longer list of painful questions. At least Emma hadn't run away with Harry. But for some reason, she'd fled the farm and then disappeared to who knew where.

How could she just vanish? It didn't make sense. There must be someone who knew what had happened to her.

That thought brought him up short. There was *Someone* who knew exactly where she was, and it was past time he asked again: *Lord, I've tried everything I can think of, but nothing has brought me any closer to finding Emma. You know where she is. Please give me some kind of sign or direction. Tell me where to look and how to find her. I love her, Lord—You know that—and it's killing me to think of her out there on her own.*

A thought flashed through Garth's mind. He clenched his jaw against it, but he had to pray it through for Emma's sake: *If there's some reason You don't want me to find her, if there's someone else You have in mind who would be better for her, help me accept that and know when it's time to give up the search.*

Even as he prayed those words, his wrestling continued. How could he give up searching? He'd promised her he would come back and they would be together. Letting go of that hope didn't seem right. But what if this was a test of his faith in the Lord as much as a test of his faithfulness to Emma?

He raised his hand in the rain: *I hear You, Lord. I know You love her even more than I do. You have a plan, and even though I have no idea what it is, I surrender her into Your care. Protect her, provide for her, and give her everything she needs for a bright future.*

The burden he'd been carrying didn't totally lift off his shoulders, but he could breathe a little easier as he rounded the bend in the road and the Chapmans' farm came into view. He looked over his shoulder at the second horse, plodding along behind him, and spurred his horse on. He cut across the field and headed for the barn.

Ducking his head, he rode through the open doorway. The scent of hay and animals greeted him. He lifted his head, thankful to finally be out of the rain. With a weary sigh, he slid off the horse and untied the rope connected to the second horse. Every bone in his body ached from the long ride, and gnawing hunger knotted his stomach.

His feet squished in his boots as he untied his bedroll from the back of the saddle. The horse nickered, and Garth stopped and patted his neck. "You did a fine job. You're a good boy."

Footsteps approached, and he looked up.

"Garth!" Grace ran into the barn and hurried toward him. She'd thrown a cape over her head and shoulders to try to keep dry. Her smile was bright in spite of the rain dripping down her face.

Rob dashed in behind her, rain running off his cap and jacket. "Boy, are we glad you're finally back."

They both looked so happy and hopeful, he hated to tell them the sorry results of his trip.

Rob slapped him on the shoulder. "We've got good news!" He pulled an envelope from his inside jacket pocket and held it out to Garth.

"What's this?"

"It's a telegram from Mum!" Grace beamed, her eyes dancing. "She received a letter from Emma."

"What?" Garth grabbed the envelope and opened it. His heart pounded hard as his eyes darted over the message. "She's in Kingston!"

Grace laughed. "Yes, she is, and she's eager to hear from you."

The air whooshed out of his chest. Emma, his Emma, was waiting for him in Kingston. "I can't believe it. How did this happen?"

Grace nodded to the telegram. "That's all we know. But it's enough, isn't it?"

"Yes! Yes, it is." Garth's throat clogged, and his eyes stung. He stepped forward and hugged Grace tight.

"I'm so happy for you, Garth," she said.

He stepped back and swiped his wet face, still trying to take in the news.

Rob grabbed his shoulder. "We've been watching for you. I was going to ride out and look for you if you didn't show up soon."

Garth's mind whirled. Emma was only a train ride away. Urgency rushed through him, filling him with renewed energy. "I should go there now."

Grace reached for his arm. "You're soaked to the skin. Why don't you come inside and dry off? Then you can have some supper and make a plan."

Garth glanced at the tired horses and then at his muddy, wet clothes. Yes, he needed to clean up and digest this news before he set out again, but his mind raced ahead. "Tomorrow morning I'll go into town and take the train down to Belleville. Then I can catch the next train east to Kingston."

The three of them worked together to unsaddle the horses and settle them in their stalls with water and feed, then they dashed through the puddles back to the house. Mabel greeted them at the back door and sent Garth upstairs to change out of his wet clothes. He rejoined them in the kitchen a few minutes later.

They filled their plates with chicken and dumplings, green beans, and applesauce, then carried them into the sitting room, where Chester rested on the couch. He sat up and Mabel placed a tray on his lap.

They pulled their chairs around him and settled in to eat their meal and hear Garth recount his trip while the fire crackled and warmed the room.

Chester listened intently, ignoring his dinner. "That must have been mighty discouraging not to find Emma."

"It was, and it made the ride home seem even longer. The rain didn't help. I had to stop and find shelter in a barn during the worst of it yesterday."

Rob's brow creased. "We wondered why it took so long for you to come back."

"All the way home," Garth continued, "I kept going over everything, trying to think of where she might've gone. But I had no idea what to do next. I admit I'd just about lost hope of ever finding her."

A slight smile lifted Mabel's lips. "Isn't that something? You'd almost given up, but God already had the answer on the way. In fact, He had it in the works long before you even left for Tweed."

Garth pondered Mabel's words, and like the sun rising over the fields, spreading light and warmth, a sense of knowing filled him. Mabel was right. God wasn't silent and distant, nor was He stingy, holding back His blessings. He had heard Garth's prayers, and all the time, He was working behind the scenes to answer them.

Tomorrow he would finally see Emma again and he could tell her how much he loved her. With his promise to return fulfilled, he'd propose, and they could build a new life together as husband and wife. A rush of gratitude flooded his heart, and he sent off his silent thanks.

A happy light shone in Rob's eyes as he looked at Garth. "This is a great answer to prayer."

"That it is." Garth exchanged a smile with Rob, then glanced at Chester, Mabel, and Grace. He was blessed to have such caring friends and his dear sister with him tonight. They understood how much it meant for him to know Emma was safe and waiting for him in Kingston. They were eager to share his joy and see what tomorrow would bring, and that made the prospect even sweeter.

Grace couldn't help noticing the change in Garth as he talked about his plans for his trip to Kingston to see Emma. The light in his eyes and the look of expectation on his face made his relief clear.

Garth turned to Chester. "May I bring Emma back here to stay with us until we leave for England . . . if she's willing?"

"Of course." Chester's eyes twinkled.

"We're counting on it," Mabel added with a warm smile.

Grace laid her hand on Garth's arm. "I'm so eager to meet her."

"I'm sure you'll love her. She doesn't have siblings, so getting to know mine will be especially meaningful to her." He sat back in his chair. "I can hardly believe I'll see her tomorrow. That will be a whole new beginning for us."

Garth's love for Emma and his intentions toward her were clear. Grace shifted her gaze to Rob, and she felt as though an arrow pierced her heart. As soon as Garth returned from Kingston, he would make arrangements for the trip to England. Rob would stay behind to help Chester and Mabel on the farm, and she would sail away to be reunited with her family. Once she said goodbye to Rob, she would probably never see him again.

She bit her lip and looked away to hide her stinging eyes. Their lives were set on two different courses. She needed to accept that and put a guard around her heart, but her stubborn heart wasn't listening. Instead, it ached at the thought of leaving Rob.

Chester shifted on the sofa and turned to Garth. "You've had a tough time of it, son, but it seems things are about to look brighter for you and Emma."

Garth released a deep breath. "I believe you're right."

Mabel nodded to Garth. "The good Lord has His eyes on both of you, and your sister, too." She shifted her gaze to Grace. "Don't ever doubt His love and goodness. He has a plan, and He's working it out."

Grace swallowed hard and nodded. She wanted to believe that was true. Looking back, there did seem to be a pattern in all that had happened: finding her old trunk, her letter to the children's home reaching her family in England, Garth coming to Canada to bring her word from her mum and sisters, Rob and Garth spiriting her away from Toronto and bringing her safely to the Chapmans' farm. All those events had fit together like pieces of a puzzle.

What about her growing feelings for Rob? Were they part of God's plan, or had she looked to Rob to meet her longing to feel loved and accepted, when that had never been God's intention for them?

"It's getting late. I better get these dishes cleaned up." Mabel stood, stacked her plate on Chester's tray, and carried it off to the kitchen.

"I'll help you," Rob said, and he rose from his chair. Grace stood as well, intending to follow Rob and Mabel.

"Rob, I'd like to have a word with you." Chester's serious tone surprised Grace. She turned and looked from Chester to Rob.

"Garth, you and Grace can stay if you'd like." Chester settled back against his pillows at the end of the sofa.

Garth rose. "I'm beat. I think I'll head upstairs and get ready for bed. I want to get an early start in the morning."

"Good night, Garth." Grace hesitated, then glanced at Rob.

Rob looked her way with an invitation in his eyes as he took a seat across from Chester. She followed Rob and sat in the chair next to his.

Chester clasped his hands and studied Rob with a solemn expression. "I had a visit from Ed Brown. He's our neighbor to the north," he added for Grace's sake.

Rob straightened in his chair. "I remember him."

"His daughter, Dorothy, is getting married this summer, and he'd like to buy our farm for them."

Grace stilled, and her gaze darted to Rob.

His jaw hardened, and he nodded, but she could clearly read the hurt in his eyes.

Chester sighed, and weary lines creased his face. "It's not what I want. I intended to pass the farm on to you when the time came, but with my health the way it is, I don't seem to have much choice. Mabel doesn't want to sell either, but she agrees with the doctor. I have to retire from farming, and I can't afford to live in town unless I sell the farm."

"I understand." Rob's voice sounded low and tight, as though holding back emotion.

Grace pressed her lips together. Oh, how her heart ached for Rob. This would change everything. What would he do now? How would he move forward and make a life for himself without this farm?

"I'm sorry, Rob." Chester's eyes glistened with tears. "You've been like a son to me, and I wish I could give you more."

Rob shook his head. "You and Mabel have already given me more than I ever expected. You took me in and gave me a home and a chance to learn skills I'll use for the rest of my life. More than that, you've shared your lives with me. I'll always be grateful, and I want to do what I can to help you through this time."

Chester's chin wobbled, and he sniffed. "Thank you, Rob. You're a fine young man. I'm real proud of you. May the good Lord return that kindness to you one hundredfold."

Rob rose and embraced Chester. "It will be all right. We'll get through this together and come out stronger on the other side."

Grace's heart melted as she watched them. This was the way a family should care for one another: living out their commitment to love each other through good times and hard times. She hoped and prayed she would experience that kind of love one day.

16

Emma walked into the café kitchen with a tray of dishes and set it on the counter. Peter lay on his back under the café's kitchen sink, working on a broken pipe. She leaned down and took a look. "How's it going?"

He banged on a pipe. "Could you hand me another towel?"

She grabbed a towel from the stack on the counter and passed it to Peter.

He huffed and banged on the pipe again. "I've got the new pipe attached, but it's leaking."

Emma wasn't sure what to say. Peter was very handy and could usually fix anything at the café that needed fixing. But he'd been under the sink for almost an hour, and she was beginning to think this plumbing problem might be too much for him.

Peter squirmed to the left. "If I can just get this pipe tightened, that should take care of it."

She stood up and looked around the kitchen. Thank goodness the lunch crowd had been light today. Still, there was a stack of dirty dishes waiting to be washed.

She glanced at the calendar hanging on the wall near the sink, and her heart gave a painful throb. It had been almost two weeks since she'd written to Garth's family in England. It was probably too soon to expect a response, but she'd hoped his mum or sisters would reply even if Garth wasn't at Bolton when her letter arrived.

The old familiar ache flooded her chest. She should be used to the pain of her unanswered questions by now, but it still crept in and stole her breath at times. Would Garth keep his promise and return to her, or had time and the experiences of war changed him so much that he no longer loved her?

No word after this many months probably meant he wasn't coming for her. She'd told herself at least a hundred times she should accept reality. But she couldn't deny the tiny flicker of hope still burning in her heart. There had to be some explanation for why he'd stayed away this long and not responded to her letters. Or was she just deceiving herself thinking there was still a chance he'd come?

Enough!

She shifted her gaze to the window above the sink. Sunshine poured through the glass, creating bright squares on the wooden floor. It was a beautiful day, and she was planning to attend the spring festival later that afternoon. She should set aside her thoughts about Garth and not let his silence put a damper on her day.

"Hand me the wrench," Peter called.

Emma's thoughts shifted back to the problem at hand. She searched through the wooden box at his feet until she found the right tool. "Here you go." Leaning down, she passed Peter the wrench.

She heard the front door open and turned that way. From this vantage point, she couldn't see who had come in. A wave of frustration coursed through her. She'd meant to turn over the *Closed* sign after she'd cleared the last table from lunch, but when the pipe had burst, she'd rushed into the kitchen to answer Margaret's frantic call. Now, with the plumbing mess and the unexpected customer, she was never going to get to the festival.

"Hello?" a man called from the café dining room.

A ripple of awareness traveled through Emma. That sounded like Garth's voice, but that couldn't be right. She'd just been thinking of him. That had to be why the man's voice sounded familiar.

"Is anyone here?" the man called again.

Emma leaned down toward Peter. "We have a customer. I'll be right back." She strode into the dining room.

A tall man with dark wavy hair stood by the door with his cap in his hand.

Recognition jolted Emma, and her steps stalled halfway across the room. All she could manage was a choked whisper. "Garth?"

A smile spread across his face. "Emma!" He hurried toward her but then stopped a few feet away. His smile faded. "Is it all right that I've come?"

"All right?" Her heart almost burst, and she rushed toward him.

He met her halfway and wrapped his arms around her, pulling her close. "Oh, Emma, I've missed you so much," he said, his voice choked with emotion.

Her tears rained down as she clung to him. "I can't believe you're here. I've been so worried. I thought I might never see you again."

"It's all right. I'm here now." He swayed back and forth, holding her tight, like she was a valuable treasure.

She pressed her cheek to his chest, and his heartbeat pounded strong and steady beneath her ear. His familiar scent of wool, soap, and sunshine filled her senses, sending a wave of comfort through her. Garth was alive! He'd survived the war, and he'd come back to her, just as he'd promised. Joy bubbled up from her heart, and she closed her eyes, too overwhelmed to say anything else.

Footsteps sounded behind her. "Hey, what's going on?"

Emma stepped back and turned, but Garth kept a protective arm around her shoulders.

Peter stood in the doorway to the kitchen, his worried gaze darting from her to Garth.

"Peter, this is Garth McAlister." She smiled at Garth, still hardly able to believe he stood beside her. "Garth, this is Peter Morton. He and his mother own the café."

Garth nodded and let his arm slip away from her shoulders. He stepped forward with his hand outstretched. "I'm glad to meet you, Peter."

Peter's expression grew more intense, and his hand fisted at his side. "You've got a lot of nerve showing up here after all this time with no word. Emma has been worried sick about you."

Garth straightened, obviously surprised by Peter's response. He stepped back beside Emma. "I've been searching for Emma ever since I returned from the war."

Peter huffed and crossed his arms. "The war ended in November. That's more than five months ago. I'd say you have a lot of explaining to do."

Heat flooded Emma's face. "Peter!"

Garth shifted his gaze to Emma. "I'm sorry. I never meant to make you worry. I've been going crazy trying to figure out why you stopped writing to me."

"What?" Emma lifted her hand to her heart. "I didn't stop writing."

Garth sent her a quizzical look. "I haven't received a letter from you since December."

She gasped. "I don't understand. I wrote to you every week, except when I was sick with the flu, and then"—she swallowed—

"when I had to leave the farm. But as soon as I got the job at the boardinghouse in Belleville, I started writing again."

"I don't know what happened. Your letters stopped in December."

Emma's heart throbbed. "Oh, Garth, I promise you I did write. When I didn't hear from you, I thought you might have been injured or taken prisoner or . . . I didn't know what to think."

He took her hand. "Where did you send your letters?"

"To your address in France."

He nodded. "That might explain it. Our unit split up after the cease-fire. Most of the men returned home right away, but a few of us moved to a new location while English officials and military leaders argued about what to do with the horses we'd been caring for all through the war. Some thought we should leave them in France, and others wanted us to bring them back to England."

Emma squeezed his hand. "I read about that in the newspaper. There was a huge public outcry, and Winston Churchill finally convinced them to bring the horses back."

"That's right. It took a few months, but in March, Rob and I sailed to England with a whole shipload of horses. As soon as we were discharged, we went to Bolton to see my family and make plans for our trip to Canada."

Peter's expression turned grim as he watched them. "Well, I don't want to interrupt your reunion. I'll go finish up in the kitchen." He turned away and walked out.

A pang struck Emma's heart, and she looked up at Garth. "I need to speak to him. I'll be right back."

Garth nodded, but concern filled his eyes.

She found Peter standing at the sink with his back to her. "I'm sorry, Peter. I hope you understand."

He slowly turned around. "I do. You told me how you felt about him. I just thought after all this time he wasn't coming." He frowned at the floor. "But it sounds like he has an explanation for his silence."

"Yes, it does." She waited, trying to think of something to say. "I'll always be grateful to you and your mother. I don't know what I would've done if you hadn't let me stay here and work at the café. Garth and I might not have been reunited without your help."

"Right." Peter rubbed his jaw, a trace of chagrin on his face. "We made it possible for you to wait for Garth, then walk away and never look back."

Emma sent him a sad smile. "Your kindness has meant the world to me. I'll always think of you fondly."

"But you'll leave with Garth."

She nodded. "I will. If that's what he has in mind."

"And that's what you really want?"

"Yes, more than anything."

He gave her a resigned half smile. "If you believe him and that's what will make you happy, then I suppose I have to let you go."

She would go with Garth no matter what Peter said, but she was glad they could part as friends. She leaned forward and kissed his cheek. "Thank you, Peter, for everything."

"You're welcome." His Adam's apple bobbed in his throat. "I hope he'll love you and care for you as he should."

Her breath caught, and she nodded. "He will. I'm sure of it."

"All right, then." Peter grabbed his hat off the hook by the back door and stepped outside.

She sent off a silent prayer as she watched him go. Peter was a good man, and he'd make a fine husband for some young woman. But she was not that woman. Her future was promised to Garth.

Finally, she could confirm her decision. She walked back into the café dining room, where Garth waited, his cap still in his hand.

Garth glanced toward the kitchen. "Is everything all right?"

"Yes." She crossed toward him. "I owe a great deal to Peter and his mother. I wanted to make sure he understands how much I appreciate what he's done for me. But he also needed to know you're the one I've been waiting for, and that changes everything."

The hopeful light returned to his eyes. "That's good to hear. Thanks for making it clear."

She smiled, happy and relieved that Garth so easily accepted what she had to say about Peter.

"We have a lot of catching up to do," he added. "Would you like to go for a walk?"

"That sounds wonderful." Emma glanced toward the front windows. "We could walk to City Park. They're holding the spring festival there today. I baked a pie and some cookies that I want to donate."

"That's a fine idea." Garth grinned. "Especially if there's some way I can get a slice of that pie."

She laughed softly, remembering how much Garth enjoyed her baking. "They're selling refreshments to raise funds for veterans' families. I'm sure you can buy a slice or two."

"Mmm. I can hardly wait."

"I can be ready in just a few minutes. Why don't you sit down? I'll go package up the pie and cookies and get my things."

Garth watched Emma walk out of the dining room, her skirt swishing with each graceful step. She was lovely, even lovelier than when he'd kissed her goodbye in 1915. Her image had grown a little fuzzy over time, but the moment she'd walked into the room, he'd felt a bolt of electricity shoot through him. Everything about her came into sharp focus: her shiny golden-brown hair, doe eyes surrounded by long dark lashes, pink cheeks, and sweet, full lips.

Oh, how he'd missed her. He closed his eyes, soaking in the exhilaration of the moment. He'd found Emma at last, and she'd saved her heart for him.

When she walked back into the dining room, she wore a small straw hat with a green ribbon and lace around the band. She'd taken off her apron and carried two pasteboard boxes, which he hoped held the pie and cookies.

He rose. "Are you ready?"

"All set," she said with a smile.

"May I carry those for you?"

A teasing light lit up her eyes. "As long as you promise not to get into the pie."

He grinned and lifted his hand. "I promise."

She passed him the boxes, and they set off down Central Street toward the park. It almost felt as if no time had passed as they easily fell into step and conversation with one another. He asked her to tell him about the past several months, and she poured out the story, starting with the flu epidemic. She explained how she and Verna had done all they could to care for their neighbors but had come down with the flu themselves.

Tears glistened in her eyes as she told him about Verna's final days. "I was still not well myself, but I sat with her until the end."

Garth's steps slowed, and he wished he wasn't carrying the boxes so he could reach for her hand. "I'm so sorry, Emma. I know how close you were to Verna."

"She was always good to me. She taught me so much."

He wanted to give her time and not pressure her, but there was so much more he wanted to know. "Jason and Harry said Mr. Gilchrest went crazy the night of Verna's funeral."

She gave a hesitant nod and looked away.

He pressed on. "I know that's the night you left the farm. What happened, Emma? Why did you run away?"

She took a few more steps before she answered. "Mr. Gilchrest went after Jason and Harry first. I could hear them yelling out in the barn. When he came back to the house, he was cursing and smashing dishes in the kitchen. I ran to my room and shut the door, but he pushed in and . . . shoved me down on the bed."

Fire flashed through Garth. "That vile man!"

"I fought back, and he was so drunk that I got away." She shuddered. "I ran outside and hid in the toolshed for a few hours. When the house was finally dark and quiet, I crept back in, gathered a few things, and set out toward town. I knew I couldn't stay at the farm any longer."

Garth clenched his jaw, fighting off his anger. Gilchrest was a wretch! He shifted his gaze to Emma. "Don't worry. I'll take care of him when we get back to the Chapmans' farm."

"No, Garth." She touched his arm. "What he did was wrong—terribly, terribly wrong—but if you strike back, what good will that do?"

"It will teach him a lesson."

She shook her head. "It's not our place to take revenge."

"He never should've treated you like that. It wasn't right."

"No, it wasn't."

Regret burned in Garth's throat. "I shouldn't have left you there with him. I knew what he was like."

"It's not your fault. You didn't know what would happen. The Lord protected me. I got away from him. That's all that matters now."

"But if I hadn't gone off to fight, I could've made sure you were safe."

"You did what you thought was right."

"Maybe. But it pains me to know you suffered so while I was away."

"I'm sure it was nothing compared to what you experienced in France." Her expression eased into a slight smile. "You're home now, the war is over, and I'm proud of you for serving so nobly."

Her reassuring words and the look of admiration shining in her eyes cooled his anger. He hated that Gilchrest had threatened Emma and frightened her so much that she had to flee the farm. But that chapter of their lives was closed. Gilchrest had no power over them now. Holding on to anger against him would only cloud their future. If Emma could let it go and move on, then so could he.

17

Emma held Garth's hand, her fingers woven through his, as they slowly walked back to the café. Spending the past few hours together at the festival had been like a wonderful dream. Knowing that he still cared for her and had searched for her all this time made her feel like she had stepped out of a cold winter day into warm summer sunshine.

He'd been so patient as he listened to her recount what had happened since she'd left the farm. He hadn't said anything about his time in France. Instead, he'd told her about going to Toronto to see his sister and then taking her to stay with the Chapmans. Connecting with Grace after all these years was truly a miracle. Thanks to Garth, his entire family would soon be reunited.

She glanced his way with a smile. She'd always treasured the relationship she and Garth shared, but spending time with him this afternoon made her realize how much he'd matured. His warmth and sense of humor were the same, but there was a new seriousness about him that showed his strength of character, and that made her certain her heart was safe with him.

"Emma"—he tightened his hold on her hand—"will you come back to the Chapmans' farm with me?"

Her breath caught. "Tonight?"

"It's too late to catch a train west today. The next one leaves tomorrow morning at nine fifteen."

She searched his face. Was he asking for more time together to renew their courtship, or was he saying he wanted them to marry and start their life together near Roslin? Either way, she was committed to Garth, and that made her decision easy. "Yes, I can be ready to leave tomorrow morning."

Relief flashed across his face. "Do you remember what I said to you before I enlisted?"

Warmth rose in her cheeks. He'd given her many sweet promises and sealed them with a kiss before he left for his training. She nodded, eager for him to continue.

He stopped by a pretty garden filled with bright-red tulips and took hold of her hands. "I love you, Emma Lafferty. I have ever since that first day you arrived at the farm."

Her throat tightened. "But I was only fifteen."

"I could tell you were someone special from the start. As our friendship grew, you were always there to lift me up and brighten my day, and I tried to do the same for you."

She nodded, remembering all the times they'd sat on the porch steps and talked while they watched the sun set. Verna usually sat nearby in the rocking chair, giving them time together while watching out for them. "I remember," she whispered.

"While I was away, your letters were a lifeline for me. They kept me sane when there was madness all around me. But even more than that, they helped me get to know you in a whole new way, and they made me love you even more. You're a treasure, and I want to ask . . . will you marry me?"

She gasped, and tears filled her eyes. "Oh, Garth. Yes, of course I'll marry you!"

He grabbed her in a fierce hug and held her close while her joyful tears overflowed. Garth loved her, truly loved her. He wanted her to be his wife and share the rest of their lives together. She wouldn't be alone anymore. They would be a family, a real family.

Finally, he stepped back and looked into her eyes. "I wish we could get married tomorrow, but there's so much we need to talk about before we can make our plans."

Emma nodded, though she wasn't sure what he meant.

A hint of regret shadowed his eyes. "I promised my family I'd escort Grace back home to England."

Her spirits deflated. "Oh yes, of course. She shouldn't have to travel alone." What would she do while Garth was away? Would Lucy and Peter let her stay on at the café? How long would he be gone?

"And I have to decide where to take my veterinary training. There's a veterinarian from my regiment who offered to oversee my training here in Canada, but Mum and the rest of the family would rather I come back to England for my training."

Emma's mind spun as she tried to imagine how it would all play out.

He focused on her again with an expectant smile. "So, what do you think?"

She blinked. "About . . ."

"Should we get married in England or Canada?"

Emma pulled in a slow deep breath. He wanted her to help make this decision. To even have a choice about her future felt overwhelming. There was nothing she wanted more than to go with him, meet his family, and be married in England. She looked up at him. "I'd love to travel to England with you and your sister, but I don't have any money saved for a trip like that."

He slipped his arm around her shoulder. "Don't worry about that, Emma. I'll take care of you from now on."

Her throat tightened. "You mean I can go with you?"

"Of course! I want you to come, but I didn't want to make you go if you'd rather not."

She stepped toward him. "I never want to be parted from you again," she whispered.

He leaned closer and kissed her forehead. "We'll be together forever. I promise."

There was a spring in Garth's steps as he and Emma approached the café, and he couldn't hold back his smile. Emma had said yes! She wanted to marry him, and she'd agreed to travel to England with him as soon as he could make the arrangements. He would take her to Bolton to meet his mum and sisters, and then they'd be married, with all the family there to enjoy the happy event. It seemed so amazing, he could hardly believe it was true. After all their trials and years of separation, they would finally be able to build a life together as husband and wife.

Hand in hand, they mounted the café's steps and crossed the porch. He pushed open the front door, and they stepped inside. The dining room tables were empty, but Peter stood near the doorway to the kitchen with two middle-aged women and three men. Two of the men wore black business suits and bowler hats. The other man was dressed in ragged work clothes and wore a gruff expression.

Who were they? Garth darted a glance at Emma, and she clutched his arm.

The taller man stepped forward, his expression stern. "Miss Lafferty, I'm sure you remember us, Constables Fieldstone and Burton from Belleville."

Her face turned pale as she gave a hesitant nod.

"We've been looking for you for some time." Fieldstone narrowed his eyes and walked toward her. "You're under arrest for the murder of Mrs. Ruby Hazelton."

Emma gasped and stepped back. "No!"

Garth pulled Emma to his side. "What are you talking about? Emma didn't murder anyone!"

Emma tightened her hold on his arm. "I told you what I heard that night. I answered all your questions."

"Then you left town without a word." Constable Fieldstone moved closer. "That wasn't wise."

Emma's eyes widened, and she shook her head. "I had to leave. I couldn't stay there."

"This is a mistake!" Garth's voice rose. "She'd never do anything like that!"

Constable Burton stepped forward and reached for Emma's arm. "Things will go much easier for you, miss, if you come along quietly."

Emma's mouth twisted, and her chin trembled.

Constable Burton pulled her away, and frantic questions darted through Garth's mind. How could this be happening? Emma would never harm anyone.

Fieldstone took handcuffs from his jacket pocket and snapped them on Emma's wrists. "Let's go." He tugged her across the room, and Burton fell in step on the other side.

Garth followed them to the door. "Where are you taking her?"

Constable Burton looked over his shoulder. "She'll spend the night at the city jail and then be transferred to Belleville tomorrow."

"Please!" Emma tried to pull away, but she was no match for them. "You have to believe me. I didn't kill Mrs. Hazelton!"

Fieldstone hustled her out the door. "You can tell that to the judge and jury."

Emma looked back, her eyes shimmering with tears.

The man in the rumpled work clothes sent them a searing grin, tipped his hat, and sauntered out the door after them.

Garth's mind spun in wild circles. This was crazy! How could his sweet Emma be arrested for murder? He stared out the door as the men descended the steps with her in tow.

One of the women behind him moaned, and Garth turned around. Was that Peter's mother or Margaret, the friend Emma had mentioned?

"Oh, this is all my fault." The thin one with gray hair raised her hands and covered her eyes.

The other woman patted her shoulder. "Now, Margaret, don't blame yourself."

"But I'm the one who convinced Emma to leave Belleville. I was certain they'd realize she didn't do it and find out who was really responsible."

Peter crossed his arms and scowled. "You know why they're accusing her."

Both women stared at him with questioning expressions.

"It's because she was a Home Child!" He huffed out a breath. "You know what people say: 'British Home Children are born in poverty and steeped in sin. They'll put strychnine in the well, burn down the house, or kill you in your beds.' "

Margaret pressed her hand to her heart. "But Emma is not like that!"

"Of course not," Peter said. "We know she's not responsible for that woman's death. But most people aren't interested in the truth. They just assume the worst, make their accusations, and let their prejudices overrule their good judgment."

Garth clenched his jaw. Peter was right. Emma's background would be held against her. He shouldn't be surprised. Many times, he'd been scorned and mistreated when people learned he was a British Home Child. The bullies at school in Roslin and others in town had used it as an excuse to torment him from the time he was fourteen until he'd enlisted and left to fight in the war. It wasn't until he became a member of Princess Patricia's infantry that he'd found acceptance and earned the respect of his peers.

Determination coursed through Garth, and he fisted his hands. "I won't let them treat Emma like that. It's not right!"

"No, it's not." Peter lifted his chin, a challenge in his eyes. "What are you going to do about it?"

Garth squared his shoulders and met Peter's gaze. "I'm going to make sure the truth comes out and Emma is set free."

Peter sent him a doubtful look. "How are you going to do that?"

"I'll tell you how. I'm going to find out who killed that woman and see that Emma has the best defense lawyer possible. Where is the closest telegraph office?"

Emma bowed her head as she walked through the train depot with the two constables. She tried to ignore the accusing frowns and painful stares of the people they passed, but it was impossible. Her face flamed, and her sore wrists chafed against the tight hand-cuffs.

How could this be happening? She'd told them she knew nothing more about Ruby Hazelton's murder, but no matter how many times she tried to make them understand, they still didn't believe her. The events of the past eighteen hours were so shocking, she could hardly make sense of them. But that didn't change the fact that she was accused of murder and would soon have to face a judge and jury. Her stomach contracted, and a shiver raced up her back.

What was she going to do? How could she prove she was innocent?

Constable Fieldstone led them to a vacant spot against the far wall. He released Emma's arm and turned to his partner. "Wait here with Miss Lafferty." Then he set off toward the ticket window while Constable Burton kept a firm hold of Emma's arm.

She lowered her head again and released a shuddering breath. *Please, Lord. I don't know what to do. I need Your help.* She waited, hoping for some reassurance or comforting thought to calm her. But all she heard were the sounds of the bustling crowd as they passed through the depot.

Her throat burned, and anguish twisted her heart. She was alone, truly alone. There was no one to help her.

"Emma!"

She lifted her head and searched the crowd. Garth strode toward her, a resolute expression on his face. Her heart swelled, and emotion clogged her throat. Garth had come! He hadn't turned his back on her, even with the shameful accusations against her.

Constable Burton tightened his grip on Emma and glared at Garth as he approached. "What do *you* want?"

Garth stopped a few feet away and lifted his hand. "I just want to speak to Miss Lafferty for a moment." His voice was calm, but his expression was firm and serious.

The constable studied him for a few seconds then finally nodded. "Make it quick."

Relief poured through Emma. Just knowing that Garth had come lifted some of the painful weight from her shoulders.

He looked into her eyes with a gaze that radiated confidence and hope. "I'm going to Belleville with you."

Constable Burton frowned and shook his head. "Miss Lafferty is already in enough trouble. You don't need to cause any more."

"I won't." Garth focused on Emma. "I've telegrammed my brother-in-law Andrew Frasier and asked him to come defend you."

She stared at him. "All the way from England?"

"Yes, and I received his reply this morning. He's taking the first ship out of Southampton tomorrow. He'll meet us in Belleville soon after he arrives in Canada."

She silently counted how many days the trip would take. "Do you think he'll come in time?"

Garth's hopeful expression clouded for a moment. He shifted his attention to the constable at her side. "How soon will Emma's case go to trial?"

Constable Burton shrugged. "The judge is the one who decides. Most likely two or three weeks."

Garth turned back to Emma. "That should be enough time for Andrew to arrive."

Emma's hopes rose, and she nodded her thanks to Garth.

Constable Fieldstone marched toward them. He glared at Garth, then at his partner. "What's *he* doing here?"

"He wanted to speak to Miss Lafferty."

Garth turned to Constable Fieldstone. "I'm informing Miss Lafferty that her legal counsel will meet us in Belleville. Until then, I expect you to treat her with courtesy and respect." He nodded toward the tracks. "And I'll be traveling on the same train to make sure that you do."

Constable Fieldstone's face turned ruddy. "We'll do our duty. You just stay away from Miss Lafferty."

"Don't worry. I'll abide by the law as long as you treat her properly."

Fieldstone stepped past Garth and gripped Emma's other arm. The two men quickly hustled her away from Garth.

"Who does he think he is?" Constable Fieldstone's gruff voice sent a chill through Emma. "I've a mind to arrest him for hindering our investigation."

"Not sure that charge would stick," his partner said.

Constable Fieldstone shook his head and muttered under his breath as they headed across the platform toward the waiting train.

Emma looked over her shoulder, searching for Garth. He moved through the crowd behind them, following at a steady pace, his gaze fixed on her. Their eyes met, and he sent her a brief, reassuring smile.

She tried to return the same, but her chin trembled and tears clogged her throat. How thankful she was for his faithfulness to her. He believed she was innocent, and that meant more to her than she could ever say. He'd proven his true character and commitment today. He loved her like no other, and her heart would always be his.

18

Grace threw the thick saddle blanket over the back of the bay mare and slid it into place.

Rob smiled. "It looks like you know what you're doing."

"The groom at the riding academy usually saddled my horse, but he taught me how to do it as well." She returned his smile, pleased that she remembered those instructions and could use them now.

Rob lifted the leather saddle. "Stand back and I'll put this on for you."

She did as he said, and in one smooth motion, he swung the heavy saddle into place on the horse's back. "There you go."

"Thanks. You seem to love working with the horses."

He gave the mare a gentle pat. "I've been doing it for years, here on the farm and in France."

Grace's smile faded. Rob rarely spoke about his wartime experiences. Were they too painful, or was he just reluctant to share that part of his life with her? Perhaps it was time she asked. "What was it like in France?"

He shot her a quick glance, then looked away, but not before she saw the pain in his eyes. He reached under for the cinch strap and pulled it through the metal ring. He was quiet for several seconds. Finally, he met her gaze. "It was more terrible than anything you can imagine."

She stilled, shaken by his words. "I'm sorry," she whispered.

Maybe she shouldn't have asked. But it couldn't be healthy to keep painful feelings bottled up inside and never speak of them to anyone.

His tense expression eased. "Every man who comes back from war has to deal with the memories."

"I know it must be hard to talk about what you experienced, but don't you think that would help?"

"Garth and I talk about it sometimes. He understands."

She pulled in a quick breath, stung by his words. But it was true. She could never understand Rob's war experiences the way Garth did.

He gave the cinch a final tug and tucked in the end of the strap, then rose and faced her. "I saw some hard things—things I wish I could forget. But I also saw acts of courage and sacrifice I'll remember for the rest of my life. There's a brotherhood that develops among the men. We were part of something bigger than ourselves, and that bonded us together."

She nodded, thankful Rob had a strong bond with those men, especially Garth. But a wave of sadness flowed through her. Soon she and Garth would leave for England. Who would Rob talk to then? Chester and Mabel were selling the farm and moving into town. Would there still be a place for Rob in their home? Who would understand his past and help him move toward a brighter future? She was taking away his best friend and leaving him behind with so much unsettled in his life. And what about the unspoken feelings growing between them? Surely, he felt them, didn't he?

Rob lowered the stirrup and tugged the saddle to make it secure. "That should do it." His painful expression had eased, though she could still see traces of sadness in the lines around his eyes.

A pang pierced her heart. How could she leave Canada and never see him again? She looked away and tried to banish that thought. She had to focus on today and not let her mind or heart run too far ahead.

"I dearly love to ride," she said. "Except I've only ever ridden sidesaddle."

He shot a quick glance at the saddle he'd placed on the horse. "I'm sorry. I didn't know that."

"It's all right. I'm sure I can manage." Mabel had given her a split skirt so she could ride astride. She smoothed down the brown fabric. The waist was a little large, but they'd cinched it with a belt.

He motioned toward the horse. "Ready?" He stepped forward to help her, but she reached for the reins and saddle horn, placed her foot in the stirrup, and pulled herself into place. A rush of pleasure filled her as she settled into the saddle and smiled down at Rob.

He chuckled. "You did that well."

"I've watched my father ride astride many times."

Rob grinned. "I'm sure you'll do fine." He quickly mounted, clicked his tongue, then led the way out of the barn.

She adjusted the reins, and her horse followed Rob's across the farmyard.

They rode around the edge of the cornfield, where the leaves of the young sprouts waved in the afternoon breeze. She lifted her face to the sun, enjoying its warmth. A light wind lifted her hair from her neck and cooled her face. She followed Rob at an easy pace as he circled the field and turned onto a path that led into a wooded area.

A few minutes later, he turned and looked over his shoulder. "There's a real pretty spot up ahead I'd like to show you."

She nodded, then ducked her head to avoid the low-hanging branch of a fir tree. Birds darted through the woods, calling to each other with their vibrant songs.

The shady path grew brighter as the evergreens gave way to birch trees with bright-white trunks. Sunshine filtered through the thin branches, and the heart-shaped leaves flickered in the breeze.

"Let's stop here." Rob slowed his horse and dismounted. He helped her down, and then motioned to the right. "It's this way."

She followed him down a path that wove between the trees. The grass was soft beneath her feet, and the scent of earth and wildflowers filled the air.

Rob stepped to the side of the path, and the view opened up to a little glen with a circle of slim birches flooded with sunlight. The trees were only a few feet taller than Grace, nothing like the large trees they'd passed on the way. Bright-green moss dotted with white and lavender wildflowers covered the forest floor.

Grace lifted her hand to her heart. "Oh, Rob, it's magical!"

He smiled and nodded, obviously pleased by her reaction.

"How did you ever find this?"

"Garth and I were out exploring one day, and we just came upon it. We kept it a secret for a few years. Then when he and Emma became close, he brought her up here so she could see it." His gaze traveled around the circle of trees and back to her. "He said she called it the fairy glen."

Grace returned his smile. "It does look like the perfect gathering spot for elves or fairies."

"It's pretty any time of year, but when these wildflowers bloom, that's the best time to come."

She studied Rob, surprised by his appreciation for the beauty of this spot and his decision to bring her here. Questions stirred her heart, especially after what he'd said about Garth bringing Emma here when they'd grown close.

Did he simply want to show it to her, or had he intended this moment to mean something more?

He crossed his arms and gazed up at the trees, a peaceful, contented expression. "Garth and I always loved coming up here."

She waited, holding her breath, hoping he'd declare his feelings and make some kind of promise for the future. But his silence stretched on, and her hopes faded away.

What did she expect? He knew she was leaving soon. Even if he was fond of her, nothing could come of it. She had to stop dreaming of something that was never going to happen. She was just torturing herself with false hopes.

But if there really was no hope, then why did he bring her here?

She pressed her lips together and steeled herself against her rising emotions. This had to stop before she said or did something foolish that she would regret. "I should go back to the house. Mabel will need help preparing dinner."

He turned toward her with a questioning look. "It's not even three o'clock."

She averted her gaze. "We have a lot to do."

Hurt flashed in his eyes. "All right. If that's what you want."

It wasn't what she wanted, but she couldn't very well tell him that. Maybe if she could steer the conversation toward a neutral topic, it would help ease the situation. "I wonder how Garth is doing in Kingston."

Rob started down the path toward the horses. "I expect he and Emma will be back soon."

"I hope she won't disappoint him."

Rob glanced over his shoulder. "Why do you say that?"

"They've been apart a long time."

"If they truly care for each other, time and distance shouldn't matter."

"But a person's feelings can change, especially when so much time has passed."

They reached the horses, and Rob turned toward her. "Garth and Emma had an understanding. I don't think she would go back on that."

"I hope she won't, but things might not work out for them."

He studied her with a curious frown. "Emma truly cares for Garth. The telegram from your mum confirmed it. Why are you all of a sudden expecting the worst?"

"I don't know. I just have a feeling something is not right." Grace lifted her hand to her forehead, where a headache was beginning to throb. Were her own hurt feelings shadowing her thoughts about Garth and Emma? Was that why this gloomy cloud had settled over her heart?

Rob reached for his horse's reins. "I hope you're wrong, especially after everything Garth has gone through to survive the war and make his way back home. That just wouldn't be fair."

Grace's throat burned, and she swallowed hard. "Life often isn't fair."

He searched her face. "Grace, what is it? What's wrong?"

"Nothing." She put her foot in the stirrup, grabbed the reins, and mounted her horse.

He rose into his saddle. "I'm sorry, Grace. This sure isn't how I'd hoped this afternoon would go."

She fixed her eyes straight ahead and urged her horse forward. He wasn't the only one who was disappointed by their outing. Her heart ached, and her hopes were dashed.

"Thanks for the ride." Garth hopped down from the back of the farm wagon at the crossroad and waved to the old man seated up front. The wagon rolled away, and Garth set off down the road toward the farm. As he walked on, memories of all that had happened since he'd left two days ago rose in his mind.

Emma's arrest had shocked him to the core. But the powerful urge to protect her had pushed past every other feeling and given him strength and clarity to do what he could for her.

That morning, he'd boarded the train and stationed himself in the passageway outside her compartment. When they reached Belleville, he'd followed Emma and the two constables to the courthouse. He'd asked to visit her, but he'd been turned away because he was not her lawyer. Friends and family were allowed to visit only on Saturday afternoons.

With no possibility of seeing Emma, he'd decided to return to the Chapmans' farm and seek the advice of his friends and sister. Surely, there was more he could do to get ready for the trial and help Emma through this terrible ordeal.

Garth trudged down the road, his spirit weary. What if Andrew didn't arrive from England in time to defend Emma? Should he find a local lawyer to represent her in case the trial was set to begin sooner than expected? If Andrew arrived before the trial, would he have enough time to prepare a strong defense?

Should Garth contact the private detective from Toronto who had helped them search for Grace? Could he help them find out who was truly responsible for Ruby Hazelton's death?

Garth heaved a sigh as he rounded the bend in the road. There was so much that needed to be done and not much time to do it.

The Chapmans' house and barn came into view, and more questions rolled through his mind. What would his friends and sister say when he told them what had happened? Would they stand with him and Emma and pray for the truth to come out, or would they distance themselves to avoid being caught up in the scandal?

Two riders came into view at the far end of the cornfield. He lifted his hand to shade his eyes. Grace and Rob rode toward the barn. He picked up his pace and waved to them.

Rob returned the wave, then set off at a gallop toward Garth. Grace followed at a steady trot. Garth turned toward the barn, thankful he could speak to Rob and Grace before he had to explain the situation to Mabel and Chester.

Rob pulled his horse to a stop a few feet from Garth and dismounted, concern in his eyes. "Are you all right?"

Garth pulled in a deep breath as he slid off the horse. "No. No, I'm not." He lowered his head and rubbed his stinging eyes.

Rob clapped a hand on Garth's shoulder. "What happened?"

Grace halted her horse nearby. Rob turned and helped her dismount, and she hurried to Garth's side. "What's wrong? Didn't you find Emma?"

Garth lifted his head, his throat aching. "I found her. She was working at the café in Kingston, just like Mum said in the telegram. We spent a few hours together at a town festival, and everything was perfect. She said she wanted to come back here with me and then go with us to England to meet the family so we could be married."

Grace nodded, as if urging him on.

"But after the festival, when we went back to the café, there were two constables waiting for her. They arrested her and took her back to Belleville this morning."

Grace gasped. "Arrested her? Whatever for?"

"They accused her of murdering the landlady at a boarding-house where she worked after she left Gilchrest's farm."

Grace lifted her hand to her mouth. "They accused her of murder?"

"Yes, but she's innocent. I'm sure of it."

Rob stared at him. "This is crazy! Emma would never kill anyone."

Garth grimaced. "Of course not, but the fact she's a British Home Child makes her the prime suspect."

Grace's eyes flashed. "*That's* no reason to accuse someone of murder."

Rob's expression hardened. "No, but far too many people think the worst of Home Children."

Garth nodded. "I'm sure that's the reason they singled out Emma instead of someone else."

Graced looked from Rob to Garth. "So, what are we going to do?"

Garth straightened, his hopes rising. "You mean you'll help me?"

"Of course we will!" Grace reached for his arm. "We'll do whatever we can."

Garth stepped forward and hugged Grace. "Thank you."

Rob slapped his back. "No need for thanks. You can count on us."

"Whatever you need, Garth," Grace said. "We'll be there for you and Emma."

His sister's caring words sent a wave of relief through Garth. Knowing that Grace and Rob were willing to stand with him and Emma through this difficult time gave his courage a boost. No matter what the charges were or how difficult it would be to defend Emma, the three of them would band together and fight to clear Emma's name, and they wouldn't give up until she was set free.

That evening after dinner, Grace took a sip of her coffee and looked across the table at her brother. He had barely touched his cherry cobbler. He shifted in his chair and gazed toward the window, as though his thoughts were miles away.

Her heart went out to him. She could understand why he would be worried and distracted. Her thoughts had been in a jumble since he'd returned with the news that Emma had been arrested and awaited trial in Belleville.

She pondered Emma's fate, and her stomach tightened. She didn't have the courage to ask what the penalty might be if Emma were found guilty, but she had a terrible feeling she already knew the answer. A shiver traveled down her arms. She cradled her warm coffee cup in her hands and tried to stave off the chill, but she couldn't banish her sobering thoughts.

Chester leaned forward. "How long until that brother-in-law of yours can get to Belleville and work on Emma's defense?"

Mabel laid her hand on his arm. "Remember what the doctor said. You can't let this upset you."

Chester waved her off. "Don't worry. I'll be fine. We've got to talk this over and help Garth figure out what to do." He turned back to Garth. "Now, tell me, what's that lawyer's name?"

"His name is Andrew Frasier. He's married to my older sister, Laura. He's actually a barrister in England."

Chester frowned. "How is that different from a lawyer?"

"He's the type of lawyer who handles cases in court."

"That's what Emma needs," Chester said. "When is he coming?"

"His telegram said he was leaving Southampton tomorrow. The voyage usually takes seven to ten days, depending on the weather."

"Good. That's not too long." Chester sat back, appearing relieved. "I expect he'll get to Belleville in time for the trial."

Grace exchanged a worried glance with Rob. She could tell his thoughts echoed hers. What would happen if Andrew Frasier didn't arrive in time? Going to trial without a lawyer would be a disaster for Emma.

Rob pushed his dessert plate aside and looked across the table at Garth. "I think you and I should head to Belleville tomorrow and see what we can learn."

Energy zinged through Grace, and she straightened. "I'll come with you."

Rob grimaced. Obviously, he wasn't in favor of the idea.

Garth shook his head. "I'm sorry, Grace. I don't think you should come."

"Why not? Rob is going, and if two heads are better than one, then three will be even better." She sent him a confident smile, hoping that would be enough to make him change his mind.

"This is serious business," Garth continued. "If we're going to prove Emma is innocent, we've got to find out what really happened."

"I know, and I want to help."

Rob turned to Grace. "We know Emma is not guilty. That means the real killer is out there. He won't like it that we're looking into what happened. It could be dangerous, and if we have to worry about protecting you while we're trying to find the murderer, that will make it more difficult."

Grace clasped her hands in her lap. Remaining calm and logical would give her the best chance of being included. "I understand what you're saying, and I agree this is a very serious matter. That's why we have to work together and do everything we can for Emma."

Garth's expression eased a bit, but Rob still seemed worried.

"The constables have already questioned everyone they believe is a possible suspect," Grace continued, "and they've decided Emma is at fault. But they obviously missed something important in their investigation. We need to find out what that is. And I think having a woman's perspective could be very helpful."

Garth glanced at Rob with a question in his eyes.

Grace's spirits rose, but she suppressed her elation. "I'm sure I can help."

Mabel clicked her tongue. "Come on, boys. It can't hurt to take Grace with you to Belleville. She has a good head on her shoulders. Who knows? She might just be the one to find out who killed that woman."

Garth studied Grace a moment more, then nodded. "All right. I suppose it's best if we stay together."

Rob crossed his arms and looked her way. Was that doubt or apprehension in his eyes? Was he concerned she might be harmed, or was he thinking she had no business going along?

She lifted her chin and turned to Mabel. "Thank you."

Mabel chuckled. "I hope you'll still want to thank me when this whole business is finished."

"I'm sure I will," Grace added with a smile. But when she shifted her gaze back to Rob, a quiver of uncertainty rose and stole her bravado.

The decision was made. She was going to Belleville to give her help and support. Garth needed her, and she would not stay behind and miss this opportunity to prove her commitment to him and Emma. With the Lord's help, they would discover the truth and make sure Emma Lafferty didn't have to pay for a crime she did not commit.

The next morning, Garth walked into the telegraph office. Rob and Grace followed him in, then stood back while Garth approached the counter.

Morning sunlight streamed through the front window and spilled across the wooden floor. The middle-aged man seated behind the counter looked up at Garth, and recognition flashed in his eyes.

Garth smiled. "Good morning, Mr. Swope."

"Garth McAlister! Good to see you. Ethan told me you were back and staying with the Chapmans."

"That's right."

Mr. Swope looked him over with a pleased smile. "Glad to see you made it home from the war."

"Thank you." Garth shifted his weight to the other foot, wishing he could get past the pleasantries. They had to catch the train to Belleville in thirty minutes, but first he needed to check on the telegram.

Mr. Swope pushed his glasses up. "So, would you like to send a telegram?"

"No, I'm expecting one from Toronto."

Mr. Swope frowned and shook his head. "Sorry. Nothing has come in for you this morning."

Garth tried to push aside his disappointment. Why didn't the private detective respond? Garth met Mr. Swope's gaze. "I'm going to Belleville today, and I'm not sure how long I'll be there. If a telegram does come for me, could you send it on to Belleville?"

Mr. Swope nodded. "I suppose we could do that."

"I'd appreciate it." Garth hesitated, thinking ahead. "I'll let you know when I'm back in town."

"That'll be fine. I'll send any telegrams addressed to you to the Belleville office until you tell me otherwise."

"Thank you."

"No problem. No problem at all." Mr. Swope looked past Garth with curiosity flickering in his eyes. "Are all three of you headed to Belleville?"

"Yes." Garth stepped back, hoping they could make their exit without having to explain anything more. It wasn't right that Emma had been accused of a crime she didn't commit, and he'd rather not spread news of her arrest around town.

"Good to see you too, Rob Lewis," Mr. Swope continued. "Glad you're both home safe." Mr. Swope's gaze zeroed in on Grace. "And who is this pretty young lady?"

"That's my sister Grace."

The older man's eyebrows rose. "I don't recall hearing you had a sister. I thought you were a Home Child without a family."

Garth clenched his jaw, irritated by the comment, but he did not have time to discuss his family. They had a train to catch.

He glanced toward Grace and Rob and caught sight of a poster on the bulletin board by the door. Grace stood in front of it, partially blocking his view, but he could see a photo of a young woman under the headline *Missing Person.*

His gut clenched, and he shifted his gaze back to Mr. Swope. "We need to be on our way. Thanks again for your help." He turned and sent Rob a piercing look. "Let's go."

As he crossed to the door, he quickly scanned the poster. It featured a photo of Grace dressed in the gown she'd worn to the St. Andrew's Ball. The words beneath the photo read, *Reward Offered for Information Leading to the Return of Miss Grace Hamilton.*

Garth led Rob and Grace outside and hurried down the steps and away from the telegraph office.

Rob pulled on his arm. "What's the rush? We have thirty minutes before our train leaves."

Garth lowered his voice. "Did you see the poster?"

"What poster?"

"The missing-person poster with Grace's photo!"

She gasped and stared at Garth.

Rob scowled toward the telegraph office. "In there?"

"Yes! Front and center on the board by the door."

"What did it say?" Grace whispered.

"The Hamiltons are offering a reward for your return."

Her face went pale, and she shook her head. "I knew they wouldn't let me go without a fight."

Rob stepped closer to Grace. "Don't worry. We won't let them take you back."

Grace turned to Garth. "What are we going to do?"

Garth's mouth went dry, and his mind spun. "I don't know." The Hamiltons were still Grace's legal guardians. How was he going to protect Grace and take her home to England when they were determined to find her and stop them?

"We haven't introduced Grace to many people," Rob said. "Maybe no one will recognize her from the poster."

The image rose in Garth's mind. "It's a full-length photograph, and her face is pretty small."

"Let's keep walking." Rob motioned down the street, and they set off together.

Rob turned to Garth. "Why do you think that private detective hasn't sent a reply to your telegrams?"

Garth huffed. "I have no idea."

Rob looked down the street. "It seems we'll have to start this investigation on our own."

"Not exactly on our own." Grace lifted her eyes toward the heavens.

Rob's mouth tugged up at the corner. "I stand corrected. We're never alone. We can call on Him for help, and that's exactly what we need to do now."

Grace's eyes glowed with a hopeful light as she looked at Rob.

Garth hardly had time to process the look Grace and Rob exchanged before Rob led them around the side of the building to a quiet spot out of view of those passing by.

"Let's pray." Rob closed his eyes and lowered his head without hesitation.

Garth looked down, grateful for his friend's solid faith.

"Father, we need Your help," Rob began. "Please protect Grace and make a way for her to be reunited with her family in England. And we're concerned for Emma, Lord. Please guide us as we search for the truth in this matter. Show us where to go and who to speak to. Please comfort Emma and give her courage through this hard time. Help her trust You and not give in to fear. Show us Your great faithfulness and mighty power as You work this all out. We pray all these things in the name of Jesus. Amen."

Rob's prayer echoed through Garth's mind, bringing him a renewed sense of calm. The Lord was with them. He would direct their steps and show them where to go and what to do. He was able to oversee events so Grace could be reunited with Mum and the family in England.

And the Lord loved Emma and was watching over her as well. He would not leave her without a defense. Even if they didn't have the help of a private detective, He could lead them to the truth that would save her.

19

G race lifted her long skirt a few inches and climbed the front steps of the Belleville Intelligencer newspaper office in the center of town. Rob walked beside her while Garth stepped ahead to pull open the door.

As they entered, Grace glanced around the dark-paneled lobby. The sound of typewriters and the hum of voices could be heard through the open door on the right. The scent of stale cigarette smoke hung in the air along with a chemical smell she guessed might be printer's ink. She turned to Rob. "I hope they'll help us."

Rob gave her a confident nod. "I'm sure they will."

They'd spent most of the train ride from Roslin to Belleville discussing how to find the information to begin building Emma's defense. After Garth told Grace and Rob what he knew about the case, they decided the newspaper office would be a good place to learn more.

Garth stepped up to the reception desk, where a young woman with red hair and freckles was seated.

She looked up. "May I help you?"

"Good morning," Garth said. "We'd like information about the death of Ruby Hazelton."

The young woman's green eyes widened. "I'm not sure I understand."

Grace joined him and smiled at the woman. "We're wondering

if it might be possible to look through past issues of the newspaper. That should help us find the information we're seeking."

The woman's confusion cleared. "Oh yes. We have an archive department that is open to the public." She pointed to the left. "Just take those stairs up to the second floor. Someone will help you there."

Grace nodded. "Thank you very much."

They climbed the stairs, walked down the hall to the archive department, and made their request. The man in charge showed them to the back room and left them to their search. Grace sniffed and grimaced. The dry, dusty scent made the room smell like an attic that was rarely used. Shelves filled with books lined the walls, and newspapers hung on rows of wooden rods.

Garth pointed at the hanging newspapers. "Mrs. Hazelton died sometime in March, so let's look for those dates."

Grace followed Garth across the room. "There should be an obituary."

"And maybe an article about her death, since it was suspicious," Rob added.

Garth took one stack of newspapers and carefully laid them on the long table in the center of the room. "Let's divide these between us."

Rob took the first section, Grace took the next, and Garth took what was left.

Grace moved to the opposite side of the table from Rob. The headlines on the front page from the March twenty-first edition read, *Paris Peace Conference Continues; Prince Albert and Queen Elisabeth of Belgium Return in Triumph.* Those were important stories, but they would not help Emma.

She turned the page, and the headline read, *Field of Honor: Canadians Who Gave Their Lives in the Great War.* Photographs of uniformed soldiers filled the page. Many looked too young to take part in battle, but they had, and they'd lost their lives.

She glanced across the table at Rob. What if he had been killed in France? What if she'd never met him? Her heart clenched, and she quickly turned the page. She did not even want to consider that painful possibility.

The headline on the next page read, *Canada Demands Full Status in League of Nations.* Grace sighed. "This is all national and international news. There's nothing about local events."

"Look in the next section," her brother said. "That should have more local news."

Grace turned a few more pages and found that Garth was correct. Stories about soldiers returning to Belleville, a charity bazaar for the local school, and a fire at a bakery filled the second section.

Her gaze traveled down the page, and she read, *Constables Investigate Death of Boardinghouse Owner.* She gasped and looked up. "Here it is!"

Rob and Garth quickly gathered around, and she read the article aloud:

"On the evening of March 18, Mrs. Ruby Hazelton was attacked and killed in the upstairs bedroom of the boardinghouse she had owned and operated for the past twenty-one years at 785 West Ridge Street in Belleville. Constables investigating the case stated there was no evidence of forced entry, and nothing seemed to be missing from the house. Constables interviewed neighbors and boarders in residence on the night of Mrs. Hazelton's death. Anyone who has information about Mrs. Hazelton's death is urged to contact Constable Fieldstone of the Belleville police service."

Rob glanced at Garth. "That doesn't tell us too much."

"But it does give us the date of the murder and the address of the boardinghouse." Garth took a small notebook and pencil from his jacket pocket and jotted down the information.

"Let's see if there is a follow-up article about the investigation." Rob pulled his newspapers over to Grace's side of the table and sat beside her.

"I'll keep searching for her obituary." Grace flipped through to the next section. "That should tell us more about her."

A few minutes later, she looked up. "I found it!" She smoothed out the page and read it aloud:

"Hazelton, Ruby (Johnson), 68. Mrs. Hazelton passed away on 18 March 1919 at her home in Belleville, Ontario. She is survived by her nephew, Ronald Johnson of Kingston, and niece, June (Johnson) Ridley of Toronto, and predeceased in death by her husband, Arnold Hazelton, her son, Liam Hazelton, and her daughters, Ruth Ann Hazelton and Lucille (Hazelton) Childs. Ruby was born 7 January 1851 in Senlac, Saskatchewan, the second of four children to Elmer and Bessie Johnson. She is predeceased by her parents and brother, Harold, and sisters, Olive and Dorothy. Although she left Saskatchewan as a teen to live in Toronto, she always considered it her home and visited frequently. She married Arnold Hazelton in 1872 and has lived in various cities across Canada since that time. In 1898, the family moved to Belleville and opened their boardinghouse shortly after. Raised in a large family, she was hardworking and a wise money manager. Ruby was shy socially and did not make friends easily; however, once a friendship was made, she hung on to it. She will be sadly missed by her family, friends, and neighbors.

Friends may pay their respects at the Fernwood Funeral Home, 350 Fernwood Avenue, Belleville, Ontario, on Tuesday, 25 March 1919, at 11 a.m. The funeral service will be held at 1 p.m., with a graveside service following at the Fernwood Cemetery."

Grace looked up. "That's sad. She had very little family left."

Rob nodded. "Only a niece and nephew, and it doesn't sound as though she had many friends in town either."

"So, what can we learn from her obituary?" Garth asked.

Grace studied it once more. "She was a widow, so we can't blame an angry husband for her death."

"Or a hostile son or daughter," Rob added.

"She ran a boardinghouse," Grace continued, "so there were others living there besides Emma when she died."

Rob straightened. "And since there was no forced entry, the other boarders should also be considered suspects. How can we get their names?"

"Maybe one of the neighbors might be able to help us," Grace said.

"Good idea." Garth rose. "Let's head over to the boardinghouse and see what we can learn."

As Grace walked down the stairs, she reviewed what they'd learned about Ruby Hazelton's death. Now that they had that information, they could begin piecing together what really happened that night.

If the private detective Garth had telegraphed agreed to come, they would pass on what they learned and give him a head start on his investigation. If they were on their own, they would give their findings to Andrew when he arrived from England.

Either way, they would do their part to help Emma.

Garth took a sip of his coffee and washed down his last bite of roasted chicken. His thoughts shifted to Emma, and his dinner congealed in his stomach.

Were they giving her a decent meal tonight? Was she able to eat her food, or was she feeling too overwhelmed and upset to eat? Did she cling to her faith in the Lord, or had fear and doubt weakened her trust in Him? Did the memory of the few hours they'd shared and his declaration of love give her the courage she needed to survive this dark time?

"Garth?"

He looked up and found Rob and Grace watching him from across the restaurant table. "Sorry, I didn't hear what you said."

Grace sent him a sympathetic smile. "I asked what you thought of Mrs. Cartwright's story about the man she saw."

He quickly recalled their conversation with Mrs. Hazelton's elderly neighbor Mrs. Ethel Cartwright. She said she'd had trouble sleeping the night of the murder and gotten up to prepare a cup of warm milk. When she looked out her kitchen window, she saw a man cross the yard between her house and Mrs. Hazelton's. It was dark and she couldn't see him clearly, but she insisted no one should have been out there at that time of night.

Garth set his coffee cup on the table. "It's not much to go on, but at least we know there's another possible suspect who was there that night."

Rob took a slice of bread from the basket in the center of the table. "I suppose the fact there was no forcible entry made the constables discount Emma's story and focus on her instead."

"What if the door was left unlocked?" Grace asked. "That man could've walked right in." She thought for a moment, then her eyes lit up. "Or what if it was locked but someone let him in?"

Rob nodded. "That could explain it. But who would let him in?"

Garth huffed. "That's what we need to find out."

They'd spent a good part of the afternoon visiting Mrs. Hazelton's neighbors. The Reynolds, the older couple who lived across the street, were eager to tell them what they knew about Ruby Hazelton and her boarders, but they hadn't seen or heard anything that night. They remembered hearing that Emma was a British Home Child, and they'd warned Mrs. Hazelton not to trust her.

Garth clenched his jaw as he recalled their spiteful words against Emma. It was so unfair and all too common.

Ethel Cartwright had been the most helpful. She seemed genuinely sad about Ruby's death and was eager to answer their questions. After she shared her story about the man she'd seen in the yard that night, they'd asked what she knew about the boarders. She told them there were two women and three men living at the boardinghouse at the time of Mrs. Hazelton's death: Emma and a woman named Margaret. She didn't know the names of the other boarders or where they'd gone after Mrs. Hazelton's death.

Garth recorded the information in his notebook, but there was very little that would actually help Emma's defense. His frustration built as the afternoon progressed, and recalling it now did nothing to ease his aggravation.

He glanced at Rob. "Without the names of the other boarders, I'm not sure we have any other leads to follow. Hopefully, we'll learn more when I speak to Emma on Saturday."

Rob's brow furrowed. "Isn't there someone else who might be able to help us?"

"What about talking to the constables?" Grace looked from Rob to Garth. "Do you think they'd tell us anything?"

Garth shook his head. "I doubt it. They didn't appreciate my shadowing their every move when they took Emma from Kingston to Belleville."

"Still, it might be worth a try," she added.

Garth thought it over, weighing the possible positives and negatives of asking the constables for information. "I need to see if the court date has been set, so I could try to speak to them then."

Grace's expression eased. "I think that's wise."

"All right. I'll go to the courthouse tomorrow morning."

Rob nodded. "Grace and I can check the telegraph office."

Garth tensed, his frustration rising again. They'd stopped by the Belleville telegraph office before going to dinner, and there was still no word from the private detective. It looked as though it would be up to Garth, Rob, and Grace to collect the information needed to build Emma's defense.

20

Grace took Rob's hand and stepped down from the front seat of the wagon. His strong, confident grip sent a wave of gratitude through her. He always made her feel safe and cherished, even with small gestures like that.

As she looked up the path to the Chapmans' farmhouse, gladness filled her heart. "It's so good to be back. It feels like coming home."

Rob fixed his gaze on the house. "I couldn't agree more." They started up the path together.

When they reached the front porch, he stopped and turned to Grace. He adjusted his grip on the suitcases and looked into her eyes. "I know this wasn't a pleasure trip, but I'm very glad we spent the time together."

Pleasant warmth flowed into her cheeks. "I'm glad as well."

These past few days had deepened their friendship and drawn her closer to Rob, but it also made the thought of their upcoming separation more painful.

Rob set down the suitcases. "Having you along on this trip made everything so much better."

Her stomach fluttered, and she glanced away.

He gently touched her cheek. "Grace, look at me."

She slowly turned toward him.

His gaze traced over her face, as though he was taking in each feature. Then he slowly leaned closer, silently asking her permission for a kiss.

Her breath caught, and longing filled her heart. She lifted her face toward his and let her eyes drift closed.

The door squeaked open behind them. Grace's eyes popped open, and Rob quickly stepped back.

"Oh, it's you two." Mabel looked out through the screen, her eyes wide. "I thought I heard a wagon pull up." She pushed open the screen door. "Why don't you come inside?"

Rob blew out a breath, and disappointment crossed his face. He picked up the suitcases and carried them into the house.

Grace's face flamed as she followed Mabel into the kitchen. Did Mabel realize Rob was about to kiss her? Would she scold them for it, or was she sorry she'd interrupted the moment?

Mabel turned and looked their way. "Where's Garth?"

Rob set down the suitcases at the bottom of the steps. "He stayed in Belleville so he can see Emma."

"But you two decided to come home?"

Rob's gaze darted from Mabel to Grace.

Grace sighed. Rob was obviously waiting for her to decide how much she wanted to tell Mabel. "My adoptive parents are circulating missing-person posters with my photograph and description."

Mabel's eyes widened. "Really?"

"Yes, we saw one in the telegraph office in Roslin," Grace continued, "and another in Belleville."

Rob took off his hat. "We didn't want to risk someone recognizing Grace, so we thought it was best to come back to the farm."

Grace didn't like cutting the trip short or making Garth stay in Belleville alone, but now that she was back, she was glad she'd agreed to return with Rob and have those few hours alone with him.

Chester walked into the kitchen. He was moving more quickly, and his color looked better. "Good to see you two. Have a seat. I'm eager to hear about your journey."

Rob and Grace sat at the kitchen table and told Chester what they'd learned in Belleville, and Mabel put on the coffeepot and bustled around the kitchen.

A few minutes later, Mabel carried over a tray filled with steaming cups of coffee and joined them at the table. She served everyone, then sat down and sent Grace a pointed look. "We had a visitor this morning. He was asking for you."

Mabel's words caught Grace mid-swallow. She coughed and lifted her hand to her heart. "He was?"

Rob frowned. "Who was it?"

Mabel reached over to the counter and picked up a small white card, then held it out to Grace.

Grace took the card, glanced at the name, and nearly dropped her cup.

Richard Findley.

A dizzy wave flooded her senses. How had he discovered she'd come to Roslin?

"Grace?" Rob studied her, seeming concerned. "Do you know him?"

"Yes. He works for my father."

Rob's eyes flashed, and he turned to Mabel. "What did he say?"

"He said he knew Grace was staying here, and he wanted to speak to her."

Rob's jaw firmed. "How did you answer him?"

"I told him, since he was a stranger, I didn't plan to give him any information about anyone."

Grace pressed a hand to her stomach. "How did he respond?"

"He said that unless Grace returns home to Toronto, Garth and Rob could be charged with kidnapping."

Grace gasped. "That's ridiculous! I'm the one who made the decision to leave."

"That's what I would've told him if I was free to speak, but I wasn't, so I just kept my mouth closed."

Rob's frown deepened. "He probably didn't appreciate that."

"No, he didn't. He smirked at me like I was a country bumpkin and said, 'You tell Grace I won't be returning to Toronto without her.'"

Grace lifted her hand to her forehead. "I can't believe this is happening. How did he find out I was staying with you?"

"I can tell you exactly how that happened." Chester's expression soured. "I asked the man point-blank, 'What gives you the idea Grace Hamilton is staying here?'"

Rob leaned forward. "And?"

Chester's eyes widened. "He said Ethan Swope told him!"

Rob groaned. "That man has a bird's nest where his brain should be!"

Mabel shook her head. "Now, Rob, I don't think you should blame Ethan. That Richard Findley could've tricked him into telling what he knows."

Rob scowled. "It wouldn't take much to fool Ethan Swope."

Chester smirked. "You're right about that."

Memories of conversations with Richard rose in Grace's mind. "Richard can be charming and persuasive. It's not hard to imagine he convinced Ethan to give him the information he wanted."

Mabel nodded. "Mr. Findley started out real friendly with us, saying how much Mr. and Mrs. Hamilton were worried about Grace and how they're longing to see her again."

Grace pressed her hand to her heart.

Rob looked her way. "We don't know if that's true. He might be making it up."

"No, I'm sure they were upset by my leaving. Look at the posters they've sent out."

Rob shook his head. "I don't have much sympathy for them. They had an opportunity to acknowledge that you were adopted and Garth was your brother by birth. Instead, they called him a liar and sent him away."

"Still, I hate to think of them being upset and worried about me."

"Grace, if you hadn't left with us when you did, they would've shipped you off to British Columbia to make sure you never learned anything more about your family in England."

That was true, but she still felt torn. Should she have found some other way to appease them? If she had waited longer, would they have changed their minds?

Understanding filled Rob's eyes. "When you get to England, you can write to the Hamiltons and let them know you're safe and explain the situation again."

Mabel set her coffee cup on the table. "I hope they'll accept it and give up the search. Richard Findley said they're convinced Garth is a scoundrel and that he lied to Grace to convince her to run away with him. That's why Findley was talking about kidnapping charges."

Grace rubbed her forehead, trying to sort out her thoughts. Why couldn't her parents believe Garth was her brother and that she had a family in England who loved her and had been searching for her all these years?

Rob laid his hand on Grace's arm. "You said Findley works for your father. What else do you know about him?"

She met Rob's gaze. "He is the assistant manager of the department store my father owns. Since my father doesn't have a son, Richard hopes to step into my father's shoes one day. I think he'd do just about anything to make that happen."

Rob's jaw tensed. "So, he meant what he said about taking you back to Toronto. It's not an empty threat."

"No, I'm afraid not." Richard was determined to please her father, and there was no telling how far he would go to bring her back. Hot tears filled her eyes. She tried to blink them away, but it was no use. "Excuse me."

She rose from her chair and fled the kitchen before she could make a blubbering fool of herself. She grabbed her suitcase by the bottom step and hurried up the stairs, trying not to drown in the waves of dread and hopelessness flooding her soul.

She would have to go back. There was no other choice. She couldn't put her friends in the middle of this struggle with her parents for control of her life. She had to protect them and put their needs above her own.

She strode into her room and dropped her suitcase by the door. Kneeling down, she reached under her bed and pulled out her bigger suitcase. She rose and placed it on the bed, then crossed to her dresser, yanked open her top drawer, and grabbed a stack of clothes.

Footsteps sounded on the stairs, and Rob appeared in her doorway. "What are you doing?"

She threw the clothes on the bed. "I'm packing. I can't stay here any longer."

"Why?"

"I have to leave. I won't put you all in danger."

Rob crossed the room toward her. "Grace, stop! You're not making sense."

She popped open the latches of the suitcase. "You don't know Richard Findley or my father. This is my only choice."

"No, it's not." He reached for her and took hold of her arms, stilling her frantic motions. "Grace, please! Slow down and listen to me."

She sucked in a shuddering breath and blinked hard to clear the tears from her eyes.

"I won't let Richard Findley make you go back to Toronto."

"He won't give up."

"And neither will I."

"But he has all my father's influence and money behind him to make sure he gets what he wants."

He looked into her eyes. "That might be true, but he doesn't love you the way I do."

She stilled, stunned by his words. "You love me?" Her voice came out in a hoarse whisper.

"Yes, I do." He pulled her close in a gentle hug. She clung to him, savoring his nearness and comforting embrace. He held her like she was a precious treasure, soothing her with his caring touch and gentle words.

"I won't let him hurt you or make you leave."

More footsteps sounded on the stairs, and a second later, Mabel and Chester looked in from the doorway.

Grace pulled back, but Rob kept an arm around her shoulders.

Mabel glanced at the suitcase on the bed. "Grace, we don't want you to go."

"That's right." Chester gave a firm nod. "We're not afraid of that Findley fellow."

Grace sniffed. "But I don't want to put you in a difficult position."

"Don't you worry about that." Mabel slipped her arm through

Chester's. "We know the real story, and we want you to see your family in England. No one should stop you from doing that."

"But the doctor said Chester needs peaceful surroundings and rest, not strangers knocking on your door, causing a commotion and making demands."

"I'm not upset," Chester insisted. "But I will be if you leave us now. I'm counting on you to help with the move next weekend."

Rob turned to Chester. "Next weekend?"

"That's right." Chester slipped his hands in his pockets, looking sheepish. "Ed Brown came by yesterday morning. He said he wants to do some painting and fix a few things around the house before his daughter's wedding. He offered us an extra two hundred dollars if we'll move out right away so he can get that work done."

Rob's eyes widened. "But . . . where will you go?"

"Reverend Paxton told us about a nice little house for rent," Mabel said. "It's just down the street from the church. We took a look at it while you were away. It's a good place. Quite a bit smaller than this house, but it will do just fine for us."

Rob looked from Mabel to Chester. "So, it's decided?"

They both nodded.

"We hope to pack up everything this week," Mabel said. "We could really use your help."

Grace's throat tightened. The Chapmans had been so kind to her, allowing her to stay with them and treating her like family. How could she refuse? "I'd be glad to stay and help with the move, if you're sure."

"We're sure!" the three of them chorused together.

Grace pulled in a deep breath to calm her nerves. They wanted her to stay, and even more surprising, Rob had said he loved her. The wonder of it all soothed her aching heart. She was more than willing to do whatever she could for Mabel and Chester. But how could they convince Richard Findley that Grace had the right to set her own course for the future? And how could she persuade him to return to Toronto without her?

Emma's hands turned cool and clammy as the guard unlocked her cell and led her down the hall toward the small, drab room where she'd been taken for questioning several times. She stepped through the doorway, and joy and relief filled her heart. Instead of the constables, Garth sat on the opposite side of the wooden table in the center of the room.

His eyes lit up. He jumped to his feet and started around the table.

"Take a seat!" the guard called, glaring at Garth. "You have twenty minutes." He stationed himself by the open doorway and leaned back against the wall.

Garth focused on Emma. "Are you all right?"

"Yes." But tears blurred her eyes. She motioned toward the table and lowered herself onto the wooden chair.

Garth took a seat on the other side of the table and reached for her hand.

"No physical contact of any kind!" the guard's harsh command rang out.

Garth slowly retracted his hand, an apology in his eyes.

"It's all right," she said softly. "I'm just glad you're here."

He forced a smile, but it didn't hide the distress in his eyes. "How are they treating you?"

She hesitated and looked away. "I'm fine." But in reality, the strange surroundings and fear of her unknown future had made her heartsick and soul weary. She had no appetite, and she'd hardly slept since she'd been arrested. The harsh interrogations always left her feeling hopeless and defeated. No one believed she was innocent. Instead, they kept hounding her for a confession.

Garth's eyes filled with concern. "We don't have long, so let me tell you what I've learned."

Emma nodded, wishing for comforting words but knowing they needed to make the most of their time together.

"The trial date is set for May 9."

She sat up straighter. "Almost two weeks away. When will your brother-in-law arrive from England?"

"He left Southampton two days ago. I expect him around May 2."

Shivers traveled down her arms. "That doesn't give him much time to prepare for the trial."

"That won't be a problem. He's an experienced barrister. We're gathering all the information he'll need."

"You and the private detective?"

Garth's brow furrowed. "He's tied up with another investigation in Toronto."

Emma's heart sank. "He's not coming? How are we going to find out who killed Mrs. Hazelton?"

"Rob and Grace have been helping me gather information and interview people. I'll be following up on what we've learned." He took a small notebook and pencil from his pocket. "Can you give me the names of the other boarders who were living there when Mrs. Hazelton died?"

She nodded. "Margaret Clarkson, Sam McDonald, Hiram Davis, and Max Clemons."

Garth quickly recorded their names. "Would any of them have a reason to be angry with Mrs. Hazelton?"

She'd turned that question over in her mind many times, but

her conclusion was always the same. "I don't think so. But I only lived there about three months, so I didn't know the men very well. Margaret and I were closer. She's the one who encouraged me to go to Kingston to stay with her sister, Lucy, after . . ." Her words dropped off. "You saw Margaret at the café the day I was arrested."

"There were two women."

"She was the taller one with gray hair." Thoughts of Margaret, Peter, and Lucy made her heart ache. Did they still believe she was innocent, or did they think she was a murderer?

He jotted something in the notebook, then looked across at her again. "Do you know where I might find any of the male boarders?"

She bit her lip, trying to recall the few conversations she'd had with them. "Max used to talk about his grown daughter, Sally. I don't know her surname, but I think she lives in Kingston. He might have gone there to stay with her. I'm not sure where Sam or Hiram would go."

Garth's eyes dimmed, and he seemed disappointed she couldn't tell him more.

She lowered her gaze to hide her hurt. That was all she knew, and it was no help at all.

Garth focused on her again. "Did Mrs. Hazelton mention anyone having a grudge against her or some other reason they might be angry with her?"

How many times had she been asked that same question? She set her jaw and looked away. This conversation was sounding more and more like the interrogations she had endured since her arrest.

"Emma, please. This is important. If we want them to drop the charges against you, we have to find out who is truly at fault."

Heat flooded her face. "Don't you think I know that?"

He sat back, hurt and confusion in his eyes.

Regret swamped her heart. "I wish I knew more, but Mrs. Hazelton didn't talk to me about her problems with friends or family. She just gave me orders and assigned the work she wanted done. That was all we talked about."

Garth nodded, his expression solemn. "I'm sorry. I don't mean to pressure you."

"Please don't apologize. I shouldn't have spoken to you as I did. I appreciate what you're trying to do, but I can't think of anyone who had a motive to kill Mrs. Hazelton."

"It could've been a robbery. One of the neighbors, Mrs. Cartwright, said she saw a man outside the boardinghouse on the night of the murder."

"But nothing was missing from inside."

"How did the constables come to that conclusion?"

"They asked me and Margaret to search Mrs. Hazelton's room. We told them it didn't look like anything had been disturbed. They searched the rest of the house."

"So, maybe it was an attempted burglary and nothing was stolen, or maybe something was taken and it just wasn't obvious. Do you think she had anything worth stealing?"

Emma sighed. "I don't know." All this speculation didn't seem to be getting them anywhere.

"If it wasn't a robbery, then it was premeditated murder, and there has to be a motive." He narrowed his eyes. "Who would benefit from her death?"

Emma rubbed her forehead, trying to focus her thoughts. An idea struck, and she looked up. "I wonder if she had a life-insurance policy."

NO JOURNEY TOO FAR 249

Garth nodded. "If she did, there would be a beneficiary. That person might also inherit the boardinghouse."

"It's an older home, but it's large and probably worth quite a bit of money. Do you think someone would kill her for that reason?"

"It's worth considering." Garth wrote in his notebook again. "Did you hear anything about a will?"

Emma shook her head. "Margaret and I left the next day. I don't know if she had a will."

Garth tapped the pencil on the table. "She doesn't have much family. The only living relatives listed in her obituary were a niece and nephew. Did she ever mention them?"

Emma was about to say no, but then she remembered a comment she'd overheard. "Mrs. Hazelton's nephew used to live at the boardinghouse, but she asked him to leave shortly before I came. That's why she had a room for me."

Garth flipped back in his notebook. "The obituary listed Ronald Johnson from Kingston as her nephew." He looked up. "Did Mrs. Hazelton say why she made him leave?"

"No, but it sounds like there was a rift between them and she was glad to see him go."

"That's helpful. I'll look into it."

"Two minutes," the guard called.

Emma's shoulders tensed. How had the time passed so quickly?

"Enough about that." Garth closed his notebook and smiled. "I don't want you to worry. You have a lot of friends who know you're innocent, and we're working together to get you out of here as soon as possible."

His words felt like a healing balm to her heart. "Oh, Garth, that's just what I needed to hear."

"Chester and Mabel send their love, and they want you to

know they're praying for you. I'm sure my family in England is keeping you in prayer as well."

Tears stung her eyes. "Thank you." She wished she could reach for his hand or give him a hug and let him know how much she appreciated what he was doing for her.

"Most of all, I want you to know I won't stop searching for answers until all of this is settled and you're released. I promise."

The shadows across her heart faded, and a tear ran down her cheek. She brushed it away and sent him a tremulous smile. "That means the world to me."

Garth's warm gaze rested on her like a blessing. It seemed as if he was about to say something else, but the guard stepped toward them.

"Time's up," he barked.

The shadows returned. She looked into Garth's eyes once more, steeled herself, then rose from her chair.

Garth stood but stayed on his side of the table. "I'll come next Saturday, and Andrew will be in to see you as soon as he arrives in town."

She nodded, her throat so tight she couldn't speak.

His eyes shimmered. "I love you, Emma."

She swallowed hard. "I love you, too."

"Let's go." The guard took her arm and hustled her toward the door.

She went along with him but glanced back at Garth, memorizing his dear face and sending him a look she hoped expressed her love and commitment. He responded with glassy eyes and a gentle smile that nearly broke her heart. Oh, how she loved him. How she longed to rush into his arms and never again leave his side.

21

The wind rushed in through the open side window of the motorcar, and Garth clamped his hand over his cap as the warm May breeze whistled past. He studied the road ahead, then turned to Andrew. His brother-in-law sat behind the wheel, handling the driving with ease.

"We're coming to the turnoff to the Chapmans' farm, just up ahead."

Andrew shifted to a lower gear, then eased the motorcar around the bend onto the rough dirt road.

They'd spent the past four days together in Belleville and Kingston, gathering information, interviewing witnesses, and preparing for Emma's trial. Andrew had visited Emma twice, and the second time, he'd convinced the guard to allow Garth to come along as his assistant.

Garth's shoulders tensed as he recalled how tired and pale Emma had looked during that last visit. She was obviously anxious about the trial and not sleeping well. It had torn his soul to see her fearful and suffering. She didn't deserve to be locked away for a crime she didn't commit. He'd forced down his anger and tried to encourage her to hold on to hope.

When Andrew wasn't meeting with Emma, he spent his time going over the facts of the case and reviewing the information Garth had gathered. Andrew believed the evidence against Emma was circumstantial, but unless they could prove someone else had committed the crime, defending Emma would still be a difficult challenge.

Garth was grateful Andrew understood the prejudice against those who'd come to Canada as British Home Children. He'd been part of an official government investigation into child emigration ten years earlier. That was how he'd learned the truth about the prejudice and mistreatment suffered by many of those children. It was also how he'd become involved with the McAlister family and fallen in love with Laura and later married her.

Garth stared at the passing fields, and the weight of the situation pressed down on him. They had to find a way to prove Emma was innocent. But how to accomplish it—that was the question. He pulled in a deep breath and lifted a prayer for mercy and justice to prevail for Emma.

The Chapmans' farmhouse and barn came into view. Garth was surprised to see three wagons parked in front of the house. Two men carrying wooden crates walked down the path from the house toward the wagons.

Andrew glanced at Garth. "It looks as though your friends are moving out." He rolled the motorcar to a stop and parked behind one of the wagons.

Garth climbed out. Across the farmyard toward the house, two more men hustled down the path, carrying the kitchen table between them. Apparently, several neighbors and friends had come to help the Chapmans pack up their home.

He spotted Rob stepping out the front door and holding it open for a young man returning to the house for another load. Garth lifted his hand and waved. Rob returned the greeting, then jogged down the path toward Garth and Andrew, meeting them in the shade of the big oak tree in the side yard.

"Hey, Garth. Glad you're back." Rob thumped him on the shoulder, then extended his hand to Andrew. "Hello, sir. It's good to see you again."

Andrew shook Rob's hand. "Thank you. And please call me Andrew."

Rob nodded. "We're very glad you're here."

Garth watched one of the men carrying a small trunk down the steps, then turned to Rob. "I didn't think Chester and Mabel were moving until mid-June."

"The buyer offered them some extra money to move out early. He wants to repaint and do some repairs before his daughter and her new husband move in."

A flicker of unease passed through Garth. Where would he and Grace stay now? Andrew planned to return to the hotel in Belleville this evening. Perhaps they would have to join him in spite of the missing-person posters with Grace's photo. Would Rob stay on with the Chapmans, or would he want to go with them to town?

Garth turned to Rob. "Where will the Chapmans go?"

"They found a rental house in Roslin. It's been a real whirlwind around here since we got back."

"Where's Grace?" Garth looked across the farmyard, searching for his sister. "I want to introduce her to Andrew."

"She was in the kitchen helping Mabel the last time I saw her." Rob turned toward the house.

As if Rob's words had conjured her, Grace stepped outside carrying a tray of glasses and a pitcher of lemonade. Garth lifted his hand and called her over, then introduced her to Andrew. She set down the tray and held out her hand to her brother-in-law.

Andrew sent her a delighted smile as he took her hand. "Grace,

I'm so pleased to finally meet you. Your sisters and Mum send their love. In fact"—he pulled a fat envelope out of his suit-coat pocket—"they wanted me to give you these letters."

Her smile spread wider. "Thank you. I loved reading the letters Garth brought when he came to Toronto. They made me feel so connected to the family, and they stirred up some very happy memories. I'm looking forward to seeing them soon."

"And they are very eager for your return to England."

Grace thanked him again and slipped the letters in her apron pocket.

As she passed out glasses of lemonade, Garth noticed Rob and Grace exchange several glances. He had watched their friendship grow over the past few weeks, but something seemed different now. The way they looked at each other made him suspect their feelings might have progressed from friendship to something more. He'd have to ask Rob about it. He couldn't think of a finer man to care for Grace, but the future was uncertain for both of them.

Grace asked about their time in Belleville and their visits with Emma. Andrew summarized what they'd learned and what they still needed to accomplish before the trial.

Rob turned to Garth. "Did you find any of the boarders or Mrs. Hazelton's nephew when you went to Kingston?"

Garth downed the last of his lemonade. "I spoke to Margaret Clarkson. She's fond of Emma, and I think she'll be a good character witness. But I couldn't find Max Clemons. I learned where Mrs. Hazelton's nephew lives, but he wasn't there both times I went to his house."

"We'll send for him." Andrew gave a firm nod. "He'll have to come testify at the trial."

"So, you haven't found any other obvious suspect?" Grace asked.

"Not yet," Andrew said. "I asked the judge to move back the trial to give me more time to prepare Emma's defense, and he agreed. It's set for the fourteenth of May now."

Grace nodded. "I'm sorry Emma has to wait that long. I'm sure this has been a very difficult time for her."

Garth clenched his jaw. He hated that Emma had to stay locked up longer, but Andrew needed that time to make sure he had uncovered every detail about the case. That would give Emma the best chance for an acquittal.

A dark-green motorcar raced up the drive and pulled in front of the first wagon. A tall, well-dressed man climbed out and looked across the farmyard. He started toward the house but then seemed to notice them and headed their way.

Garth lifted his hand to shade his eyes for a better look but didn't recognize the man. "Who's that?"

Recognition flashed through Grace, and her stomach dropped. "That's Richard Findley."

Garth turned toward Grace. "Who's Richard Findley?"

She had to force out the words. "He works for my father."

"He came here while Grace and I were in Belleville," Rob said, glaring at the man. "He's probably the one distributing those missing-person posters for her parents."

Andrew turned toward Grace. "You left home without your parents' permission?"

"I had to. They didn't believe Garth was my brother. They called him a liar and practically threw him out of the house."

Andrew's brow creased, but there was no more time to explain her decision.

Richard's piercing gaze focused on Grace as he approached their group. "Hello, Grace. I'm glad to see you're all right."

Grace clasped her hands in front of her stomach. "Richard."

He cocked an eyebrow, waiting for her to continue. When she didn't, he turned to the men. "Let me introduce myself. My name is Richard Findley. I represent Mr. Howard Hamilton, Grace's father."

Garth crossed his arms. "*Adoptive* father, you mean."

Richard flashed a disparaging look at Garth.

Andrew stepped forward and held out his hand. "I'm Andrew Frasier, Grace's legal counsel."

Grace drew in a quick breath.

"Legal counsel?" Richard's hands remained at his side, and he looked Andrew over with a skeptical glance.

Andrew lowered his hand. "That's correct."

"I don't believe Grace needs your *counsel*. Her father has a full legal team in Toronto to assist her if there's an issue."

Grace straightened her shoulders. "No, Mr. Frasier represents me."

Richard's eyes flashed, but he quickly masked his emotion. "Please, Grace, let me speak to you in private. Your parents are terribly concerned about you. They've been anxiously searching for you all this time." His smooth voice was almost convincing.

She shook her head. "Whatever you have to say to me, you can say it here, in front of my friends."

"That's right." Rob took a step closer to Grace. "We're not going to let you bully Grace into a private meeting or going back to Toronto."

Richard lifted his eyebrows to a haughty slant. "And you are?"

"Robert Lewis, Grace's . . . friend."

Richard huffed. "My, my. It seems you've made all kinds of *acquaintances* while you've been away."

Garth scowled at Richard. "I think we've heard enough. Grace is not interested in talking to you. It's time you leave."

Richard shifted his gaze to Garth. "And you must be Garth McAlister." He said Garth's name with such contempt, it sounded as though he was referring to a criminal.

Garth narrowed his eyes. "That's right. I'm Grace's brother."

Richard smirked. "That's doubtful."

Garth's face flushed, and he stepped toward Richard.

The other man's eyes widened for a split second, but he stood his ground.

"That's the truth, and if you think you can stand there and call me a liar, then you've got another thing coming."

Richard's expression darkened. "Do you deny you came to Toronto to convince Grace to run away from her family?"

"I came to bring her word from her family in England."

"Then you spirited her away without her parents' permission!"

"I didn't spirit her away!"

"Maybe we should call it kidnapping, because that's what you will be charged with if she doesn't return."

"She left of her own free will because they were going to send her away to make sure she had no contact with me or our family!"

Andrew lifted his hand and stepped between them. "Gentlemen, there's no need to let this conversation become more heated. It's a matter that can easily be resolved." He turned to Grace. "Did you leave your home in Toronto of your own free will?"

She lifted her chin. "Yes, I did."

"Do you want to stay here with your brother and your friends, or would you rather return to Toronto with Mr. Findley?"

"I want to stay here and then go to England to be reunited with my mum and sisters."

"Very well." Andrew turned to Richard. "Miss McAlister has stated her wishes, and she has the freedom to choose where she will go and with whom."

Richard shook his head. "She's not of age."

Grace's stomach plunged. It was true. Her eighteenth birthday was more than a week away.

"Her parents are still legally responsible for her, and they believe she was convinced to leave home under false pretenses." He pointed at Garth. "That man is no more her brother than I am."

"I can assure you," Andrew replied in a calm, steady voice, "Garth McAlister is Grace's brother by birth, and her family in England has been diligently searching for her for the past ten years."

Richard scoffed. "So he fooled you as well?"

Andrew's gaze turned steely. "No, he did not fool me. I'm not only Grace's legal counsel, but I am also married to her sister Laura McAlister Frasier. Garth is my brother-in-law, and he's telling the truth. Grace was wrongly emigrated to Canada as a British Home Child at the age of seven, and *that* is a situation our family has been trying to rectify for the past decade."

Richard stared at Andrew, obviously surprised by that information. "Even if that is true, the fact remains, Grace was legally adopted by Mr. and Mrs. Hamilton. She is not yet eighteen, and her parents want her to return to Toronto."

Andrew's jaw tightened. "What legal proof do you have of those statements?"

Richard's face flushed. "My word is my bond. I intend to carry out Mr. Hamilton's wishes and see that his daughter comes home."

Andrew shook his head. "There is nothing legally binding in what you've said. We won't allow you to take Grace with you."

Richard shifted his stony glare to Grace. "This is outrageous! Where is your loyalty and respect for your parents? You are a willful, ungrateful daughter."

Grace pulled in a sharp breath, stung by his words.

"That's enough! You're leaving now!" Garth grabbed Richard by the arm and hauled him toward his motorcar.

Grace's mind reeled. How could Richard say such hurtful things? One minute he was using his kindest voice to try to woo her back to her adoptive family, and the next he was spewing harsh words to demean her.

Garth shoved Richard into his motorcar and slammed the door.

The engine roared to life, and the tires spun, and the car raced down the road.

Rob slipped his arm around Grace's shoulders. "I'm sorry, Grace. Forget what he said. The man's a scoundrel."

"I'll be all right." She released a resigned sigh. "He's always been loyal to my father. I shouldn't be surprised he'd try to shame me into going back to Toronto. But I won't be swayed, no matter what he says."

Approval glowed in Rob's eyes as he looked her way, and the ache in her heart began to fade.

A sliver of the silver moon shone bright in the night sky beyond the window in Emma's cell. She lay on the narrow metal cot with her head on a flat pillow and a frayed wool blanket pulled up to her chin. The musty smell of the mattress made her grimace. It was so thin, she could feel the coiled metal springs pressing into her back.

She sighed and rolled onto her side, trying to find a more comfortable position. But comfort and sleep were elusive. Every night was the same. She lay there for hours, staring into the dark and fighting off fear and loneliness while she waited for sleep to overtake her. When she finally drifted off, restless dreams filled the few hours until sunrise.

The trial had been postponed, and that meant the possibility of freedom was pushed back again, always out of reach. As her thoughts drifted back over all that had happened in the past few months, she felt as though her life was a barren field of battered hopes.

She shifted on the cot and tried to think of something positive and hopeful. The best memory was Garth returning from the war and arriving at the café. That was such a wonderful surprise and an amazing answer to her prayers. He'd declared his love for her and asked her to go to England with him. It seemed like a wonderful dream. All she'd hoped and prayed for had finally come true, but then she'd been arrested and the dream was shattered.

Now she saw Garth only once or twice a week for a short visit, and always under the watchful eyes of the guard. There was little chance to speak about anything other than the upcoming trial.

Garth and Andrew had assured her they were working hard to discover who was truly at fault for Mrs. Hazelton's death. On their last visit, they tried to give her sagging spirits a boost, but nothing had really changed. There was no new evidence and nothing to point to anyone else as the murderer.

She rubbed her stinging eyes. *Lord, I'm so weary. Please help me find the courage to hold on and not give up hope. You know I'm innocent. No matter how hateful Mrs. Hazelton was to me, I'd never strike back at her. Please protect me and defend me and make a way for the truth to come out. Show Garth and Andrew what others have missed. Reveal the true culprit and let justice prevail.*

Her thoughts shifted to Garth, and her heart twisted. He'd put so much time and energy into the search to prove she was innocent. If his search was in vain and she was found guilty, it would be a terrible blow for him.

She closed her eyes again. *Please, Lord, for Garth's sake, don't let that happen. Keep him strong. Don't let his faith fail no matter what the outcome of the trial may be. Keep him close to You and moving forward in his life . . . even if he has to go on without me.*

She turned her face to the wall, fighting back tears and the sense of doom hovering over her like a thick cloud. She could not give up. She had to keep fighting. Pressing her eyes tight, she returned to her prayer. *I know You are good and You are faithful. You see the end from the beginning. You'll carry us through this dark time to a brighter day. I believe it. Please give me strength and help me believe.*

The sound of someone softly singing drifted through the night air toward her.

She turned her head, straining to catch the tune and words. Other prisoners in nearby cells awaited their trials, but all she'd heard from them were loud complaints and shouted curses. Who would be singing in this dark place in the middle of the night?

The song rose, and the words became clear:

"Fairest Lord Jesus,
ruler of all nature,
O thou of God and man the Son,
thee will I cherish, thee will I honor,
thou, my soul's glory, joy, and crown."

Her heart lifted as she listened to the familiar hymn. She'd sung those same words many times, standing with Garth on a Sunday morning in church before he'd left for the war. The precious memory stirred her soul, and hope flooded in.

The singer continued, and Emma raised her voice and joined in:

> *"Fair is the sunshine,*
> *Fairer still the moonlight,*
> *and all the twinkling starry host:*
> *Jesus shines brighter, Jesus shines purer*
> *than all the angels heav'n can boast."*

The truth of those lyrics washed over her, renewing her strength and boosting her courage. All of creation reflected the Lord's beauty and goodness. Even that little sliver of moonlight shining down into her cell was a reflection of His love.

The unexpected song in the night and that shimmering moonlight were the Lord's message, telling her to hold on and trust Him. No matter what happened at the trial, she was His and He was hers. And that was enough for her.

22

Grace climbed the step stool in the Chapmans' new kitchen and glanced out the window while she waited for Mabel to sort through another stack of dishes. Memories of Richard Findley's arrival at the farm ran through her mind again, but she refused to dwell on it. She'd told him her decision and endured his angry reply. Her friends had circled around her and sent him packing.

"Do you think these would fit up on this top shelf?" Mabel lifted a few platters from the kitchen table.

"I think so." Grace took the platters, placed them on the shelf, and turned back to Mabel. "Anything else?"

"I don't use these bowls very often." Mabel took them from a box at her feet. "Will these fit next to the platters?"

Grace nodded, took the offered bowls, and slid them into place. "Perfect."

They had been working together all morning, organizing the dining room and kitchen, finding a place for everything. It was a challenge since the Chapmans' new home in town was quite a bit smaller than the farmhouse. They'd already set aside a few boxes of items Mabel planned to donate to the church rummage sale.

Rob walked into the kitchen carrying a large wooden crate filled with pots and pans. He glanced up at Grace, his expression tense, then quickly looked away.

She watched him, baffled by his recent change in mood. For

some reason he seemed to be avoiding her, and she had no idea why.

He shifted his somber gaze to Mabel. "Where would you like this crate?"

"Just put it on the floor." Mabel pursed her lips as she studied him.

He lowered the crate and pushed it under the table with two others, then walked out of the kitchen without looking their way or saying another word.

As he disappeared from view, Mabel shook her head. "Rob is certainly not himself." She turned to Grace. "Did you two have an argument?"

Grace's eyes widened, and heat flooded her cheeks. "No, he's barely spoken to me the past two days."

"He hasn't told you what's bothering him?"

"No," she said, the ache in her chest growing. It didn't make sense. After they'd returned from their trip to Belleville, he'd almost kissed her. Later that evening, he'd told her he loved her and urged her not to leave. She'd been certain he was sincere, but now she wondered if he regretted his words.

Her thoughts traveled back through the past few days as she tried to understand what could've made him change his mind. The shift had happened after Richard Findley made his unexpected visit to the Chapmans' farm.

Were Richard's threats the reason Rob had taken a step back? Was he afraid Richard or her father would follow through on their threat to have him and Garth arrested for kidnapping? Frustration bubbled up, and she stifled a groan. Why couldn't Rob just tell her what was wrong? It wasn't fair for him to change the way he treated her and not explain himself. How could they work through their differences if he wouldn't be honest with her? If they couldn't communicate about problems, what did that say about the possibility of a future together?

"Grace?"

She pulled in a quick breath and looked at Mabel.

Her friend sent her a sympathetic half smile. "You can come down now."

"Oh yes, of course." Grace descended the step stool.

Mabel laid her hand on Grace's shoulder. "Don't worry about Rob. Give him time. He'll come around." She crossed to the kitchen table and lifted a stack of plates. "You know he suffered a lot his first few years in England. I think that makes him cautious about getting close to people, especially when there's a chance he might get hurt."

Grace lifted her hand to her heart. "I would never hurt Rob. Not for the world."

"I'm sure you wouldn't mean to, but I wonder if Richard Findley's visit made him think about the future and you leaving for England."

Another wave of frustration washed over Grace. Why couldn't her parents accept her decision and send her off to England with a blessing rather than hunting her down and trying to drag her back to Toronto?

Her thoughts shifted to Rob again. He hadn't told her much about his life before he met Garth at the children's home when they were fourteen. Had something she'd said or done stirred up old memories and made Rob feel she couldn't be trusted?

That thought pierced her heart. Somehow she had to assure him she truly cared and only wanted the very best for him. She wished she could tell him she loved him, but she would be leaving Canada as soon as the trial was over. After that, she had no idea if she would ever see him again.

Garth lowered the heavy clippers and stood back from the hedge to judge his progress. The flower beds and the overgrown hedge along the side of the Chapmans' property had been neglected for some time. As soon as he finished trimming the hedge, he'd start weeding. He was more skilled at working with animals than gardening, but he knew how much Chester and Mabel enjoyed spending time outside. And with Andrew back in Belleville to settle matters before Emma's trial, Garth had time to give them a head start with their new yard.

The front screen door opened, and Rob stepped out onto the wide covered porch. He pulled a handkerchief from his back pocket and wiped his forehead, then placed his hands on his hips and stared past the stack of crates piled at his feet.

Garth watched him for a few seconds, then called, "Taking a break?"

Rob jerked and turned around. "Oh, I didn't see you there."

Garth grinned. "Yes, I'd say you've been pretty preoccupied lately."

"What do you mean?"

Garth chuckled. "I mean it's obvious your thoughts have been more focused on my sister than on anything else."

Rob scowled. "Don't give me a hard time, Garth. That's the last thing I need from you."

Garth pulled back. "I'm sorry. I didn't mean to upset you."

Rob blew out a breath and shook his head. "And I didn't mean to bark at you."

Garth set down the clippers and walked over to the porch steps. "You want to talk about it?"

Rob sighed and rubbed his hand down his face.

"Did you and Grace have an argument?"

Rob cocked his head. "Why does everyone keep asking that?"

"Who is everyone?"

"Chester cornered me about an hour ago with that same question. And just now, I overheard Mabel asking Grace if we'd had a fight."

"Something must be going on. Why don't you tell me about it? Maybe I can help."

"I suppose it wouldn't hurt. I could use some advice."

"Ask away." Garth took a seat on the top step.

Rob sat beside Garth. "The day Grace and I got back from Belleville, we were walking up to the farmhouse, and . . ."

Garth waited, determined to be patient with his friend.

"I told her how much I'd enjoyed our time together and how glad I was that she'd come along, and . . . I was about to kiss her, when Mabel opened the door." He grimaced and looked down.

"If you truly have feelings for her, that's not a crime."

Rob lifted his head. "I do, but I shouldn't have done it. There's no future for us, so it wasn't fair to her. And that's not all."

Garth tensed. "Go on."

"That day, after Chester and Mabel told us about Richard Findley's first visit, Grace was so upset, she rushed out of the kitchen and ran upstairs. I went after her and found her throwing clothes in her suitcase. She was worried about Findley coming back and upsetting Chester and Mabel. She thought she had to leave, but I said I didn't want her to go, and . . . I told her I loved her."

"I see." Garth suspected their friendship had grown, but he'd been so focused on his search for Emma, and then her arrest and the upcoming trial, that he hadn't realized how strong Rob's feelings were.

"Now I don't know what to do. She wants to go to England and see her family. And of course she should." He blew out a breath and rubbed his eyes.

"Maybe after she has some time to visit them, she could come back to Canada."

"How could I ask her to do that when I have nothing to offer her?" Rob huffed a humorless laugh. "Unless you consider two hundred dollars enough to provide a promising future."

"Two hundred dollars?"

"Chester gave me the money he received from Ed Brown for moving out early. He said he wished he could give me more from the sale of the farm but that's all the money he and Mabel have now." Rob shook his head. "I wouldn't take any more from them even if he offered."

Garth nodded as the sharp contrast between his future and Rob's rose in his mind. Garth had a loving family he could rely on, a home in England if he wanted to stay, and promised training as a veterinarian. That made it possible for him to propose and hope for a future with Emma. He'd taken his freedom and stability for granted. But Rob had no security or clear plan for the future. Regret filled Garth, and he turned to his friend. "What are you going to do?"

"Chester said I could stay here with them and look for a job in town, but that's not the life for me. I'm a farmer. I want to own my own land and someday have a home and a family. That's all I've ever wanted."

Garth's throat tightened. During the war, on long winter nights, they would sit by the campfire and talk about what they'd do when they finally made it home. Rob talked about going back to the farm and working with Chester until it was time for him to take over.

Rob leaned back, looking weary. "I suppose I'll have to hire on as a farmhand somewhere and save my wages until I have enough to buy my own place." He sighed. "But that will take years. I can't expect Grace to wait that long."

"So, you're going to let her leave for England and not make plans to see her again?"

"That's not what I want, but I don't see any other option. I have to do what's best for Grace."

Garth placed his hand on his friend's shoulder. "I'm sorry, Rob. I didn't realize how much you cared for her."

"I know. I didn't want to say anything until I figured out what to do, but I'm stumped."

"There's got to be another answer."

"It's all right. I don't expect you to solve the problem, but I'm glad you're willing to listen and not box my ears for letting your sister down."

"I understand. I'll pray for you."

"Thanks." Rob leaned forward, rested his arms on his knees, and stared off across the yard. "I wish I hadn't told her how I feel. That just makes me look like a fool."

"Don't say that. I'm sure she doesn't think of you that way."

"Maybe not, but I was wrong to rush ahead and declare my feelings when there's no way I can follow through."

"Did she say how she feels about you?"

"Not in so many words, but I think she feels the same."

Garth nodded, trying to discern how to fulfill his role as best friend and brother at the same time. He owed Rob so much, but he also had to consider his sister's feelings and his family's expectations for her. "Do you want me to speak to her—try and explain things?"

"No. Please don't say anything."

"Are you sure? Maybe if I talked to her—"

Rob shook his head. "It's better if I just keep my distance. Then she can focus on preparing for her trip to England and reuniting with your family."

"All right. If you're sure that's what's best." But Garth suspected Grace truly cared for Rob and that she might not put her feelings for him aside as easily as Rob thought.

His friend gave a firm nod. "I'm sure."

Garth studied Rob's troubled expression. He didn't look as certain as his words. Still, he would have to bow to his friend's wishes. Above everything else, he owed Rob his life and so much more.

The last rays of the sunset glowed in the western sky as Grace looked out the screen door of the Chapmans' new home. The rhythmic song of crickets floated on the warm evening air, and a few birds chirped in the trees in the front yard.

Rob stood on the porch with his back to Grace and his arms crossed as he gazed out at the fading colors. Garth had gone upstairs, and Mabel and Chester were settled in the sitting room with cups of coffee and slices of cherry pie.

Grace pulled in a deep breath to steady her emotions. This was her chance to speak to Rob with no one else around to overhear their conversation. Summoning her courage, she pushed open the screen door and stepped out onto the porch.

Rob glanced over his shoulder. His gaze connected with hers for an instant before he looked away.

"It's a beautiful night," she said softly.

"Yes, it is." Was that a hint of regret in his voice, or was he simply tired from moving all the furniture and crates?

She crossed the porch to stand beside him and studied the peaceful view. Near the horizon, a pale band of gold faded to light blue. Beyond that, the color deepened to royal blue with the first few stars shining through overhead.

She waited, hoping Rob would tell her what was on his mind, but several seconds passed in silence. "It seems like you've been troubled about something the past few days."

His brow creased, and he looked down. "I'm all right."

"You don't seem all right to me." She kept her voice soft, wanting to draw him out.

The sunlight was almost gone, but a glow from the kitchen window allowed her to see his profile. A muscle in his jaw twitched, but he didn't answer.

Perhaps a direct approach would be best. "Rob, if I've said or done something that upset you, I wish you'd tell me so I can apologize and make it right."

He continued to stare out at the yard. "You haven't done anything."

"Then why don't you speak to me or look at me? Have I offended you?"

"No, you haven't."

"Then please tell me what's wrong," she said, her tone growing insistent.

His hands tightened around the top porch railing. "It's not something I want to discuss."

There had to be some way to persuade him to explain himself. Perhaps if she was more vulnerable and opened her heart, he would do the same. "You're a good man, Rob. I care about you. There's nothing you could tell me that would change my opinion of you. Whatever it is, I'll keep it in confidence." She laid her hand on his arm. "You can trust me."

He stiffened. "It's not that simple, Grace."

Stung, she lifted her hand away. "What do you mean?"

His Adam's apple bobbed in his throat. "You need to stop thinking of me in any way except as your brother's friend."

"But I don't understand. That night at the farm . . . you said you loved me."

He finally looked her way, regret burning in his eyes. "I shouldn't have said that. It's not true." He turned and walked across the porch, then stopped by the screen door and looked back. "I'm sorry, Grace. I never meant to hurt you." Without another word, he opened the screen door and stepped inside.

She stared after him, pain and confusion crushing her heart. None of this made sense. Rob was an honorable, kind man, or at least she'd thought he was. How could his feelings toward her have changed in such a short time?

Whatever the reason, he had decided she was not worth pursuing, and that felt like a dagger in her heart.

23

Grace clutched her open umbrella and sidestepped the puddles as she followed Garth and Rob toward the Brightonburg Hotel to meet Andrew on the evening before Emma's trial.

Garth held open the front door and stood back. Grace closed her umbrella, shook off the raindrops, and walked into the lobby. The paneled walls, high ceiling, and sparkling chandelier created an elegant atmosphere.

She spotted Andrew sitting in one of the four chairs grouped in the corner near the windows. A tall potted palm partially hid him from view. His head was bent as he focused on an open file in his lap. His briefcase sat at his feet.

"There he is." Garth nodded toward Andrew and started across the lobby.

Grace glanced at Rob as they followed Garth, and sadness pressed down on her heart again. The memory of their painful conversation almost a week prior filled her mind, and her throat clogged.

Rob didn't love her. Even though he hadn't explained why his feelings toward her had changed, his actions made his intentions, or lack thereof, perfectly clear. She needed to stop dreaming of a future with Rob and accept reality. They would never be more than friends, and even that was doubtful.

She swallowed hard. It was time to put Rob out of her mind

and remember she'd come to Belleville to support Garth and Emma through the trial. No matter how much Rob's change of heart hurt, she had to put her feelings aside and show her loyalty to her brother and his betrothed.

Andrew looked up as they approached, and he rose to greet them.

Garth shook his hand. "How are you doing with the preparations for the trial?"

"I'm just going over my notes now. I think we're ready." Andrew motioned to the chairs. "Shall we sit down?" They each took a seat.

Rob turned to Andrew. "What's the main focus of your defense for Emma?"

"The burden of proof rests with the prosecution. They have to prove beyond a reasonable doubt that Emma is responsible for Mrs. Hazelton's death. There are no eyewitnesses to the murder, and the evidence against Emma is circumstantial. But I'm concerned they'll use Emma's background as a Home Child to try to build the case that she is the most likely suspect. I'm afraid the prevailing prejudice may sway the jury against her."

Grace shifted in her chair and clasped her hands in her lap. "That's so unfair."

"I agree," said Andrew. "That's why calling character witnesses is so important. We have Margaret Clarkson and Reverend Paxton, as well as Garth, to speak on her behalf if needed. I'm hopeful their testimony will convince the jury it is not in Emma's character to strike back at Mrs. Hazelton, even though she was poorly treated."

Garth leaned forward. "After looking at all the evidence and interviewing witnesses, who do you think killed Mrs. Hazelton?"

Andrew's confident expression faded a bit. "There are a few

possibilities, but nothing will be clear until I'm able to question the witnesses in the courtroom."

"Who are you considering?" Garth asked.

Andrew paused for a moment, then said, "It could have been one of the other boarders or Mrs. Hazelton's niece or nephew. I also learned she was not really a widow, as most people believed. She has an ex-husband with a rather shady past."

Garth rubbed his chin. "That's interesting. Were you able to locate the other boarders?"

"We found two of the three, and that last one is an eighty-two-year-old man in poor health. I doubt he'd have the strength to carry out the murder."

Garth nodded. "So, you're going to try to prove she was killed by someone who knew her rather than by someone carrying out an attempted robbery?"

"That seems more likely," Andrew said, "but I don't want to rule out the second possibility if the boarders or relatives maintain their innocence under questioning. We have to create enough doubt in the jurors' minds to make them believe Emma is not the only possible suspect."

Grace bit her lip as she listened. Emma's fate seemed to depend on Andrew's ability to question the witnesses and see if one of them would confess under pressure. She hoped he was as skilled as Garth believed. Emma's life depended on it.

Garth and Rob exchanged a concerned look as the uncertainty of the situation seemed to settle over them as well.

Garth turned to Andrew. "How's Emma?"

"She's anxious about testifying. I'll call her only if necessary. I went over the questions I'll ask to help her prepare, but the prosecution may ask her something unexpected. I think that's her greatest concern."

Garth nodded and leaned back in his chair, looking unsettled.

"I want to go over my questions for you, but it has been a long day, and I'm rather tired. Why don't we meet tomorrow morning for breakfast at eight and talk after that?"

Garth agreed, and they all rose from their chairs.

Grace followed the men across the lobby to the front desk. While Andrew checked them in and they waited to receive the keys to their rooms, Grace turned and looked toward the front windows. Heavy rain splattered against the glass and ran down in shimmering rivulets. The wind howled, the chandelier rattled, and the lights flickered.

She hunched her shoulders against the sounds, and a shiver raced down her back. The fierce storm outside seemed a fitting reflection of the trouble that had come upon Emma and Garth. Would they be reunited and be able to move ahead with the trip to England and their wedding plans, or would Emma be found guilty and be separated from Garth forever?

Lightning flashed and lit the sky outside the hotel, quickly followed by rumbling thunder. Grace glanced at Garth, and her heart went out to him. This storm would pass and the sun would probably come out tomorrow morning, but the fateful storm in Garth's and Emma's lives wouldn't clear until the trial was over and Emma's fate was finally decided.

Emma steeled herself as she walked into the courtroom with Andrew on the second day of her trial. The day before, she'd sat through four hours of jury selection. This day's events would probably last longer and be much more difficult.

She took her seat at the wooden table up front on the left, with Andrew beside her. She glanced back, relieved to see Garth seated in the first row directly behind them. Their gazes connected and held. He nodded, his eyes and slight smile communicating a message of encouragement.

Energy flowed through her, and she returned a loving look, hoping he knew how grateful she was for all he'd done and how much she appreciated his presence.

The young woman seated next to Garth had to be his sister Grace. She wore her golden hair up with a few loose tendrils curling on each side of her face. Though her hair was a lighter color than Garth's, the shape of her face made it easy to see they were brother and sister.

Grace sent Emma an encouraging smile, and gratefulness filled Emma's heart.

Rob Lewis was seated on Grace's right. He shifted in his seat and looked around the courtroom with a somber expression. Was he uncomfortable in that stiff black suit, or was it concern for her and Garth that darkened his features?

In the next row, she spotted her friends from the café, Margaret Clarkson and Peter and Lucy Morton. Margaret sent her a brief smile, and Emma responded with a grateful nod. There were others she recognized too: Reverend Paxton, as well as Mrs. Cartwright, Mrs. Hazelton's neighbor and friend. Fellow boarders Sam McDonald and Hiram Davis sat in that same row. Andrew had told her they might be called as witnesses for the defense.

She looked at the other side of the courtroom and sucked in a startled breath. In the back corner, Eli Gilchrest sat with his head bent and his hat in his hands. Her former employer's grizzled face appeared leaner and more haggard than when she'd fled the farm in December. She shivered and looked away, trying to banish the frightening memories of what had happened on the night of Verna's funeral. Why had he been summoned? Would she have to recount those events in front of all these people? Her face burned, and her gaze darted to Garth. Did he know Eli Gilchrest was here?

She lowered her head again and tried to calm her racing heart. Andrew placed his hand on her arm. "Are you all right, Emma?"

She lifted her head. "I didn't know Eli Gilchrest would be here."

Andrew glanced at his notes. "Eli Gilchrest?"

"He's the man who owns the farm where Garth and I worked." She hadn't told Andrew why she'd left the farm. He'd never asked, but she'd have to tell him now. She started to explain, but a side door opened, and the members of the jury walked into the court-room and took their seats.

She searched their serious faces, and a sinking feeling hit her stomach. All the twelve men were dressed in dark suits, and from their stoic expressions, it looked as though they were taking this responsibility very seriously.

Please, Lord, help them discern the truth. She leaned toward Andrew. "I need to tell you about Eli Gilchrest." Andrew looked her way, and she continued. "I left the farm because he tried to attack me."

Concern flashed in Andrew's eyes. "I'm sorry. I'll need to know more, but we can wait for the first recess." He checked his watch. "The judge should be here at any moment. Then the prosecutor will give the opening statement for the Crown. What he says may be upsetting, but I'll give my opening statement after that."

She nodded. Andrew had already told her how the trial would begin, but her thoughts were so jumbled, she was glad he'd repeated it for her.

The door up front next to the judge's desk swung open, and the judge walked in wearing a long black robe and a white wig.

"All rise," the bailiff called. "The court is now in session."

Emma and Andrew stood as the judge stepped onto the raised platform and took a seat behind his desk. Emma searched his face, trying to read past his stern expression. Was he kindhearted and interested in the truth, or was he strict with a goal of ending the trial as quickly as possible? His face was heavily lined, and he appeared to be in his seventies with a long beak-like nose and piercing silver-gray eyes.

His gaze traveled around the courtroom. Then he told everyone to be seated.

Emma lowered herself into her chair, folded her hands on the table, and tried to prepare herself for what was coming, but a terrible wave of fear flooded through her. She closed her eyes. *Please be with me, Lord. I need courage and strength.*

The judge nodded to the prosecutor. "Mr. Lindhurst, you may begin."

The prosecutor rose from his table on the right and strode toward the jury. "On the night of March 18, a respected and highly valued member of our community, Mrs. Ruby Hazelton, was brutally murdered in her own home. We intend to present evidence and testimony that will prove Miss Emma Lafferty"—he turned and pointed at her—"the young lady she had kindly taken in and employed, is the one who committed that murder."

Emma shook her head and looked away from his harsh glare.

"We will prove beyond a reasonable doubt that on that fateful night, Miss Lafferty crept into Mrs. Hazelton's bedroom and suffocated her as a spiteful act of jealousy and revenge."

Emma gasped, barely able to keep from crying out against his lies.

Andrew leaned toward her. "Be calm, Emma. Our turn will come," he whispered.

She pressed her lips tight and nodded, but she had to blink back hot tears.

Mr. Lindhurst continued. "We will show that Miss Lafferty is a deeply troubled young woman who came to this country from the poverty-stricken slums of London as a British Home Child." He paused, letting that fact settle.

Emma clenched her jaw and looked down.

"Burdened by her troubled background, she was never content with her situation or the good people who took her in. Instead, she moved from place to place, unsettled and ungrateful, burying her anger about her years of hardship and perceived mistreatment until she reached a breaking point that night."

Emma's face flamed. What a terrible pack of lies!

"Out of the kindness of her heart," the prosecutor continued, "Mrs. Ruby Hazelton had taken in Miss Lafferty and given her a home at her boardinghouse. In exchange, she asked Miss Lafferty to do a few household duties. But was Miss Lafferty grateful and happy with that arrangement? No, she was not! She resented her employer and was jealous of all Mrs. Hazelton had worked so hard to gain and of the good standing she enjoyed in the eyes of her neighbors and friends.

"Finally, on the night of March 18, Miss Lafferty could stand it no longer. If she couldn't have all that Mrs. Hazelton had, then she would make sure her employer didn't live one more day to enjoy it. Miss Lafferty waited until everyone else was asleep, then crept across the hall and held a pillow over Mrs. Hazelton's face until she suffocated."

Bile rose and burned Emma's throat, and she shook her head again.

"Justice must be served! Miss Lafferty must pay for the heinous crime she committed! And as members of the jury, it will be your duty to see that she does!" Mr. Lindhurst strode to his chair, a look of satisfaction on his face.

Emma rested her hand on her midriff, trying to calm herself, but it was impossible. Who could listen to such terrible lies and not be shaken?

Andrew leaned toward her again. "It's all right, Emma. It's our turn now. I'll make sure they know the truth."

He rose and walked to the front of the courtroom. Rather than facing the jury, he focused on the prosecutor and cocked one eyebrow. "That was quite a stirring tale, Mr. Lindhurst, but it sounded more like a penny dreadful than a true account of Miss Lafferty's life and the events that night."

He turned to the jury. "I can assure you, Miss Emma Lafferty is a kind and trustworthy young woman who has been falsely accused of a crime she did not commit. We will bring forward several credible witnesses who will testify to her good character and standing among her friends and neighbors. She has overcome hardship through years of faithful service as an indentured British Home Child, and we will prove that she had nothing to do with Mrs. Ruby Hazelton's death."

He motioned toward Emma. "It is true Miss Lafferty was born in England and came to this country when she was fifteen, seeking an opportunity for a better life. But she didn't come looking for a handout or an easy life. Instead, she worked hard for six years to faithfully complete the terms of her indentured contract, and then she stayed on and worked longer than required. She did not, as Mr. Lindhurst stated, move from place to place but rather worked as a domestic on only one farm until she was twenty-two.

"At that time, she struck out on her own and took a position working for Mrs. Hazelton, whom she faithfully served until that woman's unfortunate death.

"Miss Lafferty was one of five people living with Mrs. Hazelton at that time. She was the one who heard the woman's screams and the footsteps of the murderer fleeing down the hall. She was the first to go to her employer's aid and try to help her. But it was too late. The deed was done. Mrs. Hazelton's murderer escaped before Miss Lafferty entered the room.

"Witnesses will testify that Miss Lafferty is known as a young woman who is devoted to her faith and loyal to her friends. While she waited for the return of her sweetheart, who fought valiantly in the Great War, she nursed several neighbors who became ill with the Spanish flu, putting her own health and life at risk for the good of others. It is not consistent with Miss Lafferty's character to harm Mrs. Hazelton or anyone else.

"But"—Andrew turned and looked at those seated in the courtroom—"someone is responsible for Mrs. Hazelton's death, and as the trial progresses, I'm confident the identity of that person will become clear. Miss Lafferty is innocent of all charges, and justice will be served when she is found not guilty."

A wave of relief coursed through Emma, lifting some of the shame she had felt as she'd listened to the prosecutor's dreadful statements. Surely, with such a stirring account of her character, the jury would realize she could not have killed Mrs. Hazelton.

As Andrew returned to his seat, Emma searched the faces of the jurors. Several of the men looked her way, some with scornful expressions, and others with frowns. Her chest tightened. It would take more than a stirring opening statement from Andrew to convince them of the truth.

Garth clenched his hands in his lap as he listened to the prosecutor question the first witness.

"Constable Fieldstone, can you tell us the cause of Mrs. Hazelton's death?"

The constable's eyes darted from Emma to the prosecutor again. "We believe the murderer held a pillow over the victim's face until she died of suffocation."

"Who was the first to discover Mrs. Hazelton's body?"

"Miss Lafferty. She's the one who woke the other boarders."

"And what did she tell them?"

"She said she heard screams and footsteps, then went to Mrs. Hazelton's room and found the deceased in her bed." The constable's tone made it clear he doubted Emma's statement.

The prosecutor paused and then asked, "How long would it take to suffocate someone with a pillow?"

"I'd say about three minutes, possibly longer, if the person struggled against the attacker. But if the attack began when the victim was asleep, that would give the attacker the advantage and make the process go rather quickly."

Garth glanced at Emma to see how she responded to the constable's testimony. From the rigid set of her shoulders and the way she kept looking at Andrew, he could tell she was tense. He blew out a breath and shot off a prayer for her. It had to be hard for her to listen to all that had been said and know her fate depended on the outcome of this trial.

"You said the murder happened around one o'clock in the morning and that Miss Lafferty was the one who alerted the other boarders, and then Mr. McDonald, one of the other boarders, ran to the local station for help."

"That's correct."

"You and Constable Burton arrived at Mrs. Hazelton's home to investigate the situation about quarter to two. Tell us what happened after you arrived."

"We found Mrs. Hazelton's body on the bed in her room, and a pillow was on the floor nearby. The pillow was damp in the middle on one side. We searched the house for any sign of an intruder but found none. After that, we sent word to the coroner, who came and removed Mrs. Hazelton's body. Then we searched the house again and questioned everyone who lived with Mrs. Hazelton."

"And when you questioned Miss Lafferty, what was her version of the events?"

"She said she was asleep in her room and woke up when she heard someone scream. A short time later, there was another scream, and then she heard footsteps running past her door. But that didn't make sense, because Mrs. Hazelton's room was directly across the hall from Miss Lafferty's. When I asked her about the footsteps, she changed her story and said they must have moved away from her room toward the stairs."

"So, she changed her story?" He drew out his words and looked toward the jury.

"She did, and that roused my suspicion."

"When you searched the house, did you find anything missing?"

"No sir, we did not."

"So, there was no evidence of a robbery."

"None that we found."

"Did you find any evidence of forced entry?"

"No sir. The doors were all locked. We had to wait for one of the boarders to let us in when we first arrived. The residents said Mrs. Hazelton always locked the doors before going to bed."

"So, the doors were all locked and there was no sign that anyone had broken in or stolen anything. Is that correct?"

"That's right."

Garth clenched his jaw. Everything the constable said seemed to point to Emma's guilt.

Grace sent him a worried glance, and he gave his head a slight shake. Andrew would cross-examine the constable next and hopefully knock some holes in his testimony.

Mr. Lindhurst concluded his questions and returned to his desk, looking confident with what he'd accomplished.

Andrew rose and walked toward the constable. "You stated that nothing was stolen from Mrs. Hazelton's home. How did you come to that conclusion?"

"We searched the house and asked the boarders if anything was missing. They indicated nothing looked like it was disturbed."

"And you believed them."

"I had no reason not to."

Andrew turned and paced a few steps, then faced the constable. "Do you think Mrs. Hazelton would tell her boarders where she hid her savings or valuables?"

He hesitated. "I don't know."

"According to Mrs. Hazelton's niece, Mrs. June Ridley, her aunt didn't trust banks and may have kept her savings at home." He lifted his eyebrows. "Did you find any money hidden at Mrs. Hazelton's home?"

The constable frowned. "No, we didn't."

"So, you don't actually know if there were any hidden savings in the house or if they were stolen or not."

The constable's face flushed. "No, I don't."

"Is it true you and your partner did *not* search Mrs. Hazelton's room to see if anything had been stolen but rather you asked Mrs. Clarkson and Miss Lafferty to do that?"

The constable shifted in his chair. "Yes, we knew they would be familiar with how the room normally looked and could tell us if anything was out of place."

"So, at that point in your investigation, you trusted Miss Lafferty enough to allow her to search the room for you?"

He grimaced. "Yes."

"I see. And when did your opinion of Miss Lafferty change?"

Constable Fieldstone looked away and rubbed his chin. "When I questioned her later that morning, her story was inconsistent, and she appeared uncomfortable when she was speaking to me."

"Wouldn't it make sense that a young woman who had overheard a murder and was then questioned by constables would be uncomfortable?"

"I suppose, but she seemed more than uncomfortable. She looked guilty."

Andrew shook his head. "Objection, Your Honor."

The judged glowered at the constable. "Strike that comment from the record. The jury is instructed to ignore it."

Andrew focused on the constable again. "What was it about Miss Lafferty that made you single her out as the suspect, rather than one of the other boarders?"

Garth leaned forward. Why was Andrew asking that question? It didn't sound as though it would help Emma at all.

"The other boarders were all Canadian born, from stable families. They had no reason to strike out at Mrs. Hazelton." The constable sent Emma a disdainful look. "But she's a British Home Child, an orphan with no family to speak of. In my experience, a person who has a history of hardship often becomes hardened and vengeful."

Andrew lifted his eyes to the ceiling. "So, you believe the fact that she is an English orphan makes her a prime suspect for murder?"

The constable shifted in his seat again. "I wouldn't if her story had been consistent and she'd not looked guilty when we questioned her."

Andrew turned to the judge. "Your Honor . . ."

The judge frowned at the constable. "State the facts without making assumptions."

Fieldstone nodded. "Yes sir."

Andrew paced for a moment, then turned to the constable. "You said the doors were locked."

"That's right."

"What about the windows? Could someone have climbed in through a window, crept into Mrs. Hazelton's room, and attempted a robbery?"

"None of the windows were broken."

Andrew nodded. "But isn't it true that some of the windows, four on the ground floor in fact, have broken locks and could have been used as points of entry?"

The constable blinked and gave his head a slight shake. "I don't know."

"You don't know, yet Miss Lafferty's life hangs in the balance. If Mrs. Hazelton's death could have been the result of a bungled burglary, then Miss Lafferty would not be guilty."

The constable's face twisted and reddened. "There was no evidence of anything missing, so that rules out a burglary."

"But I said a *bungled* burglary. What if Mrs. Hazelton woke up, discovered a burglar in her room, and screamed? The burglar might have wanted to keep her quiet and pressed the pillow over her face. In their struggle, she might have emitted a second scream before she fell silent, and then the intruder ran from the room."

The constable shook his head. "We've no evidence to support that theory."

"And nothing to prove it *didn't* happen that way either." Andrew looked to the judge. "No more questions, Your Honor."

Garth sat back in his chair, a small glimmer of hope rising in his mind. Perhaps Andrew could plant enough doubt to convince the jury Emma was not the only possible suspect.

24

G race checked Rob's profile as they walked back into the courtroom after the lunch recess, and her spirits sank. He had been quiet while they'd eaten a quick meal with Andrew and Garth at a restaurant down the street from the Belleville Town Hall. The focus of their conversation had been reviewing the testimony from the morning. Garth praised Andrew for the way he handled the cross-examination, and she'd added her encouragement.

Rob listened but said little. A few times, she found him watching her, as though he wanted to communicate something, but she had no idea what.

She slid into her seat at the courthouse between Garth and Rob and bent to place her handbag on the floor. When she lifted her head, her gaze connected with Rob's. Emotion flickered in his eyes.

Her breath caught, and she quickly glanced away. It wasn't fair for him to keep looking at her that way when he was the one who had put an end to their *almost* romance. Did he regret his decision now? Was that what he was trying to communicate?

She shifted away from Rob. Her thoughts should be on Emma and the next phase of the trial.

Rob leaned closer and kept his voice low. "I need to speak to you."

She tried to resist, but her gaze slid to meet his. "What is it?"

The side door opened, and the jury filed back into the courtroom.

Rob blew out a breath. "Can we talk at the next recess?"

She hesitated.

"Please." He reached over and pressed her hand.

A tremor traveled through her at his touch. "All right. At the recess."

The judge returned, and the bailiff announced that the court was back in session.

The prosecutor rose and called Margaret Clarkson to the stand.

Grace tensed. Margaret was supposed to be a defense witness. Why had she been called by the prosecution? She turned to Garth. He gave a slight shrug and returned a puzzled look.

Margaret stepped forward and was sworn in. She was dressed in a simple brown suit and small straw hat. Her dark-gray hair was pulled back in a loose bun.

"Mrs. Clarkson, will you tell the court how you're acquainted with the defendant?"

Margaret glanced at Emma. "We met at Mrs. Hazelton's boardinghouse. I lived there for three years after my husband died. Emma came to work for Mrs. Hazelton last December. She's a fine young woman, and we became good friends. I'm sure she would never hurt a soul."

The prosecutor shook his head. "Mrs. Clarkson, please confine yourself to answering the questions."

She pursed her lips, obviously displeased with the reprimand.

"What kind of work did Miss Lafferty do for Mrs. Hazelton?"

"She took care of all the housework: sweeping, scrubbing the floor, cleaning the bathrooms, changing the sheets, and handling all the laundry. Sometimes she helped in the kitchen, but Ruby was particular about meals, so she did most of the cooking herself."

"And did you ever hear Miss Lafferty complain about her work or about Mrs. Hazelton?"

Margaret hesitated and looked from Mr. Lindhurst to Emma.

"Answer the question, Mrs. Clarkson."

"She said it was hard to do everything Ruby asked, but I wouldn't call that complaining. It was the truth. Emma was still recovering from a terrible case of the flu, but Ruby didn't seem to care how hard it was for her to—"

The prosecutor lifted his hand to silence her. "Just answer the question, Mrs. Clarkson."

Margaret's frown deepened.

"Did Miss Lafferty tell you about her previous employer, Mr. Eli Gilchrest?"

"A little."

"Did she say he treated her well?"

Margaret looked down. "Not especially."

"What do you mean? How did she describe Mr. Gilchrest?"

"She said he worked her hard and didn't pay her what was promised."

"So, she wasn't satisfied with how she was treated. In fact, isn't it true she called him a harsh master and decided to run away without giving him notice?"

She shifted her gaze away. "I don't know."

"Mrs. Clarkson, I'll ask you once more, didn't she call him a harsh master and run away without notice?"

"Yes, but he—"

The prosecutor shot her a stern look, silencing the rest of her sentence. "Would you say Miss Lafferty appreciated Mrs. Hazelton taking her into her home?"

Margaret's eyes darted to Emma and then back to the prosecutor. "Emma was grateful to have a place to stay, but Ruby didn't do it out of the kindness of her heart. She only wanted her there to do the work."

The prosecutor paced a few steps away, then turned and faced Margaret. "On the night of the murder, did you hear Mrs. Hazelton scream?"

Mrs. Clarkson hesitated. "No, but—"

"Did you hear footsteps running through the house or any other unexplained noises that night?"

"I always sleep very soundly."

"So, you didn't hear anything until Miss Lafferty woke you up?"

"No, I didn't."

"Were you familiar with Mrs. Hazelton's bedroom?"

"She invited me up to her room a few times to show me her sewing projects."

"After the murder, when you looked around Mrs. Hazelton's bedroom, did you notice whether anything had been disturbed or seemed to be missing?"

"Not that I could tell."

"Did you see or hear anything that would lead you to believe someone broke into Mrs. Hazelton's home and disturbed things in her bedroom that night?"

Her lips puckered as if she'd tasted something sour. "No, I didn't."

"No more questions, Your Honor."

Grace leaned toward Garth and lowered her voice. "That certainly wasn't helpful."

"No, but you could tell she wanted to say more. Andrew will let her speak."

Grace hoped her brother was right. Though Margaret was

Emma's friend, her testimony had strengthened the case against Emma.

Andrew rose and walked forward. "Mrs. Clarkson, how would you describe Miss Lafferty's health when she first came to stay with Mrs. Hazelton?"

"She was weak and still recovering from a very bad case of the flu."

"Did she tell you how she became ill?"

"Yes, she helped care for her neighbors who were ill with the flu. She caught it from them, and she lost one of her dearest friends, who had been helping her."

"When Miss Lafferty lived at the boardinghouse, how did she treat you and the other boarders?"

Margaret smiled. "Oh, she was very respectful and spoke kindly to me and all the others. She was always looking for ways to help anyone she could."

"Can you give us some examples of how she helped others?"

"She often did extra things that weren't part of her duties, like darning socks for Mr. McDonald or sewing on buttons for Mr. Davis. She even knit a hat for Mr. Clemons when the weather grew cold. And on my birthday, she bought me a lovely bouquet of flowers and gave me a beautiful handmade card. Emma is a very thoughtful young woman."

"Mrs. Clarkson, where was Emma's room in the boarding-house?"

"Up on the third floor, across from Ruby's."

"And where was your room?"

"On the second floor, at the far end of the hall."

"Could you often hear what was going on up on the third floor?"

"No sir, I couldn't."

"That would explain why you didn't hear Mrs. Hazelton's screams on the night she was attacked by an intruder, wouldn't it?"

"Yes sir. I'm sure that's why I didn't hear them."

Andrew took a few steps and then turned back. "Were you present when the constables questioned Miss Lafferty the morning after Mrs. Hazelton died?"

"Yes, we were questioned together in the kitchen."

"How did Constable Fieldstone respond when he learned Miss Lafferty was a British Home Child?"

Margaret's eyes widened. "His whole demeanor changed. It was clear he had a low opinion of Home Children in general, especially those who came from England."

"Are you sure about that?"

"Very sure. As soon as she told him her background, you could see his expression change, and he started badgering her with more questions. I told him he had no cause to think less of her for it, but that didn't seem to change his mind."

"So, it was clear to you Constable Fieldstone had a negative opinion of Emma based on her background as a British Home Child?"

"Yes, he did."

"After the constables finished questioning you and Miss Lafferty, what did you decide to do?"

"I knew we couldn't stay at the boardinghouse any longer, so I encouraged Emma to come with me to Kingston to stay with my sister, Lucy Morton."

"So, it was your idea to leave Belleville, and you invited Emma to go with you?"

"That's right. I knew she didn't have any family, and I wanted to help her get a fresh start in a new place. We went upstairs and packed our bags. Then we took the train to Kingston that afternoon."

Grace released a slow deep breath. Andrew seemed to be laying a good foundation to show Emma's true character and raise the question of an intruder committing the murder. But would that be enough to sway the jury?

She glanced at Emma, her heart aching for her. How dreadful to be accused of such a serious crime and realize her background as a British Home Child had prejudiced so many people against her. It was frightening to think that the same thing could've happened to her since she and Emma shared a similar background.

Grace had been adopted into a wealthy and respected family and had lived a sheltered life in Toronto, but just like Emma, she'd been made to feel ashamed of her true identity and forced to keep it a secret. That was nothing like being accused of murder, but it had caused her heartache, and it made her identify all the more with how Emma must be feeling.

Emma eased back in her chair as Margaret recounted the small acts of kindness Emma had done to cheer her friends at the boardinghouse. Those weren't completely selfless acts. She had discovered that building friendships with Margaret and the other boarders had lessened her grief over losing her dear friend Verna as well as lightened the burden of not knowing what had happened to Garth.

Andrew finished questioning Margaret, and she and Andrew returned to their seats.

Mr. Lindhurst rose. "I call Mr. Eli Gilchrest to the stand."

Emma's stomach plunged as her former employer rose from his

seat in the back of the courtroom. She clasped her hands under the table and glanced back at Garth. His expression darkened as he watched their former employer walk forward and take the stand.

Once Mr. Gilchrest was sworn in and seated, the prosecutor walked forward. "Mr. Gilchrest, can you tell us how you know the defendant?"

"She worked on my farm from the time she was fifteen until last December."

"And what type of work did she do?"

"She was a domestic. Took care of the house and garden and such."

"Were any other people working for you at that time?"

Mr. Gilchrest nodded. "I took in three boys to do the work around the farm, but one of them went off to fight in the war." He looked past Emma at Garth. "And there was a woman who worked in the house—Verna Hathaway."

"So, Miss Lafferty mainly worked inside with Verna Hathaway?"

"That's right."

"How would you describe Miss Lafferty's attitude about her work?"

He frowned. "Not sure I know what you mean."

"Was she content working for you, or was she unhappy with her situation?"

"She seemed all right with it, but she talked to Verna more than me. You know how women are. I didn't get into their conversations much."

"Miss Lafferty is a British Home Child, and she worked for you under the terms of an indentured contract. Is that correct?"

"Yes."

"What did you provide for her in the arrangement?"

"She got a room, meals, clothes, and shoes. I sent her wages to the Barnardo Home, and they kept them for her."

Emma shook her head. He had not paid half of what she was owed, and she'd never seen *any* of that money. Of course, she'd never contacted the home after she ran away from the farm. She didn't want Mr. Gilchrest to know where she'd gone.

"So, from the time she was fifteen until she was twenty-two, you provided for her and gave her a chance to build a new life and learn valuable skills."

She grimaced. The prosecutor made it sound as though working for Mr. Gilchrest was a privilege, but that was far from the truth. It had been tolerable only because Garth and Verna were there. But then Garth went away to fight in the war and Verna died. She clenched her jaw and looked down at the table.

"When did Miss Lafferty leave your farm?"

"The middle of last December."

"Did she give you notice or tell you why she was leaving?"

"Nope. She just up and ran off without saying a word."

"Why did she leave like that?"

Emma lifted her head and stared at Mr. Gilchrest. Would he admit his drunken rage and tell how he'd broken into her room?

His face reddened. "Can't say. I suppose she was tired of the work and looking for a change."

"After all you'd done for her, she just left without a word? That doesn't sound like she was very loyal or grateful."

"No, she wasn't. She owed me, and that was no way to pay me back."

Emma's throat burned. There was so much he didn't explain, it almost made his words a lie.

The prosecutor nodded. "No more questions, Your Honor."

Andrew rose and walked forward. "Mr. Gilchrest, how many

British Home Children have you taken in to work on your farm over the years?"

He shrugged. "I dunno. Maybe eight or nine?"

Andrew shook his head. "No sir. You've had fourteen, and six of them were so unhappy with the way you treated them that they ran away."

Mr. Gilchrest pulled back. "It's not my fault they didn't settle in. Most of them came from workhouses or off the streets. They've got no training, no manners. Some aren't right in the head, and there's no way to get them to settle down and do what they're told. They plain don't want to do the work, so they run off."

"I wasn't able to find information about all the children you've taken in, but of the six who ran away, I learned four moved on to other situations and did well. Why weren't they content to work for you?"

The prosecutor rose. "Objection. Your Honor, Mr. Gilchrest is not on trial. How is this relevant to the case at hand?"

Andrew turned to the judge. "I'm about to make that connection, Your Honor."

The judge nodded. "Sustained. You may proceed."

"Mr. Gilchrest, isn't it true that on the night of December 16, the same day as Verna Hathaway's funeral, you became intoxicated and went on a rampage, taking up a pitchfork and threatening the two young men who worked for you?"

Gilchrest's eyes bulged. "That's a lie! I never did such a thing!"

"Mr. Gilchrest, I have a sworn statement from one of those young men. Are you sure you want to deny it?"

Gilchrest's frantic gaze darted around the courtroom. "We might've argued. I was upset about Verna's passing, but I don't remember anything about a pitchfork."

"After that confrontation, you returned to the house, cursing

NO JOURNEY TOO FAR 299

and smashing dishes, and then you turned your anger on Miss Lafferty."

He pulled back, shaking his head. "I don't know what you're talking about."

"You broke through her bedroom door and pushed Miss Lafferty down on her bed."

Several people in the courtroom gasped. Emma closed her eyes, fighting off a wave of nausea.

"It was the demon drink!" Mr. Gilchrest shouted. "I didn't hurt her!"

"The truth is, Miss Lafferty had to fight you off, and she was so frightened, she ran from the house and hid in the toolshed for several hours to avoid your wrath."

"Verna died . . . and I . . . I just had too much to drink. That's all it was. I wouldn't hurt Emma. Not really."

"But you *did* hurt her, Mr. Gilchrest. She had no choice but to run away from your farm, in spite of her weakened condition from a severe case of the Spanish flu and her grief over Verna Hathaway's death. She didn't leave because she was tired of the work or looking for a change. She ran away because she feared for her safety and her very life."

Mr. Gilchrest's chin wobbled, and tears filled his eyes. "I didn't mean to do it. I'm sorry." He broke down and lowered his head.

Emma's stomach roiled as she watched Mr. Gilchrest hunch forward and sob. For years, he'd been harsh and uncaring toward her and Garth and the others who worked on his farm. She hated what he had done to her, but more than anything else, she pitied him. He was a broken man. He had destroyed his own life through his terrible choices.

Just after three o'clock, the judge declared a twenty-minute recess. Grace's stomach fluttered as she rose from her chair and stepped into the aisle. She could feel Rob's gaze on her as they both walked out of the courtroom and into the upper hallway.

Garth followed them out. "I'll be back in a few minutes." He strode off down the hall.

She turned to Rob, her heartbeat drumming in her ears.

"Would you like to sit down?" He motioned to a nearby bench.

She nodded, then took a seat. *Lord, please help me. You know how I feel about Rob. I can't take another terrible blow to my heart.*

Rob sat quietly beside her for a few seconds, then turned toward her. "I'm afraid I haven't been honest with you, Grace."

Her breath caught. "About what?"

He leaned forward and clasped his hands between his knees. "That night on the porch when you asked me what was wrong, I didn't want to tell you, so I gave you a dishonest answer. That was wrong. I should've just told you the truth."

She searched his face, trying to understand. "I'm listening now."

He reached for her hand. "I thought it was best to pretend I didn't have feelings for you. But the truth is, I do. I care for you deeply."

Her heart surged. He cared for her, truly cared.

"I told myself I should let you go and not say anything about how I feel. That way you wouldn't be so burdened by our separation. But I saw the hurt in your eyes, and I knew I was being foolish and prideful. You deserve honest answers, even if they make you think less of me."

The warmth of his hand radiated up her arm straight to her heart. "I know you, Rob Lewis. Nothing you could say would make me think less of you."

His tense expression relaxed, and warmth filled his eyes. "That's good of you to say. I'm grateful you're so forgiving." He rubbed his thumb over the top of her hand. "I wish there was a way for us to be together, but I don't have a job, or a home of my own. How could I ask you to stay here and marry me when I have nothing to offer you?"

She blinked. "You want to marry me?"

He nodded, but his eyes clouded. "Yes, I do. But I can't ask you now, and it wouldn't be fair to make you wait several years until I am able to support you and give you a home and the life you deserve."

"I don't need a fancy home—not if I can be with you."

He lifted her hand to his lips and kissed her fingers. "Grace, you've been separated from your birth family for ten years. All that time, they've been searching for you. And now you have the chance to be reunited with them. I know how important that is to you. I can't ask you to give that up to stay here with me."

Her heart throbbed as confusing thoughts swirled through her mind. She longed to see her family in England and renew that special bond. But how could she leave Rob, especially now that he'd confessed his true feelings for her? She tightened her hold on his hand. "Then come with me to England."

His smile held a trace of sadness. "I can't live off the kindness of friends forever. I have to find a job and start supporting myself." He shook his head. "And to be honest, I don't even have the funds to pay for passage."

She pressed her lips together, desperate to find an answer that would keep them together. "I *do* want to see my family, but after that I could come back to Canada."

Tenderness shone in his eyes. "You deserve time to get to know them and see what life is like in England. There's a whole new world waiting for you there."

Her throat tightened. "But I don't want to leave you."

He looked down and pulled in a deep breath. "I know, and I feel the same. We have to believe the Lord has a plan for our lives and He'll make that plan clear to us as we put our trust in Him."

How could she trust the Lord and yield to His plan for their lives when it seemed she'd have to give up the only man who'd ever truly loved her?

Garth rounded the corner in the upper hallway and spotted Rob and Grace seated on a bench a few yards away. The look on Grace's face made it clear they were deep in conversation. He stepped back into the alcove, then leaned forward a few inches and looked around the corner. Had Rob changed his mind and decided to tell Grace how much he cared for her?

Andrew approached from the other end of the hallway. He joined Garth and checked his watch. "It's about time to get started again." He nodded toward Rob and Grace. "Shall we tell them?"

Garth shook his head. "I don't think we should interrupt them right now."

Andrew shifted his gaze to Garth. "Is there something I should know?"

Garth hesitated. He knew that his brother-in-law felt responsible for Grace. Maybe he would have an idea to help resolve the situation. "Rob and Grace have grown close, but because he doesn't have a way to provide for her, he doesn't feel he can ask her to marry him."

"I see." Andrew watched them a few more seconds. "And does she feel the same way about him?"

"I believe so, but she's torn because she wants to go home to England and see Mum and all the family."

"Do you think Rob would be a good match for Grace?"

Garth didn't have to think twice about his answer. "Yes. He has a good heart, a strong faith, and excellent character. He saved my life in France more than once, so I know he's loyal and willing to sacrifice for those he loves. But the timing doesn't seem to be right. Once he gets on his feet and can provide for her, I'd give them my blessing without hesitation. Unfortunately, I don't know how long that will take."

Andrew nodded. "She's young, but not too young to think of marriage to the right man."

Garth agreed. It was a shame Rob and Grace would be torn apart. He knew how it felt to be separated from the one you love, and he wouldn't wish that on his worst enemy, let alone his best friend and his little sister.

25

Emma rubbed her temple where a headache was beginning to build. It was the third day of the trial, and she hadn't slept well the night before. As she recalled the events of the morning, the pounding in her head grew stronger.

Mabel Chapman had been called as the first witness for the defense. She confirmed how Emma had been treated while she worked at the Gilchrest farm, then explained Emma's close relationship with Verna Hathaway, the events surrounding Verna's death, and how Emma had become ill with the flu after caring for their neighbors.

Next, Andrew called Garth to testify about Eli Gilchrest's behavior toward Emma and the other indentured workers who had lived at the farm. His testimony had built sympathy for Emma and made it clear she'd fled to Belleville to protect herself from Eli Gilchrest, not because she was a disloyal domestic who was simply unhappy with her situation.

But when the prosecutor cross-examined Garth, he asked him to describe his relationship with Emma. After Garth admitted they were engaged, the prosecutor responded with a mocking laugh, casting doubt on the validity of his testimony.

Andrew objected, but the judge allowed the prosecutor to continue that line of questioning. When Garth was excused, Emma wasn't certain if his testimony had been helpful or damaging.

Emma leaned toward Andrew and whispered, "Who will you call next?"

"Mrs. Hazelton's lawyer." He sent her a slight smile. "I hope this will be a turning point for us."

Emma blew out a breath, and a flicker of hope rose in her heart.

Andrew stood. "I call Mr. Robert Silverton to the stand."

A distinguished older man in a charcoal suit and vest walked forward and took the stand.

"Mr. Silverton, please tell the court how you were acquainted with the deceased."

"I was Mrs. Hazelton's lawyer. I took care of all her legal affairs."

"Such as preparing her will?"

"Yes."

"Is it true Mrs. Hazelton changed her will only a few months before her death?"

Mr. Silverton nodded. "That's correct. She updated her will in late November."

"What changes did she make?"

"Her original will divided her property and savings equally between her niece, June Ridley, and her nephew, Ronald Johnson. In the revised will, she left her entire estate to her niece."

Whispers traveled through the courtroom.

"Interesting." Andrew continued, "Did Mrs. Hazelton tell you why she decided to make those changes to her will?"

"She said she was unhappy with her nephew and didn't want him to throw away all she'd worked so hard to earn."

"Did she explain what he'd done that displeased her?"

"No, she didn't give me the details."

"Would you say she was upset about the situation?"

"Yes, she was quite agitated and determined to rewrite her will."

Andrew nodded. "Thank you, Mr. Silverton. No more questions."

The prosecutor studied Mr. Silverton with a frown, but he said he had no questions. Mrs. Hazelton's lawyer returned to his seat.

Andrew walked forward. "I call Mrs. June Ridley to the stand."

Mrs. Hazelton's niece stepped into the aisle and approached the witness stand. She appeared to be about thirty years old and wore an olive-green suit and a cloche hat that covered most of her red hair. As she took a seat, she looked across the courtroom with wide green eyes.

"Mrs. Ridley, will you please tell the court how you are related to Mrs. Hazelton?"

"I'm her niece. My father, Harold Johnson, was her brother."

"Your father is deceased?"

"Yes, he and my mother died when I was twelve. Aunt Ruby took us in and raised us after that."

"Us?"

"Yes, my brother, Ronald, and me."

"Mrs. Hazelton's lawyer stated that your aunt left all of her estate to you. Is that correct?"

"Yes sir. She left me the boardinghouse and everything in it."

"Did your aunt have a bank account?"

"No, I don't believe so."

"And why is that?"

"She told me she didn't trust banks and that she kept her money at home."

"Did she tell you where she kept her money?"

"No, she didn't."

"Have you searched the house?"

"Yes, but I haven't found it."

"No money?"

"She had six dollars and some coins in her purse, but that's the only money I found."

"What do you think happened to the money?"

"It must've been stolen."

The prosecutor rose. "Objection."

"Sustained." The judge looked at Mrs. Ridley.

She offered a prim nod, her eyes reflecting satisfaction.

Andrew paced a few steps away, then walked back. "Your brother, Ronald Johnson, returned to live with your aunt at the boardinghouse for a few months last year, is that correct?"

"Yes," she said. "He stayed with her from June to November."

"Do you know why he left?"

"She told him he had to leave after she caught him stealing money from her purse."

Emma stared at June Ridley. Murmurs filled the courtroom, and she looked over her shoulder. In the third row on the left, a red-faced young man glared at the witness. Was that Ronald Johnson?

"Do you know why your aunt changed her will, leaving everything to you and nothing to your brother?"

"They had a falling out over that stolen money. She suspected it wasn't the first time, and she'd had enough."

"Did she tell you she changed her will?"

"Yes. She said she was going to leave everything to me. She didn't want to see her money wasted."

"Did she tell your brother about her decision?"

"She did, but he thought it was just a threat."

Andrew nodded. "No more questions."

The prosecutor rose and walked forward. "Mrs. Ridley, you said you searched the house and found no money. Is that correct?"

"Yes. I've looked everywhere."

"Since your aunt's only income was the money she received from her boarders, is it possible she spent all those funds each month maintaining her home, providing food for six people, paying for utilities, clothing, and insurance?"

Mrs. Ridley frowned. "I doubt it."

"But you don't know that for certain, do you?"

"No, I suppose not."

"So, it's reasonable to assume there was no money hidden or stolen. Isn't that true?"

"My aunt was very thrifty. I don't think she spent everything she received."

"But you've done a thorough search and found nothing. That seems to confirm she spent it all."

"Not if it was stolen."

"Mrs. Ridley, I'm sure you'd like to believe there was a hidden fortune waiting for you in your aunt's home, but there is no evidence to back up that claim. There's also no evidence that if the money was ever there, it was stolen."

She looked away.

"Mrs. Ridley, how would you describe your relationship with your brother?"

"I see him every few months."

"When was the last time you saw him?"

"At my aunt's funeral."

"Isn't it true that you and your brother argued at the funeral?"

Her cheeks flushed. "That wasn't my fault. He spoke to Aunt Ruby's lawyer, and when he learned she cut him out of the will, he was furious. He said it was my fault, which was ridiculous. I didn't influence my aunt's decision. He's the one—"

The prosecutor held up his hand and stopped her. "Besides that unhappy exchange at the funeral, when was the last time you saw your brother?"

"Last fall when I visited my aunt."

"So, it has been several months between visits with your brother. Would you say you two have a close relationship?"

"We used to be close, but in the past few years, we've grown apart. I married and moved to Toronto, and he stayed in Belleville. Our lifestyles are different. We don't have much in common now."

"So, how is it that you claim to know why your aunt asked him to move out of the boardinghouse? Did he tell you?"

"No, she wrote to me each month. I've always been close to Aunt Ruby."

The prosecutor studied her for a few seconds. "No more questions."

Emma watched June Ridley step down and return to her seat.

Andrew looked at Emma, his eyes glowing. "Hold on to your hat."

She sent him a questioning look, but there was no time for explanations.

He rose. "I call Ronald Johnson to the stand."

The young man who had glared at June Ridley earlier sauntered forward and took the witness stand. He was short and stocky, had reddish-brown hair, and wore a wrinkled brown suit with scuffed brown shoes.

"Mr. Johnson, you are Mrs. Hazelton's nephew and Mrs. Ridley's brother. Is that correct?"

"Yes."

"Tell us, Mr. Johnson, what is your occupation?"

He hesitated. "I work at DeLorano's Restaurant as a waiter."

Andrew frowned. "Did you say you *work* at DeLorano's or *worked*? Because it's my understanding you're no longer employed there."

His gaze darted around the room. Then he lifted his chin. "That's right. I quit a while ago."

"Mr. Johnson, you didn't quit. You were fired in November, isn't that right?"

His face flushed. "Yeah, I guess that's right."

"Why were you fired?"

His mouth pulled down and he gave Andrew a sullen look. "It wasn't my fault. One of the other waiters told our boss I stole money from the till, but he was just jealous because I made more in tips than he did."

"Your former employer, Mr. DeLorano, told me you were fired because that was the third time you were suspected of stealing."

A hum of low voices rose in the courtroom.

"Order!" The judge pounded his gavel, and the people quieted.

"Mr. Johnson, isn't it true your aunt asked you to move out of the boardinghouse because she caught you stealing money from her purse?"

He scowled. "I was out of work. I had bills to pay."

"So you stole money from your aunt?"

"It was four bucks! That's all. She didn't need it."

Andrew leveled a serious gaze at him before he continued. "Have you found a new job since you were fired in November?"

Ronald's face reddened. "Not yet, but I have some good leads."

"And how have you managed to survive if you haven't had an income since November?"

He shifted in his chair. "I . . . stayed with friends. People helped me out."

Andrew leaned toward Ronald Johnson. "You've been living off the money you stole from your aunt, haven't you?"

Ronald pulled back. "No! I only took money from her that one time in November."

Andrew leaned in again. "The truth is, on the night of March 18, you entered your aunt's home through a downstairs window and climbed the stairs to the third floor to steal from her again!"

Ronald's eyes widened. "No! I didn't go there that night!"

"Oh, you went there, not only to steal that money, but to pay her back for kicking you out and threatening to cut you off!"

"She raised me! I'd never hurt her!"

Andrew's stare drilled into him. "You knew she hid her money in her bedroom, didn't you?"

His shook his head. "I didn't know where she kept it!"

"You not only knew her secret hiding place, but you went there that night to take what you believed your aunt owed you."

"No!"

"But she heard you. She woke up and screamed, and the only way to stop her was to hold that pillow over her mouth and silence her forever." Andrew's voice rose. "You killed her, didn't you, Mr. Johnson?"

"I didn't mean to!" He cowered, shaking his head. "I just wanted to keep her quiet!"

Emma gasped and covered her mouth. Pandemonium broke out in the courtroom. The judge called for order, then instructed the bailiff to take Ronald Johnson into custody. Ruby Hazelton's nephew hung his head as he was escorted out.

Andrew spoke briefly to the judge and strode back toward Emma with a triumphant smile.

Emma stood on trembling legs and turned to Garth, but she was so stunned, she couldn't speak. His eyes shimmered as he reached over the low wooden divider and pulled her in for a hug. She clung to him, and her tears overflowed.

"It's all right, Emma. Everything will be all right now." His voice choked off, and he held her tight against his chest.

Andrew laid his hand gently on her shoulder. "Emma, the judge has something to say. We need to sit down."

Garth kissed the top of her head and released her, blinking back the moisture in his eyes.

Her hands shook as she took her seat again and looked up at the judge.

He instructed everyone to be seated. When the courtroom was finally quiet, he focused on Emma. Though his gaze seemed serious, Emma detected a mixture of warmth and relief in his eyes. "All charges against Miss Emma Lafferty are hereby dismissed. She is free to go. The court is adjourned." He banged his gavel and rose from his seat.

Applause broke out from the witnesses and spectators.

Emma rose, still stunned by how quickly everything had changed. She wouldn't have to go back to her cell or fear for her future. She could walk out of the courtroom, hand in hand with Garth, and nothing would ever keep them apart again. She was free!

Garth, Grace, and Rob walked around the divider.

Garth shook hands with Andrew. "Thank you. Thank you so much."

Andrew smiled, relief evident on his face. "I'm grateful it turned out as it did."

Rob nodded to Andrew. "That was amazing. How did you know Ronald Johnson was the murderer?"

"After I spoke to June Ridley yesterday, I thought her brother might be guilty, but I wasn't sure until he began to squirm under my questions."

Grace's eyebrows rose. "But you didn't mention you suspected him."

"I didn't want to raise false hopes. It all depended on how he responded under the pressure of testifying."

The courtroom began to clear, but Margaret, Peter, and Lucy waited by the rear door.

Emma turned to Garth and motioned toward her friends. "I want to speak to them."

He nodded. "Of course."

She strode up the aisle and held out her hand to Margaret. "Thank you so much for coming and for what you said."

Margaret pulled her in for a quick hug. "I'm so happy they cleared your name. I should've guessed Ronald was the one behind all this trouble. Ruby never should've let him stay at the boardinghouse. She told me he had a gambling problem, but she wanted to help him get a fresh start."

"I'm just glad the truth came out." Emma turned to Lucy and Peter and thanked them as well.

"I wish they would've called me to testify," Peter added with a smile. "I would've told them they were crazy to think you'd hurt anyone."

Emma returned his smile, grateful for his loyal friendship. "Thank you, Peter."

"We better be on our way. We need to catch the train back to Kingston." Lucy touched Emma's shoulder. "You take care of yourself, my dear. And, remember, you'll always have friends in Kingston. I hope you'll come back and see us sometime."

"I'd like that." She sent Peter a final smile before the three of them walked out the door. Memories of the time she'd spent with them at the café rose and filled her with gratitude. The Lord had provided good friends when she'd needed them most, and Margaret, Lucy, and Peter were among the finest.

Garth joined her. "Ready to go?"

She looked up at him, her heart overflowing. "So very ready."

He slipped his arm around her back, and they walked out together.

Garth held Emma's hand as they strolled down the moonlit street the evening after the trial. Rain had fallen earlier, dampening the pavement and making it shine beneath the streetlamps. They had just finished a delicious dinner with Andrew, Rob, and Grace at a small Italian restaurant where they'd been made to feel like family. The other three walked a few feet ahead of them now, leading the way back to their hotel. Garth slowed his steps, hoping he and Emma could have a bit of privacy.

Emma smiled at him. "You look happy."

"I am. The trial is over and you're free. Now we can make our plans to travel to England."

"I still feel a bit amazed by it all." She gazed up at the star-studded sky as the moon peeked out from the edge of a silver cloud. "It's certainly a wonderful answer to our prayers."

He nodded, a rush of gratefulness filling him. "We must never forget what the Lord has done for us through Andrew."

"You did your part as well, gathering all that information and visiting me to keep my spirits up. I'll always remember that." She looked his way with shining eyes. "Thank you for standing by me, Garth. You've shown me what true love looks like. I'm so grateful."

His chest expanded, and he slipped his arm around her shoulders, gently bringing her close. She'd faithfully waited for him all those years, proving her love for him. How could he do any less? Their journey to this day had been long and difficult, but all they'd endured had made their love grow stronger.

He stopped and took both her hands in his. "I love you, Emma. I have since you were fifteen, and I plan to keep on loving you until we're both old and gray." Gazing at her sweet face, he memorized each feature, all so beautiful to him.

Her eyes glowed as she looked up at him. "And I love you, so very much."

He touched her cheek and leaned closer. She lifted her face, and her eyes fluttered closed. His lips brushed hers, and she responded, offering him the sweetest kiss he could've imagined. His heart pounded, and he savored her nearness, wishing the kiss didn't have to end. But he eased back and rested his forehead against hers. He could wait. They would be married soon, and then they'd have a lifetime to enjoy their love.

He tenderly brushed a strand of hair from her cheek. "We better catch up or they'll come looking for us."

"If we must," she said with a trace of teasing in her eyes.

He chuckled and squeezed her hand. He'd found the one he loved, and he planned to never let her go. After all the years of hardship and separation, they would finally be able to make plans to establish a home and family of their own. As they put their trust in the Lord, He would carry them through new challenges that would surely come their way.

They set off down the street, intent on catching up with their friends.

Up ahead, Rob slowed and looked back at them. "Are you two coming?"

"We're here," Garth called before winking at Emma.

She sent him a secret smile that gave him a delightful shot of energy all the way to his toes.

When they reached the hotel, Rob held the door open for them and glanced at Garth. "Everything all right?"

"Couldn't be better," Garth replied with a grin.

His friend slapped him on the shoulder. "Glad to hear it."

They entered the hotel lobby, where Andrew and Grace waited for them.

As they walked to the front desk, Grace turned to Emma. "Would you like to stay with me in my room? I have two beds, and I'd be very happy for the company."

Emma nodded and smiled. "Thank you, Grace. That's so kind. I'd like that very much."

The clerk at the front desk lifted his hand. "Mr. Frasier?"

Andrew turned toward him. "Yes?"

"A telegram arrived for you, sir." The clerk held out an envelope.

Andrew accepted the telegram. "Thank you." He tore open the envelope, read the message, and looked up with a smile. "This is good news." He motioned them all closer.

"What is it?" Garth asked.

Andrew lifted the telegram. "Katie gave birth to a baby boy this morning! Five pounds, twelve ounces. They named him Steven Garth Tillman."

Garth's jaw dropped. "They named him after me?"

"Well, he's named after his father and you," Andrew added with a chuckle.

Garth laughed. What an honor. His new nephew would carry his name. He couldn't wait to introduce Emma to his twin sister and the rest of the family and then meet the newest nephew.

Emma took his arm. "How wonderful!"

"Any other news?" Garth asked.

Andrew's gaze dropped to the telegram, and his smile faded. "Nothing urgent. Just some estate business I can take care of when we return."

Garth patted Emma's hand on his arm. "We'll have to send them a telegram in the morning and let them know the results of the trial. We can even tell them when to expect our return."

Andrew tucked the telegram in his pocket. "Good idea. I'll check on securing our tickets and send that telegram tomorrow."

Garth stayed close to Emma's side as they walked toward the elevator. He hated to say good night to her, especially after such a momentous day, but he could tell she was tired and needed her rest.

"Shall we all meet for breakfast tomorrow morning at eight o'clock?" Andrew asked. Everyone agreed. The elevator doors slid open, and Andrew, Rob, and Grace walked in.

Garth lifted Emma's hand to his lips and kissed her fingers. "See you in the morning."

She sent him a loving look that made his heart race once more, and then they stepped into the elevator and joined their friends.

26

J ust before eight o'clock the next morning, Grace and Emma
decided not to wait for the slow elevator and took the hotel
stairs down to meet the men for breakfast. While rounding the
first landing, Grace pondered the plan for the day. Would they
return to Roslin, or would they wait in Belleville until they were
ready to take the train east to board the ship to England? How
many more days would she have with Rob?

That last question sent a pang through her heart. Now that she
knew how much he cared for her, their parting would be even
harder. But if they had to be separated, at least she could go knowing he loved her.

As they descended the last flight, Emma smoothed the skirt of
the light-green dress Grace had given her. "I've never worn such a
beautiful dress."

Grace smiled. "It's the perfect color. You look lovely."

Emma's cheeks flushed pink. "Thank you for the dress and the
compliment. I hope Garth likes it."

"I'm sure he will."

When Emma had first tried on the dress, they realized it was a
bit loose, but they tied a sash around her waist and fixed the problem. Then Grace had helped Emma put her hair up in a pretty
style that showed off her heart-shaped face, soft brown eyes, and
elegant neck. Garth was bound to be impressed.

They reached the main floor and walked into the lobby. Andrew, Garth, and Rob waited in the corner by a potted palm.

As if sensing Grace's arrival, Rob looked up. He smiled at her, but in his eyes, she read that same mixture of regret and sadness she felt about their coming parting.

As she crossed to meet him, a prayer rose from her heart: *Help me find my way, Lord. Give me courage. I don't want to spoil what little time we have left.*

Rob greeted them both but kept his focus on Grace.

"Good morning." She sent him her brightest smile.

Andrew motioned toward the entrance to the hotel restaurant. "I've reserved a table for us."

Rob fell in step with Grace as they walked toward the restaurant. "Did you sleep well?"

She was about to say yes and keep up her cheerful front, but her throat constricted, and she shook her head. "I didn't fall asleep until after midnight."

His face fell. "I'm sorry, Grace."

"It's not your fault," she said softly.

"But it is. I wish there was something I could say that would help."

She lifted her gaze to meet his. If only they could have a few moments alone to continue their conversation and reassure each other, but they reached their table. He pulled out her chair, and she took a seat.

The waiter arrived and poured their coffee. He offered them menus and answered a question for Andrew before striding off to the kitchen.

Andrew laid his menu aside. "Before we order, I have something important I want to discuss."

Grace looked up, curious to hear what was on Andrew's mind.

"The telegram I received last night announcing the birth of Katie and Steven's son also included the news that our estate manager resigned. His father is ill, so he must return to the family farm in Yorkshire."

Grace glanced around the table, uncertain why Andrew wanted to discuss the resignation of the estate manager.

"So, it's important that I find a new estate manager as soon as possible," Andrew continued. "I need someone who not only has experience in farming and has the wisdom and character to oversee our crops and herds but also understands the perspective of our tenant farmers." He turned to Rob. "I wondered if you might be interested in the position."

Grace's heart leaped, and she could hardly hold back a squeal of delight.

Rob's eyes widened, and he stared at Andrew. "You're offering me the position of estate manager?"

"Yes. Garth tells me you've had years of experience caring for the Chapmans' land and animals and proven you're a trustworthy fellow with sterling character." His grin spread wider. "And I believe you have serious intentions toward Grace."

Rob's face lit up. "I do! And I'm honored you'd think of me."

"There's a house included and some land you could farm yourself, as well as a salary equal to the position." Andrew thought for a moment. "You probably saw the house when you visited Bolton. It's the stone cottage you passed as you came up the main drive to the estate."

Garth leaned forward. "Remember, I told you Mum, Laura, and Katie lived there until Laura got married."

Rob's eyes widened again. "*That's* the estate manager's house?"

Garth nodded and grinned. "It's very nice, and there's plenty of room."

Andrew focused on Rob. "Would you be willing to come back to England with us as Bolton's estate manager?"

Rob shifted his gaze to Grace, the question in his eyes.

She clasped her hands, barely able to contain her joy. "I do hope you'll consider it."

Rob turned to Andrew. "I'd be glad to go with you and help manage the estate. Thank you."

Hearty congratulations filled the air.

Garth slapped Rob on the shoulder. "Now that you're coming to England, you can be my best man!"

Rob grinned. "I'd like nothing better."

Grace's heart soared. What a blessing! This position was a perfect match for Rob's skills and desires. It would give them time together for a true courtship and a chance for them both to get to know her family. The future was an open door, and she and Rob would walk through it together.

Grace tucked her arm through Rob's as they walked through the Belleville railway station, hope and expectation making her steps light. They would travel by train to Roslin to visit Mabel and Chester, and then in three days they would head east to Quebec City and board a ship bound for England.

As they stopped by a row of benches in the middle of the station, Grace glanced at the other travelers. Several men dressed in business suits and women wearing stylish dresses and hats sat on benches nearby. A few families with children also waited for the arrival of the next train. Were they as excited as she was to be setting off on such an important journey?

Rob checked his watch. "We still have twenty minutes until the train arrives."

She smiled up at him. "I'm so happy you're coming to England with me. It's still hard to believe."

He grinned. "I know. I keep recalling Andrew's conversation to make sure it really happened."

She nodded. "It did, and very soon you'll be the new estate manager of Bolton. I'm so proud and happy for you, Rob."

"It's a great opportunity, but knowing we're going to England together is even more important to me."

Joy tingled through Grace. She had so much to look forward to, and Rob would be with her every step of the way.

Across the station, Andrew waited in line at the ticket counter. "It's certainly kind of Andrew to buy my ticket," Rob said.

"Yes, he's been very kind. I don't know how we'll ever repay him." Andrew had become like a trusted older brother. She couldn't wait to become reacquainted with Laura and meet their children. Knowing she'd soon see her mum and Katie and all her nieces and nephews was almost too wonderful to believe.

Rob glanced back in the direction they'd come from. "I wonder if Garth found a porter."

Grace stood on tiptoe and spotted Emma and Garth speaking to a porter near the entrance. She pointed them out to Rob.

He nodded. "It looks like Garth has the luggage taken care of."

Just past Rob's shoulder, she noticed a couple walking directly toward them. Shock hit her full force. She gasped and clutched Rob's arm.

"What is it?" he asked.

"My parents!" Judith and Howard Hamilton crossed the last few yards and stopped in front of her.

Her mother wore a burgundy coat with a thick fur collar and a large burgundy hat covered with ostrich plumes, though it was a warm spring day. Her face was flushed and her expression anxious. "Grace, we've been so worried about you!"

"I'm all right. You've no reason to worry." Grace infused strength into her words, but they still carried a slight tremor.

Her father glared at Rob, then turned toward Grace. "No reason? You disappear for more than a month and you expect us not to worry?"

"I know it was unexpected. I hoped my note would explain why I had to leave. I didn't mean to cause you any pain."

"But you gave us no idea where you'd gone or who you were with!" Her mother's voice rose as her gaze darted from Rob to Grace. "How could you treat us like that after all we've done for you?"

Her father laid his hand on his wife's arm. "Judith, if we're going to have a productive conversation, you need to remain calm."

Her mother sniffed and tossed her head. "Very well."

Her father turned back to Grace. "Richard told us he found you on a farm near Roslin and that you refused to come home." His forehead creased. "I don't understand. He said you'd hired a lawyer."

She looked away, trying to pull her thoughts together, then faced her father again. "Richard was respectful at first, but when I told him I wasn't going back to Toronto with him, he became very rude and threatening. Andrew stepped in to help. He is a lawyer—a barrister, in fact—but I didn't hire him. He's married to my sister Laura."

Her mother moaned and raised her hand to her forehead. "Her *sister*! Oh, this is too much."

"Judith, please." Her father took a deep breath and straightened his shoulders. "After you left, we hired a private investigator to look into the claim that you had a family in England."

Surprise rippled through Grace. "I'm sure he found it was true."

Her father hesitated, then nodded. "He did. I want you to know we didn't purposely try to mislead you. From the beginning, we were told you were an orphan with no living family. That's what we believed all these years. Then one day two young men arrived at our home, and one of them claimed he was your long-lost brother." Her father's voice carried an appeal for understanding. "Surely, you can see why we doubted his word and suspected his motives."

"Garth's visit was a surprise, but I told you I remembered him and the rest of my family in England."

"I thought that was wishful thinking on your part. I know some young women go through a time of resistance when they're coming of age. I couldn't imagine that what he said was true. How did he know where to find you?"

It was time to tell them the rest of the story and appeal to them to accept her decision. "I discovered my old trunk in the attic with my name painted on top, along with the name of the children's home I passed through. I wrote to the children's home and asked for information about my siblings. They sent the letter to my family in England. That's how Garth knew my address in Toronto."

Tired lines crossed her father's face. "That explains some of it. But why didn't you tell us you found the trunk or that you wrote to the children's home?"

Her throat tightened. "I suppose I should have, but every time I asked about my birth family, you said you knew nothing about them and that I should let everyone believe I was born into your family." She shook her head. "I couldn't continue living a lie."

Tears flooded her mother's eyes. "We were only trying to do what was best. We wanted to protect you from the shame of being known as a Home Child."

Grace bristled. "Perhaps *you're* ashamed that I was a Home Child, but *I'm* not."

Her father's eyebrows drew down in a V. "That's *not* what she meant."

"My past can't be denied, and it shouldn't be hidden. I was wrongfully sent to Canada without my mum's knowledge or permission after she became ill and couldn't care for us. She expected to get well and reclaim us from the home, but we were shipped off before she had a chance."

Her parents exchanged pained looks.

"I don't know why they told you I was an orphan. Maybe they thought it would be easier to place me with a family, but that was a lie. I have a family in England who has been searching for me for ten years, and once they discovered where I was, they went to great lengths to send Garth here to bring me home."

Her father slowly nodded, then shifted his gaze to Rob. "I remember seeing you at our home. Who are you?"

Grace started to reply, but Rob pressed her arm.

"My name is Robert Lewis." He stood tall, his tone confident and respectful. "I was also born in England, and I've known Garth for many years. We served together in Princess Patricia's Canadian Light Infantry in the war. I've recently been hired to manage the Frasier family estate near St. Albans in England." He raised his chin. "And I love Grace."

Her mother gasped and lifted a hand to her mouth.

Her father's eyes widened. "You love her?"

Grace's heart expanded with love for Rob. How brave he was to face her father and proclaim his feelings so honestly.

"Yes sir, I do. I'm going to England with her to meet her mum and the rest of the family there. I intend to court her properly. And when the time is right, I hope to ask for her hand."

Her mother's chin quivered. "You want to marry our Grace?"

"Yes ma'am. That is my fondest hope."

Garth strode across the station toward them with Emma hurrying along beside him. His panicked gaze darted from her parents to Grace. "Is everything all right?"

"Yes." Grace turned to her parents. "Father, Mother, I'm sure you remember my brother, Garth McAlister."

Her mother nodded, then took her handkerchief from her purse and dabbed at her eyes and nose.

Her father studied him a moment. "Yes, I remember, and I believe I owe you an apology, young man. It seems I misjudged the situation." He held out his hand.

Garth's eyes widened for a second, and then he reached out and shook her father's hand. "Thank you, sir."

Her father released Garth's hand. "I'm sorry for the way I spoke to you at our home. We were told Grace had no living relatives when we took her in, but I've recently learned that's not the case."

"Grace has a large and loving family, and they're eagerly awaiting her return to England."

Her father nodded. "That's what we've been told." He turned to Grace. "So, that's your decision? You won't reconsider and come home with us?"

Grace pressed her lips tight, fighting to stay in control of her emotions. "I need to go to England to see my mum and sisters. I hope you'll try to understand."

His eyes turned glassy, and he looked down for a moment. "I confess it saddens me, but my deepest wish has always been for your happiness." He lifted his gaze to meet hers once more. "I can

understand why you're curious to meet your . . . first family, but I
hope you'll always remember you have family here in Canada as
well."

Her mother dabbed at her eyes again. "Yes, please don't forget
us."

A knot formed in Grace's throat, and she had to force out her
words. "I won't forget you. I'll write, and perhaps one day you'd
like to visit us there."

"We'd like that very much, wouldn't we, Howard?" Her mother
sniffed and then pulled a blue velvet box from her purse. "We
want to give you this." She held out the box.

Grace accepted it. "What is it?"

Her mother's eyes filled again. "It's your birthday gift."

Grace blinked. Her birthday! With all the excitement surrounding the trial and Rob confessing his feelings for her, she'd
totally forgotten her birthday had passed.

"You're eighteen now, a young woman who will move into the
next phase of life."

Grace lifted the lid. Inside lay a beautiful pearl necklace. "Oh,
it's lovely." She looked at her mother and father. "Thank you. This
is very kind."

Her father watched her, tenderness in his eyes. "We love you,
Grace. I hope you'll remember the good times and think of us
fondly."

Grace's throat tightened, and she nodded. "I will."

Her mother opened her arms. Grace stepped into her embrace and patted her mother's back, wishing she could ease her
distress.

"I'm sorry, Grace." Her mother's muffled voice was filled with
emotion. "I should've listened and tried harder to understand.
Maybe then you wouldn't feel the need to leave us now."

Grace stepped back and blinked away her own tears. "Every young woman needs to step out on her own path and follow where the Lord leads her. My path takes me to England, but I'll always be grateful for you and all you've done for me."

Her mother sniffed. "If you must go, I want to send you off with my love."

Grace swiped at her cheeks. "Thank you, Mother. That means a great deal to me."

Her mother turned to Rob. "Promise me you'll take good care of our Grace. She's a jewel. You'll never find another girl like her."

Grace stared at her mother. What a gift to hear those words of love and acceptance!

"I know that's true, Mrs. Hamilton," Rob said. "And you can be sure I'll treasure Grace always."

Andrew approached and stepped into the circle, obviously curious about the couple who had joined them.

Grace flashed a pointed look his way. "Andrew, these are my adoptive parents, Howard and Judith Hamilton."

His eyes widened for a split second. "Oh, hello. It's good to meet you. I'm Andrew Frasier." He held out his hand to Howard.

Her father shook his hand. "You're the lawyer. I understand you're married to Grace's . . . sister?"

"That's right. I'm Laura's husband and Grace's brother-in-law."

Her father grimaced, obviously still struggling to accept Grace's relationship with her family but making an effort to be civil. "Richard told us you've recently taken part in a murder trial."

Grace exchanged a glance with Rob. Richard must have asked a lot of questions around town to learn that fact.

"I defended Miss Emma Lafferty." Andrew motioned toward Emma. "She was falsely accused, but she has been cleared of all charges."

Her mother's eyes bulged. "You're the woman who was accused of murder?"

Emma's face flamed. "Yes ma'am."

Grace stepped closer to Emma. "Andrew handled her defense with such skill that the man who was responsible confessed under questioning."

"That's right." Garth slipped his arm around Emma's shoulders. "Andrew proved Emma was innocent. We're engaged, and we plan to marry soon after we arrive in England."

Her father looked back at Grace. "Well, that all sounds very *interesting.*" He checked his watch, still appearing unsettled, even after the explanations. "Our train back to Toronto doesn't depart until twelve thirty. Would you like to join us for a meal?"

"That's kind of you, Father," Grace said, "but we're leaving for Roslin very soon."

He nodded, resignation in his eyes. "All right, my dear." He stepped forward, and Grace met him in the middle for a slightly awkward hug. "Take care of yourself, and write soon," he said.

"I will." She held on for a moment, then stepped back.

"Goodbye, Grace." Her mother sent Grace a teary-eyed smile, then took her husband's arm.

"Goodbye," Grace called as she watched them turn and walk away. When they disappeared out the front door, she melted against Rob. "I can't believe they came."

"They love you, Grace. Even with all their faults and the misunderstandings, they want what's best for you."

"I wasn't sure of that before, but I am now."

"It's hard for them to let you go, but I admire the way they handled themselves."

Grace nodded, thankful they'd been able to clear the air before she left for England.

The stationmaster's voice rang out, announcing the arrival of the ten-forty-five train to Roslin.

Andrew picked up his bag and motioned toward the doors leading to the platform. "Time to go."

Rob grinned at Grace. "Are you ready for your adventure?"

She laughed and returned a smile. "As long as you're going with me."

"There's nowhere else I'd rather be." He took her hand, and they walked through the doors together.

Grace leaned forward, watching out the motorcar's side window as Andrew drove under the stone archway guarding the entrance to his estate.

Andrew looked over his shoulder from the front seat. "Welcome to Bolton."

Her heartbeat picked up speed, and she smiled at Rob, seated next to her. His eyes shone, reflecting the same joy she felt at this special homecoming.

They rounded a curve, and Andrew pointed out the window. "The estate manager's cottage is just ahead."

A stone house appeared through the trees, and Grace's eyes widened. When Andrew had told them it was a cottage, she'd imagined a small cozy dwelling, but this was a large two-storied stone house surrounded by a thriving garden and several fruit trees. "Oh, it's lovely!"

Rob ducked his head to get a better view, and his smile spread wider. "I remember being impressed when I saw it on my first visit, but I'd forgotten what it looked like." He turned and winked at Grace. She squeezed his hand, thinking ahead to the day they would share that home and begin their new life together.

They continued up the drive past large open meadows dotted with wildflowers. A few trees were scattered across the parkland, and sheep grazed on the lush green grass. They drove across a narrow stone bridge that spanned a rippling stream lined with rocks, small trees, and bushes.

Andrew glanced back at them again. "Just around this curve, you'll see the family home."

Grace tightened her hold on Rob's hand as Bolton House came into view. The family's three-storied manor house was beautifully crafted from golden-brown stone, with more windows and chimneys than she could count. Tall green hills rose behind the house, and the contrast in colors made the building seem to glow in the afternoon light. Grace shook her head in amazement and wonder.

The motorcar rolled to a stop in front of the house, and the second car, carrying Garth and Emma, parked behind them.

Grace looked at Rob, joy thrumming through her. "I'm so excited to see Mum and all the family."

He sent her an encouraging smile. "I'm sure they're just as eager to see you."

The heavy oak front door opened, and a tall butler with gray hair, deep-set eyes, and a long nose walked out, followed by a younger footman dressed in livery. The footman sprang forward and opened the motorcar door for Grace, then opened Andrew's door.

The butler nodded to Andrew. "Welcome home, Mr. Frasier."

"Thank you, Sterling. Will you see to our luggage?"

"Yes sir." The butler motioned to the footman, who hustled into action.

Garth and Emma climbed out of the second motorcar and crossed the gravel drive toward them.

The front door of the house opened again, and adults and children streamed out. Grace quickly searched their faces.

"Grace!" Mum hurried toward her, her eyes glistening. Memories from years ago came rushing back. Mum's brown hair was now laced with silver, and lines crinkled around her eyes, but the same love flowed from her smile.

Grace's heart swelled. "Mum!"

Before Grace could say another word, Mum drew her into her arms and wrapped her in a tight hug. The scent of lavender and roses filled the air around them, sending a comforting wave through Grace.

"Oh, my girl! My dear, dear girl!" Emotion hushed Mum's voice.

Grace's eyes stung as she held tightly to Mum. For so long she'd ached to know she was loved and cherished by her family, especially her dear mum. She swallowed back her tears. "It's all right, Mum. I'm home now."

Mum held on a few more seconds, and then she leaned back but didn't let go. Instead, she placed her hands on Grace's shoulders and smiled. "You're so tall and lovely, and you look so much like Laura." Mum laughed softly through her tears, then traced her fingers down the side of Grace's face. "My little Gracie is home at last."

All around them other members of the family greeted each other with hugs and handshakes. The children moved among the adults, eager to be acknowledged and introduced.

Mum released her with a teary smile. "I'm sure the others want to say hello."

Laura stepped forward with a glowing smile. She was tall and elegantly dressed with her blond hair pulled up in a pretty style. Her blue eyes reflected kindness and warmth. "Welcome home, Grace." She leaned in and kissed Grace's cheek, then hugged her.

"I'm so glad to be here. Thank you for all you and Andrew did to search for us."

Laura sniffed and patted Grace's back. "I only wish we could've connected with you sooner."

Grace stepped back and smiled through her tears. "All in the Lord's good time."

Katie came forward next. She was shorter than Laura and had auburn hair and pretty hazel eyes. Her figure was softly rounded, reminding Grace that she'd recently given birth to a baby boy.

As she gazed at Grace, her smile melted away and her chin trembled. "Oh, Gracie, I'm so sorry I didn't keep us together. I know I promised I would, but—"

Grace pulled her sister into her arms. "It's all right, Katie. I know you did everything you could. And from what Garth tells me, you're the one who suffered the most."

Katie stepped back and wiped a tear from her cheek. "That's long past. Life is good now. The Lord has blessed us all."

"Yes, He has."

"We're thrilled to have you home," Katie said. "I can't wait to catch up and hear all about your years in Toronto."

Grace nodded, her heart warmed by her sister's tender words and the powerful sense of connection they still shared. "I want to hear all about your life here—how you met Steven, and so much more. It will be fun exchanging stories."

Grace turned to Rob and took his hand. "I'm sure you remember Rob Lewis."

Several family members nodded and welcomed Rob.

Steven shook Rob's hand. "Good to see you again, Rob. Andrew says you've agreed to take on the estate manager's position."

"That's right. I'm looking forward to it. I hope you'll help me learn the ropes."

"I'd be glad to bring you up to speed as soon as you've had a chance to rest up from your journey." The two men continued talking, and Grace smiled, happy to see how easily they conversed.

Mum walked over and embraced Garth. "Welcome home, son. We're all so grateful for what you've done to bring Grace back to us. Thank you."

He kissed Mum's cheek and stepped back. "Thank you for praying for us. I couldn't have done it without Him guiding me each step of the way."

Mum nodded, her face glowing with pride and affection. She turned to Emma and held out both hands. "And this must be Emma."

Garth's fiancée offered a shy smile as she took Mum's hands. "Yes ma'am."

Mum offered her a gentle smile. "We're so glad you've come, and I'm happy to hear you'll be joining our family very soon."

Garth grinned and exchanged a smile with Emma. "That's right. Emma has agreed to marry me as soon as we can make the arrangements."

"I'm very happy for you both. And since you're soon to be my daughter-in-law, I hope you'll call me Mum."

Emma's cheeks flushed. "Thank you. I'd like that."

Grace's throat tightened as she watched Mum interact with Emma. The dear girl had been through so much, from years of being scorned as a Home Child to being falsely accused of murder. It was past time she received the love and acceptance she so richly needed and deserved.

Mum slipped her arm around Emma's shoulders and guided her toward the house. "We'll give you a few days to settle in, and then we can begin working on your wedding plans."

"Tea is ready in the library," Laura announced. "Let's all gather there and continue our conversations."

As Grace watched her family move toward the house, a warm wave of happiness filled her. She might have been missing from the family for ten years, but she could tell the love she remembered still burned brightly in each of their hearts. They had offered her a warm welcome and given assurance that there was a special place in the family for Rob and Emma.

Rob stepped up beside her. "Glad to be home?"

She met his gaze. "Yes, so very glad."

He placed his arm around her shoulders and exhaled a contented sigh. "You're finally back with those who love you most, and that includes me." Affection and a hint of mischief twinkled in his eyes as he leaned down and gave her a kiss as tender and light as a summer breeze.

His message of love flew straight to her heart, washing away the shadows of the past. No longer would she have to hide her true identity or live a life pretending to be someone she was not. She had finally found the freedom, love, and acceptance she'd longed for—in the Lord and in her relationships with Rob and her family.

The journey had been long and challenging, and it had taken her farther than she'd ever imagined going, but the Lord's love and light had shone on the path and guided her home at last.

Epilogue

Garth looked in the small mirror on the church-choir-room wall, and his fingers tangled in his tie. Why couldn't he get this right? Beads of perspiration gathered on his brow. He huffed and shook out his hands.

Rob looked over his shoulder in the mirror. "Having trouble?"

"You could say that," Garth muttered.

"Turn around. I'll give you a hand."

"Thanks." Garth faced Rob, lifted his chin, and continued tapping his foot with nervous energy. He could hear the voices of friends and family gathering in the sanctuary for the ceremony. Had Emma arrived at the church yet? That question shot another rush of energy through him.

He looked at Rob. "I don't know why I'm so flustered."

"This is an important day." Rob undid Garth's tie and started again. "I'd be surprised if you weren't a bit nervous."

Garth blew out a breath and studied his friend's face. They'd grown as close as brothers in the past ten years, and he was thankful Rob was with him today. "We've been through a lot together, haven't we?"

Rob's gaze met Garth's, and a smile tipped up the corners of his mouth. "From the children's home in London, to our years in Canada, then the war in France, and now back to England to celebrate your wedding day."

"And yours is not too far away."

Rob's grin spread wide, and he gave Garth's tie a final tug. "It can't come soon enough for me."

Garth glanced toward the door leading to the sanctuary and grew serious again. "I hope everything will go well today for Emma's sake. She deserves a perfect wedding."

Rob clamped his hand on Garth's shoulder. "It will. Your family will make sure of it."

Garth nodded, grateful that was true. In only five weeks, his mum and sisters had helped Emma plan the wedding—everything from ordering invitations and having her dress made to choosing the menu for the wedding breakfast and selecting the flowers.

Andrew and Rob had gone with him to the tailor to select his new suit. They had also helped him make the arrangements for his and Emma's wedding trip to Cornwall. The whole family had come together to make sure their wedding would be a wonderful day for them to enjoy. He was blessed to be surrounded by so much kindness and support.

The door to the choir room opened, and Reverend Jacobs peeked in. "Are you gentlemen ready?"

Garth turned to Rob, and his friend sent him a confident smile. Garth looked back at the reverend. "Yes sir. We're ready."

They walked out of the choir room and entered the sanctuary through the side door. A few people turned and looked their way with smiles as the low hum of conversation continued. The women wore stylish hats and beautiful summer dresses, and the men were dressed in formal suits.

Garth walked up to the front, followed by Rob. He saw Mum seated with Laura in the first row on the left. Next to them sat Katie and Steven. Andrew would be walking Emma down the aisle, and Laura and Andrew's sons were serving as page boys.

Their daughter, Lillian, was one of Emma's young bridesmaids. Katie and Steven's two young children waited for them at home under the watchful eye of the housekeeper.

Mum smiled at Garth with shining eyes. His throat tightened, and he nodded to her and returned a grateful smile. Her example of love and trust in the Lord had been a great inspiration to him. How thankful they all were that she had survived the terrible illness that had almost taken her life ten years ago. But the Lord had healed her and reunited their family. It was a gift and a miracle he would always cherish.

The first notes of the organ rose and vibrated through Garth, and a rush of excitement filled him. Rob looked his way, his expression reflecting the strong bond of brotherhood they'd shared for so many years. Garth nodded to Rob, then straightened his shoulders and stepped into place to wait for his bride.

Organ music flowed from the sanctuary past the closed doors into the vestibule, where Emma waited with Andrew and the wedding party. The tempo of the joyful song matched the beat of her heart and brought tears to her eyes. On this day, she and Garth would say their vows before God, family, and friends and become husband and wife. She'd dreamed of their wedding for so long, it was hard to grasp that it had finally arrived.

Grace stepped beside Emma and adjusted her bridal veil. Grace wore a pretty pale pink gown, a broad-brimmed hat, and a tender smile for Emma. "You look lovely. Garth will be thrilled when he sees you."

"Thank you," Emma whispered. She wished she could hug her soon-to-be sister-in-law, but she held her wedding bouquet of white orchids and pale-pink roses in one hand, and her other arm was linked with Andrew's. She would be sure to give Grace an extra-long hug after the ceremony.

During their sea voyage to England and their time together at Bolton, they had become close friends. She was grateful Grace would walk down the aisle as her maid of honor.

Grace touched her fingers to her lips and blew Emma a kiss. "God bless you, Emma. I hope you and Garth enjoy every minute of your special day."

"Thank you for everything you've done. We never could've been ready without your help."

"I was happy to do my part."

Emma looked over her shoulder at the three little bridesmaids. Lillian and two of Andrew's young cousins, Anne and Mary, were dressed in matching pale-pink dresses. Each one wore a floral crown and looked like an angel.

Andrew glanced at his sons, Andy and Matthew. "Pay attention, boys. It's almost time." The two stopped fidgeting and took their place in line.

The doors opened, and Andrew patted Emma's hand. "Ready?"

She pulled in a trembling breath and nodded to him. They stepped into the sanctuary and started up the aisle. On both sides of the church, people rose and turned to watch as they passed.

Emma returned a few smiles, then focused forward, past the smiling crowd of friends and family to the altar, where Garth waited for her. As soon as he came into view, joy surged in her heart and she had to force herself to stay in step with Andrew and not rush to Garth's side. She knew that once they were together, she would feel calm and be able to enjoy the ceremony.

Garth gazed at her, and the tender look of affection in his glistening eyes made her heart ache with love for him. How blessed

she was to find such a fine man with a true heart. His faithful love
had been an anchor for her through the most difficult days of her
life. He had proven his commitment to her over and over, and
now she would pledge her love to him and spend the rest of her
life living out those promises.

A prayer of thanks rose from her heart to the One who had
watched over them all their lives. He might have allowed trials to
come their way, but they'd never had to face them alone. His love
and grace had guided them and carried them through. His promises were sure, and that gave her confidence to take this next important step.

They approached the altar, and Andrew smiled down at Emma.
He put her hand in Garth's and stepped back. Garth moved into
place next to her with a smile just for her. Assurance and joy filled
her soul. Garth loved her, and she loved him, and they were ready
to begin this new journey together.

Grace took Rob's hand and walked out of the cool stone church
and into the warm sunshine in the churchyard. All around them
friends and family lined the walkway, waiting to send off the bride
and groom. Happy chatter filled the air as people exchanged greet-
ings and commented on the meaningful ceremony, the lovely
bride, and the handsome groom.

Garth and Emma had asked for a few private moments after
they signed the register in the reverend's office.

Grace was glad to give them a chance to catch their breath and
perhaps even share a kiss before they stepped out to greet everyone.

Rob leaned down and whispered in Grace's ear. "You look very
fetching in that dress."

She laughed softly. "Fetching?"

His face reddened, and he shrugged, but his eyes shone with humor. "You should take that as a compliment, you know."

She squeezed his hand, sending him a teasing smile. "I'm glad to hear you think I'm fetching."

He lifted his eyes toward the blue sky. "Aw, Grace, you are more than fetching."

"Am I indeed?"

He laughed and gently pulled her to his side. "I'm looking forward to the day you and I will sign that registry and start our life together."

Joy bubbled up from her heart, and her smile bloomed. "So am I, Rob. So am I."

"Here they come!" Andy's voice rang out, and the crowd turned toward the open doorway.

Hand in hand, Garth and Emma stepped into the sunlight, their smiles bright and their faces glowing with happiness. A cheer rose around them, and flower petals flew up into the air, showering them like a blessing from above.

"Congratulations!" Laura called as she clasped Andrew's arm.

"Best wishes to you!" Katie tossed a handful of rose petals in the air, with Steven grinning at her side.

"God bless you both!" Mum waved, her eyes filled with happy tears.

"Hurrah!" Rob yelled, then beamed at Garth and Emma.

"We love you!" Grace called, joining the chorus of well-wishers lining the path. She couldn't help thinking of how far they had all come. Only a few months before, she had bent to her adoptive parents' wishes and hidden the fact she was a British Home Child as she prepared to launch into Toronto society and seek a husband. Now she was reunited with her birth family and proud of them and her past. Best of all, the man she loved stood at her side to share it all.

Garth and Emma dashed past, laughing and calling out thanks to family and friends. Colorful flower petals swirled in the air around them as they hurried to Andrew's motorcar.

Rob slipped his arm around Grace. She leaned her head on his shoulder, and her heart overflowed with gratitude for the joyous day and the wonderful vision of the future that filled her with anticipation and hope for them all.

Author's Note

Dear Reader,

I hope you enjoyed reading *No Journey Too Far*, the second book of the McAlister-family novels, and learning more about British Home Children. I wanted to continue the story not only to tell what happened to Grace and Garth but also to highlight some of the challenges British Home Children faced when they became young adults. After they finished their indentured contracts, many had to strike out on their own and find ways to make a living and provide for themselves. Some of the young men went off to fight in World War I or World War II, and not all of them survived. Those who did often hid the fact they'd come to Canada as Home Children because of the stigma and prejudice against them.

Even though they faced those obstacles, many British Home Children went on to build successful lives and strong families. Through hard work and strength of character, they became important members of Canadian society and made many significant contributions. Today, more than 10 percent of Canadians are descendants of British Home Children, though many are still unaware of that fact.

Have you read *No Ocean Too Wide*, the first book about the McAlister family? If not, I hope you'll purchase a copy so you can read the beginning of the story and learn more about the hardships and challenges faced by young children who went to Canada as British Home Children.

The British Home Children Advocacy & Research Association was a wonderful resource for my research. Lori Oschefski (the CEO) and those who work with her answered many of my questions and provided outstanding information through their website, Facebook group, newsletters, articles, and books they recommended. I hope *No Ocean Too Wide* and *No Journey Too Far* give people the opportunity to learn about British Home Children and honor their memory. If you'd like to investigate the topic further, these are some of the resources I used in my research:

- The British Home Children Advocacy & Research Association: www.britishhomechildren.com
- The British Home Children Advocacy & Research Association Facebook group: www.facebook.com/groups/Brit ishhomechildren
- *The Camera and Dr. Barnardo: Based on the exhibition staged by the National Portrait Gallery, London, July–November 1974*, compiled by Valerie Lloyd
- *The Golden Bridge: Young Immigrants to Canada, 1833–1939*, by Marjorie Kohli
- *Labouring Children: British Immigrant Apprentices to Canada, 1869–1924*, by Joy Parr
- *Nation Builders: Barnardo Children in Canada*, by Gail H. Corbett
- *Promises of Home: Stories of Canada's British Home Children*, by Rose McCormick Brandon

Blessings and happy reading,
Carrie

Readers Guide

1. Had you heard about British Home Children before you read *No Journey Too Far*? What is one thing you learned that made an impression on you about child emigration and British Home Children in particular?

2. What were some of the challenges British Home Children faced when they grew up? Which of these were highlighted in the book?

3. Garth served in World War I. What do you think were his motivations to enlist, and how did they relate to him being a British Home Child?

4. Grace was adopted into a wealthy family, but her adoptive parents wanted her to hide the fact that she was a British Home Child. Why did they make that decision, and what did you think of their reasons for making it?

5. Friendship played a key role in this story: Garth and Rob shared a strong bond, and Emma relied on Margaret, Peter, and Lucy. What acts of friendship did you notice in the story, and how did they affect the characters?

6. Emma faced many challenges in this story—Eli Gilchrest's attack, fleeing the farm, working for Ruby Hazelton at the board-

inghouse, concern for Garth when his letters stopped, and then being accused of murder. Which of these do you think was the most challenging for her, and why?

7. Rob fell in love with Grace, but he decided to distance himself from her. What did you think of his decision? How would you have counseled him to handle the situation?

8. Grace was raised in the city, and she learned some new skills when she stayed with the Chapmans on their farm, with some humorous results. Which skill do you think was the most challenging for her, and why?

9. Andrew traveled all the way from England to act as Emma's defense attorney. What did you think of Andrew and how he handled Emma's defense? Were you surprised by the outcome of the trial, or did you guess who murdered Ruby Hazelton before it was revealed?

10. The theme passage for *No Journey Too Far* is Psalm 9:9–10 (NIV): "The LORD is a refuge for the oppressed, and a stronghold in times of trouble. Those who know your name trust in you, for you, LORD, have never forsaken those who seek you." How do you see the truths of those verses shown in the story?

Acknowledgments

I am very grateful for all those who have given me their support and encouragement and provided information in the process of writing this book. Without your help, it never would have been possible! I'd like to say thank you to the following people:

- My husband, Scott, who always provides great feedback and constant encouragement when I talk about my characters and plot, the editing process, and what's happening next. Your love and support have allowed me to follow my dreams and write the books of my heart. I will be forever grateful for you!
- Steve Laube, my literary agent, for his patience, guidance, and wise counsel. You have been a great advocate who has represented me well. I feel very blessed to be your client, and I appreciate you!
- Becky Nesbitt, Linda Washington, Laura Wright, and Cara Iverson—my gifted editors—who helped me shape the story and then polished it so readers will be able to truly enjoy it.
- Lori Oschefski, Norma Cook, and all the members of the British Home Children Advocacy & Research Association Facebook group. Many told me their stories and shared photographs of their family members who were British Home Children. Sharing those firsthand experiences made the writing of this book possible.

- Joe Perez, the talented cover designer, who did a great job creating a beautiful cover that represents the story so well. I appreciate the opportunity to give input and work together to fine-tune the design.
- Leslie Calhoun, Lori Addicott, Laura Barker, and the entire Multnomah team for their great work with marketing, publicity, production, and sales. This book would stay hidden on my computer if not for your creative ideas and hard work. Thank you!
- Amy Renaud, for her help with Canadian research. The photos and information you shared were a great help in writing this story. I appreciate the time and effort you gave to help me learn more about the setting and life in Canada in the early 1900s.
- Cara Putman, attorney and fellow author, helped me understand courtroom procedure and think through those tricky murder-trial scenes. I appreciate your insight and practical help. Any errors are mine alone.
- Cathy Gohlke and Terri Gillespie, fellow authors and friends, who constantly encourage me to trust the Lord for grace to write stories that will transform hearts and draw people closer to Him. You both are a great blessing in my life! Let's keep pressing on to serve the Lord with the gift of writing.
- Shirley Turansky, my mother-in-law, for all the ways you cheer me on and help me spread the word about my books. It's a blessing to have someone like you in my life who is so supportive!
- My dear readers, especially those in Carrie's Reading Friends Facebook group, who encourage me with their kind reviews and help me spread the word about my

books. Your thoughtful posts and emails keep me going! Happy reading, dear friends!

- Most of all, I thank my Lord and Savior, Jesus Christ, for His love, wonderful grace, and faithful provision. I am grateful for the gifts and talents You have given me, and I hope to always use them in ways that bless You and bring You glory.

About the Author

CARRIE TURANSKY has loved reading since she first visited the library as a young child and checked out a tall stack of picture books. Her love for writing began when she penned her first novel at age twelve. She is now the award-winning author of more than twenty inspirational romance novels and novellas.

Carrie and her husband, Scott—who is a pastor, author, and speaker—have been married for forty-two years and make their home in New Jersey. They often travel together on ministry trips and to visit their five adult children and seven grandchildren. Carrie also leads the women's ministry at her church, and when she's not writing, she enjoys spending time working in her flower gardens and cooking healthful meals for friends and family.

She loves to connect with reading friends through her website, http://carrieturansky.com, and via Facebook, Pinterest, and Twitter.

Read the First Book in the Epic McAlister Family Saga

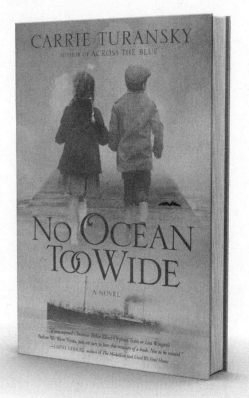

Learn more at
carrieturansky.com